Praise for Amy Tan

*The Hundred Secret Senses*

"Powerful . . . engrossing . . . [an] effortless mix of invention."
—*Chicago Tribune*

"Kwan, in particular, is a memorable creation . . . at once innocent and wise. . . . We could all do with such a sister."
—*The New York Times Book Review*

"Compelling . . . Tan is a wonderful writer, a master at dialogue and description. In Kwan, she's created a woman so vivid, you can almost see her badly permed hair, hear her raspy voice, smell the garlic on her hands." —*The Hartford Courant*

"Funny, entertaining, and thought-provoking."
—*Houston Chronicle*

"Kwan is a great raconteur, a great talker, a great fictional invention." —*San Jose Mercury News*

"Delightful, intriguing, meaningful." —*The Kansas City Star*

"No one will deny the pleasure of Tan's seductive prose and the skill with which she unfolds the many-layered narrative."
—*Publishers Weekly*

## ABOUT THE AUTHOR

Amy Tan is the author of the internationally bestselling novels *The Joy Luck Club; The Kitchen God's Wife; The Hundred Secret Senses; The Bonesetter's Daughter; Saving Fish from Drowning;* a memoir, *The Opposite of Fate;* and two children's books, *The Moon Lady* and *Sagwa,* which was adapted as a PBS production, for which she served as a creative consultant and writer. Tan was also a coproducer and coscreenwriter of the film version of *The Joy Luck Club,* and her essays and stories have appeared in numerous magazines and anthologies. She is the librettist for the opera *The Bonesetter's Daughter* and a member of The Rock Bottom Remainders, a literary garage band that raises money for charity. Her work has been translated into thirty languages. She lives with her husband in San Francisco and New York.

# THE
# HUNDRED
# SECRET
# SENSES

## AMY TAN

PENGUIN BOOKS

PENGUIN BOOKS

Published by the Penguin Group
Penguin Group (USA) Inc., 375 Hudson Street, New York, New York 10014, U.S.A.
Penguin Group (Canada), 90 Eglinton Avenue East, Suite 700, Toronto,
Ontario, Canada M4P 2Y3 (a division of Pearson Penguin Canada Inc.)
Penguin Books Ltd, 80 Strand, London WC2R 0RL, England
Penguin Ireland, 25 St Stephen's Green, Dublin 2, Ireland (a division of Penguin Books Ltd)
Penguin Group (Australia), 250 Camberwell Road, Camberwell,
Victoria 3124, Australia (a division of Pearson Australia Group Pty Ltd)
Penguin Books India Pvt Ltd, 11 Community Centre, Panchsheel Park, New Delhi – 110 017, India
Penguin Group (NZ), 67 Apollo Drive, Rosedale, North Shore 0632,
New Zealand (a division of Pearson New Zealand Ltd)
Penguin Books (South Africa) (Pty) Ltd, 24 Sturdee Avenue,
Rosebank, Johannesburg 2196, South Africa

Penguin Books Ltd, Registered Offices:
80 Strand, London WC2R 0RL, England

First published in the United States of America by G. P. Putnam's Sons 1995
Published in Penguin Books 2010

5   7   9   10   8   6   4

PUBLISHER'S NOTE
This novel is a work of fiction. Any references to historical events; to real people, living or dead;
or to real locales are intended only to give the fiction a sense of reality and authenticity. Names,
characters, places, and incidents either are the product of the author's imagination or are used
fictitiously, and their resemblence, if any, to real-life counterparts is entirely coincidental.

THE LIBRARY OF CONGRESS HAS CATALOGED THE HARDCOVER EDITION AS FOLLOWS:
Tan, Amy.
The hundred secret senses / Amy Tan.
p.   cm.
ISBN 0-399-14114-6 (hc.)
ISBN 978-0-14-311908-1 (pbk.)
I. Title.
PS3570.A48H86   1995   95-31791 CIP
813'.54—dc20

Printed in the United States of America
*Designed by Claire Naylon Vaccaro*

FOR FAITH

To write this story, I depended on the indulgence, advice, conversations, and sustenance of many: Babalu, Ronald Bass, Linden and Logan Berry, Dr. Thomas Brady, Sheri Byrne, Joan Chen, Mary Clemmey, Dr. Asa DeMatteo, Bram and Sandra Dijkstra, Terry Doxey, Tina Eng, Dr. Joseph Esherick, Audrey Ferber, Robert Foothorap, Laura Gaines, Ann and Gordon Getty, Molly Giles, Amy Hempel, Anna Jardine, Peter Lee Kenfield, Dr. Eric Kim, Gus Lee, Cora Miao, Susanne Pari, the residents of Pei Sa Bao village, Robin and Annie Renwick, Gregory Atsuro Riley, the Rock Bottom Remainders, Faith and Kirkpatrick Sale, Orville Schell, Gretchen Schields, the staff of Shelburne House Library, Kelly Simon, Dr. Michael Strong, Daisy Tan, John Tan, Dr. Steven Vandervort, Lijun Wang, Wayne Wang, Yuhang Wang, Russell Wong, the people of Yaddo, and Zo.

I thank them, but do not hold them accountable for the felicitous and sometimes unwitting ways in which they contributed to the truth of this fiction.

I

# THE GIRL
# WITH YIN EYES

My sister Kwan believes she has yin eyes. She sees those who have died and now dwell in the World of Yin, ghosts who leave the mists just to visit her kitchen on Balboa Street in San Francisco.

"Libby-ah," she'll say to me. "Guess who I see yesterday, you guess." And I don't have to guess that she's talking about someone dead.

Actually, Kwan is my half sister, but I'm not supposed to mention that publicly. That would be an insult, as if she deserved only fifty percent of the love from our family. But just to set the genetic record straight, Kwan and I share a father, only that. She was born in China. My brothers, Kevin and Tommy, and I were born in San Francisco after my father, Jack Yee, immigrated here and married our mother, Louise Kenfield.

Mom calls herself "American mixed grill, a bit of everything white, fatty, and fried." She was born in Moscow, Idaho, where she was a champion baton twirler and once won a county fair prize for growing a deformed potato that had the profile of Jimmy Durante. She told me she dreamed she'd one day grow up to be different—thin, exotic, and noble like Luise Rainer, who won an Oscar playing O-lan in *The Good*

*Earth.* When Mom moved to San Francisco and became a Kelly girl instead, she did the next-best thing. She married our father. Mom thinks that her marrying out of the Anglo race makes her a liberal. "When Jack and I met," she still tells people, "there were laws against mixed marriages. We broke the law for love." She neglects to mention that those laws didn't apply in California.

None of us, including my mom, met Kwan until she was eighteen. In fact, Mom didn't even know Kwan *existed* until shortly before my father died of renal failure. I was not quite four when he passed away. But I still remember moments with him. Falling down a curly slide into his arms. Dredging the wading pool for pennies he had tossed in. And the last day I saw him in the hospital, hearing what he said that scared me for years.

Kevin, who was five, was there. Tommy was just a baby, so he was in the waiting room with my mom's cousin, Betty Dupree—we had to call her Aunt Betty—who had moved out from Idaho as well. I was sitting on a sticky vinyl chair, eating a bowl of strawberry Jell-O cubes that my father had given me from his lunch tray. He was propped up in bed, breathing hard. Mom would cry one minute, then act cheerful. I tried to figure out what was wrong. The next thing I remember, my father was whispering and Mom leaned in close to listen. Her mouth opened wider and wider. Then her head turned sharply toward me, all twisted with horror. And I was terror-struck. How did he know? How did Daddy find out I flushed my turtles, Slowpoke and Fastpoke, down the toilet that morning? I had wanted to see what they looked like without their coats on, and ended up pulling off their heads.

"Your daughter?" I heard my mom say. "Bring her back?" And I was sure that he had just told her to bring me to the pound, which is what he did to our dog Buttons after she chewed up the sofa. What I recall after that is a jumble: the bowl of Jell-O crashing to the floor, Mom staring at a photo, Kevin grabbing it and laughing, then me seeing this tiny black-and-white snapshot of a skinny baby with patchy hair. At some point, I heard my mother shouting: "Olivia, don't argue, you have to leave now." And I was crying, "But I'll be good."

Soon after that, my mother announced: "Daddy's left us." She also told us she was going to bring Daddy's other little girl from China to live in our house. She didn't say she was sending me to the pound, but I still cried, believing everything was vaguely connected—the headless turtles whirling down the toilet, my father abandoning us, the other girl who was coming soon to take my place. I was scared of Kwan before I ever met her.

When I was ten, I learned that my father's kidneys had killed him. Mom said he was born with four instead of the usual two, and all of them were defective. Aunt Betty had a theory about why this happened. She *always* had a theory, usually obtained from a source like the *Weekly World News*. She said he was supposed to be a Siamese twin. But in the womb, my father, the stronger twin, gobbled up the weaker one and grafted on the two extra kidneys. "Maybe he also had two hearts, two stomachs, who knows." Aunt Betty came up with this scenario around the time that *Life* magazine ran a pictorial about Siamese twins from Russia. I saw the same story: two girls, Tasha and Sasha, conjoined at the hip, too heartbreakingly beautiful to be freaks of nature. This must have been in the mid-sixties, around the time I learned fractions. I remember wishing we could exchange Kwan for those Siamese twins. Then I'd have two half sisters, which equaled a whole, and I figured all the kids on the block would try to be our friends, hoping we'd let them watch as we jumped rope or played hopscotch.

Aunt Betty also passed along the story of Kwan's birth, which was not heartbreaking, just embarrassing. During the war, she said, my father had been a university student in Guilin. He used to buy live frogs for his supper at the outdoor market from a young woman named Li Chen. He later married her, and in 1944 she gave birth to their daughter, the skinny baby in the picture, Kwan.

Aunt Betty had a theory about the marriage as well. "Your dad was good-looking, for a Chinese man. He was college-educated. And he spoke English like me and your mom. Now why would he marry a little peasant girl? Because he *had to,* that's why." By then, I was old enough to know what *had to* meant.

Whatever the case, in 1948, my father's first wife died of a lung disease, perhaps TB. My father went to Hong Kong to search for work. He left Kwan in the care of his wife's younger sister, Li Bin-bin, who lived in a small mountain village called Changmian. Of course, he sent money for their support — what father would not? But in 1949, the Communists took over China, and it was impossible for my father to return for his five-year-old daughter. So what else could he do? With a heavy heart, he left for America to start a new life and forget about the sadness he left behind. Eleven years later, while he was dying in the hospital, the ghost of his first wife appeared at the foot of his bed. "Claim back your daughter," she warned, "or suffer the consequences after death!" That's the story my father gave just before he died — that is, as told by Aunt Betty years later.

Looking back, I can imagine how my mom must have felt when she first heard this. Another wife? A daughter in China? We were a modern American family. We spoke English. Sure, we ate Chinese food, but take-out, like everyone else. And we lived in a ranch-style house in Daly City. My father worked for the Government Accounting Office. My mother went to PTA meetings. She had never heard my father talk about Chinese superstitions before; they attended church and bought life insurance instead.

After my father died, my mother kept telling everyone how he had treated her "just like a Chinese empress." She made all sorts of grief-stricken promises to God and my father's grave. According to Aunt Betty, at the funeral, my mother vowed never to remarry. She vowed to teach us children to do honor to the Yee family name. She vowed to find my father's firstborn child, Kwan, and bring her to the United States.

The last promise was the only one she kept.

MY MOTHER has always suffered from a kind heart, compounded by seasonal rashes of volunteerism. One summer, she was a foster mother for Yorkie Rescue; the house still stinks of dog pee. For two Christmases, she dished out food to the homeless at St. Anthony's Dining Room; now she goes away to Hawaii with whoever is her current boyfriend. She's circulated petitions, done fund-raising, served on boards of alternative-health groups. While her enthusiasm is genuine, eventually, always, it runs out and then she's on to something new. I suspect she thought of Kwan as a foreign exchange student she would host for a year, a Chinese Cinderella, who would become self-sufficient and go on to have a wonderful American life.

During the time before Kwan came, Mom was a cheerleader, rallying my brothers and me to welcome a big sister into our lives. Tommy was too little to do anything except nod whenever Mom said, "Aren't you excited about having another big sister?" Kevin just shrugged and acted bored. I was the only one who did jumping jacks like a gung-ho recruit, in part because I was ecstatic to learn Kwan would be *in addition* to me, not *instead of.*

Although I was a lonely kid, I would have preferred a new turtle or even a doll, not someone who would compete for my mother's already divided attention and force me to share the meager souvenirs of her love. In recalling this, I know that my mother loved me — but not absolutely. When I compared the amount of time she spent with others — even total strangers — I felt myself sliding further down the ranks of favorites, getting bumped and bruised. She always had plenty of room in her life for dates with men or lunch with her so-called gal pals. With me, she was unreliable. Promises to take me to the movies or the public pool were easily erased with excuses or forgetfulness, or worse, sneaky variations of what was said and what was meant: "I hate it when you pout, Olivia," she once told me. "I didn't guarantee I'd *go* to the swim club with you.

I said I would *like to.*" How could I argue my need against her intention?

I learned to make things not matter, to put a seal on my hopes and place them on a high shelf, out of reach. And by telling myself that there was nothing inside those hopes anyway, I avoided the wounds of deep disappointment. The pain was no worse than the quick sting of a booster shot. And yet thinking about this makes me ache again. How is it that as a child I knew I should have been loved more? Is everyone born with a bottomless emotional reservoir?

So of course, I didn't want Kwan as my sister. Just the opposite. Which is why I made great efforts in front of my mother to appear enthusiastic. It was a distorted form of inverse logic: If hopes never come true, then hope for what you don't want.

Mom had said that a big sister was a bigger version of myself, sweet and beautiful, only more Chinese, and able to help me do all kinds of fun things. So I imagined not a sister but another me, an older self who danced and wore slinky clothes, who had a sad but fascinating life, like a slant-eyed version of Natalie Wood in *West Side Story,* which I saw when I was five. It occurs to me only now that my mother and I both modeled our hopes after actresses who spoke in accents that weren't their own.

One night, before my mother tucked me in bed, she asked me if I wanted to pray. I knew that praying meant saying the nice things that other people wanted to hear, which is what my mom did. So I prayed to God and Jesus to help me be good. And then I added that I hoped my big sister would come soon, since my mother had just been talking about that. When I said, "Amen," I saw she was crying and smiling proudly. Under my mother's eye I began to collect welcome presents for Kwan. The scarf my aunt Betty gave me for my birthday, the orange blossom cologne I received at Christmas, the gooey Halloween candy—I lovingly placed all these scratchy, stinky, stale items into a box my mother had marked "For Olivia's big sister." I convinced myself I had become so good that soon Mom would realize we didn't need another sister.

My mother later told my brothers and me how difficult it was to find Kwan. "In those days," she said, "you couldn't just write a letter, stick a stamp on it, and send it to Changmian. I had to cut through *mounds* of red tape and fill out dozens of forms. And there weren't too many people who'd go out of their way to help someone from a communist country. Aunt Betty thought I was crazy! She said to me, 'How can you take in a nearly grown girl who can't speak a word of English? She won't know right from wrong or left from right.' "

Paperwork wasn't the only obstacle Kwan had to unknowingly surmount. Two years after my father died, Mom married Bob Laguni, whom Kevin today calls "the fluke in our mother's history of dating foreign imports—and that's only because she thought Laguni was Mexican instead of Italian." Mom took Bob's name, and that's how my brothers and I also ended up with Laguni, which I gladly changed to Bishop when I married Simon. The point is, Bob never wanted Kwan to come in the first place. And my mom usually put his wishes above everyone else's. After they divorced—I was in college by then—Mom told me how Bob pressured her, just before they were married, to cancel the paperwork for Kwan. I think she intended to and forgot. But this is what she told me: "I watched you pray. You looked so sweet and sad, asking God, 'Please send me my big sister from China.' "

I WAS NEARLY SIX by the time Kwan came to this country. We were waiting for her at the customs area of San Francisco Airport. Aunt Betty was also there. My mother was nervous and excited, talking nonstop: "Now listen, kids, she'll probably be shy, so don't jump all over her. . . . And she'll be skinny as a beanpole, so I don't want any of you making fun of her. . . ."

When the customs official finally escorted Kwan into the lobby where we were waiting, Aunt Betty pointed and said, "That's her. I'm telling you that's her." Mom was shaking her head. This person looked like a strange old lady, short and chubby, not exactly the starving waif Mom pictured or the glamorous teenage sister I had in mind. She was dressed in drab gray pajamas, and her broad brown face was flanked by two thick braids.

Kwan was anything but shy. She dropped her bag, fluttered her arms, and bellowed, "Hall-oo! Hall-oo!" Still hooting and laughing, she jumped and squealed the way our new dog did whenever we let him out of the garage. This total stranger tumbled into Mom's arms, then Daddy Bob's. She grabbed Kevin and Tommy by the shoulders and shook them. When she saw me, she grew quiet, squatted on the lobby floor, and held out her arms. I tugged on my mother's skirt. "Is *that* my big sister?"

Mom said, "See, she has your father's same thick, black hair."

I still have the picture Aunt Betty took: curly-haired Mom in a mohair suit, flashing a quirky smile; our Italo-American stepfather, Bob, appearing stunned; Kevin and Tommy mugging in cowboy hats; a grinning Kwan with her hand on my shoulder; and me in a frothy party dress, my finger stuck in my bawling mouth.

I was crying because just moments before the photo was taken, Kwan had given me a present. It was a small cage of woven straw, which she pulled out of the wide sleeve of her coat and handed to me proudly. When I held it up to my eyes and peered between the webbing, I saw a six-legged monster, fresh-grass green, with saw-blade jaws, bulging eyes, and whips for eyebrows. I screamed and flung the cage away.

At home, in the bedroom we shared from then on, Kwan hung the cage with the grasshopper, now missing one leg. As soon as night fell, the grasshopper began to chirp as loudly as a bicycle bell warning people to get out of the road.

After that day, my life was never the same. To Mom, Kwan was a handy baby-sitter, willing, able, and free. Before my mother took off for an afternoon at the beauty parlor or a shopping trip with her gal pals, she'd tell me to stick to Kwan. "Be a good little sister and explain to her anything she doesn't understand. Promise?" So every day after school, Kwan would latch on to me and tag along wherever I went. By the first grade, I became an expert on public humiliation and shame. Kwan asked so many dumb questions that all the neighborhood kids thought she had come from Mars. She'd say: "What M&M?" "What ching gum?" "Who this Popeye Sailor Man? Why one eye gone? He bandit?" Even Kevin and Tommy laughed.

With Kwan around, my mother could float guiltlessly through her honeymoon phase with Bob. When my teacher called Mom to say I was running a fever, it was Kwan who showed up at the nurse's office to take me home. When I fell while roller-skating, Kwan bandaged my elbows. She braided my hair. She packed lunches for Kevin, Tommy, and me. She tried to teach me to sing Chinese nursery songs. She soothed me when I lost a tooth. She ran the washcloth over my neck while I took my bath.

I should have been grateful to Kwan. I could always depend on her. She liked nothing better than to be by my side. But instead, most of the time, I resented her for taking my mother's place.

I remember the day it first occurred to me to get rid of Kwan. It was summer, a few months after she had arrived. Kwan, Kevin, Tommy, and I were sitting on our front lawn, waiting for something to happen. A couple of Kevin's friends sneaked to the side of our house and turned on the sprinkler system. My brothers and I heard the telltale spit and gurgle of water running into the lines, and we ran off just before a dozen sprinkler heads burst into spray. Kwan, however, simply stood there, getting soaked, marveling that so many springs had erupted out of the earth all at once. Kevin and his friends were howling with laughter. I shouted, "That's not nice."

Then one of Kevin's friends, a swaggering second-grader whom all the little girls had a crush on, said to me, "Is that dumb Chink your sister? Hey, Olivia, does that mean you're a dumb Chink too?"

I was so flustered I yelled, "She's not my sister! I hate her! I wish she'd go back to China!" Tommy later told Daddy Bob what I had said, and Daddy Bob said, "Louise, you better do something about your daughter." My mother shook her head, looking sad. "Olivia," she said, "we don't ever hate anyone. 'Hate' is a *terrible* word. It hurts you as much as it hurts others." Of course, this only made me hate Kwan even more.

The worst part was sharing my bedroom with her. At night, she liked to throw open the curtains so that the glare of the street lamp poured into our room, where we lay side by side in our matching twin beds. Under this "beautiful American moon," as she called it, Kwan would jabber away in Chinese. She kept on talking while I pretended to be asleep. She'd still be yakking when I woke up. That's how I became the only one in our family who learned Chinese. Kwan infected me with it. I absorbed her language through my pores while I was sleeping. She pushed her Chinese secrets into my brain and changed how I thought about the world. Soon I was even having nightmares in Chinese.

In exchange, Kwan learned her English from me—which, now that I think of it, may be the reason she has never spoken it all that well. I was not an enthusiastic teacher. One time, when I was seven, I played a mean trick on her. We were lying in our beds in the dark.

"Libby-ah," Kwan said. And then she asked in Chinese, "The delicious pear we ate this evening, what's its American name?"

"Barf," I said, then covered my mouth to keep her from hearing my snickers.

She stumbled over this new sound—"bar-a-fa, bar-a-fa"—before she said, "Wah! What a clumsy word for such a delicate taste. I never ate such good fruit. Libby-ah, you are a lucky girl. If only my mother did not die." She could segue from just about any topic to the tragedies of her former life, all of which she conveyed to me in our secret language of Chinese.

Another time, she watched me sort through Valentine's Day cards

I had spilled onto my bed. She came over and picked up a card. "What's this shape?"

"It's a heart. It means love. See, all the cards have them. I have to give one to each kid in my class. But it doesn't really mean I love everyone."

She went back to her own bed and lay down. "Libby-ah," she said. "If only my mother didn't die of heartsickness." I sighed, but didn't look at her. This again. She was quiet for a few moments, then went on. "Do you know what heartsickness is?"

"What?"

"It's warming your body next to your family, then having the straw roof blow off and carry you away."

"Oh."

"You see, she didn't die of lung sickness, no such thing."

And then Kwan told me how our father caught a disease of too many good dreams. He could not stop thinking about riches and an easier life, so he became lost, floated out of their lives, and washed away his memories of the wife and baby he left behind.

"I'm not saying our father was a bad man," Kwan whispered hoarsely. "Not so. But his loyalty was not strong. Libby-ah, do you know what loyalty is?"

"What?"

"It's like this. If you ask someone to cut off his hand to save you from flying off with the roof, he immediately cuts off both hands to show he is more than glad to do so."

"Oh."

"But our father didn't do this. He left us when my mother was about to have another baby. I'm not telling you lies, Libby-ah, this is true. When this happened, I was four years old by my Chinese age. I can never forget lying against my mother, rubbing her swollen belly. Like a watermelon, she was this big."

She reached out her arms as far as she could. "Then all the water in her belly poured out as tears from her eyes, she was so sad." Kwan's arms fell suddenly to her sides. "That poor starving baby in her belly ate a hole in my mother's heart, and they both died."

I'm sure Kwan meant some of this figuratively. But as a child, I saw everything Kwan talked about as literal truth: chopped-off hands flying out of a roofless house, my father floating on the China Sea, the little baby sucking on his mother's heart. The images became phantoms. I was like a kid watching a horror movie, with my hands clapped to my eyes, peering anxiously through the cracks. I was Kwan's willing captive, and she was my protector.

At the end of her stories, Kwan would always say: "You're the only one who knows. Don't tell anyone. Never. Promise, Libby-ah?"

And I would always shake my head, then nod, drawn to allegiance through both privilege and fear.

One night, when my eyelids were already heavy with sleep, she started droning again in Chinese: "Libby-ah, I must tell you something, a forbidden secret. It's too much of a burden to keep inside me any longer."

I yawned, hoping she'd take the hint.

"I have yin eyes."

"What eyes?"

"It's true. I have yin eyes. I can see yin people."

"What do you mean?"

"Okay, I'll tell you. But first you must promise never to tell anyone. Never. Promise, ah?"

"Okay. Promise."

"Yin people, they are those who have already died."

My eyes popped open. "What? You see dead people? . . . You mean, *ghosts*?"

"Don't tell anyone. Never. Promise, Libby-ah?"

I stopped breathing. "Are there ghosts here now?" I whispered.

"Oh yes, many. Many, many good friends."

I threw the covers over my head. "Tell them to go away," I pleaded.

"Don't be afraid. Libby-ah, come out. They're your friends too. Oh see, now they're laughing at you for being so scared."

I began to cry. After a while, Kwan sighed and said in a disappointed voice, "All right, don't cry anymore. They're gone."

So that's how the business of ghosts got started. When I finally came out from under the covers, I saw Kwan sitting straight up, illuminated by the artificial glow of her American moon, staring out the window as if watching her visitors recede into the night.

The next morning, I went to my mother and did what I promised I'd never do: I told her about Kwan's yin eyes.

NOW THAT I'm an adult, I realize it wasn't my fault that Kwan went to the mental hospital. In a way, she brought it on herself. After all, I was just a little kid then, seven years old. I was scared out of my mind. I had to tell my mother what Kwan was saying. I thought Mom would just ask her to stop. Then Daddy Bob found out about Kwan's ghosts and blew his stack. Mom suggested taking her to Old St. Mary's for a talk with the priest. But Daddy Bob said no, confession wouldn't be enough. He booked Kwan into the psychiatric ward at Mary's Help instead.

When I visited her there the following week, Kwan whispered to me: "Libby-ah, listen, I have secret. Don't tell anyone, ah?" And then she switched to Chinese. "When the doctors and nurses ask me questions, I treat them like American ghosts—I don't see them, don't hear them, don't speak to them. Soon they'll know they can't change me, why they must let me go." I remember the way she looked, as immovable as a stone palace dog.

Unfortunately, her Chinese silent treatment backfired. The doctors thought Kwan had gone catatonic. Things being what they were back in the early 1960s, the doctors diagnosed Kwan's Chinese ghosts as a serious mental disorder. They gave her electroshock treatments, once, she said, then twice, she cried, then over and over again. Even today it hurts my teeth to think about that.

The next time I saw her at the hospital, she again confided in me. "All that electricity loosened my tongue so I could no longer stay silent as a fish. I became a country duck, crying *gwa-gwa-gwa!*—bragging about the World of Yin. Then four bad ghosts shouted, 'How can you tell our secrets?' They gave me a *yin-yang tou*—forced me to tear out half my hair. That's why the nurses shaved everything off. I couldn't stop pulling, until one side of my head was bald like a melon, the other side hairy like a coconut. The ghosts branded me for having two faces: one loyal, one traitor. But I'm not a traitor! Look at me, Libby-ah. Is my face loyal? What do you see?"

What I saw paralyzed me with fear. She looked as if she'd been given a crew cut with a hand-push lawn mower. It was as bad as seeing an animal run over on the street, wondering what it once had been. Except I knew how Kwan's hair used to be. Before, it flowed past her waist. Before, my fingers swam through its satin-black waves. Before, I'd grab her mane and yank it like the reins of a mule, shouting, "Giddyap, Kwan, say hee-haw!"

She took my hand and rubbed it across her sandpapery scalp, whispering about friends and enemies in China. On and on she went, as if the shock treatments had blown off the hinges of her jaw and she could not stop. I was terrified I'd catch her crazy talking disease.

To this day, I don't know why Kwan never blamed me for what happened. I'm sure she knew I was the one who got her in trouble. After she came back from Mary's Help, she gave me her plastic ID bracelet as a souvenir. She talked about the Sunday-school children who came to the hospital to sing "Silent Night," how they screamed when an old man yelled, "Shut up!" She reported that some patients there were possessed by ghosts, how they were not like the nice yin people she knew, and this was a real pity. Not once did she ever say, "Libby-ah, why did you tell my secret?"

Yet the way I remember it is the way I have always felt—that I betrayed her and that's what made her insane. The shock treatments, I believed, were my fault as well. They released all her ghosts.

THAT WAS more than thirty years ago, and Kwan still mourns, "My hair sooo bea-you-tiful, shiny-smooth like waterfall, slippery-cool like swimming eel. Now look. All that shock treatment, like got me bad home permanent, leave on cheap stuff too long. All my rich color—burnt out. All my softness—crinkle up. My hairs now just stiff wires, pierce message to my brain: No more yin-talking! They do this to me, hah, still I don't change. See? I stay strong."

Kwan was right. When her hair grew back, it was bristly, wiry as a terrier's. And when she brushed it, whole strands would crackle and rise with angry static, popping like the filaments of light bulbs burning out. Kwan explained, "All that electricity doctor force into my brain, now run through my body like horse go 'round racetrack." She claims that's the reason she now can't stand within three feet of a television set without its hissing back. She doesn't use the Walkman her husband, George, gave her; she has to ground the radio by placing it against her thigh, otherwise no matter what station she tunes it to, all she hears is "awful music, boom-pah-pah, boom-pah-pah." She can't wear any kind of watch. She received a digital one as a bingo prize, and after she strapped it on, the numbers started mutating like the fruits on a casino slot machine. Two hours later the watch stopped. "I gotta jackpot," she reported. "Eight-eight-eight-eight-eight. Lucky numbers, bad watch."

Although Kwan is not technically trained, she can pinpoint in a second the source of a fault in a circuit, whether it's in a wall outlet or a photo strobe. She's done that with some of my equipment. Here *I* am, the commercial photographer, and *she* can barely operate a point-and-shoot. Yet she's been able to find the specific part of the camera or cable or battery pack that was defective, and later, when I ship the camera to Cal Precision in Sacramento for troubleshooting, I'll find she was exactly right. I've also seen her temporarily activate a dead cordless phone just by pressing her fingers on the back recharger nodes. She can't explain any of this, and neither can I. All I can say is, I've seen her do these things.

The weirdest of her abilities, I think, has to do with diagnosing ailments. She can tell when she shakes hands with strangers whether they've ever suffered a broken bone, even if it healed many years before. She knows in an instant whether a person has arthritis, tendinitis, bursitis, sciatica — she's really good with all the musculoskeletal stuff — maladies that she calls "burning bones," "fever arms," "sour joints," "snaky leg," and all of which, she says, are caused by eating hot and cold things together, counting disappointments on your fingers, shaking your head too often with regret, or storing worries between your jaw and your fists. She can't cure anybody on the spot; she's no walking Grotto of Lourdes. But a lot of people say she has the healing touch. Like her customers at Spencer's, the drugstore in the Castro neighborhood where she works. Most of the people who pick up their prescriptions there are gay men — "bachelors," she calls them. And because she's worked there for more than twenty years, she's seen some of her longtime customers grow sick with AIDS. When they come in, she gives them quickie shoulder rubs, while offering medical advice: "You still drink beer, eat spicy food? Together, *same* time? Wah! What I tell you? Tst! Tst! How you get well do this? Ah?" — as if they were little kids fussing to be spoiled. Some of her customers drop by every day, even though they can receive home delivery free. I know *why.* When she puts her hands on the place where you hurt, you feel a tingling sensation, a thousand fairies dancing up and down, and then it's like warm water rolling through your veins. You're not cured, but you feel released from worry, becalmed, floating on a tranquil sea.

Kwan once told me, "After they die, the yin bachelors still come visit me. They call me *Doctor* Kwan. Joking, of course." And then she added shyly in English: "Maybe also for respect. What you think, Libby-ah?" She always asks me that: "What you think?"

No one in our family talks about Kwan's unusual abilities. That would call attention to what we already know, that Kwan is wacky, even by Chinese standards — even by San Francisco standards. A lot of the stuff she says and does would strain the credulity of most people who are not on antipsychotic drugs or living on cult farms.

But I no longer think my sister is crazy. Or if she is, she's fairly harmless, that is, if people don't take her seriously. She doesn't chant on the sidewalk like that guy on Market Street who screams that California is doomed to slide into the ocean like a plate of clams. And she's not into New Age profiteering; you don't have to pay her a hundred fifty an hour just to hear her reveal what's wrong with your past life. She'll tell you for free, even if you don't ask.

Most of the time, Kwan is like anyone else, standing in line, shopping for bargains, counting success in small change: "Libby-ah," she said during this morning's phone call, "yesterday, I buy two-for-one shoes on sale, Emporium Capwell. Guess how much I don't pay. You guess."

But Kwan is odd, no getting around that. Occasionally it amuses me. Sometimes it irritates me. More often I become upset, even angry — not with Kwan but with how things never turn out the way you hope. Why did I get Kwan for a sister? Why did she get me?

Every once in a while, I wonder how things might have been between Kwan and me if she'd been more normal. Then again, who's to say what's normal? Maybe in another country Kwan would be considered ordinary. Maybe in some parts of China, Hong Kong, or Taiwan she'd be revered. Maybe there's a place in the world where everyone has a sister with yin eyes.

. . .

KWAN'S NOW NEARLY FIFTY, whereas I'm a whole twelve years younger, a point she proudly mentions whenever anyone politely asks which of us is older. In front of other people, she likes to pinch my cheek and remind me that my skin is getting "wrinkle up" because I smoke cigarettes and drink too much wine and coffee—bad habits she does not have. "Don't hook on, don't need stop," she's fond of saying. Kwan is neither deep nor subtle; everything's right on the surface, for anybody to see. The point is, no one would ever guess we are sisters.

Kevin once joked that maybe the Communists sent us the wrong kid, figuring we Americans thought all Chinese people looked alike anyway. After hearing that, I fantasized that one day we'd get a letter from China saying, "Sorry, folks. We made a mistake." In so many ways, Kwan never fit into our family. Our annual Christmas photo looked like those children's puzzles, "What's Wrong with This Picture?" Each year, front and center, there was Kwan—wearing brightly colored summer clothes, plastic bow-tie barrettes on both sides of her head, and a loony grin big enough to burst her cheeks. Eventually, Mom found her a job as a busgirl at a Chinese-American restaurant. It took Kwan a month to realize that the food they served there was supposed to be Chinese. Time did nothing to either Americanize her or bring out her resemblance to our father.

On the other hand, people tell me I'm the one who takes after him most, in both appearance and personality. "Look how much Olivia can eat without gaining an ounce," Aunt Betty is forever saying. "Just like Jack." My mother once said, "Olivia analyzes every single detail to death. She has her father's accountant mentality. No wonder she became a photographer." Those kinds of comments make me wonder what else has been passed along to me through my father's genes. Did I inherit from him my dark moods, my fondness for putting salt on my fruit, my phobia about germs?

Kwan, in contrast, is a tiny dynamo, barely five feet tall, a miniature bull in a china shop. Everything about her is loud and clashing.

She'll wear a purple checked jacket over turquoise pants. She whispers loudly in a husky voice, sounding as if she had chronic laryngitis, when in fact she's never sick. She dispenses health warnings, herbal recommendations, and opinions on how to fix just about anything, from broken cups to broken marriages. She bounces from topic to topic, interspersing tips on where to find bargains. Tommy once said that Kwan believes in free speech, free association, free car-wash with fill-'er-up. The only change in Kwan's English over the last thirty years is in the speed with which she talks. Meanwhile, she thinks her English is great. She often corrects her husband. "Not *stealed*," she'll tell George. "*Stolened*."

In spite of all our obvious differences, Kwan thinks she and I are exactly alike. As she sees it, we're connected by a cosmic Chinese umbilical cord that's given us the same inborn traits, personal motives, fate, and luck. "Me and Libby-ah," she tells new acquaintances, "we same in here." And she'll tap the side of my head. "Both born Year the Monkey. Which one older? You guess. Which one?" And then she'll squash her cheek against mine.

Kwan has never been able to correctly pronounce my name, Olivia. To her, I will always be Libby-ah, not plain Libby, like the tomato juice, but Libby-ah, like the nation of Muammar Qaddafi. As a consequence, her husband, George Lew, his two sons from a first marriage, and that whole side of the family all call me Libby-ah too. The "ah" part especially annoys me. It's the Chinese equivalent of saying "hey," as in "Hey, Libby, come here." I asked Kwan once how she'd like it if I introduced her to everyone as "Hey, Kwan." She slapped my arm, went breathless with laughter, then said hoarsely, "I like, I like." So much for cultural parallels, Libby-ah it is, forever and ever.

I'm not saying I don't love Kwan. How can I not love my own sister? In many respects, she's been more like a mother to me than my real one. But I often feel bad that I don't want to be close to her. What I mean is, we're *close* in a manner of speaking. We know things about each other, mostly through history, from sharing the same closet, the same toothpaste, the same cereal every morning for twelve years, all the routines and habits of being in the same family. I really think Kwan is sweet, also loyal, extremely loyal. She'd tear off the ear of anyone who said an unkind word about me. That counts for a lot. It's just that I wouldn't want to be closer to her, not the way some sisters are who consider themselves best friends. As it is, I don't share everything with her the way she does with me, telling me the most private details of her life — like what she told me last week about her husband:

"Libby-ah," she said, "I found mole, big as my nostril, found on — what you call this thing between man legs, in Chinese we say *yinnang*, round and wrinkly like two walnut?"

"Scrotum."

"Yes-yes, found big mole on scrotum! Now every day–every day, must examine Georgie-ah, his scrotum, make sure this mole don't start grow."

To Kwan, there are no boundaries among family. Everything is open for gruesome and exhaustive dissection — how much you spent on your vacation, what's wrong with your complexion, the reason you look as doomed as a fish in a restaurant tank. And then she wonders why I don't make her a regular part of my social life. She, however, invites me to dinner once a week, as well as to every boring family gathering — last week, a party for George's aunt, celebrating the fact that she received her U.S. citizenship after fifty years, that sort of thing. Kwan thinks only a major catastrophe would keep me away. She'll worry aloud: "Why you don't come last night? Something the matter?"

"Nothing's the matter."

"Feel sick?"

"No."

"You want me come over, bring you orange? I have extra, good price, six for one dollar."

"Really, I'm *fine*."

She's like an orphan cat, kneading on my heart. She's been this way all my life, peeling me oranges, buying me candy, admiring my report cards and telling me how smart I was, smarter than she could ever be. Yet I've done nothing to endear myself to her. As a child, I often refused to play with her. Over the years, I've yelled at her, told her she embarrassed me. I can't remember how many times I've lied to get out of seeing her.

Meanwhile, she has *always* interpreted my outbursts as helpful advice, my feeble excuses as good intentions, my pallid gestures of affection as loyal sisterhood. And when I can't bear it any longer, I lash out and tell her she's crazy. Before I can retract the sharp words, she pats my arm, smiles and laughs. And the wound she bears heals itself instantly. Whereas I feel guilty forever.

IN RECENT MONTHS, Kwan has become even more troublesome. Usually after the third time I say no to something, she quits. Now it's as though her mind is stuck on automatic rewind. When I'm not irritated by her, I worry that maybe she's about to have a nervous breakdown again. Kevin said she's probably going through menopause. But I can tell it's more than that. She's more obsessed than usual. The ghost talk is becoming more frequent. She mentions China in almost every conversation with me, how she must go back before everything changes and it's too late. Too late for what? She doesn't know.

And then there's my marriage. She simply won't accept the fact that Simon and I have split up. In fact, she's purposely trying to sabotage the divorce. Last week, I gave a birthday party for Kevin and invited this guy I was seeing, Ben Apfelbaum. When he told Kwan he worked as a voice talent for radio commercials, she said, "Ah, Libby-ah and me too, both talent for get out of tricky situation, also big talent for get own way. Is true, Libby-ah?" Her eyebrows twitched. "You husband, Simon, I think he agree with me, ah?"

"My soon-to-be *ex*-husband." I then had to explain to Ben: "Our divorce will be final five months from now, December fifteenth."

"Maybe not, maybe not," Kwan said, then laughed and pinched my arm. She turned to Ben: "You meet Simon?"

Ben shook his head and started to say, "Olivia and I met at the —"

"Oh, very handsome," Kwan chirped. She cupped her hand to the side of her mouth and confided: "Simon look like Olivia twin brother. Half Chinese."

"Half *Hawaiian*," I said. "And we don't look alike at all."

"What you mother father do?" Kwan scrutinized Ben's cashmere jacket.

"They're both retired and live in Missouri," said Ben.

"Misery! Tst! Tst!" She looked at me. "This too sad."

Every time Kwan mentions Simon, I think my brain is going to implode from my trying not to scream in exasperation. She thinks that because I initiated the divorce I can take it back.

"Why not forgive?" she said after the party. She was plucking at the dead blooms of an orchid plant. "Stubborn and anger together, very bad for you." When I didn't say anything, she tried another tack: "I think you still have strong feeling for him — mm-hm! Very, very strong. Ah — see! — look you face. So red! This love feeling rushing from you heart. I right? Answer. I right?"

And I kept flipping through the mail, scrawling MOVED across any envelope with Simon Bishop's name on it. I've never discussed with Kwan why Simon and I broke up. She wouldn't understand. It's too complex. There's no one event or fight I can put my finger on to say, "That was the reason." Our breakup was the result of many things: a wrong beginning, bad timing, years and years of thinking habit and silence were the same as intimacy. After seventeen years together, when I finally realized I needed more in my life, Simon seemed to want less. Sure, I loved him — too much. And he loved me, only not enough. I just want someone who thinks I'm number one in his life. I'm not willing to accept emotional scraps anymore.

But Kwan wouldn't understand that. She doesn't know how people can hurt you beyond repair. She believes people who say they're sorry. She's the naive, trusting type who believes everything said in television commercials is certifiable truth. Look at her house: it's packed to the gills with gadgets—Ginsu knives, slicers and dicers, juicers and french-fry makers, you name it, she's bought it, for "only nineteen ninety-five, order now, offer good until midnight."

"Libby-ah," Kwan said on the phone today. "I have something must tell you, very important news. This morning I talk to Lao Lu. We decide: You and Simon shouldn't get divorce."

"How nice," I said. "You decided." I was balancing my checkbook, adding and subtracting as I pretended to listen.

"Me and Lao Lu. You remember him."

"George's cousin." Kwan's husband seemed to be related to just about every Chinese person in San Francisco.

"No-no! Lao Lu not cousin. How you can forget? Lots times I already tell you about him. Old man, bald head. Strong arm, strong leg, strong temper. One time loose temper, loose head too! Chopped off. Lao Lu say—"

"Wait a minute. Someone without a head is now telling *me* what to do about my marriage?"

"Tst! Chopped head off over one hundred year ago. Now look fine, no problem. Lao Lu think you, me, Simon, we three go China, everything okay. Okay, Libby-ah?"

I sighed. "Kwan, I really don't have time to talk about this now. I'm in the middle of something."

"Lao Lu say cannot just balance checkbook, see how much you got left. Must balance life too."

How the hell did Kwan know I was balancing my checkbook?

That's how it's been with Kwan and me. The minute I discount her, she tosses in a zinger that keeps me scared, makes me her captive once again. With her around, I'll never have a life of my own. She'll always claim a major interest.

Why do I remain her treasured little sister? Why does she feel that I'm the most important person in her life?—the most! Why does she say over and over again that even if we were not sisters, she would feel this way? "Libby-ah," she tells me, "I never leave you."

No! I want to shout, I've done nothing, don't say that anymore. Because each time she does, she turns all my betrayals into love that needs to be repaid. Forever we'll know: She's been loyal, someday I'll have to be.

But even if I cut off both my hands, it'd be no use. As Kwan has already said, she'll never release me. One day the wind will howl and she'll be clutching a tuft of the straw roof, about to fly off to the World of Yin.

"Let's go! Hurry come!" she'll be whispering above the storm. "But don't tell anyone. Promise me, Libby-ah."

# 2

# FISHER OF MEN

Before seven in the morning, the phone rings. Kwan is the only one who would call at such an ungodly hour. I let the answering machine pick up.

"Libby-ah?" she whispers. "Libby-ah, you there? This you big sister . . . Kwan. I have something important tell you. . . . You want hear? . . . Last night I dream you and Simon. Strange dream. You gone to bank, check you savings. All a sudden, bank robber run through door. Quick! You hide you purse. So bank robber, he steal everybody money but yours. Later, you gone home, stick you hand in purse—ah!—where is?—gone! Not money but you heart. Stolened! Now you have no heart, how can live? No energy, no color in cheek, pale, sad, tired. Bank president where you got all you savings, he say, 'I loan you my heart. No interest. You pay back whenever.' You look up, see his face—you know who, Libby-ah? You guess. . . . Simon! Yes-yes, give you his heart. You see! Still love you. Libby-ah, do you believe? Not just dream . . . Libby-ah, you listening me?"

. . .

BECAUSE OF KWAN, I have a talent for remembering dreams. Even today, I can recall eight, ten, sometimes a dozen dreams. I learned how when Kwan came home from Mary's Help. As soon as I started to wake, she would ask: "Last night, Libby-ah, who you meet? What you see?"

With my half-awake mind, I'd grab on to the wisps of a fading world and pull myself back in. From there I would describe for her the details of the life I'd just left—the scuff marks on my shoes, the rock I had dislodged, the face of my true mother calling to me from underneath. When I stopped, Kwan would ask, "Where you go before that?" Prodded, I would trace my way back to the previous dream, then the one before that, a dozen lives, and sometimes their deaths. Those are the ones I never forget, the moments just before I died.

Through years of dream-life, I've tasted cold ash falling on a steamy night. I've seen a thousand spears flashing like flames on the crest of a hill. I've touched the tiny grains of a stone wall while waiting to be killed. I've smelled my own musky fear as the rope tightens around my neck. I've felt the heaviness of flying through weightless air. I've heard the sucking creak of my voice just before life snaps to an end.

"What you see after die?" Kwan would always ask.

I'd shake my head. "I don't know. My eyes were closed."

"Next time, open eyes."

For most of my childhood, I thought everyone remembered dreams as other lives, other selves. Kwan did. After she came home from the psychiatric ward, she told me bedtime stories about them, yin people: a woman named Banner, a man named Cape, a one-eyed bandit girl, a half-and-half man. She made it seem as if all these ghosts were our friends. I didn't tell my mother or Daddy Bob what Kwan was saying. Look what happened the last time I did that.

When I went to college and could finally escape from Kwan's world, it was already too late. She had planted her imagination into mine. Her ghosts refused to be evicted from my dreams.

"Libby-ah," I can still hear Kwan saying in Chinese, "did I ever tell you what Miss Banner promised before we died?"

I see myself pretending to be asleep.

And she would go on: "Of course, I can't say exactly how long ago this happened. Time is not the same between one lifetime and the next. But I think it was during the year 1864. Whether this was the Chinese lunar year or the date according to the Western calendar, I'm not sure. . . ."

Eventually I would fall asleep, at what point in her story I always forgot. So which part was her dream, which part was mine? Where did they intersect? Every night, she'd tell me these stories. And I would lie there silently, helplessly, wishing she'd shut up.

Yes, yes, I'm sure it was 1864. I remember now, because the year sounded very strange. Libby-ah, just listen to it: *Yi-ba-liu-si.* Miss Banner said it was like saying: Lose hope, slide into death. And I said, No, it means: Take hope, the dead remain. Chinese words are good and bad this way, so many meanings, depending on what you hold in your heart.

Anyway, that was the year I gave Miss Banner the tea. And she gave me the music box, the one I once stole from her, then later returned. I remember the night we held that box between us with all those things inside that we didn't want to forget. It was just the two of us, alone for the moment, in the Ghost Merchant's House, where we lived with the Jesus Worshippers for six years. We were standing next to the holy bush, the same bush that grew the special leaves, the same leaves I used to make the tea. Only now the bush was chopped down, and Miss Banner was saying she was sorry that she let General Cape kill that bush. Such a sad, hot night, water streaming down our faces, sweat and tears, the cicadas screaming louder and louder, then falling quiet. And later, we stood in this archway, scared to death. But we were also happy. We were happy to learn we were unhappy for the same reason. That was the year that both our heavens burned.

Six years before, that's when I first met her, when I was fourteen and she was twenty-six, maybe younger or older than that. I could never tell the ages of foreigners. I came from a small place in Thistle Mountain, just south of Changmian. We were not Punti, the Chinese who claimed they had more Yellow River Han blood running through their veins, so everything should belong to them. And we weren't one of the Zhuang tribes either, always fighting each other, village against village, clan against clan. We were Hakka, Guest People—hnh!—meaning, guests not invited to stay in any good place too long. So we lived in one of many Hakka roundhouses in a poor part of the mountains, where you must farm on cliffs and stand like a goat and unearth two wheelbarrows of rocks before you can grow one handful of rice.

All the women worked as hard as the men, no difference in who carried the rocks, who made the charcoal, who guarded the crops from bandits at night. All Hakka women were this way, strong. We didn't bind our feet like Han girls, the ones who hopped around on stumps as black and rotten as old bananas. We had to walk all over the mountain to do our work, no binding cloths, no shoes. Our naked feet walked right over those sharp thistles that gave our mountain its famous name.

A suitable Hakka bride from our mountains had thick calluses on her feet and a fine, high-boned face. There were other Hakka families living near the big cities of Yongan, in the mountains, and Jintian, by the river. And the mothers from poorer families liked to match their sons to hardworking pretty girls from Thistle Mountain. During marriage-matching festivals, these boys would climb up to our high villages and our girls would sing the old mountain songs that we had brought from the north a thousand years before. A boy had to sing back to the girl he wanted to marry, finding words to match her song. If his voice was soft, or his words were clumsy, too bad, no marriage. That's why Hakka people are not only fiercely strong, they have good voices, and clever minds for winning whatever they want.

We had a saying: When you marry a Thistle Mountain girl, you get three oxen for a wife: one that breeds, one that plows, one to carry your old mother around. That's how tough a Hakka girl was. She never complained, even if a rock tumbled down the side of the mountain and smashed out her eye.

That happened to me when I was seven. I was very proud of my wound, cried only a little. When my grandmother sewed shut the hole that was once my eye, I said the rock had been loosened by a ghost horse. And the horse was ridden by the famous ghost maiden Nunumu—the *nu* that means "girl," the *numu* that means "a stare as fierce as a dagger." Nunumu, Girl with the Dagger Eye. She too lost her eye when she was young. She had witnessed a Punti man stealing another man's salt, and before she could run away, he stabbed his dagger in her face. After that, she pulled one corner of her headscarf over her blind eye. And her other eye became bigger, darker, sharp as a cat-eagle's. She robbed only Punti people, and when they saw her dagger eye, oh, how they trembled.

All the Hakkas in Thistle Mountain admired her, and not just because she robbed Punti people. She was the first Hakka bandit to join the struggle for Great Peace when the Heavenly King came back to us for help. In the spring, she took an army of Hakka maidens to Guilin, and the Manchus captured her. After they cut off her head, her lips were still moving, cursing that she would return and ruin their families for one hundred generations. That was the summer I lost my eye. And when I told everyone about Nunumu galloping by on her ghost horse, people said this was a sign that Nunumu had chosen me to be her messenger, just as the Christian God had chosen a Hakka man to be the Heavenly King. They began to call me Nunumu. And sometimes, late at night, I thought I could truly see the Bandit Maiden, not too clearly, of course, because at that time I had only one yin eye.

Soon after that, I met my first foreigner. Whenever foreigners arrived in our province, everyone in the countryside—from Nanning to Guilin—talked about them. Many Westerners came to trade in foreign mud, the opium that gave foreigners mad dreams of China. And some came to sell weapons—cannons, gunpowder, rifles, not the fast, new ones, but the slow, old kind you light with a match, leftovers from foreign battles already lost. The missionaries came to our province because they heard that the Hakkas were God Worshippers. They wanted to help more of us go to their heaven. They didn't know that a God Worshipper was not the same as a Jesus Worshipper. Later we all realized our heavens were not the same.

But the foreigner I met was not a missionary. He was an American general. The Hakka people called him Cape because that's what he always wore, a large cape, also black gloves, black boots, no hat, and a short gray jacket with buttons—like shiny coins!—running from the waist to his chin. In his hand he carried a long walking stick, rattan, with a silver tip and an ivory handle carved in the shape of a naked woman.

When he came to Thistle Mountain, people from all the villages poured down the mountainsides and met in the wide green bowl. He arrived on a prancing horse, leading fifty Cantonese soldiers, former boatmen and beggars, now riding ponies and wearing colorful army uniforms, which we heard were not Chinese or Manchu but leftovers from wars in French Africa. The soldiers were shouting, "God Worshippers! We are God Worshippers too!"

Some of our people thought Cape was Jesus, or, like the Heavenly King, another one of his younger brothers. He was very tall, had a big mustache, a short beard, and wavy black hair that flowed to his shoulders. Hakka men also wore their long hair this way, no pigtail anymore, because the Heavenly King said our people should no longer obey the laws of the Manchus. I had never seen a foreigner before and had no way of knowing his true age. But to me, he looked old. He had skin the color of a turnip, eyes as murky as shallow water. His face had sunken spots and sharp points, the same as a person with a wasting disease. He seldom smiled, but laughed often. And he spoke harsh words in a donkey bray. A man always stood by his side, serving as his go-between, translating in an elegant voice what Cape said.

The first time I saw the go-between, I thought he looked Chinese. The next minute he seemed foreign, then neither. He was like those lizards that become the colors of sticks and leaves. I learned later this man had the mother blood of a Chinese woman, the father blood of an American trader. He was stained both ways. General Cape called him *yiban ren*, the one-half man.

Yiban told us Cape had just come from Canton, where he became friends with the Heavenly King of the Great Peace Revolution. We were all astounded. The Heavenly King was a holy man who had been born a Hakka, then chosen by God to be his treasured younger son, little brother to Jesus. We listened carefully.

Cape, Yiban said, was an American military leader, a supreme general, the highest rank. People murmured. He had come across the sea to China, to help the God Worshippers, the followers of Great Peace. People shouted, "Good! Good!" He was a God Worshipper himself, and he admired us, our laws against opium, thievery, the pleasures of the dark parts of women's bodies. People nodded, and I stared with my one eye at the naked lady on the handle of Cape's walking stick. He said that he had come to help us win our battle against the Manchus, that this was God's plan, written more than a thousand years before in the Bible he was holding. People pushed forward to see. We knew that same plan. The Heavenly King had already told us that the Hakka people would inherit the earth and rule God's Chinese kingdom. Cape reported the Great Peace soldiers had already captured many cities, had gathered much money and land. And now, the struggle was ready to move north — if only the rest of the God Worshippers in Thistle Mountain would join him as soldiers. Those who fought, he added, would share in the bounty — warm clothes, plenty to eat, weapons, and later, land of their own, new status and ranks, schools and homes, men and women separate. The Heavenly King would send food to their families left behind. By now, everybody was shouting, "Great Peace! Great Peace!"

Then General Cape tapped his walking stick on the ground. Everyone grew quiet again. He called Yiban to show us the gifts the Heavenly King had asked him to bring. Barrels of gunpowder! Bushels of rifles! Baskets of French African uniforms, some torn and already stained with blood. But everyone agreed they were still very fine. Everybody was saying, "Hey, see these buttons, feel this cloth." That day, many, many people, men and women, joined the army of the Heavenly King. I could not. I was too young, only seven, so I was very unhappy inside. But then the Cantonese soldiers passed out uniforms—only to the men, none to the women. And when I saw that, I was not as unhappy as before.

The men put on their new clothes. The women examined their new rifles, the matches for lighting them. Then General Cape tapped his walking stick again and asked Yiban to bring out his gift to us. We all pressed forward, eager to see yet another surprise. Yiban brought back a wicker cage, and inside was a pair of white doves. General Cape announced in his curious Chinese that he had asked God for a sign that we would be an ever victorious army. God sent down the doves. The doves, General Cape said, meant we poor Hakkas would have the rewards of Great Peace we had hungered for over the last thousand years. He then opened the cage door and pulled out the birds. He threw them into the air, and the people roared. They ran and pushed, jumping to catch the creatures before they could fly away. One man fell forward onto a rock. His head cracked open and his brains started to pour out. But people jumped right over him and kept chasing those rare and precious birds. One dove was caught, the other flew away. So someone ate a meal that night.

My mother and father joined the struggle. My uncles, my aunts, my older brothers, nearly everyone over thirteen in Thistle Mountain and from the cities down below. Fifty or sixty thousand people. Peasants and landowners, soup peddlers and teachers, bandits and beggars, and not just Hakkas, but Yaos and Miaos, Zhuang tribes, and even the Puntis who were poor. It was a great moment for Chinese people, all of us coming together like that.

I was left behind in Thistle Mountain to live with my grandmother. We were a pitiful village of scraps, babies and children, the old and the lame, cowards and idiots. Yet we were happy, because just as he had promised, the Heavenly King sent his soldiers to bring us food, more kinds than we could have ever imagined in a hundred years. And the soldiers also brought us stories of great victories: How the Heavenly King had set up his new kingdom in Nanjing. How taels of silver were more plentiful than rice. What fine houses everyone lived in, men in one compound, women in another. What a peaceful life—church on Sunday, no work, only rest and happiness. We were glad to hear that we now lived in a time of Great Peace.

The following year, the soldiers came with rice and salt-cured fish. The next year, it was only rice. More years passed. One day, a man who had once lived in our village returned from Nanjing. He said he was sick to death of Great Peace. When there is great suffering, he said, everyone struggles the same. But when there is peace, no one wants to be the same. The rich no longer share. The less rich envy and steal. In Nanjing, he said, everyone was seeking luxuries, pleasures, the dark places of women. He said the Heavenly King now lived in a fine palace and had many concubines. He allowed his kingdom to be ruled by a man possessed with the Holy Ghost. And General Cape, the man who rallied all the Hakkas to fight, had joined the Manchus and was now a traitor, bound by a Chinese banker's gold and marriage to his daughter. Too much happiness, said the man who returned, always overflows into tears of sorrow.

We could feel in our stomachs the truth of what this man said. We were hungry. The Heavenly King had forgotten us. Our Western friends had betrayed us. We no longer received food or stories of victory. We were poor. We had no mothers, no fathers, no singing maidens and boys. We were bitter cold in the wintertime.

The next morning, I left my village and went down the mountain. I was fourteen, old enough to make my own way in life. My grandmother had died the year before, but her ghost didn't stop me. It was the ninth day of the ninth month, I remember this, a day when Chinese people were supposed to climb the heights, not descend from them, a day for honoring ancestors, a day that the God Worshippers ignored to prove they abided by a Western calendar of fifty-two Sundays and not the sacred days of the Chinese almanac. So I walked down the mountain, then through the valleys between the mountains. I no longer knew what I should believe, whom I could trust. I decided I would wait for a sign, see what happened.

I arrived at the city by the river, the one called Jintian. To those Hakka people I met, I said I was Nunumu. But they didn't know who the Bandit Maiden was. She was not famous in Jintian. The Hakkas there didn't admire my eye that a ghost horse had knocked out. They pitied me. They put an old rice ball into my palm and tried to make me a half-blind beggar. But I refused to become what people thought I should be.

So I wandered around the city again, thinking about what work I might do to earn my own food. I saw Cantonese people who cut the horns off toes, Yaos who pulled teeth, Puntis who pierced needles into swollen legs. I knew nothing about drawing money out of the rotten parts of other people's bodies. I continued walking until I was beside the low bank of a wide river. I saw Hakka fishermen tossing big nets into the water from little boats. But I had no nets, no little boat. I did not know how to think like a fast, sly fish.

Before I could decide what to do, I heard people along the riverbank shouting. Foreigners had arrived! I ran to the dock and watched two Chinese *kuli* boatmen, one young, one old, walking down a narrow plank, carrying boxes and crates and trunks from a large boat. And then I saw the foreigners themselves, standing on the deck — three, four, five of them, all in dull black clothes, except for the smallest one, who had clothing and hair the shiny brown of a tree-eating beetle. That was Miss Banner, but of course I didn't know it at the time. My one eye watched them all. Their five pairs of foreign eyes were on the young and old boatmen balancing their way down the long, thin gangplank. On the shoulders of the boatmen were two poles, and in the saggy middle a large trunk hung from twisted ropes. Suddenly, the shiny brown foreigner ran down the plank — who knew why? — to warn the men, to ask them to be more careful. And just as suddenly, the plank began to bounce, the trunk began to swing, the men began to sway, and the five foreigners on the boat began to shout. Back and forth, up and down — our eyes leapt as we watched those boatmen clenching their muscles and the shiny foreigner flapping her arms like a baby bird. In the next moment, the older man, at the bottom of the plank, gave one sharp cry — I heard the crack, saw his shoulder bone sticking out. Then two *kuli*s, one trunk, and a shiny-clothed foreigner fell with great splashes into the water below.

I ran to the river edge. The younger *kuli* had already swum to shore. Two fishermen in a small boat were chasing the contents that had spilled out of the trunk, bright clothing that billowed like sails, feathered hats that floated like ducks, long gloves that raked the water like the fingers of a ghost. But nobody was trying to help the injured boatman or the shiny foreigner. The other foreigners would not; they were afraid to walk down the plank. The Punti people on the shore would not; if they interfered with fate, they would be responsible for those two people's undrowned lives. But I didn't think this way. I was a Hakka. The Hakkas were God Worshippers. And the God Worshippers were fishers of men. So I grabbed one of the bamboo poles that had fallen in the water. I ran along the bank and stuck this out, letting the ropes dangle downstream. The *kuli* and the foreigner grabbed them with their eager hands. And with all my strength, I pulled them in.

Right after that the Punti people pushed me aside. They left the injured boatman on the ground, gasping and cursing. That was Lao Lu, who later became the gatekeeper, since with a broken shoulder he could no longer work as a *kuli*. As for Miss Banner, the Puntis dragged her higher onto the shore, where she vomited, then cried. When the foreigners finally came down from the boat, the Puntis crowded around them, shouting, "Give us money." One of the foreigners threw small coins on the ground, and the Puntis flocked like birds to devour them, then scattered away.

The foreigners loaded Miss Banner in one cart, the broken boatman in another. They loaded three more carts with their boxes and crates and trunks. And as they made their way to the mission house in Changmian, I ran behind. So that's how all three of us went to live in the same house. Our three different fates had flowed together in that river, and became as tangled and twisted as a drowned woman's hair.

It was like this: If Miss Banner had not bounced on the plank, Lao Lu never would have broken his shoulder. If his shoulder had not broken, Miss Banner never would have almost drowned. If I hadn't saved Miss Banner from drowning, she never would have been sorry for breaking Lao Lu's shoulder. If I hadn't saved Lao Lu, he never would have told Miss Banner what I had done. If Miss Banner hadn't known this, she never would have asked me to be her companion. If I hadn't become her companion, she wouldn't have lost the man she loved.

THE GHOST MERCHANT'S HOUSE was in Changmian, and Changmian was also in Thistle Mountain, but north of my village. From Jintian it was a half-day's journey. But with so many trunks and moaning people in carts, we took twice as long. I learned later that *Changmian* means "never-ending songs." Behind the village, higher into the mountains, were many caves, hundreds. And when the wind blew, the mouths of the caves would sing *wu! wu!* —just like the voices of sad ladies who have lost sons.

That's where I stayed for the last six years of my life — in that house. I lived with Miss Banner, Lao Lu, and the missionaries — two ladies, two gentlemen, Jesus Worshippers from England. I didn't know this at the time. Miss Banner told me many months later, when we could speak to each other in a common tongue. She said the missionaries had sailed to Macao, preached there a little while, then sailed to Canton, preached there another little while. That's also where they met Miss Banner. Around this time, a new treaty came out saying the foreigners could live anywhere in China they pleased. So the missionaries floated inland to Jintian, using West River. And Miss Banner was with them.

The mission was a large compound, with one big courtyard in the middle, then four smaller ones, one big fancy main house, then three smaller ones. In between were covered passageways to connect everything together. And all around was a high wall, cutting off the inside from the outside. No one had lived in that place for more than a hundred years. Only foreigners would stay in a house that was cursed. They said they didn't believe in Chinese ghosts.

Local people told Lao Lu, "Don't live there. It's haunted by fox-spirits." But Lao Lu said he was not afraid of anything. He was a Cantonese *kuli* descended from ten generations of *kuli*s! He was strong enough to work himself to death, smart enough to find the answer to whatever he wanted to know. For instance, if you asked him how many pieces of clothing did the foreign ladies own, he wouldn't guess and say maybe two dozen each. He would go into the ladies' rooms when they were eating, and he would count each piece, never stealing any, of course. Miss Banner, he told me, had two pairs of shoes, six pairs of gloves, five hats, three long costumes, two pairs of black stockings, two pairs of white stockings, two pairs of white undertrousers, one umbrella, and seven other things that may have been clothing, but he could not determine which parts of the body they were supposed to cover.

Through Lao Lu, I quickly learned many things about the foreigners. Only later did he tell me why local people thought the house was cursed. Many years before, it had been a summer mansion, owned by a merchant who died in a mysterious and awful way. Then his wives died, four of them, one by one, also in mysterious and awful ways, youngest first, oldest last, all of this happening from one full moon to the next.

Like Lao Lu, I was not easily scared. But I must tell you, Libby-ah, what happened there five years later made me believe the Ghost Merchant had come back.

# THE DOG
# AND THE BOA

Ever since we separated, Simon and I have been having a custody spat over Bubba, *my* dog. Simon wants visitation rights, weekend walks. I don't want to deny him the privilege of picking up Bubba's poop. But I hate his cavalier attitude about dogs. Simon likes to walk Bubba off leash. He lets him romp through the trails of the Presidio, along the sandy dog run by Crissy Field, where the jaws of a pit bull, a rottweiler, even a mad cocker spaniel could readily bite a three-pound Yorkie-chihuahua in half.

This evening, we were at Simon's apartment, sorting through a year's worth of receipts for the free-lance business we haven't yet divided. For the sake of tax deductions, we decided "married filing joint return" should still apply.

"Bubba's a dog," Simon said. "He has the right to run free once in a while."

"Yeah, and get himself killed. Remember what happened to Sarge?"

Simon rolled his eyes, his look of "Not that again." Sarge had been Kwan's dog, a scrappy Pekingese-Maltese that challenged any male dog on the street. About five years ago, Simon took him for a walk—off leash—and Sarge tore open the nose of a boxer. The owner of the boxer presented Kwan with an eight-hundred-dollar veterinary bill. I insisted Simon should pay. Simon said the boxer's owner should, since his dog had provoked the attack. Kwan squabbled with the animal hospital over each itemized charge.

"What if Bubba runs into a dog like Sarge?" I said.

"The boxer started it," Simon said flatly.

"Sarge was a vicious dog! You were the one who let him off leash, and Kwan ended up paying the vet bill!"

"What do you mean? The boxer's owner paid."

"Oh no, he didn't. Kwan just said that so you wouldn't feel bad. I told you that, remember?"

Simon twisted his mouth to the side, a grimace of his that always preceded a statement of doubt. "I don't remember that," he said.

"Of course you don't! You remember what you *want* to remember."

Simon sneered. "Oh, and I suppose you don't?" Before I could respond, he held up his hand, palm out, to stop me. "I know, I know. *You* have an indelible memory! *You* can never forget a thing! Well, let me tell you, your recollection of every last detail has nothing to do with memory. It's called holding a goddamn grudge."

WHAT SIMON SAID has annoyed me all night long. Am I really the kind of person who hangs on to resentments? No, Simon was being defensive, throwing back barbs. Can I help it if I was born with a knack for remembering all sorts of things?

Aunt Betty was the first person to tell me I had a photographic memory; her comment made me believe I would grow up to be a photographer. She said this because I once corrected her in front of a bunch of people on her account of a movie we had all seen together. Now that I've been making my living behind the camera lens for the last fifteen years, I don't know what people mean by photographic memory. How

I remember the past isn't like flipping through an indiscriminate pile of snapshots. It's more selective than that.

If someone asked me what my address was when I was seven years old, the numbers wouldn't flash before my eyes. I'd have to relive a specific moment: the heat of the day, the smell of the cut lawn, the slap-slap-slap of rubber thongs against my heels. Then once again I'd be walking up the two steps of the poured-concrete porch, reaching into the black mailbox, heart pounding, fingers grasping — Where is it? Where's that stupid letter from Art Linkletter, inviting me to be on his show? But I wouldn't give up hope. I'd think to myself, Maybe I'm at the wrong address. But no, there they are, the brass numbers above, 3-6-2-4, complete with tarnish and rust around the screws.

That's what I remember most, not addresses but pain — that old lump-in-the-throat conviction that the world had fingered me for abuse and neglect. Is that the same as a grudge? I wanted so much to be a guest on *Kids Say the Darndest Things*. It was the kiddie route to fame, and I wanted once again to prove to my mother that I was special, in spite of Kwan. I wanted to snub the neighborhood kids, to make them mad that I was having more fun than they would ever know. While riding my bicycle around and around the block, I'd plot what I'd say when I was finally invited to be on the show. I'd tell Mr. Linkletter about Kwan, just the funny stuff — like the time she said she loved the movie *Southern Pacific*. Mr. Linkletter would raise his eyebrows and round his mouth. "Olivia," he'd say, "doesn't your sister mean *South* Pacific?" Then people in the audience would slap their knees and roar with laughter, and I'd glow with childish wonder and a cute expression.

Old Art always figured kids were so sweet and naive they didn't know they were saying embarrassing things. But all those kids on the show knew precisely what they were doing. Why else didn't they ever mention the *real* secrets — how they played night-night nurse and dickie doctor, how they stole gum, gunpowder caps, and muscle magazines from the corner Mexican store. I knew kids who did those things. They were the same ones who once pinned down my arms and peed on me, laughing and shouting, "Olivia's sister is a retard." They sat on me until I started crying, hating Kwan, hating myself.

To soothe me, Kwan took me to the Sweet Dreams Shoppe. We were sitting outside, licking cones of rocky road ice cream. Captain, the latest mutt my mother had rescued from the pound, whom Kwan had named, was lying at our feet, vigilantly waiting for drips.

"Libby-ah," Kwan said, "what this word, lee-tahd?"

"Reee-tard," I corrected, lingering over the word. I was still angry with Kwan and the neighbor kids. I took another tongue stab of ice cream, thinking of retarded things Kwan had done. "Retard means *fantou*," I said. "You know, a stupid person who doesn't understand anything." She nodded. "Like saying the wrong things at the wrong time," I added. She nodded again. "When kids laugh at you and you don't know why."

Kwan was quiet for the longest time, and the inside of my chest began to feel tickly and uncomfortable. Finally she said in Chinese: "Libby-ah, you think this word is me, *retard*? Be honest."

I kept licking the drips running down the side of my cone, avoiding her stare. I noticed that Captain was also watching me attentively. The tickly feeling grew, until I let out a huge sigh and grumbled, "Not really." Kwan grinned and patted my arm, which just about drove me crazy. "Captain," I shouted. "Bad dog! Stop begging!" The dog cowered.

"Oh, he not begging," Kwan said in a happy voice. "Only hoping." She petted his rump, then held her cone above the dog's head. "Talk English!" Captain sneezed a couple of times, then let go with a low *wuff*. She allowed him a lick. *"Jang Zhongwen!* Talk Chinese!" Two high-pitched yips followed. She gave him another lick, then another, sweet-talking him in Chinese. And it annoyed me to see this, how any dumb thing could make her and the dog instantly happy.

Later that same night Kwan asked me again about what those kids had said. She pestered me so much I thought she really was retarded.

Libby-ah, are you sleeping? Okay, sorry, sorry, go back to sleep, it's not important. . . . I only wanted to ask you again about this word, *retard*. Ah, but you're sleeping now, maybe tomorrow, after you come home from school. . . .

Funny, I was thinking how I once thought Miss Banner was this way, *retard*. She didn't understand anything. . . . Libby-ah, did you know I taught Miss Banner to talk? Libby-ah? Sorry, sorry, go back to sleep, then.

It's true, though. I was her teacher. When I first met her, her speech was like a baby's! Sometimes I laughed, I couldn't help it. But she did not mind. The two of us had a good time saying the wrong things all the time. We were like two actors at a temple fair, using our hands, our eyebrows, the fast twist of our feet to show each other what we meant. That's how she told me about her life before she came to China. What I thought she said was this:

She was born to a family who lived in a village far, far west of Thistle Mountain, across a tumbling sea. It was past the country where black people live, beyond the land of English soldiers and Portuguese sailors. Her family village was bigger than all these lands put together. Her father owned many ships that crossed this sea to other lands. In these lands, he gathered money that grew like flowers, and the smell of this money made many people happy.

When Miss Banner was five, her two little brothers chased a chicken into a dark hole. They fell all the way to the other side of the world. Naturally, the mother wanted to find them. Before the sun came up and after the sun came down, she puffed out her neck like a rooster and called for her lost sons. After many years, the mother found the same hole in the earth, climbed in, and then she too fell all the way to the other side of the world.

The father told Miss Banner, We must search for our lost family.

45

So they sailed across the tumbling sea. First they stopped at a noisy island. Her father took her to live in a large palace ruled by tiny people who looked like Jesus. While her father was in the fields picking more flower-money, the little Jesuses threw stones at her and cut off her long hair. Two years later, when her father returned, he and Miss Banner sailed to another island, this one ruled by mad dogs. Again he put Miss Banner in a large palace and went off to pick more flower-money. While he was gone, the dogs chased Miss Banner and tore at her dress. She ran around the island, searching for her father. She met an uncle instead. She and this uncle sailed to a place in China where many foreigners lived. She did not find her family there. One day, as she and the uncle lay in bed, the uncle became hot and cold at the same time, rose up in the air, then fell into the sea. Lucky for her, Miss Banner met another uncle, a man with many guns. He took her to Canton, where foreigners also lived. Every night, the uncle laid his guns on the bed and made her polish them before she could sleep. One day, this man cut off a piece of China, one with many fine temples. He sailed home on this floating island, gave the temples to his wife, the island to his king. Miss Banner met a third uncle, a Yankee, also with many guns. But this one combed her hair. He fed her peaches. She loved this uncle very much. One night, many Hakka men burst into their room and took her uncle away. Miss Banner ran to the Jesus Worshippers for help. They said, Fall on your knees. So she fell on her knees. They said, Pray. So she prayed. Then they took her inland to Jintian, where she fell in the water and prayed to be saved. That's when I saved her.

Later on, as Miss Banner learned more Chinese words, she told me about her life again, and because what I heard was now different, what I saw in my mind was different too. She was born in America, a country beyond Africa, beyond England and Portugal. Her family village was near a big city called *Nu Ye*, sounds like Cow Moon. Maybe this was New York. A company called Russia or Russo owned those ships, not her father. He was a clerk. The shipping company bought opium in India—

those were the flowers — then sold it in China, spreading a dreaming sickness among Chinese people.

When Miss Banner was five, her little brothers did not chase chickens into a hole, they died of chicken pox and were buried in their backyard. And her mother did not puff her neck out like a rooster. Her throat swelled up and she died of a goiter disease and was buried next to her sons. After this tragedy, Miss Banner's father took her to India, which was not ruled by little Jesuses. She went to a school for Jesus-worshipping children from England, and they were not holy but naughty and wild. Later, her father took her to Malacca, which was not ruled by dogs. She was talking about another school, where the children were also English and even more disobedient than the ones in India. Her father sailed off to buy more opium in India but never returned — why, she did not know, so she grew many kinds of sadness in her heart. Now she had no father, no money, no home. When she was still a young maiden, she met a man who took her to Macao. Lots of mosquitoes in Macao; he died of malaria there and was buried at sea. Then she lived with another man, this one an English captain. He helped the Manchus, fought the God Worshippers, earned big money for each city he captured. Later, he sailed home, bearing many looted temple treasures for England and his wife. Miss Banner then went to live with another soldier, a Yankee. This one, she said, helped the God Worshippers, fought against the Manchus, also earned money by looting the cities he and the God Worshippers burned to the ground. These three men, Miss Banner told me, were not her uncles.

I said to her, "Miss Banner-ah, this is good news. Sleeping in the same bed with your uncles is not good for your aunts." She laughed. So you see, by this time, we could laugh together because we understood each other very well. By this time, the calluses on my feet had been exchanged for an old pair of Miss Banner's tight leather shoes. But before this happened, I had to teach her how to talk.

To begin, I told her my name was Nunumu. She called me Miss

Moo. We used to sit in the courtyard and I would teach her the names of things, as if she were a small child. And just like a small child, she learned eagerly, quickly. Her mind wasn't rusted shut to new ideas. She wasn't like the Jesus Worshippers, whose tongues were creaky old wheels following the same grooves. She had an unusual memory, extraordinarily good. Whatever I said, it went in her ear then out her mouth.

I taught her to point to and call out the five elements that make up the physical world: metal, wood, water, fire, earth.

I taught her what makes the world a living place: sunrise and sunset, heat and cold, dust and heat, dust and wind, dust and rain.

I taught her what is worth listening to in this world: wind, thunder, horses galloping in the dust, pebbles falling in water. I taught her what is frightening to hear: fast footsteps at night, soft cloth slowly ripping, dogs barking, the silence of crickets.

I taught her how two things mixed together produce another: water and dirt make mud, heat and water make tea, foreigners and opium make trouble.

I taught her the five tastes that give us the memories of life: sweet, sour, bitter, pungent, and salty.

One day, Miss Banner touched her palm on the front of her body and asked me how to say this in Chinese. After I told her, she said to me in Chinese: "Miss Moo, I wish to know many words for talking about my breasts!" And only then did I realize she wanted to talk about the feelings in her heart. The next day, I took her wandering around the city. We saw people arguing. Anger, I said. We saw a woman placing food on an altar. Respect, I said. We saw a thief with his head locked in a wooden yoke. Shame, I said. We saw a young girl sitting by the river, throwing an old net with holes into the shallow part of the water. Hope, I said.

Later, Miss Banner pointed to a man trying to squeeze a barrel that was too large through a doorway that was too small. "Hope," Miss Banner said. But to me, this was not hope, this was stupidity, rice for brains. And I wondered what Miss Banner had been seeing when I was naming those other feelings for her. I wondered whether foreigners had feelings that were entirely different from those of Chinese people. Did they think all our hopes were stupid?

In time, however, I taught Miss Banner to see the world almost exactly like a Chinese person. Of cicadas, she would say they looked like dead leaves fluttering, felt like paper crackling, sounded like fire roaring, smelled like dust rising, and tasted like the devil frying in oil. She hated them, decided they had no purpose in this world. You see, in five ways she could sense the world like a Chinese person. But it was always this sixth way, her American sense of importance, that later caused troubles between us. Because her senses led to opinions, and her opinions led to conclusions, and sometimes they were different from mine.

For most of my childhood, I had to struggle *not* to see the world the way Kwan described it. Like her talk about ghosts. After she had the shock treatments, I told her she had to pretend she didn't see ghosts, otherwise the doctors wouldn't let her out of the hospital.

"Ah, keep secret," she said, nodding. "Just you me know."

When she came home, I then had to pretend the ghosts *were* there, as part of our secret of pretending they weren't. I tried so hard to hold these two contradictory views that soon I started to see what I wasn't supposed to. How could I not? Most kids, *without* sisters like Kwan, imagine that ghosts are lurking beneath their beds, ready to grab their feet. Kwan's ghosts, on the other hand, sat *on* the bed, propped against her headboard. I saw them.

I'm not talking about filmy white sheets that howled "Ooooooohh." Her ghosts weren't invisible like the affable TV apparitions in *Topper* who moved pens and cups through the air. Her ghosts looked alive. They chatted about the good old days. They worried and complained. I even saw one scratching our dog's neck, and Captain thumped his leg and wagged his tail. Apart from Kwan, I never told anyone what I saw. I thought I'd be sent to the hospital for shock treatments. What I saw seemed so real, not at all like dreaming. It was as though someone *else's* feelings had escaped, and my eyes had become the movie projector beaming them into life.

I remember a particular day—I must have been eight—when I was sitting alone on my bed, dressing my Barbie doll in her best clothes. I heard a girl's voice say: *"Gei wo kan."* I looked up, and there on Kwan's bed was a somber Chinese girl around my age, demanding to see my doll. I wasn't scared. That was the other thing about seeing ghosts: I always felt perfectly calm, as if my whole body had been soaked in a mild tranquilizer. I politely asked this little girl in Chinese who she was. And she said, *"Lili-lili, lili-lili,"* in a high squeal.

When I threw my Barbie doll onto Kwan's bed, this *lili-lili* girl picked it up. She took off Barbie's pink feather boa, peered under the matching satin sheath dress. She violently twisted the arms and legs. "Don't break her," I warned. The whole time I could feel her curiosity, her wonder, her fear that the doll was dead. Yet I never questioned why we had this emotional symbiosis. I was too worried that she'd take Barbie home with her. I said, "That's enough. Give her back." And this little girl pretended she didn't hear me. So I went over and yanked the doll out of her hands, then returned to my bed.

Right away I noticed the feather boa was missing. "Give it back!" I shouted. But the girl was gone, which alarmed me, because only then did my normal senses return, and I knew she was a ghost. I searched for the feather boa—under the covers, between the mattress and the wall, beneath both twin beds. I couldn't believe that a ghost could take something real and make it disappear. I hunted all week for that feather boa, combing through every drawer, pocket, and corner. I never found it. I decided that the girl ghost really had stolen it.

Now I can think of more logical explanations. Maybe Captain took it and buried it in the backyard. Or my mom sucked it up into the vacuum cleaner. It was probably something like that. But when I was a kid, I didn't have strong enough boundaries between imagination and reality. Kwan saw what she believed. I saw what I *didn't* want to believe.

When I was a little older, Kwan's ghosts went the way of other childish beliefs, like Santa Claus, the Tooth Fairy, the Easter Bunny. I did not tell Kwan that. What if she went over the edge again? Privately I replaced her notions of ghosts and the World of Yin with Vatican-endorsed saints and a hereafter that ran on the merit system. I gladly subscribed to the concept of collecting goody points, like those S&H green stamps that could be pasted into booklets and redeemed for toasters and scales. Only instead of getting appliances, you received a one-way ticket to heaven, hell, or purgatory, depending on how many good and bad deeds you'd done and what other people said about you. Once you made it to heaven, though, you didn't come back to earth as a ghost, unless you were a saint. This would probably not be the case with me.

I once asked my mom what heaven was, and she said it was a permanent vacation spot, where all humans were now equal—kings, queens, hoboes, teachers, little kids. "Movie stars?" I asked. Mom said I could meet all kinds of people, as long as they had been nice enough to get into heaven. At night, while Kwan rattled on with her Chinese ghosts, I would list on my fingers the people I wanted to meet, trying to put them in some sort of order of preference, if I was limited to meeting, say, five a week. There was God, Jesus, and Mary—I knew I was supposed to mention them first. And then I'd ask for my father and any other close family members who might have passed on—although not Daddy Bob. I'd wait a hundred years before I put him on my dance card. So that took care of the first week, sort of boring but necessary. The next week was when the good stuff would begin. I'd meet famous people, if they were already dead—the Beatles, Hayley Mills, Shirley Temple,

Dwayne Hickman—and maybe Art Linkletter, the creep, who'd finally realize why he should have had me on his dumb show.

By junior high, my version of the afterlife was a bit more somber. I pictured it as a place of infinite knowledge, where all things would be revealed—sort of like our downtown library, only bigger, where pious voices enumerating what thou shall and shall not do echoed through loudspeakers. Also, if you were slightly but not hopelessly bad, you didn't go to hell, but you had to pay a huge fine. Or maybe if you did something worse, you went to a place similar to continuation school, which was where all the bad kids ended up, the ones who smoked, ran away from home, shoplifted, or had babies out of wedlock. But if you had followed the rules, and didn't wind up a burden on society, you could advance right away to heaven. And there you'd learn the answers to all the stuff your catechism teachers kept asking you, like:

What should we learn as human beings?

Why should we help others less fortunate than ourselves?

How can we prevent wars?

I also figured I'd learn what happened to certain things that were lost, such as Barbie's feather boa and, more recently, my rhinestone necklace, which I suspected my brother Tommy had filched, even though he said, "I didn't take it, swear to God." What's more, I wanted to look up the answers to a few unsolved mysteries, like: Did Lizzie Borden kill her parents? Who was the Man in the Iron Mask? What really happened to Amelia Earhart? And out of all the people on death row who had been executed, who was actually guilty and who was innocent? For that matter, which felt worst, being hanged, gassed, or electrocuted? In between all these questions, I'd find the proof that it was my father who told the truth about how Kwan's mother died, not Kwan.

By the time I went to college, I didn't believe in heaven and hell anymore, none of those metaphors for reward and punishment based on absolute good and evil. I had met Simon by then. He and I would get stoned with our friends and talk about the afterlife: "It just doesn't make sense, man—I mean, you live for less than a hundred years, then everything's added up and, boom, you go on for billions of years after that, either lying on the proverbial beach or roasting on a spit like a hot dog." And we couldn't buy the logic that Jesus was the only way. That meant that Buddhists and Hindus and Jews and Africans who had never even heard of Christ Almighty were doomed to hell, while Ku Klux Klan members were not. Between tokes, we'd speak while trying not to exhale: "Wow, what's the point in that kind of justice? Like, what does the universe learn after that?"

Most of our friends believed there was nothing after death—lights out, no pain, no reward, no punishment. One guy, Dave, said immortality lasted only as long as people remembered you. Plato, Confucius, Buddha, Jesus—they were immortal, he said. He said this after Simon and I attended a memorial service for a friend, Eric, whose number came up in the draft and who was killed in Vietnam.

"Even if they weren't really the way they're now remembered?" Simon asked.

Dave paused, then said, "Yeah."

"What about Eric?" I asked. "If people remember Hitler longer than Eric, does that mean Hitler is immortal but Eric isn't?"

Dave paused again. But before he could answer, Simon said firmly, "Eric was great. Nobody will ever forget Eric. And if there's a paradise, that's where he is right now." I remember I loved Simon for saying that. Because that's what I felt too.

How did those feelings disappear? Did they vanish like the feather boa, disappear when I wasn't looking? Should I have tried harder to find them again?

It's not just grudges that I hang on to. I remember a girl on my bed. I remember Eric. I remember the power of inviolable love. In my memory, I still have a place where I keep all those ghosts.

# 4

# THE GHOST MERCHANT'S HOUSE

$\text{M}$y mother has another new boyfriend, Jaime Jofré. I don't have to meet him to know he'll have charm, dark hair, and a green card. He'll speak with an accent and my mother will later ask me, "Isn't he passionate?" To her, words are more ardent if a man must struggle to find them, if he says *"amor"* with a trill rather than ordinary "love."

Romantic though she is, my mother is a practical woman. She wants proof of love: Give and you should receive. A bouquet, ballroom dancing lessons, a promise of eternal fidelity—it must be up to the man to decide. And there's also Louise's corollary of sacrificial love: Give up smoking for him and receive a week at a health spa. She prefers the Calistoga Mud Baths or the Sonoma Mission Inn. She thinks men who understand this kind of exchange are from emerging nations—she would never say "the third world." A colony under foreign dictatorship is excellent. When emerging nation isn't available, she'll settle for Ireland, India, Iran. She firmly believes that men who have suffered from oppression and a black-market economy know there's more at stake. They try harder to win you over. They're willing to deal. Through these guiding thoughts, my mother has found true love as many times as she's quit smoking for good.

Hell yes, I'm furious with my mother. This morning she asked if she could drop by to cheer me up. And then she spent two hours comparing my failed marriage with hers to Bob. A lack of commitment, an unwillingness to make sacrifices, no give, all take—those are the common faults she's noticed in Simon and Bob. And she and I both "gave, gave, gave from the bottom of our hearts." She bummed a cigarette from me, then a match.

"I saw it coming," she said, and inhaled deeply. "Ten years ago. Remember that time Simon went to Hawaii and left you home when you had the flu?"

"I told him to go. We had nonrefundable airline tickets and he could sell only one." Why was I defending him?

"You were sick. He should have been giving you chicken soup rather than cavorting on the beach."

"He was cavorting with his grandmother. She'd had a stroke." I was starting to sound as whiny as a kid.

She gave me a sympathetic smile. "Sweetie, you don't have to be in denial anymore. I know what you're feeling. I'm your mother, remember?" She stubbed out her cigarette before assuming her matter-of-fact, social worker manner: "Simon didn't love you enough, because *he* was lacking, not you. You are abundantly lovable. There is *nothing wrong with you.*"

I gave a stiff nod. "Mom, I really should get to work now."

"You go right ahead. I'll just have another cup of coffee." She looked at her watch and said, "The exterminators flea-bombed my apartment at ten. Just to be safe, I'd like to wait another hour before I go back."

And now I'm sitting at my desk, unable to work, completely drained. What the hell does she know about my capacity for love? Does she have any idea how many times she's hurt me without knowing it? She complains that all that time she spent with Bob was a big waste. What about me? What about the time she didn't spend with me? Wasn't that a waste too? And why am I now devoting any energy to thinking about this? I've been reduced to a snivelly little kid again. There I am, twelve years old, facedown on my twin bed, a corner of the pillow stuffed into my mouth so that Kwan can't hear my mangled sobs.

"Libby-ah," Kwan whispers, "something matter? You sick? Eat too much Christmas cookie? Next time I don't make so sweet. . . . Libby-ah, you like my present? You don't like, tell me, okay? I make you another sweater. You tell me what color. Knit it take me only one week. I finish, wrap up, like surprise all over again. . . . Libby-ah? I think Daddy Mommy come back from Yosemite Park bring you beautiful present, pictures too. Pretty snow, mountaintop . . . Don't cry! No! No! You not mean this. How you can *hate* you own mother? . . . Oh? Daddy Bob too? *Ah, zemma zaogao.* . . ."

Libby-ah, Libby-ah? Can I turn on the light? I want to show you something. . . .

Okay, okay! Don't get mad! I'm sorry. I'm turning it off. See? It's dark again. Go back to sleep. . . . I was going to show you the pen that fell out of Daddy Bob's trouser pocket. . . . You tilt it one way, you see a lady in a blue dress. You tilt it the other way, wah! —the dress falls down. I'm not lying. See for yourself. I'll turn on the light. Are you ready? . . . Oh, Libby-ah, your eyes are swollen big as plums! Put the wet towel back over them. Tomorrow they won't itch as much. . . . The pen? I saw it sneaking out of his pocket when we were at Sunday mass. He didn't notice because he was pretending to pray. I know it was just pretend, mm-hmm, because his head went this way—*booomp!*—and he was snoring. *Nnnnnnnhhh!* It's true! I gave him a little push. He didn't wake up, but his nose stopped making those sounds. Ah, you think that's funny? Then why are you laughing?

So anyway, after a while I looked at the Christmas flowers, the candles, the colored glass. I watched the priest waving the smoky lantern. Suddenly I saw Jesus walking through the smoke! Yes, Jesus! I thought he had come to blow out his birthday candles. I told myself, Finally I can see him—now I am a Catholic! Oh, I was so excited. That's why Daddy Bob woke up and pushed me down.

I kept smiling at Jesus, but then I realized—ah?—that man was not Jesus but my old friend Lao Lu! He was pointing and laughing at me. "Fooled you," he said. "I'm not Jesus! Hey, you think he has a bald head like mine?" Lao Lu walked over to me. He waved his hand in front of Daddy Bob. Nothing happened. He touched his little finger light as a fly on Daddy Bob's forehead. Daddy Bob slapped himself. He slowly pulled the nasty pen from Daddy Bob's pocket and rolled it into a fold of my skirt.

"Hey," Lao Lu said. "Why are you still going to a foreigners' church? You think a callus on your butt will help you see Jesus?"

Don't laugh, Libby-ah. What Lao Lu said was not polite. I think he was remembering our last lifetime together, when he and I had to sit on the hard bench for two hours every Sunday. Every Sunday! Miss Banner too. We went to church for so many years and never saw God or Jesus, not Mary either, although back then it was not so important to see her. In those days, she was also mother to baby Jesus but only concubine to his father. Now everything is Mary this and that!—*Old St. Mary's, Mary's Help, Mary Mother of God, forgiving me my sins*. I'm glad she got a promotion. But as I said, in those days, the Jesus Worshippers did not talk about her so much. So I had to worry only about seeing God and Jesus. Every Sunday, the Jesus Worshippers asked me, "Do you believe?" I had to say not yet. I wanted to say yes to be polite. But then I would have been lying, and when I died maybe they would come after me and make me pay two kinds of penalty to the foreign devil, one for not believing, another for pretending that I did. I thought I couldn't see

Jesus because I had Chinese eyes. Later I found out that Miss Banner never saw God or Jesus either. She told me she wasn't a religious kind of person.

I said, "Why is that, Miss Banner?"

And she said, "I prayed to God to save my brothers. I prayed for him to spare my mother. I prayed that my father would come back to me. Religion teaches you that faith takes care of hope. All my hopes are gone, so why do I need faith anymore?"

"Ai!" I said. "This is too sad! You have no hopes?"

"Very few," she answered. "And none that are worth a prayer."

"What about your sweetheart?"

She sighed. "I've decided he's not worth a prayer either. He deserted me, you know. I wrote letters to an American navy officer in Shanghai. My sweetheart's been there. He's been in Canton. He's even been in Guilin. He knows where I am. So why hasn't he come?"

I was sad to hear that. At the time, I didn't know her sweetheart was General Cape. "I still have many hopes of finding my family again," I said. "Maybe I should become a Jesus Worshipper."

"To be a true worshipper," she said, "you must give your whole body to Jesus."

"How much do you give?"

She held up her thumb. I was astonished, because every Sunday she preached the sermon. I thought this should be worth two legs at least. Of course, she had no choice about preaching. No one understood the other foreigners, and they couldn't understand us. Their Chinese was so bad it sounded just like their English. Miss Banner had to serve as Pastor Amen's go-between. Pastor Amen didn't ask. He said she must do this, otherwise no room for her in the Ghost Merchant's House.

So every Sunday morning, she and Pastor stood by the doorway to the church. He would cry in English, "Welcome, welcome!" Miss Banner would translate into Chinese: "Hurry-come into God's House! Eat rice after the meeting!" God's House was actually the Ghost Merchant's family temple. It belonged to his dead ancestors and their gods. Lao Lu thought the foreigners showed very bad manners picking this place for God's House. "Like a slap in the face," he said. "The God of War will drop horse manure from the sky, you wait and see." Lao Lu was that way—you make him mad, he'll pay you back.

The missionaries always walked in first, Miss Banner second, then Lao Lu and I, as well as the other Chinese people who worked in the Ghost Merchant's House—the cook, the two maids, the stableman, the carpenter, I forget who else. The visitors entered God's House last. They were mostly beggars, a few Hakka God Worshippers, also an old woman who pressed her hands together and bowed three times to the altar, even though she was told over and over again not to do that anymore. The newcomers sat on the back benches—I'm guessing this was in case the Ghost Merchant came back and they needed to run away. Lao Lu and I had to sit up front with the missionaries, shouting "Amen!" whenever the pastor raised his eyebrows. That's why we called him Pastor Amen—also because his name sounded like "Amen," Hammond or Halliman, something like that.

As soon as we flattened our bottoms on those benches, we were not supposed to move. Mrs. Amen often jumped up, but only to wag her finger at those who made too much noise. That's how we learned what was forbidden. No scratching your head for lice. No blowing your nose into your palm. No saying "Shit" when clouds of mosquitoes sang in your ear—Lao Lu said that whenever anything disturbed his sleep.

That was another rule: No sleeping except when Pastor Amen prayed to God, long, boring prayers that made Lao Lu very happy. Because when the Jesus Worshippers closed their eyes, he could do the same and take a long nap. I kept my eye open. I would stare at Pastor Amen to see if God or Jesus was coming down from the heavens. I had seen this happen to a God Worshipper at a temple fair. God entered an ordinary man's body and threw him to the ground. When he stood up again, he had great powers. Swords thrust against his stomach bent in

59

half. But no such thing ever happened to Pastor Amen. Although one time when Pastor was praying, I saw a beggar standing at the door. I remembered that the Chinese gods sometimes did this, came disguised as beggars to see what was going on, who was being loyal, who was paying them respect. I wondered if the beggar was a god, now angry to see foreigners standing at the altar where he used to be. When I looked back a few minutes later, the beggar had disappeared. So who knows if he was the reason for the disasters that came five years later.

At the end of the prayer time, the sermon would begin. The first Sunday, Pastor Amen spoke for five minutes—talk, talk, talk!—a lot of sounds that only the other missionaries could understand. Then Miss Banner translated for five minutes. Warnings about the devil. Amen! Rules for going to heaven. Amen! Bring your friends with you. Amen! Back and forth they went, as if they were arguing. So boring! For two hours, we had to sit still, letting our bottoms and our brains grow numb.

At the end of the sermon, there was a little show, using the music box that belonged to Miss Banner. Everyone liked this part very much. The singing was not so good, but when the music started, we knew our suffering was almost at an end. Pastor Amen lifted both hands and told us to rise. Mrs. Amen walked to the front of the room. So did the nervous missionary named Lasher, like *laoshu*, "mouse," so that was what we called her, Miss Mouse. There was also a foreign doctor named Swan, which sounded like *suan-le*, "too late"—no wonder sick people were scared to see him. Dr. Too Late was in charge of opening Miss Banner's music box and winding it with a key. When the music started, the three of them sang. Mrs. Amen had tears pouring from her eyes. Some of the old country people asked out loud if the box contained tiny foreigners.

Miss Banner once told me the music box was a gift from her father, the only memory of her family that she had left. Inside, she kept a little album for writing down her thoughts. The music, she said, was actually a German song about drinking beer, dancing, and kissing pretty girls.

But Mrs. Amen had written new words, which I heard a hundred times but only as sounds: "We're marching with Jesus on two willing feet, when Death turns the corner, our Lord we shall meet." Something like that. You see, I remember that old song, but this time the words have new meaning. Anyway, that was the song we heard every week, telling everyone to go outside to eat a bowl of rice, a gift from Jesus. We had many beggars who thought Jesus was a landlord with many rice fields.

The second Sunday, Pastor Amen spoke for five minutes, Miss Banner for three. Then Pastor for another five minutes, Miss Banner for one. Everything became shorter and shorter on the Chinese side, and the flies drank from our sweat for only one and a half hours that Sunday. The week after that it was only one hour. Later, Pastor Amen had a long talk with Miss Banner. The following week, Pastor Amen spoke for five minutes, Miss Banner spoke the same amount. Again Pastor spoke for five minutes, Miss Banner the same amount. But now she didn't talk about rules for going to heaven. She was saying, "Once upon a time, in a kingdom far away, there lived a giant and the filial daughter of a poor carpenter who was really a king. . . ." At the end of each five minutes, she would stop at a very exciting part and say something like: "Now I must let Pastor speak for five minutes. But while you wait, ask yourself, Did the tiny princess die, or did she save the giant?" After the sermon and story were over, she told people to shout "Amen" if they were ready to eat their free bowl of rice. Ah, big shouts!

Those Sunday sermons became very popular. Many beggars came to hear Miss Banner's stories from her childhood. The Jesus Worshippers were happy. The rice-eaters were happy. Miss Banner was happy. I was the only one who worried. What if Pastor Amen learned what she was doing? Would he beat her? Would the God Worshippers pour coals over my body for teaching a foreigner to have a disobedient Chinese tongue? Would Pastor Amen lose face and have to hang himself? Would the people who came for rice and stories and not Jesus go to a foreigners' hell?

When I told Miss Banner my worries, she laughed and said no such thing would happen. I asked her how she knew this. She said, "If everyone is happy, what harm can follow?" I remembered what the man who returned to Thistle Mountain had said: "Too much happiness always overflows into tears of sorrow."

WE HAD five years of happiness. Miss Banner and I became great and loyal friends. The other missionaries remained strangers to me. But from seeing little changes every day, I knew their secrets very well. Lao Lu told me about shameful things he saw from outside their windows, also strange things he saw when he was inside their rooms. How Miss Mouse cried over a locket holding a dead person's hair. How Dr. Too Late ate opium pills for his stomachache. How Mrs. Amen hid pieces of Communion bread in her drawer, never eating it, just saving it for the end of the world. How Pastor Amen reported to America that he had made one hundred converts when really it was only one.

In return, I told Lao Lu some of the secrets I had seen myself. That Miss Mouse had feelings for Dr. Too Late, but he didn't notice. That Dr. Too Late had strong feelings for Miss Banner, and she pretended not to notice. But I did not tell him that Miss Banner still had great feelings for her number-three sweetheart, a man named Wa-ren. Only I knew this.

For five years, everything was the same, except for these small changes. That was our life back then, a little hope, a little change, a little secret.

And yes, I had my secrets too. My first secret was this. One night, I dreamed I saw Jesus, a foreign man with long hair, long beard, many followers. I told Miss Banner, except I forgot to mention the part about the dream. So she told Pastor Amen, and he put me down for a hundred converts—that's why I knew it was only one. I didn't tell Miss Banner to correct him. Then he would have been more ashamed that his hundred converts was not even one.

My second secret was much worse.

This happened soon after Miss Banner told me she had lost her family and her hopes. I said I had so much hope I could use my leftovers to wish her sweetheart would change his mind and return. This pleased her very much. So that's what I prayed for, for at least one hundred days.

One evening, I was sitting on a stool in Miss Banner's room. We were talking, talking, talking. When we ran out of the usual complaints, I asked if we could play the music box. Yes, yes, she said. I opened the box. No key. It's in the drawer, she said. Ah! What's this? I picked up an ivory carving and held it to my eye. It was in the shape of a naked lady. Very unusual. I remembered seeing something like it once. I asked her where the little statue had come from.

"It belonged to my sweetheart," she said. "The handle of his walking stick. When it broke off, he gave it to me as a remembrance."

Wah! That's when I knew Miss Banner's sweetheart was the traitor, General Cape. All this time, I had been praying for him to come back. Just thinking about it shriveled my scalp.

So that was my second secret: that I knew who he was. And the third was this: I started praying he would stay away.

Let me tell you, Libby-ah, I didn't know how much she hungered for love, any kind. Sweet love didn't last, and it was too hard to find. But rotten love!—there was plenty to fill the hollow. So that's what she grew accustomed to, that's what she took as soon as it came back.

# 5

# LAUNDRY DAY

Just like clockwork, the phone rings at eight. That makes it the third morning in a row Kwan's called at the exact moment that I'm buttering toast. Before I can say hello, she blurts out: "Libby-ah, ask Simon — name of stereo fix-it store, what is?"

"What's wrong with your stereo?"

"Wrong? Ahhhh . . . too much noise. Yes-yes, I play radio, it go *cccccchhhhhhhhssss*."

"Did you try adjusting the frequency?"

"Yes-yes! I often adjust."

"How about standing back from the stereo? Maybe you're conducting a lot of static today. It's supposed to rain."

"Okay-okay, maybe try that first. But just case, you call Simon, ask him store name."

I'm in a good mood. I want to see how far she'll carry her ruse. "I know the store," I say, and search for a likely-sounding name. "Yeah, it's Bogus Boomboxes. On Market Street." I can practically hear Kwan's mind whirring and clicking into alternate mode.

Finally she laughs and says, "Hey, you bad girl — lie! No such name."

"And no such stereo problem," I add.

"Okay-okay. You call Simon, tell him Kwan say Happy Birthday."

"Actually, I was going to call him for the same reason."

"Oh, you so bad! Why you torture me, embarrass this way!" She lets out a wheezy laugh, then gasps and says, "Oh, and Libby-ah, after call Simon, call Ma."

"Why? Is her stereo broken too?"

"Don't joke. Her heart feel bad."

I'm alarmed. "What's wrong? Is it serious?"

"Mm-hmm. So sad. You remember new boyfriend she have, I May Hopfree?"

"*High*-may ho-*fray*," I pronounce slowly. "Jaime Jofré."

"I always remember, I May Hopfree. And that's what he do! Turn out he married already. Chile lady. She show up, pinch his ear, take home."

"No!" A ripple of glee flows into my cheeks, and I mentally slap myself.

"Yes-yes, Ma so mad! Last week she buy two loveboat cruise ticket. Hopfree say use your Visa, I pay you back. Now no pay, no cruise, no refund. Ah! Poor Ma, always find wrong man. . . . Hey, maybe I do matchmake for her. I choose better for her than she choose herself. I make good match, bring me luck."

"What if it's not so good?"

"Then I must fix, make better. My duty."

After we hang up, I think about Kwan's duty. No wonder she sees my impending divorce as a personal and professional failure on her part. She still believes she was our spiritual *mei-po*, our cosmic match-maker. And I'm hardly in the position to tell her that she wasn't. I was the one who asked her to convince Simon we were destined to be to-gether, linked by the necessity of fate.

SIMON BISHOP AND I met more than seventeen years ago. At that moment in our lives, we were willing to place all our hopes on the ridiculous — pyramid power, Brazilian *figa* charms, even the advice of Kwan and her ghosts. We both were terribly in love, I with Simon, he with someone else. The someone else happened to have died before I ever met Simon, although I didn't know that until three months later.

I spotted Simon in a linguistics class at UC Berkeley, spring quarter 1976. I noticed him right away because like me he had a name that didn't fit with his Asian features. Eurasian students weren't as common then as they are now, and as I stared at him, I had the sense I was seeing my male doppelgänger. I started wondering how genes interact, why one set of racial characteristics dominates in one person and not in another with the same background. I once met a girl whose last name was Chan. She was blond-haired and blue-eyed, and no, she wearily explained, she was not adopted. Her father was Chinese. I figured that her father's ancestors had engaged in secret dalliances with the British or Portuguese in Hong Kong. I was like that girl, always having to explain about my last name, why I didn't look like a Laguni. My brothers look almost as Italian as their last name implies. Their faces are more angular than mine. Their hair has a slight curl and is a lighter shade of brown.

Simon didn't look like any particular race. He was a perfectly balanced blend, half Hawaiian-Chinese, half Anglo, a fusion of different racial genes and not a dilution. When our linguistics class formed study groups, Simon and I drifted toward the same one. We didn't mention what we so obviously shared.

I remember the first time he brought up his girlfriend, because I had been hoping he didn't have one. Five of us were cramming for a midterm. I was listing the attributes of Etruscan: a dead language, as well as an isolate, unrelated to other languages . . . In the middle of my summary, Simon blurted: "My girlfriend, Elza, she went on a study tour of Italy and saw these incredible Etruscan tombs."

We looked at him—like, So? Mind you, Simon didn't say, "My girl-friend, who, by the way, is as dead as this language." He talked about her in passing, as if she were alive and well, traveling on Eurail and sending postcards from Tuscany. After a few seconds of awkward silence, he looked sheepish and mumbled the way people do when they're caught arguing with themselves while walking down the sidewalk. Poor guy, I thought, and at that moment my heartstrings went *twing*.

After class, Simon and I would often take turns buying each other coffee at the Bear's Lair. There we added to the drone of hundreds of other life-changing conversations and epiphanies. We discussed primi-tivism as a Western-biased concept. Mongrelization as the only long-term answer to racism. Irony, satire, and parody as the deepest forms of truth. He told me he wanted to create his own philosophy, one that would guide his life's work, that would enable him to make *substantive* changes in the world. I looked up the word *substantive* in the dictionary that night, then realized I wanted a substantive life too. When I was with him, I felt as if a secret and better part of myself had finally been un-leashed. I had dated other guys to whom I felt attracted, but those re-lationships seldom went beyond the usual good times induced by all-night parties, stoned conversations, and sometimes sex, all of which soon grew as stale as morning breath. With Simon, I laughed harder, thought more deeply, felt more passionately about life beyond my own cubbyhole. We could volley ideas back and forth like tennis pros. We wrestled with each other's minds. We unearthed each other's past with psychoanalytic gusto.

I thought it was eerie how much we had in common. Both of us had lost a parent before the age of five, he a mother, I a father. We both had owned pet turtles; his died after he accidentally dropped them into a chlorinated swimming pool. We both had been loners as kids, abandoned to caretakers—he to two unmarried sisters of his mother's, I to Kwan.

"My mom left me in the hands of someone who talked to ghosts!" I once told him.

"God! I'm amazed you aren't crazier than you already are." We laughed, and I felt giddy about our making fun of what had once caused me so much pain.

"Good ol' Mom," I added. "She's the quintessential social worker, totally obsessed with helping strangers and ignoring the homefront. She'd rather keep an appointment with her manicurist than lift a finger to help her kids. Talk about phony! It wasn't that she was pathological, but, you know—"

And Simon jumped in: "Yeah, even benign neglect can hurt for a lifetime." Which was *exactly* what I was feeling but couldn't put into words. And then he clinched my heart: "Maybe her lack of attention is what made you as strong as you are today." I nodded eagerly as he went on: "I was thinking that, because my girlfriend—you know, Elza—well, she lost both parents when she was a baby. Talk about strong-willed—whew!"

That's how we were together, intimate in every way—up to a point. I sensed we were attracted to each other. From my end it was a strong sexual charge. From his it was more like static cling—which he easily shook off: "Hey, Laguni," he'd say, and put his hand firmly on my shoulder. "I'm bushed, gotta run. But if you want to go over notes this weekend, give me a call." With this breezy sendoff, I'd trudge back to my apartment, nothing to do on a Friday night, because I had turned down a date hoping that Simon would ask me out. By then I was stupid-in-love with Simon—goo-goo-eyed, giggly-voiced, floaty-headed, infatuated in the worst way. There were so many times when I lay in bed, disgusted that I was twitching with unspent desire. I wondered: Am I crazy? Am I the only one who's turned on? Sure, he has a girlfriend. So what? As everyone knows, when you're in college and changing your mind about a million things, a current girlfriend can turn into a former one overnight.

But Simon didn't seem to know that I was flirting with him. "You know what I like about you?" he asked me. "You treat me like a good buddy. We can talk about anything and we don't let the other thing get in the way."

"The other what?"

"The fact that we are . . . Well, you know, the opposite-sex thing."

"Really?" I said, faking astonishment. "You mean, I'm a girl but you're a — I had no idea!" And then we both broke into hearty guffaws.

At night I'd cry angrily, telling myself that I was a fool. I vowed many times to give up any hope of romance with Simon — as if it were possible to will myself *not* to be in love! But at least I knew how to put on a good front. I continued to play the jovial good buddy, listening with a smile on my face and a cramp in my heart. I expected the worst. And sure enough, sooner or later, he would bring up Elza, as though he knew she was on my mind as well.

Through three months of masochistic listening I came to know the minutiae of her life: That she lived in Salt Lake City, where she and Simon had grown up, tussling with each other since the fifth grade. That she had a two-inch scar on the back of her left knee the shape and color of an earthworm, a mysterious legacy from infancy. That she was athletic; she kayaked, backpacked, and was an expert cross-country skier. That she was musically gifted, a budding composer, who had studied with Artur Balsam at a famous summer music camp in Blue Hill, Maine. She'd even written her own thematic variation on the Goldberg Variations. "Really?" I said to each praiseworthy thing he said about her. "That's amazing."

The strange thing is, he kept speaking about her in the present tense. Naturally I thought she was alive in the present time. Once, Simon pointed out I had smeared lipstick on my teeth, and as I hurriedly rubbed it off, he added, "Elza doesn't wear makeup, not even lipstick. She doesn't believe in it." I wanted to scream, What's there to believe!? You either wear makeup or you don't! By then I wanted to smack her, a girl so morally upright she had to be the most odious hominid ever to walk planet Earth, in her non–animal hide shoes. Even if Elza had been sweet and insipid, it wouldn't have mattered, I still would have despised her. To me, Elza didn't *deserve* Simon. Why should she have him as one of her perks of life? She deserved an Olympic gold medal for Amazon discus-throwing. She deserved a Nobel Peace Prize for saving retarded baby whales. She deserved to play organ for the Mormon Tabernacle Choir.

Simon, on the other hand, deserved me, someone who could help him discover the recesses of his soul, the secret passageways that Elza had barricaded with constant criticism and disapproval. If I complimented Simon—told him what he had said was profound, for example—he'd say, "You think so? Elza says one of my biggest faults is going along with whatever's nice and easy, that I don't think things through hard enough."

"You can't believe everything that Elza says."

"Yeah, that's what she says too. She hates it when I just go along with what's been handed to me as truth. She believes in trusting your own intuitions, sort of like that guy who wrote *Walden*, what's his name, Thoreau. Anyway, she thinks it's important for us to argue, to get to the marrow of what we believe and why."

"I hate to argue."

"I don't mean argue in the sense of a fight. More of a debate, like what you and I do."

I hated being compared and falling short. I tried to sound playful. "Oh? So what do *you two* debate?"

"Like whether celebrities have a responsibility as symbols and not just as people. Remember when Muhammad Ali refused to be drafted?"

"Sure," I lied.

"Elza and I both thought he was great, taking a personal stand like that against the war. But then he wins back the heavyweight title and later President Ford invites him to the White House. Elza said, 'Can you believe it?' I said, 'Hell, if I were invited, I'd go to the White House too.'

And she said, 'By a *Republican* president? During an election year?' She wrote him a letter."

"The president?"

"No, Muhammad Ali."

"Oh, right. Of course."

"Elza says you can't just talk politics or watch it happen on television. You have to do something, otherwise you're part of it."

"Part of what?"

"You know, hypocrisy. It's the same as corruption."

I imagined Elza looking like Patty Hearst, wearing a beret and combat fatigues, an automatic rifle perched on her hip.

"She believes all people should take an active moral position on life. Otherwise the world's going to end in thirty years or less. A lot of our friends say she's a pessimist. But she thinks she's the real optimist, because she wants to *do* something to change the world in a positive way. If you think about it, she's right."

While Simon grew more expansive about Elza's ridiculous opinions, I'd be dreamily analyzing his features, how chameleonlike they were. His face would change—from Hawaiian to Aztecan, Persian to Sioux, Bengali to Balinese.

"What kind of name is Bishop?" I asked one day.

"On my father's side, missionary eccentrics. I'm descended from *the* Bishops—you know?—the family of Oahu Island fame. They went to Hawaii in the eighteen hundreds to convert lepers and heathens, then ended up marrying royalty and owning half the island."

"You're kidding."

"Unfortunately, I'm also from the side of the family that didn't inherit any of the wealth, not a single pineapple orchard or golf course. On my mother's side, we're Hawaiian-Chinese, with a couple of royal princesses swimming in the gene pool. But again, no direct access to beachfront property." And then he laughed. "Elza once said I inherited from the missionary side of my family the laziness of blind faith, and from my royal Hawaiian side a tendency to use others to take care of my needs rather than working to fulfill them myself."

"I don't think that's true, that stuff about inherited nature, as if we're destined to develop into a certain kind of person without choice. I mean, hasn't Elza ever heard of *determinism*?"

Simon looked stumped. "Hmmm," he said, thinking. For a moment, I felt the satisfaction of having vanquished a competitor with a subtle and deft move.

But then he remarked: "Doesn't the doctrine of determinism say that all events and even human choices follow natural laws, meaning it kind of goes along with what Elza was saying?"

"What I mean is," and I began to stammer as I tried to recall what I'd skimmed over in philosophy class. "I mean, how do we define *natural*? Who's to say what's natural and what's not?" I was flailing, trying to keep my pathetic self above water. "Besides, what's her background?"

"Her folks are Mormon, but they adopted her when she was a year old and named her Elsie, Elsie Marie Vandervort. She doesn't know who her biological parents were. But ever since she was six, before she knew how to read music, she could hear a song just once, then play it exactly, note for note. And she especially loved music by Chopin, Paderewski, Mendelssohn, Gershwin, Copland—I forget the others. Later she discovered every single one of them was either Polish or Jewish. Isn't that weird? So that made her think she was probably a Polish Jew. She started calling herself Elza instead of Elsie."

"I like Bach, Beethoven, and Schumann," I said smartly, "but that doesn't make me a German."

"It wasn't just that. When she was ten, something happened which will sound really bizarre, but I swear it's true, because I saw part of it. She was in the school library, flipping through an encyclopedia, and she saw a photo of some crying kid and his family being rounded up by soldiers. The caption said they were Jews being taken to Auschwitz. She didn't know where Auschwitz was or even that it was a concentration camp. But she literally smelled something horrible that made her shake and gag. And then she fell to her knees and started chanting: 'Osh-vee-en-shim, osh-vee-en-shim,' something like that. The librarian shook her, but Elza wouldn't stop—she couldn't. So the librarian dragged her to the school nurse, Mrs. Schneebaum. And Mrs. Schneebaum, who was Polish, heard Elza chanting 'Osh-vee-en-shim' and freaked. She thought Elza was saying this to make fun of her. Well, get this: It turned out 'Oświęcim' is the way you say 'Auschwitz' in Polish. After Elza came out of her trance, she knew her parents were Polish Jews who had survived Auschwitz."

"What do you mean, she knew?"

"She just *knew*—like the way hawks know to hover on a stream of air, the way rabbits freeze with fear. It's knowledge that can't be taught. She said her mother's memories passed from heart to womb, and they're now indelibly printed on the walls of her brain."

"Come on!" I said dismissively. "She sounds like my sister Kwan."

"How so?"

"Oh, she just makes up any old theory to suit whatever she believes. Anyway, biological instinct and emotional memories aren't the same thing. Maybe Elza read or heard about Auschwitz before and didn't remember. You know how people see old photos or movies and later think they were personal memories. Or they have a déjà vu experience—and it's just a bad synapse feeding immediate sensory perception into long-term memory. I mean, does she even *look* Polish or Jewish?" And right after I said that I had a dangerous thought. "You have a picture of her?" I asked as casually as possible.

While Simon dug out his wallet, I could feel my heart revving like a race car, about to confront my competition. I feared she would look devastatingly beautiful—a cross between Ingrid Bergman illuminated by airport runway lights and Lauren Bacall sulking in a smoke-filled bar.

The photo showed an outdoorsy girl, backlit by a dusk-hour glow, frizzy hair haloing a sullen face. Her nose was long, her chin childishly small, her lower lip curled out in mid-utterance, so that she looked like a bulldog. She was standing next to a camping tent, arms akimbo, hands perched on chunky hips. Her cutoff jeans were too tight, sharply creased at the crotch. There was also her ridiculous T-shirt, with its "Question Authority" in lumpy letters stretched over the mounds of her fatty breasts.

I thought to myself, Why, she isn't gorgeous. She isn't even button-nose cute. She's as plain as a Polish dog without mustard. I was trying to restrain a smile, but I could have danced the polka I was so happy. I knew that comparing myself with her that way was superficial and ir-relevant. But I couldn't help feeling happily superior, believing I was prettier, taller, slimmer, more stylish. You didn't have to like Chopin or Paderewski to recognize that Elza was descended from Slavic peasant stock. The more I looked, the more I rejoiced. To finally see the demons of my insecurity, and they were no more threatening than her cherub-faced kneecaps.

What the hell did Simon see in her? I tried to be objective, look at her from a male point of view. She was athletic, there was that. And she certainly gave the impression of being smart, but in an intimidating, ob-noxious way. Her breasts were far bigger than mine; they might be in her favor—if Simon was stupid enough to like fleshy globules that would someday sag to her navel. You might say that her eyes were interesting, slanted and catlike. Although on second glance, they were disturbing, smudged with dark hollows. She stared straight into the camera and her look was both penetrating and vacant. Her expression suggested that she knew the secrets of the past and future and they were all sad.

I concluded Simon had confused loyalty with love. After all, he had known Elza since childhood. In a way, you had to admire him for that. I handed the picture back to him, trying not to appear smug. "She seems *awfully* serious. Is that something you inherit being a Polish Jew?"

Simon studied the photo. "She can be funny when she wants. She can do impersonations of anyone — gestures, speech patterns, foreign accents. She's hilarious. She can be. Sometimes. But." He paused, struggling. "But you're right. She broods a lot about how things can be better, why they should be, until she goes into a funk. She's always been that way, moody, serious, I guess you might even say depressed. I don't know where that comes from. Sometimes she can be so, you know, unreasonable," and he trailed off, seemingly troubled, as if he were now viewing her from a new light and her features were glaringly unattractive.

I hoarded these observational tidbits as weapons to use in the future. Unlike Elza, I would become a *true* optimist. I would take action. In contrast to her lugubriousness, I would be buoyant. Instead of being a critical mirror, I would admire Simon's insights. I too would take active political stands. But I'd laugh often and show Simon that life with a spiritual soul mate didn't have to be all doom and gloom. I was determined to do whatever was necessary to unseat her from Simon's heart.

After seeing Elza's picture, I thought she would be easy to displace. Foolish me, I didn't know I would have to pry Simon from the clutches of a ghost. But that day, I was so happy I even accepted an invitation from Kwan to come to dinner. I brought my laundry, and just to be pleasant, I pretended to listen to her advice.

Libby-ah, let me do this. You don't know how to use my washing machine. Not too much soap, not too much hot, always turn the pockets inside out. . . .

Libby-ah, ai-ya, why do you have so many black clothes? You should wear pretty colors! Little flowers, polka dots, purple is a good color for you. White, I don't like. Not because of superstition. Some people think that white means death. No such thing. In the World of Yin, there are many, many colors you don't even know, because you can't see them with your eyes. You have to use your secret senses, imagine them when you are full of genuine feelings and memories, both happy and sad. Happy and sad sometimes come from the same thing, did you know this?

Anyway, white I don't like because it's too easy to get dirty, too hard to clean. It's not practical. I know, because in my last lifetime, I had to wash lots of white laundry—lots, lots, lots. That was one of the ways I earned my room in the Ghost Merchant's House.

On the First Day of each week I had to wash. On the Second Day, I ironed what I had washed. The Third Day was for polishing shoes and mending clothes. The Fourth Day was for sweeping the courtyard and passageways, the Fifth Day for mopping the floors and wiping the furniture in God's House. The Sixth Day was for important business.

I liked the Sixth Day the most. Together Miss Banner and I walked around the village, handing out pamphlets called "The Good News." Even though the paper contained English words turned into Chinese, I couldn't read them. Since I couldn't read, I couldn't teach Miss Banner to read. And in the poor parts of the village that we walked through, nobody knew how to read either. But people were glad to take those pamphlets. They used them to stuff inside their winter clothes. They put them over rice bowls to keep out flies. They pasted them over cracks in walls. Every few months, a boat from Canton came and brought more boxes of these pamphlets. So every week, on the Sixth Day, we had plenty to hand out. We didn't know that what we really were giving those people was plenty of future trouble.

When we returned to the Ghost Merchant's House, happy and empty-handed, Lao Lu would put on a little show for us. He would climb up a column, then walk quickly along the edge of the roof, while we gasped and cried, "Don't fall!" Then he would turn around and pick up a brick and place this on his head, then a teacup on top of that, then a bowl, a plate, all sorts of things of different sizes and weights. Again he would walk along that skinny edge, while we screamed and laughed. I think he was always trying to recover face from that time he fell into the water with Miss Banner and her trunk.

The Seventh Day, of course, was for going to God's House, then resting in the afternoon, talking in the courtyard, watching the sunset, the stars, or a lightning storm. Sometimes I plucked leaves from a bush that grew in the courtyard. Lao Lu always corrected me: "That's not a bush. It's a holy tree. See here." He would stand with his arms straight out, like a ghost walking in the night, claiming that the spirit of nature now flowed from the tree's limbs into his. "You eat the leaves," he said, "and you find peace, balance in yourself, piss on everyone else." So every Sunday, I used those leaves to make a tea, like a thank-you gift to Lao Lu for his show. Miss Banner always drank some too. Each week, I would say, "Hey, Lao Lu, you are right, the tea from this bush makes a person feel peaceful." Then he would say, "That's not just any dog-pissing bush, it's a holy tree." So you see, those leaves did nothing to cure him of cursing, too bad.

After the Seventh Day, it was the First Day all over again, the one I'm now going to talk about. And as I said, I had to wash the dirty clothes.

I did my washing in the large walled passageway just outside the kitchen. The passageway had a stone-paved floor and was open to the sky but shaded by a big tree. All morning long, I kept big pots of water and lime boiling, two pots because the missionaries didn't allow me to have men and ladies swimming together in the same hot water. One pot I scented with camphor, the other with cassia bark, which smells like cinnamon. Both were good for keeping away cloth-eating moths. In the camphor water, I boiled white shirts and the secret underclothes of Pastor Amen and Dr. Too Late. I boiled their bedding, the cloths they used to wipe their noses and brows. In the pot with cassia bark, I boiled the blouses, the secret underclothes of the ladies, their bedding, the cloths they used to wipe their lady noses.

I laid the wet clothes on the wheel of an old stone mill, then rolled the stone to squeeze out the water. I put the squeezed clothes into two baskets, men and ladies still separate. I poured the leftover cassia water over the kitchen floor. I poured the leftover camphor water over the passageway floor. And then I carried the baskets through the gateway, into the back area, where there were two sheds along the wall, one for a mule, one for a buffalo cow. Between these two sheds was a rope stretched very tight. And this is where I hung the laundry to dry.

On my left side was another wall, and a gateway that led into a large strolling garden, bounded by high stone walls. It was a beautiful place, once tamed by the hands of many gardeners, now neglected and wild. The stone bridges and ornamental rocks still stood, but the ponds underneath were dried up, no fish only weeds. Everything was tangled together—the flowering bushes, the branches of trees, weeds and vines. The pathways were thick with the leaves and blossoms of twenty seasons, so soft and cool on my feet. The paths rolled up and down in surprising ways, letting me dream I was climbing back up Thistle Mountain. The top of one of these hills was just big enough for a small pavilion. Inside the pavilion were stone benches covered with moss. In the middle of the stone floor was a burnt spot. From this pavilion, I could look over the wall, see the village, the limestone peaks, the archway going into the next mountain valley. Every week, after I washed the clothes, I soaked duck eggs in leftover lime and buried them in the garden to let them cure. And when I was done with that, I stood in the pavilion, pretending the world I saw beyond the wall was mine. I did this for several years, until one day Lao Lu saw me standing there. He said, "Ai, Nunumu, don't go up there anymore, that's where the Punti merchant died, in the pavilion."

Lao Lu said the merchant was standing there one evening, with his four wives down below. He gazed at the sky and saw a cloud of black birds. The merchant cursed them, then burst into flames. Wah! The fire roared, the merchant's fat hissed and spattered. Below, his terrified wives yowled, smelling the pungent odor of fried chili and garlic. All at once, the fire went out, and smoke in the shape of the merchant rose and blew away. When his wives crept up to the pavilion, they found no ash, only his feet and shoes remained. Also, the smell, terrible and delicious at the same time.

After Lao Lu told me that, I worried about that smell every time I hung the laundry, every time I went into the garden to bury my eggs. I smelled camphor, cassia, dead leaves, and flowering bushes. But the day that I'm now talking about, I thought I smelled the Ghost Merchant, his fear of death, very strong, chili and garlic, maybe a little vinegar too. It was a day of great heat, during the month when the cicadas unbury themselves after lying four years in the ground. They were singing, the males shrieking for females, each one trying to be the loudest. I kept my one eye aimed toward the gateway, just in case the Ghost Merchant was in there, looking for his feet. I heard a rustling sound, dry leaves crackling, twigs snapping, and black birds rushed up out of the bushes and scattered in the sky. The cicadas fell silent.

My bones were trembling. I wanted to run away. But I heard the Ghost Bandit Maiden inside me say, "Scared? How can you be scared of a Punti merchant with no feet? Go inside and see where he is." I was now both scared and ashamed to be scared. I carefully went to the gateway, peeked in. When the cicadas began to buzz, I ran into the garden, my feet crunching dead leaves. I darted onto the stone bridge, past the dry pond, over the hills rolling up and down. When the buzzing turned into clacks, I stopped, knowing the cicadas would soon exhaust themselves and fall quiet. Using their song, I ran and stopped, ran and stopped, until I was standing at the bottom of the hill big enough for a small pavilion. I circled its bottom when the clacking stopped, and stared at a man sitting on a stone bench, eating a tiny banana. I had never heard of a ghost eating a banana. Of course, since then, other ghosts have told me that they sometimes pretend to eat bananas, although never ones with lots of black bruises, which is what this man's banana had.

When the man saw me, he leapt to his feet. He had a peculiar but elegant face, not Chinese, not foreign. He wore gentleman's clothes. I had seen this man before, I was sure of it. Then I heard sounds coming from the other side of the hill, a loud stream of water splashing on rocks, a man sighing, feet crunching twenty seasons of leaves. I saw the flash of a silver-tipped walking stick, the hollowed face of the man who owned it. His hands were busy closing the many buttons of his trousers. This was General Cape, and the elegant man with the banana was the one-half man called Yiban.

Wah! Here was the man I had prayed would return to Miss Banner. I later prayed that he would stay away, but I must not have asked God that as many times.

Cape barked to Yiban, and then Yiban said to me, "Little Miss, this gentleman is a famous Yankee general. Is this the house where the God-worshipping foreigners live?"

I didn't answer. I was remembering what the man who came back to Thistle Mountain had said: that General Cape had turned traitor against the Hakkas. I saw General Cape looking at my shoes. He spoke again, and Yiban translated: "The lady who gave you those leather shoes is a great friend of the general. She is anxious to see him."

So the shoes with my feet inside led the two men to Miss Banner. And Yiban was right. She was anxious to see General Cape. She threw her arms around him and let him lift her in the air. She did this in front of Pastor Amen and Mrs. Amen, who although they were husband and wife never touched each other, not even in their own room—that's what Lao Lu told me. Late at night, when everyone was supposed to be asleep but was not, Miss Banner opened her door and General Cape quickly walked from his room into hers. Everyone heard this; we had no windows, only wooden screens.

I knew Miss Banner would call the general into her room. Earlier that evening, I had told her Cape was a traitor to Hakka people, that he would be a traitor to her as well. She became very angry with me, as if

I were saying these things to curse her. She said General Cape was a hero, that he had left her in Canton only to help the God Worshippers. So then I told her what the man who returned to Thistle Mountain had said: that General Cape had married a Chinese banker's daughter for gold. She said my heart was rotten meat and my words were maggots feeding on gossip. She said if I believed these things about General Cape, then I would no longer be her loyal friend.

I said to her, "When you already believe something, how can you suddenly stop? When you are a loyal friend, how can you no longer be one?" She didn't answer.

Late at night, I heard the music box play, the one her father had given her when she was a young girl. I heard the music that made tears pour from Mrs. Amen's eyes, but now the music was making a man kiss a girl. I heard Miss Banner sigh, again and again. And her happiness was so great it spilled over, leaked into my room, and turned into tears of sorrow.


I've started doing my laundry at Kwan's house again. Simon used to take care of the wash — that was one of the nice things about being married to him. He liked to tidy up the house, snap fresh sheets and smooth them onto the bed. Since he left, I've had to wash my own clothes. The coin-op machines are in the basement of my building, and the mustiness and dim light give me the willies. The atmosphere preys on my imagination. But then, so does Kwan.

I always wait until I run out of clean underwear. And then I throw three bagfuls of laundry into the car and head for Balboa Street. Even now, as I stuff my clothes into Kwan's dryer, I think about that story she told me the day I was so hopeful with love. When she got to the part about joy turning into sorrow, I said, "Kwan, I don't want to hear this anymore."

"Ah? Why?"

"It bums me out. And right now, I want to stay in a good mood."

"Maybe I tell you more, don't become bum. You see mistake Miss Banner do—"

"Kwan," I said, "I don't want to hear about Miss Banner. *Ever.*"

What power! What relief! I was amazed how strong Simon made me feel. I could stand up to Kwan. I could decide whom I should listen to and why. I could be with someone like Simon, who was down-to-earth, logical, and sane.

I never thought that he too would fill my life with ghosts.

II

# 6

# FIREFLIES

The night Simon kissed me for the first time was when I finally learned the truth about Elza. The spring quarter had ended and we were walking in the hills behind the Berkeley campus, smoking a joint. It was a warm June night, and we came upon an area where tiny white lights were twinkling in the oak trees as if it were Christmas.

"Am I hallucinating?" I asked.

"Fireflies," Simon answered. "Aren't they amazing?"

"Are you sure? I don't think they exist in California. I've never seen them before."

"Maybe some student bred them for a work-study experiment and let them go."

We sat on the scabby trunk of a fallen tree. Two flickering bugs were zigzagging their way toward each other, their attraction looking haphazard yet predestined. They flashed on and off like airplanes headed for the same runway, closer and closer, until they sparked for an instant as one, then extinguished themselves and flitted darkly away.

"That's romance for you," I said.

Simon smiled and looked right at me. He awkwardly put his arm around my waist. Ten seconds passed, twenty seconds, and we hadn't moved. My face grew hot, my heart was beating fast, as I realized we were crossing the confines of friendship, about to leap over the fence and run for the wilds. And sure enough, our mouths, like those fireflies, bobbed and weaved toward each other. I closed my eyes when his lips reached mine, both of us trembly and tentative. Just as I pressed in closer to let him take me into a more passionate embrace, he released me, practically pushed me. He started talking in an apologetic tone.

"Oh God, I'm sorry. I really like you, Olivia. A lot. It's complicated, though, because of—well, you know."

I flicked a bug off the trunk, stared at it dumbly as it twirled on its back.

"You see, the last time I saw her, we had a terrible fight. She got very angry with me, and I haven't seen her since. That was six months ago. The thing is, I still love her. But—"

"Simon, you don't have to explain." I stood up on shaky legs. "Let's just forget it, okay?"

"Olivia, sit down. Please. I have to tell you. I want you to understand. This is important."

"Let go of me. Forget it, okay? Oh, shit! Just pretend it never happened!"

"Wait. Come back. Sit down, please sit down. Olivia, I have to tell you this."

"What the hell for?"

"Because I think I love you too."

I caught my breath. Of course, I would have preferred if he hadn't qualified his declaration with "I think" and "too," as if I could be part of an emotional harem. But infatuated as I was, "love" was enough to act as both balm and bait. I sat down.

"If you hear what happened," he said, "maybe you'll understand why it's taken me so long to tell you how I feel about you."

My heart was still pounding wildly with a strange mixture of anger and hope. We sat in nervous silence for a few minutes. When I was ready, I said in a cool voice, "Go ahead."

Simon cleared his throat. "This fight Elza and I had, it was in December, during the quarter break. I was back in Utah. We had planned to go cross-country skiing in Little Cottonwood Canyon. The week before, we'd been praying for new snow, and then it finally came in truckloads, three feet of fresh powder."

"She didn't want to go," I guessed, trying to hurry up the story.

"No, we went. So we were driving up the canyon, and I remember we were talking about the SLA and whether giving food to the poor made extortion and bank robbery less reprehensible. Out of the blue, Elza asked me, 'What do you feel about abortion?' And I thought I heard wrong. 'Extortion?' I said. And she said, 'No, abortion.' So I said, 'You know, like what we said before, about *Roe versus Wade*, that the decision didn't go far enough.' She cut me off and said, 'But what do you *really* feel about abortion?'"

"What did she mean, really feel?"

"That's what I asked. And she said slowly, enunciating every syllable: 'I mean emotionally, what do you feel?' And I said, 'Emotionally, I think it's fine.' Then she blew up: 'You didn't even think about the question! I'm not asking you about the weather. I'm asking you about the lives of human beings! I'm talking about the real life of a woman versus the potential life in her womb!'"

"She was hysterical." I was eager to emphasize Elza's volatile and unreasonable nature.

He nodded. "At the trailhead, she jumped out of the car, really pissed, threw on her skis. Just before she took off, she screamed, 'I'm pregnant, you idiot. And there's no way I'm having this baby and ruining my life. But it tears me up to abort it and you're just sitting there, smiling, saying it's fine.'"

"Omigod. Simon. How were you supposed to know?" So that was it, I thought: Elza had wanted to get married, and confronted with the prospect, Simon had refused. Good for him.

"I was stunned," Simon continued. "I had no idea. We were always careful about birth control."

"You think she slipped up on purpose?"

He frowned. "She's not that kind of person." He seemed defensive.

"What did you do?"

"I put on my skis, followed her tracks. I kept shouting for her to wait, but she went over a crest and I couldn't see her anymore. God, I remember how beautiful it was that day, sunny, peaceful. You know, you never think terrible things can happen when the weather's nice." He laughed bitterly.

I thought he was through—since that day he and Elza hadn't seen each other, end of story, time for the sequel, me. "Well," I said, trying to sound sympathetic, "the least she could have done was given you a chance to discuss the situation before jumping all over you."

Simon leaned forward and buried his face in his hands. "Oh God!" he said in an anguished voice.

"Simon, I understand, but it wasn't your fault, and now it's over."

"No, wait," he said hoarsely. "Let me finish." He stared at his knees, took a few deep breaths. "I got to this steep fire road, and there was an out-of-bounds sign. Just beyond that, she was sitting at the top of a ledge, hugging herself, crying. I called to her and she looked up, really pissed. She pushed off and headed down this steep wide-open bowl. I can still see it: The snow, it was incredible, pristine and bottomless. And she was gliding down, taking the fall line. But about halfway down, she hit some heavier snow, her skis sank, and she sagged to a stop."

I looked at Simon's eyes. They were fixed on something faraway and lost, and I became scared.

"I yelled her name as loud as I could. She was mashing her poles against the snow, trying to kick up the tips of her skis. I yelled again—

'Goddamnit, Elza!' — and I heard this sound, like a muffled gunshot, and then it was perfectly quiet again. She turned around. She was squinting — she must have been blinded by the sun. I don't think she saw it — the slope, two hundred yards above her. It was slowly tearing, no sound, like a giant zipper opening up. The seam became a crack, an icy blue shadow. And then it was snaking fast, straight across. The crack slipped down a little, and it was huge, glassy as an ice rink. Then everything began to rumble, the ground, my feet, my chest, my head. And Elza — I could tell she knew. She was struggling to get out of her skis."

Like Elza, I knew what was coming. "Simon, I don't think I want to hear any more of this —"

"She threw off her skis and her backpack. She was jumping through the snow, sinking to her hips. I started yelling, 'Go to the side!' And then the mountain collapsed and all I could hear was this train roar, trees snapping, whole stands of them, popping like toothpicks."

"Oh God," I whispered.

"She was swimming on top of the crud — that's what you're supposed to do, swim, swim, keep swimming. And then . . . she was swallowed up . . . gone. Everything creaked and settled, then grew absolutely still. I could smell pine pitch from the broken trees. My mind was going a million miles a minute. Don't panic, I told myself, if you panic it's all over. I skied down the side, between the trees where the snow was intact. I kept telling myself, Remember where she went under. Look for skis sticking up. Use one of your skis as a marker. Dig with your pole. Spread out in a widening circle.

"But when I got to the bottom, nothing looked the way it did from the top. The point I'd marked in my head, shit, it wasn't there, just this huge field of rubbly snow, heavy as wet cement. I was stumbling around, feeling like I was in one of those nightmares where your legs are paralyzed."

"Simon," I said, "you don't have to —"

But he kept talking: "All of a sudden this strange calm hit me, the eye of the hurricane. I could see Elza in my mind, where she was. We were so connected. She was guiding me with her thoughts. I shoved my way across to where I thought she was. I started to dig with one of my skis, telling her I'd have her out soon. And then I heard a helicopter. Thank God! I waved like mad, then two ski patrol guys were jumping out with a rescue dog and avalanche probes. I was so nuts I was saying how aerobically fit she was, what her heart rate was, how many miles she ran every week, where they should dig. But the ski patrol guys and the dog started going down the slope in a zigzag pattern. So I kept digging in the same area where I was sure she was. Pretty soon, I heard the dog yelping, and the guys shouting down below that they'd found her. That surprised me, that she wasn't where I thought she was. When I got down to where the ski patrol guys were, I saw they had her top half uncovered. I was shoving my way through, sweaty and out of breath, thanking them, telling them how great they were, because I could see she was okay. She was there, right there, all along she'd been only two feet under the surface. I was so damn happy to see she was alive."

"Oh, thank God," I whispered. "Simon, until you said that, you know what? I actually thought —"

"Her eyes were already open. But she was stuck, crouched on her side with her hands cupped together in front of her mouth, like this, which was what I'd taught her to do, to push out an air pocket so you can breathe longer. I was laughing and saying, 'God, Elza, I can't believe you were calm enough to remember that part about the air pocket.' Only the rescue guys were now pushing me back, saying, 'We're sorry, man, but she's gone.' And I said, 'What the fuck are you talking about? She's still there, I can see her, get her out.' And one of the guys put his arm on my shoulder and said, 'Hey, bud, we've been digging for an hour and the avalanche was reported an hour before that. The most she ever had was twenty, twenty-five minutes tops.'

"And I yelled back, 'It's been *ten minutes*!' I was so crazed—you know what I thought? That Elza told them to say that because she was still mad at me. I pushed past them. You see, I was going to tell her that I knew—I knew in my heart and my gut—how special life is, how hard it is to give it up, yours or anyone else's."

I put my hand on Simon's shoulder. He was sucking in air like an asthmatic. "When I reached her," he said, "I scraped out the snow stuck in her mouth. And, and, and—and that's when I realized she wasn't breathing, you know, she wasn't really breathing into that little air space I had taught her to make. And, and, and I saw how dark her face was, the tears frozen in her open eyes, you know, and I said, 'Elza, please, come on, please don't do this, please don't be scared.' I grabbed her hands like this—oh God, oh shit, they were so cold—but she wouldn't stop, she wouldn't . . . She was—"

"I know," I said softly.

Simon shook his head. "She was praying, you see, hands cupped together like this, the way I had taught her. And even though I already knew, oh shit, oh Jesus, even though I knew she wasn't really saying anything, I could hear her, she was crying, 'Please, God, please, please, please don't let me die.' "

I turned away. My throat was making stupid noises as I tried not to cry. I didn't know what to say, how to console him. And I know I should have felt horrible sadness, great sympathy for Simon, which I did feel. But to be completely honest, what I felt most of all was gut-wrenching fear. I had hated her, wished her dead, and now it was as if I'd killed her. I would have to pay for this. It would all come back to me, the full karmic circle, like Kwan and the mental hospital. I looked at Simon. He was gazing clear-eyed at the silhouettes of oak trees, the sparks of fireflies.

"You know, most of the time I know that she's gone," he said with an eerie calm. "But sometimes, when I think about her, our favorite song will come on the radio. Or a friend of hers from Utah will call right at that moment. And I don't think it's just coincidence. I sense her. She's there. Because, you see, we were connected, really connected, in every way. It wasn't just physical, that was the least of it. It was like well . . . can I read you something she wrote?"

I nodded blankly. Simon took out his wallet and unfolded a sheet of paper taped at the seams. "She sent this to me about a month before the accident, as part of my birthday present." I listened with a sickened heart.

" 'Love is tricky,' " he read in a quavery voice. " 'It is never mundane or daily. You can never get used to it. You have to walk with it, then let it walk with you. You can never balk. It moves you like the tide. It takes you out to sea, then lays you on the beach again. Today's struggling pain is the foundation for a certain stride through the heavens. You can run from it but you can never say no. It includes everyone.' " Simon folded the letter back up. "I still believe that," he said.

I was desperately trying to figure out what the words meant. But my mind was churning everything I had heard into frothy gibberish. Did he read the letter to say that's what he wanted from me?

"That was beautiful." I was ashamed I couldn't think of anything else to say.

"God! You don't know how relieved I am, I mean, being able to talk to you about her." His eyes were shiny, speedy, his words spilled out with abandon. "It's like she's the only one who *knows* me, really knows me. It hits me all the time, and I know I need to let her go. But I'll be walking around campus thinking, No, she can't be gone. And then I see her, her same wavy hair, only when she turns around, it's someone else. But no matter how many times I'm wrong, I can't stop looking for her. It's like being addicted, going through the worst kind of withdrawal. I find her in everything, everyone." His eyes locked crazily on mine. "Like your voice. When I first met you, I thought it sounded a lot like hers."

I must have jumped a couple of inches, because Simon quickly added, "You have to understand I was sort of whacked-out when I met you. It was only three months after she, you know, had the accident. I wanted to believe she was still alive, living in Utah, that she was mad at me, that's why I hadn't seen her in a while. . . . Actually, now that I think about it, you two don't sound that much alike, not really." He traced a finger around my knuckles. "I never wanted to love anyone else. I figured it was enough, what Elza and I had. I mean, I figure most people never have that kind of love in a whole lifetime—you know what I mean?"

"You were lucky."

He kept stroking my knuckles. "And then I remembered what she wrote about not running away from love, not saying no. That you can't." He glanced up at me. "Anyway, that's why I had to tell you everything, so I can be open with you from here on out. And so you'd understand that I also have these other feelings, besides what I have for you, and if I'm not always there . . . well, you know."

I could barely breathe. I whispered in the softest possible voice, "I understand. I do. Really, I do." And then we both stood up and, without another word between us, walked out of the hills and back to my apartment.

What should have been one of the most romantic nights of my life was a nightmare for me. The whole time we made love I had the sense that Elza was watching us. I felt as if I were having sex during a funeral. I was afraid to make a sound. Yet Simon didn't act bereaved or guilty at all. You wouldn't have known he had just told me the saddest story I'd ever heard. He was like other lovers on first nights, eager to show me how versatile and experienced he was, worried he wasn't pleasing me, soon ready for a second round.

Afterward, I lay in bed, sleepless, thinking about music by Chopin and Gershwin, what they could possibly have in common. I could picture Elza's cherub-faced kneecaps, one of them with a beatific smile, and I wondered how a little baby could get a scar the shape and color of an earthworm. I thought about her eyes—what memories of hope and pain and violence had she inherited? Love moves you like the tide, she had said. I saw her floating on the wave of an avalanche.

By dawn, I could see Elza as Simon had. Her head was surrounded by a halo of light, her skin was as soft as a cherub's wings. And her icy blue eyes could see everything, the past into the future. She would always be dangerously beautiful, as pristine and alluring as a slope of fresh, bottomless snow.

LOOKING BACK, I can see I was an idiot to continue with Simon. But I was young, I was stupid-in-love. I confused a pathetic situation with a romantic one, sympathy with a mandate to save Simon from sorrow. And I've always been a magnet for guilt. My father, then Kwan, now Elza. I felt guilty about every bad thought I'd ever had about Elza. As penance, I sought her approval. I became her conspirator. I helped resuscitate her.

I remember the time I suggested to Simon that we go backpacking in Yosemite. "You told me how much Elza loved nature," I said. "I was thinking, if we went, well, she'd be there too." Simon looked grateful that I understood, and for me that was enough, that this was the way our love would grow. I just had to wait a bit. That's what I reminded myself later, when we were camped at a place called Rancheria Falls. Above us was a magnificent canopy of stars. It was so vast, so vivid, and my hope was the same. I struggled in my heart, then my brain to tell Simon this, but it all came out sounding trite. "Simon, look," I said. "Do you realize they're the same stars that the first lovers on earth saw?"

And Simon breathed in and exhaled deeply. I could tell he did this not with wonder but with informed sadness. So I was quiet, I understood, the way I said I would. I knew he was thinking about Elza again. Maybe he was thinking that she used to see these same stars. Or that she once expressed a similar thought, only more elegantly. Or that in the dark my voice was hers, with the same overly passionate tone, the one I used to express ordinary ideas, the one she would have used to save the whole damn world.

And then I felt myself becoming smaller yet denser, about to be crushed by the weight of my own heart, as if the laws of gravity and balance had changed and I was now violating them. I stared once again at those sharp little stars, twinkling like fireflies. Only now they were splotched and melting, and the night heaven was tilting and whirling, too immense to hold itself up any longer.

# THE HUNDRED
# SECRET SENSES

The way I embraced Elza's former life, you'd have thought she was once my dearest, closest friend. When Simon and I had to pick recipes for Thanksgiving, we chose Elza's oyster-and-chestnut stuffing over my Chinese sticky-rice-and-sausage. We drank our coffee out of two-handled ceramic mugs Elza had made at a summer camp for musically gifted children. In the evenings and on weekends, we played Elza's favorite tapes: songs by the Blues Project, Randy Newman, Carole King, as well as a rather bathetic symphony that Elza herself had composed, which her college orchestra had recently performed and recorded as a memorial to her. To Simon, I said the music was living proof of her beliefs. But secretly, I thought it sounded like alley cats yowling on garbage night, with a finale of cans crashing as a well-aimed shoe flew out the window.

Then December rolled around, and Simon asked me what special gift I wanted for Christmas. The radio was playing holiday songs, and I was trying to think what Simon would want for Elza—a donation in her name to the Sierra Club? a collection of Gershwin records? That's when I heard Yogi Yorgesson singing "Yingle Bells."

The last time I had heard that song I was twelve, when I thought sarcasm was the height of cool. That year, I gave Kwan a Ouija board for Christmas. While she stared in bafflement at the old-fashioned letters and numbers, I told her she could use the Ouija to ask American ghosts how to spell English words. She patted the board and said, "Wunnerful, so useful." My stepfather threw a fit.

"Why do you feel you have to make fun of her?" Daddy Bob said to me sternly. Kwan examined the Ouija board, more puzzled than before.

"It was just a joke, okay?"

"Then it's a mean joke and you have a mean heart to do it." He grabbed my hand and jerked me up, saying, "Young lady, Christmas is over for you."

Alone, in the bedroom, I turned on the radio. That's when I heard "Yingle Bells" playing. The song was supposed to be a "yoke," like Kwan's present. I was crying bitterly: How was I being mean to Kwan if she didn't even *know* it? Besides, I reasoned, if I was being mean, which I wasn't, she deserved it, she was so wacko. She invited people to play funny jokes on her. And what was so wrong about having fun on Christmas? It was the holier-than-thou people who were mean. Well, if everyone thought I was bad, I'd show them what bad was.

I turned the radio way up. I imagined the volume knob was Daddy Bob's big Italian nose, and I twisted it so hard it broke off, and now Yogi Yorgesson was singing "laughing all the way—ha-ha-ha!" at the top of his lungs while Daddy Bob was swearing, "Olivia, turn off that goddamn radio," which was not a Christian thing to say, especially on Christmas. I pulled the plug with a vengeance. Later Kwan came into the bedroom and told me she liked my spelling gift "oh very-very much."

"Stop acting so retarded," I growled. And I kept my face looking as mean as I could, but it scared me to see how much I had hurt her.

Now here was Simon asking me what I wanted for Christmas. Once again I was listening to "Yingle Bells" on the radio. And I wanted to cry out that being understanding gets you nowhere. At that moment, I knew what I really wanted for Christmas. I wanted to pull the plug. I wanted Elza dead.

But after six months of acting like the noble runner-up, how could I suddenly tell Simon I wanted to kick Elza's ghostly butt out of our bed? I imagined packing her photos, her records, her irritating kitsch into a box. "For safekeeping," I'd tell Simon, "while I do some spring cleaning." Then I'd load the box into the trunk of my car and late at night I'd drive to Lake Temescal. I'd weigh the box down with bleach bottles filled with sand, dump the whole mess into the dark moonless water, and watch the bubbles surface as my nemesis sank into liquid oblivion.

And later, what would I say to Simon, what explanation would I give him? "God, it's terrible, but the box with all of Elza's things? —it was stolen. I can't believe it either. The burglars must have thought it was valuable. I mean, it is, but just to you and me. God, you're right, I don't know why they didn't take the stereo."

He'd notice my evasive eyes, the corners of my mouth turned up in an irrepressible smile. I'd have to confess what I'd done, what I really felt about Elza and her two-handled coffee mugs. He'd be pissed, and that would be the end of Simon and me. If that was the case, to hell with him. But after I had exhausted my imaginary self with variations of this pyrrhic victory, I was lost. I couldn't let go of Simon any more than he could Elza.

It was in this wretched and murderous frame of mind that I sought an accomplice to do the dirty deed. I called Kwan.

I DISCREETLY OUTLINED the situation to my sister. I didn't say I was in love with Simon. To Kwan? And suffer her sisterly chuckles, endless teasing, and crackpot advice? I said Simon was a friend.

"Ah! Boyfriend," she guessed, all excited.

"No. Just a friend."

"Close friend."

"*Just* a friend."

"Okay-okay, now I understand you meaning."

I told her that one of Simon's friends had died in an accident. I said that Simon was sad, that he couldn't let go of this friend who was dead. He was obsessed, it was unhealthy. I said it might help him if he heard from this friend as a yin person. Knowing how suggestible Kwan was, also how eager she was to help me in any way, I made the requirements as clear as possible.

"Maybe," I hinted, "Simon's dead friend can tell him they must both start a new life. He must forget about her, never mention her name."

"Ah! She was girlfriend."

"No, just a friend."

"Ah, like you, *just* friend." She smiled, then asked, "Chinese too?"

"Polish, I think. Maybe also Jewish."

"Tst! Tst!" Kwan shook her head. "Polish-Jewish, very hard to find, so many dead Polish-Jewish. Many dead Chinese people too, but I have many connection for Chinese—this yin person know that yin person, easier for me to find if Chinese. But Polish-Jewish—ah!—maybe she don't even go to Yin World, maybe go someplace else."

"The next world is *segregated*? You can go to the World of Yin only if you're Chinese?"

"No-no! Miss Banner, she not Chinese, she go to Yin World. All depend what you love, what you believe. You love Jesus, go Jesus House. You love Allah, go Allah Land. You love sleep, go sleep."

"What if you don't believe in anything for sure before you die?"

"Then you go big place, like Disneyland, many places can go try—you like, you decide. No charge, of course."

As Kwan continued to ramble, I imagined an amusement park filled with ex–insurance agents dressed in hand-me-down angel costumes, waving fake lightning bolts, exhorting passersby to take an introductory tour of Limbo, Purgatory, the Small World of Unbaptized Infants.

Meanwhile, there'd be hordes of former Moonies and est followers signed up for rides called the Pandemonium, the Fire and Brimstone, the Eternal Torture Rack.

"So who goes to the World of Yin?"

"Lots people. Not just Chinese, also people have big regret. Or people think they miss big chance, or miss wife, miss husband, miss children, miss sister." Kwan paused and smiled at me. "Also, people miss Chinese food, they go Yin World, wait there. Later can be born into other person."

"Oh, you mean yin people are those who believe in reincarnation."

"What mean recarnation?"

"Reincarnation. You know, after you die, your spirit or soul or whatever can be reborn as another human being."

"Yes, maybe this same thing, something like that. You not too picky, can come back fast, forty-nine days. You want something special—born to this person, marry that person—sometimes must wait long time. Like big airport, can go many-many places. But you want first class, window seat, nonstop, or discount, maybe have long delay. Hundred year at least. Now I tell you something, secret, don't tell anyone, ah. Many yin people, next life, guess who they want be. You guess."

"President of the United States."

"No."

"The Who."

"Who?"

"Never mind. Who do they want to be?"

"Chinese! I telling you true! Not French, not Japanese, not Swedish. Why? I think because Chinese food best, fresh and cheap, many-many flavors, every day different taste. Also, Chinese family very close, friends very loyal. You have Chinese friend or family one lifetime, stay with you ten thousand lifetime, good deal. That's why so many Chinese people live in world now. Same with people from India. Very crowded there. India people believe many lifetime too. Also, I hear India food not too bad, lots spicy dishes, curry flavors too. Course, Chinese curry still best. What you think, Libby-ah? You like my curry dish? You like, I can make for you tonight, okay?"

I steered Kwan back to the matter of Elza. "So what's the best way to go about finding Simon's friend? Where do Polish Jews usually go?"

Kwan started muttering: "Polish-Jewish, Polish-Jewish. So many places can go. Some believe nothing after die. Some say go in-between place, like doctor waiting room. Others go Zion, like fancy resort, no one ever complaining, no need tip, good service anyway." She shook her head, then asked, "How this person die?"

"A skiing accident in Utah. Avalanche. It's like drowning."

"Ah!—waterski affa lunch! Stomach too full, no wonder drown."

"I didn't say after lunch. I said—"

"No lunch? Then why she drown? Cannot swim?"

"She didn't drown! She was buried in the snow."

"Snow!" Kwan frowned. "Then why you say she drown?"

I sighed, about to go insane.

"She very young?"

"Twenty-one."

"Tst! This too sad. Happen when?"

"About a year ago."

Kwan clapped her hands. "How could I forgotten! My bachelor friend! Toby Lipski. Lipski, sound like 'ski.' Jewish too. Oh!—very funny yin person. Last year he die, liver cancer. He tell me, 'Kwan, you right, too much drinking at disco club, bad for me, very-very bad. When I come back, *no more drinking*. Then I can have long life, long love, *long* penis.' Last part, course he just joking. . . ." Kwan looked at me to make sure she'd made her point about the evils of alcohol. "Toby Lipski also tell me, 'Kwan, you need yin favor, you ask for Toby Lipski.' Okay. Maybe I ask Toby Lipski find this girl. What's name?"

"Elza."

"Yes-yes, Elza. First I must send Toby message, like write letter with my mind." She squeezed her eyes shut and tapped the side of her head. Her eyes flew back open. "Send to Yin World. Everything with mind and heart together, use hundred secret sense."

"What do you mean, secret sense?"

"Ah! I already tell you so many time! You don't listen? Secret sense not really secret. We just call secret because everyone has, only forgotten. Same kind of sense like ant feet, elephant trunk, dog nose, cat whisker, whale ear, bat wing, clam shell, snake tongue, little hair on flower. Many things, but mix up together."

"You mean instinct."

"Stink? Maybe sometimes stinky—"

"Not stink, *instinct*. It's a kind of knowledge you're born with. Like . . . well, like Bubba, the way he digs in the dirt."

"Yes! Why you let dog do that! This not sense, just nonsense, mess up you flower pot!"

"I was just making a—ah, forget it. What's a secret sense?"

"How I can say? Memory, seeing, hearing, feeling, all come together, then you know something true in you heart. Like one sense, I don't know how say, maybe sense of tingle. You know this: Tingly bones mean rain coming, refreshen mind. Tingly skin on arms, something scaring you, close you up, still pop out lots a goose bump. Tingly skin top a you brain, oh-oh, now you know something true, leak into you heart, still you don't want believe it. Then you also have tingly hair in you nose. Tingly skin under you arm. Tingly spot in back of you brain—that one, you don't watch out, you got a big disaster come, mm-hm. You use you secret sense, sometimes can get message back and forth fast between two people, living, dead, doesn't matter, same sense."

"Well, whatever you need to do," I said. "But put a rush on it."

"Wah!" Kwan snorted. "You think I work post office—shop late, mail Christmas Eve, deliver Christmas Day, everything rush-rush-rush? No such thing here, no such thing there either! Anyway, in Yin World, no need save time. Everything already too late! You want reach someone, must sense that person feeling, that person sense youself feeling. Then —*pung!*—like happy accident when two self run into each other."

"Well, whatever. Just be sure to tell this Toby guy that the woman's name is Elza Vandervort. That's her adopted name. She doesn't know who her real parents were. She thinks they were Polish Jews who had been in Auschwitz. And she may be thinking about Chopin, musical stuff."

"Wah! You talking too fast."

"Here, I'll write it down for you."

Only afterward did I consider the irony of the whole matter: that I was helping Kwan with her illusions so that she could help Simon let go of his.

Two weeks later, Kwan told me Toby had hit a jackpot. He had set a date with Elza for the night of the next full moon. Kwan said that people in the World of Yin were very bad about making appointments, because nobody used a calendar or a clock anymore. The best method was to watch the moon. That was why so many strange things happened when the moon was at its brightest, Kwan said: "Like porch light, telling you guests welcome-welcome, come inside."

I STILL FEEL GUILTY over how easy it was to fool Simon. It went like this.

I mentioned to him we'd been invited to Kwan's for dinner. He accepted. The moment we walked in her house, Kwan said, "Ohhhh, so good-looking." As if he'd been prompted, Simon said to Kwan, "You're kidding. You don't look twelve years older than Olivia." Then Kwan beamed and said, "Ohhhh, good manner too."

The curry wasn't bad, the conversation wasn't too painful. Kwan's husband and her stepsons chatted excitedly about a fistfight they'd witnessed in the parking lot of Safeway. Throughout the dinner, Kwan did not act that weird, although she did ask Simon nosy questions about his parents. "Which one Chinese? Mother side. But not Chinese? . . . Ah, Hawaii-ah, I know, Chinese already premix. She do hula-hula dance? . . . Ah. Dead? So young? Ai, so sad. I see hula-hula once on TV, hip go 'round like wash machine, wavy hands like flying bird. . . ."

When Simon went to the bathroom, she gave me a wink and whispered loudly: "Hey! Why you say he just friend? This look on you face, his face, hah, not just friend! I right?" And then she broke into gales of belly laughter.

After dinner, on cue, George and the boys went to the family room to watch *Star Trek*. Kwan told Simon and me to come to the living room; she had something important to say. We sat down on the couch, Kwan in her easy chair. She pointed to the fake fireplace with its gas heater insert.

"Too cold?" she asked.

We shook our heads.

Kwan folded her hands in her lap. "Simon," she said, smiling like a genie, "tell me—you like my little sister, ah?"

"Kwan," I warned, but Simon was already answering her: "Very much."

"Hmm-mm." She looked as pleased as a cat after a tongue bath. "Even you don't tell me, I already see this. Mm-hmm . . . You know why?"

"I guess it's apparent," Simon said with a sheepish grin.

"No-no, you parent not telling me. I know—in here," and she tapped her forehead. "I have yin eyes, mm-hm, yin eyes."

Simon gave me a searching look, as if to ask, Help me out, Olivia—what's going on? I shrugged.

"Look there." Kwan was pointing to the fireplace. "Simon, what you see?"

He leaned forward, then made a stab at what he must have thought was a Chinese game. "You mean those red candles?"

"No-no, you see *fireplace*. I right?"

"Oh, yeah. Over there, a fireplace."

"You see fireplace. I see something else. A yin person standing there, somebody already dead."

Simon laughed. "Dead? You mean like a ghost?"

"Mm-hm. She say her name—Elsie." Good old Kwan, she accidentally said Elza's name wrong in exactly the right way. "Simon-ah, maybe you know this girl Elsie? She saying she know you, mm-hm."

His smile gone, Simon now sat forward. "Elza?"

"Oh, now she sooo happy you remember her." Kwan poised her ear toward the imaginary Elza, listening attentively. "Ah? . . . Ah. Okay-okay." She turned back to us. "She saying you won't believe, she already meet many famous music people, all dead too." She consulted the fireplace. "Oh? . . . Oh . . . Oh! . . . Ah, ah. No-no, stop, Elsie, too many name! You saying so many famous people name I can't repeat! Okay, one . . . Showman? No? I not pronouncing right?"

"Chopin?" I hinted.

"Yes-yes. Chopin too. But this one she say name like Showman. . . . Oh! Now understand—*Schumann*!"

Simon was mesmerized. I was impressed. I didn't know before that Kwan knew anything about classical music. Her favorite songs were country-western tunes about heartbroken women.

"She also saying so happy now meet her mother, father, big brother. She mean other family, not adopt-her one. Her real name she say sound like Wawaski, Wakowski, I think Japanese name. . . . Oh? Not Japanese? . . . Mm. She say Polish. Polish-Jewish. What? . . . Oh, okay. She saying her family die long time ago, because auto in ditch."

"Auschwitz," I said.

"No-no. Auto in ditch. Yes-yes, I right, auto go in ditch, turn over, crash!" Kwan cupped her right ear. "Lots time, beginning very hard understand what yin person saying. Too excited, talk too fast. Ah? . . ." She cocked her head slightly. "Now she saying, grandparents, they die this place, Auschwitz, wartime Poland." Kwan looked at me and gave me a wink, then quickly turned back to the fireplace with a surprised and concerned expression. "Ai-ya! Tst! Tst! Elsie, you suffer too much. So sad. Oh." Kwan touched her knee. "She saying, auto accident, this how she got scar on her little baby leg."

I didn't think I had written down that detail about Elza's scar. But I must have, and was glad I had. It added a nice authentic touch.

Simon blurted out a question: "Elza, the baby. What about the baby you were going to have? Is it with you?"

Kwan looked at the fireplace, puzzled, and I held my breath. Shit! I forgot to mention the damn baby. Kwan concentrated on the fireplace. "Okay-okay." She turned to us and brushed the air with one nonchalant hand. "Elsie say no problem, don't worry. She met this person, very nice person suppose be her baby. He not born yet, so didn't die. He have only small waiting time, now already born someone else."

I exhaled in relief. But then I saw that Kwan was staring at the fireplace with a worried face. She was frowning, shaking her head. And just as she did this, the top of my head began to tingle and I saw sparks fly around the fireplace.

"Ah," Kwan said quietly, more hesitantly. "Now Elsie saying you, Simon, you must no longer think about her. . . . Ah? Mm-hm. This wrong, yes-yes — too much waste you life think about her. . . . Ah? Hm. You must forget her, she say, yes, *forget!* — never say her name. She have new life now. Chopin, Schumann, her mommy, daddy. You have new life too. . . ."

And then Kwan told Simon that he should grab me before it was too late, that I was his true-love girl, that he'd be forever sorry if he missed this good chance of many lifetimes. She went on and on about how honest and sincere I was, how kind, how loyal, how smart. "Oh, maybe she not so good cook, not yet, but you patient, wait and see. If not, I teach her."

Simon was nodding, taking it all in, looking sad and grateful at the same time. I should have been ecstatic right then, but I was nauseated. Because I also had seen Elza. I had heard her.

She wasn't like the ghosts I saw in my childhood. She was a billion sparks containing every thought and emotion she'd ever had. She was a cyclone of static, dancing around the room, pleading with Simon to hear her. I knew all this with my one hundred secret senses. With a snake's tongue, I felt the heat of her desire to be seen. With the wing of a bat, I knew where she fluttered, hovering near Simon, avoiding me. With my tingly skin, I felt every tear she wept as a lightning bolt against my heart. With the single hair of a flower, I felt her tremble, as she waited for Simon to hear her. Except I was the one who heard her—not with my ears but with the tingly spot on top of my brain, where you know something is true but still you don't want to believe it. And her feelings were not what came out of Kwan's well-meaning mouth. She was pleading, crying, saying over and over again: "Simon, don't forget me. Wait for me. I'm coming back."

I NEVER TOLD KWAN what I saw or heard. For one thing, I didn't want to believe it was anything but a hallucination. Yet over these last seventeen years, I've come to know that the heart has a will of its own, no matter what you wish, no matter how often you pull out the roots of your worst fears. Like ivy, they creep back, latching on to the chambers in your heart, leeching out the safety of your soul, then slithering through your veins and out your pores. On countless nights, I've awakened in the dark with a recurring fever, my mind whirling, scared about the truth. Did Kwan hear what I heard? Did she lie for my sake? If Simon found out we'd tricked him, what would he do? Would he realize he didn't love me?

On and on the questions came, and I let them pile up, until I was certain our marriage was doomed, that Elza would pull it down. It was an avalanche waiting to happen, balanced on one dangerous and slippery question: Why are we together?

And then the sun would climb above the sill. Morning light would make me squint. I'd look at the clock. I'd rise and touch the faucets of the shower. I'd adjust the hot and the cold, then awaken my mind with water sprayed hard against my skin. And I'd be grateful to return to what was real and routine, confined to the ordinary senses I could trust.

# 8

# THE CATCHER
# OF GHOSTS

I had the Internal Revenue Service to thank for leading us to the altar.

We had been living together for three years, two of those post-college. In keeping with our shared dream to "make a substantive difference," we worked in the human services field. Simon was a counselor for Clean Break, which helped troubled teens with criminal records. I was an outreach worker for Another Chance, a program for pregnant drug addicts. We didn't earn much, but after we saw how much withholding tax the IRS took out of our monthly paychecks, we calculated how much we would save if we filed a joint return: a whole three hundred forty-six dollars a year!

With this sum dangling before our impoverished eyes, we debated whether it was right for the government to favor married couples. We both agreed that taxes were an insidious form of government coercion. But why give the government three hundred forty-six dollars to buy more weapons? We could use that money to buy new stereo speakers. It was definitely Simon who suggested we get married, I remember. "What do you think?" he said. "Should we be co-opted and file jointly?"

The wedding took place near the Rhododendron Gardens of Golden Gate Park, a site we figured was both free and romantically al fresco. But that June day, the fog rolled in on an arctic breeze, whipping our clothes and hair around, so that in the wedding photos we and our guests look deranged. While the Universal Life Church minister was intoning the blessing of the marriage, a park official announced loudly, "Excuse me, folks, but you need a permit to hold a gathering like this." So we rushed through the exchange of vows, packed up the wedding picnic and gifts, and hauled them back to our cramped apartment on Stanyan Street.

As icing to our ruined cake, the wedding gifts included none of the practical things we desperately needed to replace our ragtag assortment of sheets, towels, and kitchenware. Most of our friends provided joke gifts of the marital-aids variety. My former stepfather, Bob, gave us a crystal vase. Simon's parents presented us with an engraved sterling tray.

The rest of my family tried to outdo one another in finding that "special something" that our future grandchildren would inherit as heirlooms. From my mother, it was an original metal sculpture of a man and woman embracing, a work of art that Bharat Singh, her boyfriend of the moment, had made. My brother Tommy supplied us with a vintage pachinko machine, which he played every time he visited. Kevin gave us a case of red wine, which we were supposed to let age fifty years. But after a few impromptu weekend parties with friends, we had a fine collection of empty bottles.

Kwan's gift was actually quite beautiful, surprisingly so. It was a Chinese rosewood box with a carved lid. When I lifted the lid, the music of "The Way We Were" broke out in a stiff and mindless rhythm. In the jewelry compartment was a package of tea. "Make good feeling last long time," Kwan explained, and gave me a knowing look.

. . .

FOR THE FIRST SEVEN YEARS of our marriage, Simon and I went out of our way to agree on almost everything. For the next seven, we seemed to do the opposite. We didn't debate as he and Elza had on important issues, such as due process, affirmative action, and welfare reform. We argued over petty matters: Does food taste better if you heat the pan before putting olive oil in it? Simon yes, me no. We didn't have blowouts. But we squabbled often, as if from habit. And this made us ill-tempered with each other, less than loving.

As to our hopes, our dreams, our secret desires, we couldn't talk about those. They were too vague, too frightening, too important. And so they stayed inside us, growing like a cancer, a body eating away at itself.

In retrospect, I'm amazed how long our marriage lasted. I wonder about the marriages of other people, our friends, if they continue out of habit, or lethargy, or some strange combination of fear feeding into hope, then hope unleashing fear. I never thought our marriage was worse than anyone else's. In some respects, I felt ours was better than most. We made a nice-looking couple at dinner parties. We kept our bodies in shape, had a decent sex life. And we had one very big thing in common, our own business, public relations, mostly for nonprofit and medical groups.

Over the years, we developed a steady roster of clients—the National Kidney Foundation, the Brain Tumor Research Foundation, Paws for a Cause, a couple of hospitals, and one lucrative account, a sleaze-ball clinic that insisted on print ads using a lot of before-and-after photos of liposucted female buttocks. Simon and I worked out of a room in our apartment. I was the photographer, designer, desktop typographer, and pasteup artist. Simon was the copywriter, client manager, print buyer, and accounts receivable department. In matters of aesthetics, we treated each other with careful respect. We sought agreement in brochure layouts, type sizes, and headlines. We were extremely professional.

Our friends used to say, "You two are so lucky." And for years I wanted to believe we were as lucky as they enviously thought we were. I reasoned that the quarrels we had were only minor irritations, like slivers under the skin, dents on the car, easy enough to remove once we got around to it.

And then, almost three years ago now, Dudley, my godfather, a retired accountant whom I hadn't seen since babyhood, died and left me stocks in a small gene-splicing company. They weren't worth much when he died. But by the time the executor passed them along to me, the gene company had gone public, the stocks had split a couple of times, and thanks to the commercial miracles of DNA, Simon and I had enough money to buy, even with inflated San Francisco prices, a decent house in a terrific neighborhood. We did, that is, until my mother suggested that I share my luck with my brothers and Kwan. After all, she pointed out, Dudley was Daddy's friend and not anyone I had been especially close to. She was right, but I was hoping Kevin, Tommy, and Kwan would say, "Keep it, thanks for the thought." So much for hope. The one who surprised me the most was Kwan. She shrieked and danced like a contestant on *Wheel of Fortune*. After we cut up the inheritance pie and removed a hefty wedge for taxes, Simon and I had enough for a down payment on a modest house in an iffy neighborhood.

As a result, our search for a home took more than a year. Simon had suggested a 1950s fixer-upper in the fog-ridden Sunset district, which he thought we could sell in a few years for double our investment. What I had in mind was more of a shabby Victorian in up-and-coming Bernal Heights, a place we could remodel as home sweet home and not an investment. "You mean hovel sweet hovel," Simon said, after viewing one property.

We didn't see eye to eye on what we called "future potential." The potential, of course, had more to do with us. We both knew that living in a small dump required the kind of fresh, exuberant love in which nothing mattered except happily snuggling for warmth in the same cramped double bed. Simon and I had long before progressed to a king-size bed and an electric blanket with dual controls.

One foggy summer Sunday, we spotted an Open House sign for a co-op in a six-unit building on the fringe of Pacific Heights. By fringe, I mean that it was hanging on to neighborhood chic by a tattered thread. The building's backside rested in the Western Addition, where windows and doors were covered with saw-proof steel bars. And it was fully three blocks and two tax brackets away from the better streets of Pacific Heights, populated by families who could afford dog-walkers, au pairs, and two second homes.

In the common hallway, Simon picked up a sales leaflet riddled with hyphenated disclaimers. " 'A semi-luxurious, bi-level, lower Pacific Heights co-op,' " he read out loud, " 'located in a prestigious, once-grandiose Victorian mansion constructed in 1893 by the quite-famous architect Archibald Meyhew.' " Amazingly, the leaflet also boasted of ten rooms and a parking space, all for an asking price only a tad out of our budget. Everything else we had seen that was affordable had no more than five rooms, six if it lacked a garage.

I rang the bell for unit five. "It's a good price for the neighborhood," I remarked.

"It's not even a condo," said Simon. "With co-ops, I hear you have to go by loony rules to even change the wattage of your light bulbs."

"Look at that banister. I wonder if it's the original woodwork. Wouldn't that be great?"

"It's faux. You can tell by the lighter swirls. They're too regular."

Since Simon seemed to be quashing all interest in the place, I was going to suggest we leave. But then we heard rapid footsteps on the staircase and a man calling: "I'll be with you in a sec." Simon casually clasped his hand around mine. I couldn't remember the last time he had done that. Despite his criticisms, he must have liked the building's possibilities, enough anyway to want us to have the appearance of a happily married couple, sturdy in our finances, sufficiently stable to last through the escrow period.

The real estate agent and, as it turned out, creator of the sales sheet was a nattily dressed, balding young guy named Lester Roland or Roland Lester. He had the annoying habit of frequently clearing his throat, thus giving the impression he was either lying or on the verge of making an embarrassing confession.

He handed us a business card. "Have you bought in this neighborhood before, Mr. and Mrs. uh — ?"

"Bishop. Simon and Olivia," Simon answered. "We live in the Marina district now."

"Then you know this is one of *the* best residential areas of the city."

Simon acted blasé. "Pacific Heights, you mean, not the Western Addition."

"Well! You must be old pros at this. Want to see the basement first, I suppose."

"Yep. Let's get that over with."

Lester dutifully showed us the separate meters and hot water tanks, the common boiler and the copper pipes, while we both made experienced, noncommittal grunts. "As you'll notice" — Lester cleared his throat — "the foundation is the original brick."

"Nice." Simon nodded approvingly.

Lester frowned and gave us a moment of profound silence. "I mention this because" — he coughed — "as you may already know, most banks won't finance a building with a brick foundation. Earthquake fears, you know. But the owner is willing to carry a second mortgage, and at comparable market rates, if you qualify, of course."

Here it is, I thought, the reason why the place is for sale so cheap. "Has there been a problem with the building?"

"Oh no, not at all. Of course, it's gone through the usual settling, cosmetic cracks and such. All classic buildings get a few wrinkles — that's the privilege of age. Hell, we should all look so good at a hundred! And you also have to bear in mind this old painted lady has already survived the 'eighty-nine quake, not to mention the big one of 'aught-six. You can't say that about the newer buildings, can you now?"

Lester sounded all too eager, and I started smelling the unpleasant mustiness of a dump. In dark corners, I saw piles of beaten suitcases, their mouse-gnawed leather and cracked vinyl ashy with dust. In another storage area was an assortment of rusted heavy things—automobile parts, barbells, a metal toolbox—a monument to some prior tenant's overproduction of testosterone. Simon let go of my hand.

"The unit comes with only one garage space," said Lester. "But luckily, the man in unit two is blind and you can rent his space for a second car."

"How much?" Simon asked, just as I announced, "We don't have a second car."

Like a cat, Lester looked serenely at both of us, then said to me, "Well, that saves a lot of trouble, doesn't it." We started climbing a narrow stairwell. "I'm taking you up the back entry, what was once the servants' staircase, leading to the available unit. Oh, and by the way, a couple of blocks down—walking distance, you know?—there's a terrific private school, absolutely top-notch. By the third grade, those little monsters know how to tear apart a 386 computer and upgrade it to a 486. Incredible what they can teach your kids these days!"

And this time, Simon and I said in the same two beats, "No kids." We looked at each other, startled. Lester smiled, then said, "Sometimes that's very wise."

EARLIER IN OUR MARRIAGE, having children was the one big dream we shared. Simon and I were infatuated with the possibilities of our genetic merger. He wanted a girl who looked like me, I wanted a boy who looked like him. After six years of taking my temperature daily, of abstaining from alcohol between periods, of having sex by clockwork, we went to a fertility specialist, Dr. Brady, who told us Simon was sterile.

"You mean Olivia is sterile," Simon said.

"No, the tests indicate it's you," Dr. Brady answered. "Your medical records also report that your testicles didn't descend until you were three."

"What? I don't remember that. Besides, they're descended now. What does that have to do with anything?"

That day we learned a lot about the fragility of sperm, how sperm has to be kept cooler than body temperature; that's why the testicles hang outside, natural air-conditioning. Dr. Brady said that Simon's sterility wasn't simply a matter of low sperm count or low motility, that he had been sterile probably since pubescence, meaning since his first ejaculation.

"But that's impossible," Simon said. "I already know I can—well, it can't be. The tests are wrong."

Dr. Brady said in a voice practiced at consoling a thousand disbelieving men: "I assure you, sterility has nothing whatsoever to do with masculinity, virility, sexual drive, erection, ejaculation, or your ability to satisfy a partner." I noticed the doctor said "a partner" and not "your wife," as if to include many possibilities, past, present, and future. He then went on to discuss the contents of ejaculate, the physics of an erection, and other trivia that had nothing to do with the tiny duck rain boots that sat on our dresser, the Beatrix Potter books my mother had already collected for her future grandchild, the memory of a pregnant Elza screaming at Simon from the top of an avalanche-prone slope.

I knew Simon was thinking about Elza, wondering whether she had been wrong about the pregnancy. If so, that made her death all the more tragic, based on one stupid mistake after another. I also knew Simon had to be considering that Elza might have lied, that she hadn't been pregnant at all. But why? And if she had been pregnant, who had been her other lover? Why, then, did she lash out at Simon? None of the possible answers made any sense.

Ever since our yin-talk session with Kwan years before, Simon and I had avoided bringing up Elza's name. Now we found ourselves doubly tongue-tied, unable to discuss Simon's sterility, the questions it raised about Elza or, for that matter, our feelings about artificial insemination and adoption. Year after year, we avoided talking about babies, real, imagined, or hoped for, until there we were, on this third-floor landing, both of us informing this odious stranger named Lester, "No kids," as if we'd made our decision years earlier and it was as final then as it was now.

LESTER WAS SEARCHING through dozens of keys strung on a wire. "It's here somewhere," he muttered. "Probably the last one. Yep, wouldn't you know it—voilà!" He swung open the door and tapped his hand against the wall until he found the light switch. The apartment felt familiar at first—as if I had secretly visited this place a thousand times before, the rendezvous house of nightly dreams. There they were: the heavy wooden double doors with panes of wavy old glass, the wide hallway with its wainscoting of dark oak, the transom window throwing a shaft of light glittery with ancient dust. It was like coming back to a former home, and I couldn't decide whether my sense of familiarity was comforting or oppressive. And then Lester cheerily announced that we should start by looking at the "reception parlor," and the feeling evaporated.

"The architecture is what we call Eastlake and gothic revival," Lester was telling us. He went on to explain how the place had become a boardinghouse for itinerant salesmen and war widows in the twenties. In the forties, "gothic revival" evolved into "handyman special" when the building was converted into twenty-four dinky studios, cheap wartime housing. In the sixties, it became student apartments, and during the real estate boom of the early eighties, the building was again reincarnated, this time into the present six "semi-luxurious" co-ops.

I figured "semi-luxurious" referred to the cheap-glass chandelier in the foyer. "Semi-funky" would have been a more honest way to describe the apartment, which embodied an incongruous mix of its former incarnations. The kitchen with its Spanish-red tiles and wood-laminate cupboards had lost all traces of its Victorian lineage, whereas the other rooms were still generously decorated with useless gingerbread spandrels and plaster friezes in the corners of the ceilings. The radiator pipes no longer connected to radiators. The brick fireplaces had had their jowls bricked over. Hollow-core doors made do for recently improvised closets. And through Lester's grandiloquent real estate parlance, useless Victorian spaces had sprung important new purposes. A former stair landing backlit by a panel of amber glass became "the music hall"—perfect, I imagined, for a string quartet of midgets. What were once the suffocating quarters of a bottom-of-the-rung laundry maid now became at Lester's suggestion "the children's library," *not* that there was an adult library. And half of a once commodious dressing room with a built-in cedar wardrobe—the other half was in the adjoining apartment—was now "the scriptorium." We listened patiently to Lester, words skittering out of his mouth like cartoon dogs on fresh-waxed linoleum, frantically going nowhere.

He must have noticed our dwindling interest; he toned down the bluster, changed tack, and aimed us toward "the excellent economics of classic lines and a little bit of elbow grease." We made a perfunctory inspection of the remaining rooms, a maze of cubbyholes, similarly inflated with pseudobaronial terms: the nursery, the breakfast parlor, the water closet, the last being an actual closet big enough only for one toilet and its seated occupant, knees pressed against the door. In a modern apartment, the whole floor space would have amounted to no more than four average-size rooms at best.

Only one room, on the top floor, remained to be seen. Lester invited us to climb the narrow staircase to the former attic, now "the grand boudoir." There, the jaws on our cynical faces dropped. We gazed about slowly like people awestruck from sudden religious conversion. Before us was an enormous room with ceilings that sloped into walls. It was equivalent in floor space to the entire nine rooms below. And in contrast to the musty darkness of the third floor, the attic was light and airy, painted clean white. Eight dormer windows jutted out of the sloped ceiling, leading our eyes into the cloud-spotted sky. Below our feet, wide-plank floors gleamed, shiny as an ice rink. Simon took my hand again and squeezed it. I squeezed back.

This had potential. Together, I thought, Simon and I could dream up ways to fill the emptiness.

THE DAY WE MOVED IN, I began stripping layers from the walls of the former nursery, soon to be dubbed my "inner sanctum." Lester had said that the original walls were mahogany with inlays of burl, and I was eager to uncover this architectural treasure. Aided by the dizzying fumes of paint thinner, I imagined myself an archaeologist digging through the strata of former lives whose histories could be reconstructed by their choice of wall coverings. First to peel off was a yuppie skin of Chardonnay-colored latex, stippled to look like the walls of a Florentine monastery. This was followed by flaky crusts of the preceding decades—eighties money green, seventies psychedelic orange, sixties hippie black, fifties baby pastels. And beneath those rolled off sheaves of wallpaper in patterns of gold-flocked butterflies, cupids carrying baskets of primroses, the repetitious flora and fauna of past generations who stared at these same walls during sleepless nights soothing a colicky baby, a feverish toddler, a tubercular aunt.

A week later, with raw fingertips, I reached a final layer of plaster and then the bare wood, which was not mahogany, as Lester had said, but cheap fir. Where it was not charred it was blackened with mildew, the probable result of an overzealous turn-of-the-century firehose. While I'm not someone prone to violence, this time I kicked at the wall so hard one of the boards caved in and exposed masses of coarse gray hair. I let out a tremendous scream, grade-B horror movie in pitch, and Simon bounded into the room, waving a trowel — as if *that* would have been an effective weapon against a mass murderer. I pointed an accusing finger toward the hairy remains of what I believed was an age-old unsolved crime.

After an hour, Simon and I had torn off nearly all of the damaged and rotting wood. On the floor lay piles of hair resembling giant rats' nests. It was not until we called in a contractor to install drywall that we discovered we had removed bushels of horsehair, a form of Victorian insulation. The contractor also said that horsehair made for effective soundproofing. Well-to-do Victorians, we learned, constructed their homes so that one would not have to listen to anything as indelicate as a trill of sexual ecstasy or the trumpet blasts of indigestion emanating from adjoining rooms.

I mention this because Simon and I didn't bother to put back the horsehair, and at first I believed that had something to do with the strange acoustics we began to experience in the first month. The space between our wall and the adjoining apartment's had become a hollow shaft about a foot in width. And this shaft, I thought, served as a sounding board, capable of transmitting noises from the entire building, then converting them into thumps, hisses, and what sometimes sounded like lambada lessons being conducted upstairs in our bedroom.

Whenever we tried to describe our noise problem, I would imitate what I had heard: *Tink-tink-tink, whumpa-whumpa-whumpa, chh-chh-shhh.* Simon would compare the noise to a possible source: the tapping of an out-of-tune piano key, the flitter of mourning doves, the scraping of ice. We perceived the world so differently — that's how far apart we had grown.

There was another strange aspect to all this: Simon never seemed to be at home when the creepiest sounds occurred — like the time I was in the shower and heard the theme to *Jeopardy* being whistled, a melody I found especially haunting since I couldn't get the annoying tune out of my mind the rest of the day. I had the feeling I was being stalked.

A structural engineer suggested that the racket might be coming from the useless radiator pipes. A seismic safety consultant told me that the problem might be simply the natural settling of a wood-frame building. With a little imagination, he explained, you might think creaks and groans were all sorts of things, doors slamming, people running up and down the stairs—although he had never known of anyone else who complained of the sound of glass breaking followed by snickers of laughter. My mother said it was rats, possibly even raccoons. She'd had that problem once herself. A chimneysweep diagnosed pigeons nesting in our defunct flues. Kevin said that dental fillings can sometimes transmit radio waves and I should see Tommy, who was my dentist. The problems persisted.

Strangely enough, our neighbors said they weren't bothered by any unusual sounds, although the blind man below us acidly mentioned that he could hear us playing our stereo too loud, especially in the mornings. That's when he did his daily Zen meditation, he said.

When my sister heard the thumps and hisses, she came up with her own diagnosis: "The problem not some*thing* but some*body*. Mm-hm." As I continued to unpack books, Kwan walked around my office, her nose upraised, scenting like a dog in search of its favorite bush. "Sometime ghost, they get lost," she said. "You want, I try catch for you." She held out one hand like a divining rod.

I thought of Elza. Long ago, she had vanished from conversation, but she managed to dwell in the back of my brain, frozen in time, like a tenant under rent control who was impossible to evict. Now, with Kwan's ghosts, she had wriggled her way out.

"It's not ghosts," I said firmly. "We took out the insulation. The room's like an echo chamber."

Kwan dismissed my explanation with an authoritative sniff. She placed her hand over a spot on the floor. She wandered about the room, her hand quivering, tracking like a bloodhound. She emitted a series of "hmmms," each growing more conclusive: "HHhhmm! HhhmmMM!" Finally she stood in the doorway, absolutely still.

"Very strange," she said. "Someone here, I feel this. But not ghost. Living person, full of electricity, stuck in wall, also under floor."

"Well!" I joked. "Maybe we should charge this person rent."

"Living people always more trouble than ghost," Kwan continued. "Living people bother you because angry. Ghost make trouble only because sad, lost, confused."

I thought of Elza, pleading for Simon to hear her.

"Ghost, I know how catch," said Kwan. "My third auntie teach me how. I call ghost—'Listen me, ghost!'—one heart speaking each other." She gazed upward, looking sincere. "If she old woman, show her old slippers, leather bottoms already soft, very comfortable wear. If she young girl, show comb belong her mother. Little girl always love own mother hair. I put this treasure ghost love so much in big oil jar. When she go in—quick!—I put lid on tight. Now she ready listen. I tell her, 'Ghost! Ghost! Time you go Yin World.' "

Kwan looked at my frowning face and added: "I know—I know! In America don't have big oil jar, maybe don't even know what kind I mean. For American ghost, must use something else—like maybe big Tupperware. Or travel suitcase, Samsonite kind. Or box from very fancy store, not discount place. Yes-yes, this better idea, I think. Libby-ah, what's a name that fancy store, everybody know everything cost so much? Last year Simon bought you hundred-dollar pen there."

"Tiffany."

"Yes-yes, Tiffany! They give you blue box, same color like heaven. American ghost love heaven, pretty clouds. . . . Oh, I know. Where music box I give you wedding time? Ghost love music. Think little people inside play song. Go inside see. My last lifetime, Miss Banner have music box like this—"

"Kwan, I have work to do—"

"I know—I know! Anyway, you don't have ghost, you got living person sneak in you house. Maybe he did some sort a bad thing, now hiding, don't want get caught. Too bad I don't know how catch loose person. Better you call FBI. Ah—I know! Call that man on TV show, *American Most Wanted*. You call. I telling you, every week, they catch someone." So much for Kwan's advice.

And then something else occurred, which I tried to pass off as coincidence. Elza came back into our lives in rather dramatic fashion. One of her college classmates, who had gone on to become a producer of New Age music, revived a number of pieces Elza had composed called *Higher Consciousness*. The music later became the sound track to a television series on angels, which was ironic, as Simon pointed out, since Elza was not fond of Christian mythology. But then, overnight it seemed, everyone was wild for anything having to do with angels. The series received huge ratings, a CD of the sound track sold moderately well, and Simon started finding new self-worth in Elza's small fame. I never thought I'd hate angels so much. And Simon, who once loathed New Age music, would play her album whenever friends came over. He would casually remark that the composer had dedicated the music to him. Why's that, they would ask. Well, they had been lovers, best friends. Naturally, this caused some friends to smile at me in a consoling way, which I found maddening. I would then explain matter-of-factly that Elza had died before I met Simon. Yet somehow it sounded more like a confession, as if I'd said I had killed her myself. And then silence would permeate the room.

So along with all the sound effects in our house, I tried to pretend I wasn't bothered by Elza's music. I tried to ignore the increasing distance between Simon and me. I tried to believe that in matters of marriage, as with earthquakes, cancer, and acts of war, people such as myself were immune to unexpected disaster. But to pretend that all was right with the world, I first had to know what was wrong.

# 9
# KWAN'S FIFTIETH

Simon and I never replaced the cheap-glass chandelier. When we first moved in, we found it offensive, a glaring insult to good taste. Later, the fixture became a joke. And soon it was merely a source of light we took for granted. It was there but not noticed, except when one of the bulbs burned out. We even tried to rid ourselves of this reminder by buying a dozen light bulbs from a blind-veterans' organization, sixty watts each, guaranteed to last fifty thousand hours, forever in foyer-light years. But then five out of six bulbs burned out within the year. We never got around to putting up the ladder to change them. With one bulb burning, the chandelier was practically invisible.

One night, this was about six months ago now, that last bulb gave out with a small pop, leaving us in darkness. Simon and I were about to go to our usual neighborhood restaurant for an after-work supper. "I'll buy some real bulbs tomorrow," said Simon.

"Why not a whole new light fixture?"

"What for? This one's not so bad. Come on, let's go. I'm hungry."

As we walked to the restaurant, I was wondering about what he had said, or rather, how he had said it, as if he didn't care about our life to-gether anymore. Tacky was now good enough for us.

The restaurant was half empty. Soft, soporific music was playing in the background, white noise, the kind no one really listens to. While glancing at a menu I knew by heart, I noticed a couple in their fifties seated across from us. The woman wore a sour expression. The man seemed bored. I watched them awhile longer. They chewed, buttered bread, sipped water, never making eye contact, never saying a word. They didn't seem to be having a fight. They just acted resigned, dis-connected from both happiness and discomfort. Simon was studying the wine list. Did we ever order anything except the house white?

"You want to share a bottle of red this time?" I said.

He didn't look up. "Red has all that tannin. I don't want to wake up at two in the morning."

"Well, let's get something different. A fumé blanc maybe."

He handed me the wine list. "I'm just going to have the house Chablis. But you go ahead."

As I stared at the list, I began to panic. Suddenly, everything about our life seemed predictable yet meaningless. It was like fitting all the pieces of a jigsaw puzzle only to find the completed result was a repro-duction of corny art, great effort leading to trivial disappointment. Sure, in some ways we were compatible—sexually, intellectually, profession-ally. But we weren't *special,* not like people who truly belonged to each other. We were partners, not soul mates, two separate people who hap-pened to be sharing a menu and a life. Our whole wasn't greater than the sum of our parts. Our love wasn't destined. It was the result of a tragic accident and a dumb ghost trick. That's why he had no great pas-sion for me. That's why a cheap chandelier fit our life.

When we arrived home, Simon flopped on the bed. "You've been awfully quiet," he said. "Anything wrong?"

"No," I lied. Then: "Well, I don't know, exactly." I sat on my side of the bed and started to page through a shopping catalogue, waiting for him to ask me again.

Simon was now using the television remote to change channels every five seconds: a news flash about a kidnapped little girl, a *telenovela* in Spanish, a beefy man selling exercise equipment. As pieces of televised life blipped past me, I tried to gather my emotions into coherent logic Simon could understand. But whatever I'd been stifling hit me in a jumble and ached in my throat. There was the fact that we couldn't talk about Simon's sterility—not that I wanted to have children at this point in our lives. And the spooky sounds in the house, how we pretended they were normal. And Elza, how we couldn't talk about her, yet she was everywhere, in the memory of lies Kwan had told during her yin-talk session, in the damn music Simon played. I was going to suffocate if I didn't make drastic changes in my life. Meanwhile, Simon was still bouncing from one channel to the next.

"Do you know how irritating that is?" I said tersely.

Simon turned off the TV. He rolled over to face me, propped on one arm. "What's wrong?" He looked tenderly concerned.

My stomach clenched. "I just wonder sometimes, Is this all there is? Is this how we're going to be ten, twenty years from now?"

"What do you mean, is this all?"

"You know, living here in this funky house, putting up with the noise, the tacky chandelier. Everything feels stale. We go to the same restaurant. We say the same things. It's the same old shit over and over again."

He looked puzzled.

"I want to *love* what we do as a couple. I want us to be closer."

"We're together twenty-four hours a day as it is."

"I'm not talking about work!" I felt like a small child, hungry and hot, itchy and tired, frustrated that I couldn't say what I really wanted to. "I'm talking about us, what's important. I feel like we're stagnating and mold is growing around the edges."

"I don't feel that way."

"Admit it, our life together won't be any better next year than it is today. It'll be worse. Look at us. What do we share now besides doing the same work, seeing the same movies, lying in the same bed?"

"Come on. You're just depressed."

"Of course I'm depressed! Because I can see where we're headed. I don't want to become like those people we saw in the restaurant tonight—staring at their pasta, nothing to say to each other except, 'How's the linguini?' As it is, we never talk, not really."

"We talked tonight."

"Yeah, sure. How the new client is a neo-Nazi. How we should put more in our SEP account. How the co-op board wants to raise the dues. That's not real talk! That's not real life. That's not what's important in *my* life."

Simon playfully rubbed my knee. "Don't tell me you're having a mid-life crisis? People had those only in the seventies. Besides, today there's Prozac."

I brushed his hand away. "Stop being so condescending."

He put his hand back. "Come on, I'm joking."

"Then why do you always joke about important things?"

"Hey, you're not the only one. I wonder about my life too, you know, how long I have to do the things that really matter."

"Yeah? Like what?" I sneered. "What matters to you?"

He paused. I imagined what he was going to say: the business, the house, having enough money to retire early.

"Go on. Tell me."

"Writing," he finally said.

"You already write."

"I don't mean what I write now. Do you really think that's all I'm about—writing brochures on cholesterol and sucking fat out of flabby thighs? Gimme a break."

"What, then?"

"Stories." He looked at me, waiting for a reaction.

"What kind?" I wondered if he was making this up on the spot.

"Stories about real life, people here, or in other countries, Madagascar, Micronesia, one of those islands in Indonesia where no tourists have ever been."

"Journalism?"

"Essays, fiction, whatever allows me to write about the way I see the world, where I fit in, questions I have. . . . It's hard to explain."

He started to remove the catalogue from my hand. I grabbed it back. "Don't." We were on the defensive again.

"All right, stay in your goddamn funk!" he shouted. "So we're not perfect. We slip up. We don't talk enough. Does that make us miserable failures? I mean, we're not homeless or sick or working in mindless jobs."

"What, I'm supposed to be happy thinking, 'Gee, someone else has it worse than I do'? Who do you think I am—Pollyanna?"

"Shit! What do you want?" he snapped. "What could possibly make you happy?"

I felt stuck in the bottom of a wishing well. I was desperate to shout what I wanted, but I didn't know what that was. I knew only what it wasn't.

Simon lay back on the pillow, his hands locked over his chest. "Life's always a big fucking compromise," he said. He sounded like a stranger. "You don't always get what you want, no matter how smart you are, how hard you work, how good you are. That's a myth. We're all hanging in the best we can." He exhaled a cynical laugh.

And then I spit out what I had been afraid to say: "Yeah, well, I'm sick of hanging in as Elza's lousy replacement."

Simon sat up. "What the hell does Elza have to do with this?" he asked.

"Nothing." I was being stupid and childish, but I couldn't stop. A few tense minutes went by before I said: "Why do you have to play that goddamn CD all the time and tell everyone she was your girlfriend?"

Simon stared at the ceiling. He sighed sharply, a signal he was just about to give up. "What's going on?"

"I just want us, you know, to have a better life," I stammered. "Together." I couldn't meet his eyes. "I want to be important to you. I want you to be important to me. . . . I want us to have dreams together."

"Yeah, what kind of dreams?" he said hesitantly.

"That's the point—I don't know! That's what I want us to talk about. It's been so long since we had dreams together, we don't even know what that means anymore."

We were at a standstill. I pretended to read my magazine. Simon went to the bathroom. When he returned, he sat on the bed and put his arm around me. I hated myself for crying, but I couldn't stop. "I don't know, I don't know," I kept sobbing. He patted my eyes with a tissue, wiped my nose, then eased me down on the bed.

"It's all right," he consoled. "You'll see, tomorrow, it'll be all right."

But his niceness made me despair even more. He wrapped himself around me, and I tried to choke back my sobs, pretending to be calmed, because I didn't know what else to do. And then Simon did what he always did when we didn't know what else to do—he started to make love. I stroked his hair, to let him think this was what I wanted too. But I was thinking, Doesn't he worry about what's going to happen to us? Why doesn't he worry? We're doomed. It's just a matter of time.

The next morning, Simon surprised me. He brought me coffee in bed and brightly announced, "I've been thinking about what you said last night—about having a dream together. Well, I have a plan."

Simon's idea was to draw up a wish list: something we could do together, which would allow us to define what he called the creative parameters of our life. We talked openly, excitedly. We agreed the dream should be risky but fun, include exotic travel, good food, and most important, a chance to create something that was emotionally satisfying.

We did not mention romance. "That takes care of the dream part," he said. "Now we have to figure out how to make it happen."

At the end of our three-hour discussion, we had conjured up a proposal that we would mail to a half-dozen travel and food magazines. We would offer to write and photograph a story on village cuisine of China; this would involve a junket to serve as the model for future food and folk-culture articles, possibly a book, a lecture tour, maybe even a cable TV series.

It was the best talk Simon and I had had in years. I still didn't think he completely understood my fears and despair, but he had responded in the best way he could. I wanted a dream. He made a plan. And when I thought about it, wasn't that enough to give us hope?

I realized we had about a one-zillionth-percent chance of getting even a nibble on our proposal. But once the letters were out in the universe, I felt better, as if I'd hauled off my old life to Goodwill. Whatever came next had to be better.

A FEW DAYS after Simon and I had our tête-à-tête, my mother called with a reminder to bring my camera to Kwan's house that evening. I looked at the calendar. Shit, I had completely forgotten we were supposed to go to Kwan's for her birthday. I ran upstairs to the bedroom, where Simon was watching Super Bowl highlights, his lanky body stretched across the rug in front of the TV. Bubba was lying next to him, chewing on a squeaky toy.

"We have to be at Kwan's in an hour. It's her birthday."

Simon groaned. Bubba jumped up into sitting position, front paws paddling, whining for his leash.

"No, Bubba, you have to stay." He slumped to the floor, head on paws, gazing at me with woeful eyes.

"We'll stay long enough to be social," I offered, "then skip out early."

"Oh, sure," said Simon, eyes still on the screen. "You know how Kwan is. She'll never let us leave early."

"Well, we have to go. It's her fiftieth."

I scanned the bookshelves to find something that might pass for a birthday gift. An art book? No, I decided, Kwan wouldn't appreciate it, she has no aesthetic sense. I looked in my jewelry box. How about this silver-and-turquoise necklace I hardly ever wear? No, my sister-in-law gave me that, and she'd be at the party. I went downstairs to my office, and that's where I spotted it: a mock-tortoiseshell box slightly larger than a pack of cards, perfect accompaniment for Kwan's kitschy junk. I had bought the box while Christmas shopping two months before. At the time, it looked like one of those all-purpose gifts, compact enough to tuck in my purse, just in case someone, for instance a client, surprised me with a Christmas present. But this year, no one did.

I went to Simon's study and rummaged around in his desk for wrapping paper and ribbon. In the bottom left-hand drawer, tucked in the back, I found a misplaced diskette. I was about to file it in Simon's storage box, when I noticed the index name he had written on the label: "Novel. Opened: 2/20/90." So he *was* trying to write something important to him after all. He'd been working on it for a long time. I felt wounded that he hadn't shared this with me.

At that point, I should have respected Simon's privacy and filed the diskette away. But how could I not look? There was his heart, his soul, what mattered to him. I turned on the computer with shaky hands, slipped in the diskette. I called up the file named "Chap. 1." A screenful of words flashed on a blue background, and then the first sentence: *From the time she was six, Elise could hear a song once, then play it from memory, a memory inherited from her dead grandparents.*

I scrolled through the first page, then the second. This is schlock, this is drivel, I kept telling myself. I read page after page, gorging myself on poison. And I imagined her, Elza, stroked by his fingertips, gazing back at him on the screen. I could see her smirking at me: "I came back. That's why you've never been happy. I've been here all along."

CALENDARS DON'T MEASURE time for me anymore. Kwan's birthday was six months ago, a lifetime ago. After I came home from her party, Simon and I fought viciously for another month. The pain seemed to last forever, but love disintegrated in a second. He camped out in his study, then moved out at the end of February, which now feels so long ago I can't even remember what I did the first few weeks alone.

But I'm getting used to the change. No routines, no patterns, no old habits, that's the norm for me now. It suits me. As Kevin told me last week at his birthday party, "You look good, Olivia, you really do."

"It's the new me," I said in a flip tone. "I'm using a new face cream, fruit acids."

I've surprised everyone by how well I've been doing—not just coping, but actually carving out a new life. Kwan is the only one who thinks otherwise.

Last night on the phone, she had this to say: "You voice, so tired-sounding! Tired live alone, I think. Simon same way. Tonight two you come my house eat dinner, like old time, just be friend—"

"Kwan, I don't have time for this."

"Ah, so busy! Okay, not tonight. Tomorrow, too busy again? You come tomorrow, ah."

"Not if Simon's there."

"Okay-okay. Just you come tonight. I make you potsticker, your favorite. Also give you wonton take home for you freezer."

"No talking about Simon, right?"

"No talk, just eat. Promise."

. . .

I'M INTO my second helping of potstickers. I keep waiting for Kwan to slip in some mention of my marriage. She and George are talking heatedly about Virginia, a cousin of George's dead wife, in Vancouver, whose nephew in China wants to immigrate to Canada.

George is chewing a mouthful. "His girlfriend wanted to catch a ride to Canada too. Forced him to marry her. My cousin, she had to start the paperwork all over again. Everything was almost approved, now — Hey! Go back to the end of the line. Wait eighteen more months."

"Two hundred dollar, new paperwork." Kwan reaches for a green bean with her chopsticks. "Many-many hour wasted, going this office, that office. Then what? Surprise — baby pop out."

George nods. "My cousin said, 'Hey, why didn't you wait? Now we have to add the baby, start the application process over again.' The nephew said, 'Don't tell the officials we got a baby. The two of us, we come first, go to college, find high-paying jobs, buy a house, car. Later, we find a way to bring the baby, one, two years from now.' "

Kwan puts her rice bowl down. "Leave baby behind! What sort a thinking this?" She glares at me, as if I were the one with child abandonment ideas. "College, money, house, job — where you think find such things? Who pay for college, big down payment?"

I shake my head. George grumbles, and Kwan makes a disgusted face. "Bean not tender, too old, no taste."

"So? What happened?" I ask. "Are they bringing the baby?"

"No." Kwan puts down her chopsticks. "No baby, no nephew, no wife. Virgie move San Francisco soon. America don't have immigration for nephew, Auntie Virgie can't sponsor. Now the nephew mother in China, sister to Virgie, she blame us lose her son's good chance!"

I wait for further explanation. Kwan pokes the air with her chopsticks. "Wah! Why you think you son so important? Own sister don't consider how much trouble! You son spoil. I already smell from here. *Hwai dan*. Bad egg."

"You told her this?"

"Never meet her."

"Then why is she blaming you?"

"Blame in letter because Virgie tell her we invite her stay with us."

"Did you?"

"Before not. Now letter say this, we invite. Otherwise she loose face. Next week, she come."

Even with constant exposure to Kwan, I don't think I will ever understand the dynamics of a Chinese family, all the subterranean intricacies of who's connected to whom, who's responsible, who's to blame, all that crap about losing face. I'm glad my life isn't as complicated.

At the end of the night, Kwan hands me a video. It's of her birthday party, the same day Simon and I had our major blowout, the one that led to our end.

I remember that I had raced upstairs, where Simon was getting dressed. I opened a dormer window and held up his diskette and shouted, "Here's your fucking novel! Here's what's important to you!" And then I let go of the diskette.

We shouted at each other for an hour, and then I said in a calm and detached voice the words that were more terrible than any curse: "I want a divorce." Simon shocked me by saying, "Fine," then stomped down the stairs, banged the door, and was gone. Not five minutes later, the phone rang. I made myself as unemotional as I could. No hurt, no anger, no forgiveness. Let him beg. On the fifth ring, I picked it up.

"Libby-ah?" It was Kwan, her voice shy and girlish. "Ma call you? You coming? Everyone already here. Lots food . . ."

I mumbled some sort of excuse.

"Simon sick? Just now? . . . Oh, food poison. Okay, you take care him. No-no. He more important than birthday." And when she said that, I was determined that Simon would no longer be more important than anything in my life, not even Kwan. I went to the party alone.

"Very funny video," Kwan is now saying, as she sees me to the door.

"Maybe no time watch. Take anyway." And so the evening ends, without one mention of Simon.

Once home, I am forlorn. I try watching television. I try to read. I look at the clock. It's too late to call anyone. For the first time in six months, my life seems hollow and I'm desperately lonely. I see Kwan's video lying on the dresser. Why not? Let's go to a party.

I've always thought home videos are boring, because they're never edited. You see moments from your life that never should be replayed. You see the past happening as the present, yet you already know what's coming.

This one opens with blinking holiday lights, then pans out to show we are at the Mediterranean doorway of Kwan and George's house on Balboa Street. With the blurry sweep of the camera, we enter. Even though it's the end of January, Kwan always keeps the holiday decorations up until after her birthday. The video captures it all: plastic wreaths hung over aluminum-frame windows, the indoor-outdoor green-and-blue carpeting, the fake-wood-grain paneling, and a mish-mash of furniture bought at warehouse discount centers and Saturday tag sales.

The back of Kwan's permed hair looms into the frame. She calls out in her too loud voice: "Ma! Mr. Shirazi! Welcome-welcome, come inside." My mother and her boyfriend of the moment bounce into view. She's wearing a leopard-print blouse, leggings, and a black velour jacket with gold braid trim. Her bifocals have a purple gradient tint. Ever since her facelift, my mother has been wearing progressively more outrageous clothes. She met Sharam Shirazi at an advanced salsa dance class. She told me she liked him better than her last beau, a Samoan, because he knows how to hold a lady's hand, "not like a drumstick." Also, by my mother's estimation, Mr. Shirazi is quite the lover boy. She once whispered to me: "He does things maybe even you young people don't do." I didn't ask what she meant.

Kwan stares back at the camera to make sure George has recorded our mother's arrival properly. And then more people arrive. The video swerves toward them: Kwan's two stepsons, my brothers, their wives, their cumulative four children. Kwan greets them all, shouting out each child's name—"Melissa! Patty! Eric! Jena!"—then motions to George to get a shot of the kids grouped together.

Finally, there's my arrival. "Why so late!" Kwan complains happily. She grabs my arm and escorts me to the camera so that our faces fill the screen. I look tired, embarrassed, red-eyed. It's obvious I want to escape.

"This my sister, Libby-ah," Kwan is saying to the camera. "My *favorite* best sister. Which one older? You guess. Which?"

In the next few scenes, Kwan acts as if she were on amphetamines, bouncing off the walls. There she is, standing next to her fake Christmas tree. She points to ornaments, gestures like the gracious hostess of a game show. There she is, picking up her presents. She exaggerates their heaviness, then shakes, tilts, smells each one before reading the name tag of the lucky recipient. Her mouth rounds in fake astonishment: "For *me*?" And then she laughs gruffly and holds up all ten fingers, closing and opening them like a flashing signal: "Fifty years!" she shouts. "Can you believe? No? How 'bout forty?" She comes closer to the camera and nods. "Okay-okay, forty."

The camera ricochets from one ten-second scene to the next. There they are, my mother sitting on Mr. Shirazi's lap: someone yells for them to kiss and they gladly oblige. Next are my brothers in the bedroom, watching ESPN; they wave to the camera with sloshing cans of beer. Now my sisters-in-law, Tabby and Barbara, are helping Kwan in the kitchen; Kwan holds up a coin-shaped slice of pork and cries, "Taste! Come close, taste!" In another bedroom, kids are huddled around a computer game; they cheer each time a monster has been killed. And now the whole family and I are standing in the buffet line, finding our way to a dining table which has been enlarged by the addition of a mah jong table at one end and a card table at the other.

I see a close-up of myself: I wave, toast Kwan, then go back to stabbing at my plate with a plastic fork, all the usual party behavior. But the camera is heartlessly objective. Anyone can see it in my face: my expressions are bland, my words are listless. It's so obvious how depressed I am, entirely resistant to what life has to offer. My sister-in-law Tabby is talking to me, but I'm staring vacantly at my plate. The cake arrives and everyone breaks into the Happy Birthday song. The camera pans the room and finds me on the sofa, setting into motion a tabletop toy of steel balls that make a perpetual and annoying *clack-clack* sound. I look like a zombie.

Kwan opens her presents. The Hummel knockoff of skating children is from her coworkers at the drugstore. "Oh, so cute-cute," she croons, putting it next to her other figurines. The coffee maker is from my mother. "Ah, Ma! How you know my other coffee machine broken?" The silk blouse in her favorite color, red, is from her younger stepson, Teddy. "Too good to wear," Kwan laments with joy. The silver-plated candlestick holders are from her other stepson, Timmy; she puts candles in them, then sets them on the table he helped her refinish last year. "Just like First Lady in White House!" she gloats. The clay-blob sculpture of a sleeping unicorn is from our niece Patty; Kwan puts this carefully on the mantel, promising: "I never sell it, even when Patty become famous artist and this worth one million dollar." The daisy-patterned bathrobe is from her husband. She looks at the designer-soundalike label: "Ohhhh. Giorgio Laurentis. Too expensive. Why you spend so much?" She shakes her finger at her husband, who smiles, bashfully proud.

Another pile is set in front of Kwan. I fast-forward through the unveiling of placemats, a clothes steamer, a monogrammed tote bag. Finally I see her picking up my present. I press the Stop button, then hit Play.

". . . Always save best for last," she's proclaiming. "Must be very-very special, because Libby-ah my favorite sister." She unties the ribbon, puts it aside for safekeeping. The wrapping paper falls away. She purses her lips, staring at the tortoiseshell box. She turns it slowly from top to bottom, then lifts off the top and looks inside. She touches her hand to one cheek and says, "Beautiful, so useful too." She holds up the box for video-recorded history: "See?" she says, grinning. "Travel soap dish!"

In the background, you can hear my strained voice. "Actually, it's not for soap. It's for, you know, jewels and stuff."

Kwan looks at the box again. "Not for soap? For jews? Ohhh!" She holds up the box again, giving it more respect. Suddenly she brightens. "George, you hear? My sister Libby-ah say I deserve good jews. Buy me diamond, big diamond put in travel soap dish!"

George grunts and the camera swings wildly as he calls out: "The two sisters, stand by the fireplace." I'm protesting, explaining that I have to go home, that I have work to do. But Kwan is pulling me up from the sofa, laughing and calling to me, "Come-come, lazy girl. Never too busy for big sister."

The video camera whirs. Kwan's face freezes into a grin, as if she's waiting for a flash to go off. She squeezes me tight, forcing me to be even closer to her, then murmurs in a voice full of wonder, "Libby-ah, my sister, so special, so good to me."

And I'm on the verge of tears, both in the video and now watching my life happen over again. Because I can't deny it any longer. Any second, my heart is going to break.

III

III

# 10

# KWAN'S KITCHEN

Kwan says to come over at six-thirty, which is what time she always says to come over, only usually we don't start eating until closer to eight. So I ask if dinner will *really* be ready at six-thirty, otherwise I'll come later, because I am *really* busy. Six-thirty for sure, she says.

At six-thirty, George answers the door, bleary-eyed. He isn't wearing his glasses, and his thin patch of hair looks like an advertisement for anti–static cling products. He's just been promoted to manager at a Food-4-Less store in the East Bay. When he first started working there, Kwan didn't notice the 4 in the store's name, and even with reminders she still calls it Foodless.

I find her in the kitchen, cutting off the stems of black mushrooms. The rice hasn't been washed, the prawns haven't been deveined. Dinner is two hours away. I thump my purse down on the table, but Kwan is oblivious to my irritation. She pats a chair.

"Libby-ah, sit down, I have something must tell you." She slices mushrooms for fully half a minute more before dropping her bombshell. "I was talking to a yin person." She's now speaking in Chinese.

I sigh deeply, letting her know I am not in the mood for this line of conversation.

"Lao Lu, you also know him, but not in this lifetime. Lao Lu said that you must stay together with Simon. This is your *yinyuan,* the fate that brings lovers together."

"And why is this my fate?" I say unpleasantly.

"Because in your last lifetime together, you loved someone else before Simon. Later, Simon trusted you with his whole life that you loved him too."

I almost fall off my chair. I have never told Kwan or anyone else the real reason we are getting divorced. I've said simply that we've grown apart. And now here's Kwan talking about it—as if the whole damn universe, dead and alive, knows.

"Libby-ah, you must believe," she says in English. "This yin friend, he say Simon telling you true. You think he love you less, she more—no!—why you think like this, always compare love? Love not like money. . . ."

I am livid to hear her defending him. "Come on, Kwan! Do you realize how crazy-stupid you sound? If anyone else heard you talking like this, they'd think you were nuts! If there really are ghosts, why don't I ever see them? Tell me that, huh."

She's now slicing open the backs of the prawns, pulling out their black intestines, leaving on their shells. "One time you can see," she says calmly. "Little-girl time."

"I was pretending. Ghosts come from the imagination, not the World of Yin."

"Don't say 'ghost.' To them this like racist word. Only bad yin person you call ghost."

"Oh, right. I forgot. Even dead people have become politically correct. Okay, so what do these *yin* people look like? Tell me. How many of them are here tonight? Who's sitting in this chair? Mao Tse-tung? Chou En-lai? How about the Dowager Empress?"

"No-no, they not here."

"Well, tell them to drop by! Tell them I want to see them. I want to ask them if they have degrees in marriage counseling."

Kwan spreads newspapers on the floor to catch the grease from the stove. She slides the prawns into a hot pan and instantly the roar of blistering oil fills the kitchen. "Yin people want come, that's when come," she says above the din. "They never saying when, because treat me just like close family—come by no invitation, 'Surprise, we here.' But most times, come for dinner, when maybe one two dish not cook right. They say, 'Ah! This sea bass, too firm, not flaky, maybe cook one minute too much. And these pickle-turnips, not crunchy enough, should make sound like walk in snow, crunch-crunch, then you know ready eat. And this sauce—tst!—too much sugar, only foreigner want eat it.' "

Blah, blah, blah. It's so ludicrous! She's describing precisely what she, George, and his side of the family do all the time, the kind of talk I find boring as hell. It makes me want to laugh and scream at the same time, hearing her version of the pleasures of the afterlife described as amateur restaurant reviewing.

Kwan dumps the glistening prawns into a bowl. "Most yin people very busy, working hard. They want relax, come to me, for good conversation, also because say I'm excellent cook." She looks smug.

I try to trap Kwan in her own faulty logic: "If you're such an excellent cook, why do they come so often and criticize your cooking?"

Kwan frowns and sticks out her lower lip—as if I could be stupid enough to ask such a question! "Not real criticize, just friendly way open-talk, be frank like close friend. And don't really come eat. How can eat? They already dead! Only pretend eat. Anyway, most times they praise my cooking, yes, saying they never so lucky enough eat such good dish. Ai-ya, if only can eat my green-onion pancake, then can die oh so happy. But—too late—already dead."

"Maybe they should try take-out," I grumble.

Kwan pauses for a moment. "Ah-ha-ha, funny! You make joke." She pokes my arm. "Naughty girl. Anyway, yin people like come visit me, talk about life already gone, like banquet, many-many flavors. 'Oh,' they say, 'now I remember. This part I enjoy, this I not enjoy enough. This I eat up too fast. Why I don't taste that one? Why I let this piece my life gone spoiled, complete wasted?' "

Kwan pops a prawn into her mouth, slides it around from cheek to cheek, until she has extricated the shell intact minus every bit of flesh. I'm always amazed that she can do this. To me, it looks like a circus stunt. She smacks her lips approvingly. "Libby-ah," she says, holding up a small plate of golden shreds, "you like dried scallop?" I nod. "Georgie cousin Virgie send me from Vancouver. Sixty dollar one pound. Some people think too good for everyday. Should save best for later on." She throws the scallops into a pan of sliced celery. "To me, best time now. You wait, everything change. Yin people know this. Always ask me, 'Kwan, where best part my life gone? Why best part slip through my fingers like fast little fish? Why I save for last, find out later last already come before?' . . . Libby-ah, here, taste. Tell me, too salty, not salty enough?"

"It's fine."

She continues: " 'Kwan,' they telling me, 'you still alive. You can still make memory. You can make good one. Teach us how make good one so next time we remember what not suppose forget.' "

"Remember what?" I ask.

"Why they want come back, of course."

"And you help them remember."

"I already help many yin people this way," she brags.

"Just like Dear Abby."

She considers this. "Yes-yes, like Dear Abby." She's visibly pleased with the comparison. "Many-many yin people in China. America too, plenty." And then she starts to tally them on her fingers: "That young police officer—come my house time my car get stolen?—last lifetime he missionary in China, always saying 'Amen, Amen.' That pretty girl, work at bank now watch over my money so good, she another — bandit girl, long time ago rob greedy people. And Sarge, Hoover, Kirby, now Bubba, doggies, all them so loyal. Last lifetime they same one person. You guess who."

I shrug. I hate this game, the way she always inveigles me into her delusions.

"You guess."

"I don't know."

"Guess."

I throw my hands up. "Miss Banner."

"Ha! You guess wrong!"

"All right, tell me. Who, then?"

"General Cape!"

I slap my forehead. "Of course." I have to admit the whole idea of my dog's being General Cape is rather amusing.

"Now you know reason why first dog name Captain," Kwan adds.

"I named him that."

She wags her finger. "Demote him lower rank. You smart, teach him lesson."

"Teach him! Pff. That dog was so dumb. He wouldn't sit, wouldn't come, all he could do was beg for food. And then he ran away."

Kwan shakes her head. "Not run away. Run over."

"What?"

"Mm-hm. I see, didn't want tell you, you so little. So I say, Oh, Libby-ah, doggie gone, run away. I not lying. He run away to street before run over. Also, my English then not so good. Run away, run over, sound same to me. . . ." As Kwan belatedly speaks of Captain's death, I feel a twinge of childlike sadness, of wanting things back, of believing I can change the fact that I was less than kind to Captain if only I could see him one more time.

"General Cape, last lifetime no loyalty. That's why come back doggie so many times. He choose himself do this. Good choice. Last lifetime he so bad—so bad! I know because his one-half man told me. Also I can see . . . Here, Libby-ah, *huang ∂o-zi,* big bean sprout, see how yellow? Bought fresh today. Break off tails. You see any rotten spot, throw away. . . ."

General Cape, he was rotten too. He threw away other people. Nunumu, I told myself, you pretend General Cape is not here. I had to pretend for a long time. For two months, General Cape lived in the Ghost Merchant's House. For two months, Miss Banner opened her door every night to let him in. For those same two months, she didn't speak to me, not as her loyal friend. She treated me as if I were her servant. She pointed to spots on the bosom part of her white clothes, spots she claimed I had not washed out, spots I knew were the dirty fingerprints of General Cape. On Sundays, she preached exactly what Pastor Amen said, no more good stories. And there were other great changes during that time.

At meals, the missionaries, Miss Banner, and General Cape sat at the table for foreigners. And where Pastor Amen used to sit, that's where General Cape put himself. He talked in his loud, barking voice. The others, they just nodded and listened. If he raised his soup spoon to his lips, they raised their spoons. If he put his spoon down to say one more boast, they put their spoons down to listen to one more boast.

Lao Lu, the other servants, and I sat at the table for Chinese. The man who translated for Cape, his name, he told us, was Yiban Johnson, One-half Johnson. Even though he was half-and-half, the foreigners decided he was more Chinese than Johnson. That's why he had to sit at our table as well. At first, I didn't like this Yiban Johnson, what he said—how important Cape was, how he was a hero to both Americans and Chinese. But then I realized: What he spoke was what General Cape put in his mouth. When he sat at our dinner table, he used his own words. He talked to us openly, like common people to common people. He was genuinely polite, not pretending. He joked and laughed. He praised the food, he did not take more than his share.

In time, I too thought he was more Chinese than Johnson. In time, I didn't even think he looked strange. His father, he told us, was American-born, a friend of General Cape's from when they were little boys. They went to the same military school together. They were kicked out together. Johnson sailed to China with an American company doing the cloth trade, Nankeen silk. In Shanghai, he bought the daughter of a poor servant as his mistress. Just before she was about to have his child, Johnson told her, "I'm going back to America, sorry, can't take you with me." She accepted her fate. Now she was the leftover mistress of a foreign devil. The next morning, when Johnson awoke, guess who he saw hanging from the tree outside his bedroom window?

The other servants cut her down, wrapped a cloth around the red neck gash where the rope had twisted life out of her body. Because she had killed herself, they held no ceremonies. They put her in a plain wood coffin and closed it up. That night, Johnson heard a crying sound. He rose and went into the room where the coffin lay. The crying grew louder. He opened the box, and inside he found a baby boy, lying between the legs of the dead mistress. Around the baby's neck, just under his tiny chin, was a red mark, thick as a finger, the same half-moon shape of the rope burn on his mother.

Johnson took that baby who was one-half his blood to America. He put the baby in a circus, told people the hanging story, showed them the mysterious rope-burn scar. When the boy was five, his neck was bigger, his scar looked smaller, and nobody paid to see if it was mysterious anymore. So Johnson went back to China with the circus money and his half-blood son. This time, Johnson took up the opium trade. He went from one treaty-port city to another. He made a fortune in each city, then gambled each fortune away. He found a mistress in each city, then left each mistress behind. Only the little Yiban cried to lose so many mothers. That was who taught him to speak so many Chinese dialects—

Cantonese, Shanghainese, Hakka, Fukien, Mandarin—those mistress-mothers. English he learned from Johnson.

One day, Johnson ran into his old schoolmate Cape, who now worked for any kind of military army—the British, the Manchus, the Hakkas, it didn't matter which—whoever would pay him. Johnson said to Cape, "Hey, I have a big debt, lots of trouble, can you loan your old friend some money?" As proof that he would repay him, Johnson said, "Borrow my son. Fifteen years old and he speaks many languages. He can help you work for any army you choose."

Since that day, for the next fifteen years, young Yiban Johnson belonged to General Cape. He was his father's never paid debt.

I asked Yiban: Who does General Cape fight for now—the British, the Manchus, the Hakkas? Yiban said Cape had fought for all three, had made money from all three, had made enemies among all three. Now he was hiding from all three. I asked Yiban if it was true that General Cape had married a Chinese banker's daughter for gold. Yiban said Cape married the banker's daughter not just for gold, but for the banker's younger wives as well. Now the banker was looking for him too. Cape, he said, was addicted to golden-millet dreams, riches that could be harvested in one season, then plowed under, gone.

I was happy to hear that I was right about General Cape, that Miss Banner was wrong. But in the next instant, I became sick with sadness. I was her loyal friend. How could I be glad, watching this terrible man devour her heart?

Then Lao Lu spoke up: "Yiban, how can you work for such a man? No loyalty, not to country, not to family!"

Yiban said, "Look at me. I was born to a dead mother, so I was born to no one. I have been both Chinese and foreign, this makes me neither. I belonged to everyone, so I belong to no one. I had a father to whom I am not even one-half his son. Now I have a master who considers me a debt. Tell me, whom do I belong to? What country? What people? What family?"

We looked at his face. In all my life, I had never seen a person so intelligent, so wistful, so deserving to belong. We had no answer for him.

That night, I lay on my mat, thinking about those questions. What country? What people? What family? To the first two questions, I knew the answers right away. I belonged to China. I belonged to the Hakkas. But to the last question, I was like Yiban. I belonged to no one else, only myself.

Look at me, Libby-ah. Now I belong to lots of people. I have family, I have you. . . . Ah! Lao Lu says no more talking! Eat, eat before everything gets cold.

# 11

# NAME CHANGE

As it turns out, Kwan was right about the sounds in the house. There *was* someone in the walls, under the floors, and he was full of anger and electricity.

I found out after our downstairs neighbor, Paul Dawson, was arrested for making crank phone calls to thousands of women in the Bay Area. My automatic response was sympathy; after all, the poor man was blind, he was lonely for companionship. But then I learned the nature of his calls: he had claimed to be a member of a cult that kidnapped "morally reprehensible" women and turned them into "sacrificial village dolls," destined to be penetrated by male cult members during a bonding rite, then eviscerated alive by their female worker bees. To those who laughed at his phone threats, he said, "Would you like to hear the voice of a woman who also thought this was a joke?" And then he played a recording of a woman screaming bloody murder.

When the police searched Dawson's apartment, they found an odd assortment of electronic equipment: tape recorders hooked up to his telephone, redialers, voice changers, sound-effects tapes, and more. He hadn't limited his terrorist activities to the telephone. Apparently, he felt the prior owners of our apartment also had been too noisy, inconsiderate of his morning Zen meditations. When they temporarily moved out during a remodeling phase, he punched holes in his ceiling and installed speakers and bugging devices underneath the upstairs floor, enabling him to monitor the doings of his third-floor neighbors and spook them with sound effects.

My sympathy immediately turned into rage. I wanted Dawson to rot in jail. For all this time, I had been driven nearly crazy with thoughts of ghosts—one in particular, even though I would have been the last to admit so.

But I'm relieved to know what caused the sounds. Living alone edges my imagination toward danger. Simon and I see each other only for business reasons. As soon as we're fiscally independent, we'll divorce ourselves from our clients as well. In fact, he's coming over later to deliver copy for a dermatologist's brochure.

But now Kwan has dropped by, uninvited, while I'm in the middle of a phone call to the printer's. I let her in, then return to my office. She's brought some homemade wontons, which she is storing in my freezer, commenting loudly on the lack of provisions in my fridge and cupboards: "Why mustard, pickles, but no bread, no meat? How you can live like this way? And beer! Why beer, no milk?"

After a few minutes, she comes into my office, a huge grin on her face. In her hands is a letter I had left on the kitchen counter. It's from a travel magazine, *Lands Unknown*, which has accepted Simon's and my proposal for a photo essay on village cuisines of China.

When the letter arrived the day before, I felt as though I had won the lottery only to remember I'd thrown my ticket away. It's a cruel joke played on me by the gods of chance, coincidence, and bad luck. I've spent the better part of the day and night gnawing on this turn of events, playing out scenarios with Simon.

I pictured him scanning the letter, saying, "God! This is unbelievable! So when are we going?"

"We're not," I'd say. "I'm turning it down." No hint of regret in my voice.

Then he'd say something like: "What do you mean, turning it down?"

And I'd say, "How could you even *think* we'd go together?"

Then maybe—and this really got my blood boiling—maybe he'd suggest that *he* would still go, and take along another photographer.

So I'd say, "No, you're not, because *I'm* going and I'm bringing along another writer, a *better* writer." And then the whole thing would escalate into a volley of insults about morals, business ethics, and comparative talent, variations of which kept me awake most of the night.

"Ohhhh!" Kwan is now cooing, waving the letter with joy. "You and Simon, going to China! You want, I go with you, be tour guide, do translation, help you find lots bargains. Of course, pay my own way. For long time I want go back anyway, see my auntie, my village—"

I cut her off: "I'm not going."

"Ah? Not going? Why not?"

"You know."

"I know?"

I turn around and look at her. "Simon and I are getting divorced. Remember?"

Kwan ponders this for two seconds, before answering: "Can go like friends! Why not just friends?"

"Drop it, Kwan, *please*."

She looks at me with a tragic face. "So sad, so sad," she moans, then walks out of my office. "Like two starving people, argue-argue, both throw out rice. Why do this, why?"

When I show Simon the letter, he is stunned. Are those actually tears? In all the years I've known him, I've never seen him cry, not at sad movies, not even when he told me about Elza's death. He swipes at the wetness on his cheeks. I pretend not to notice. "God," he says, "the thing we wished for so much came through. But we didn't."

We're both quiet, as if to remember our marriage with a few moments of respectful silence. And then, in a bid for strength, I take a deep breath and say, "You know, painful as it's been, I think the breakup has been good for us. I mean, it forces us to examine our lives separately, you know, without assuming our goals are the same." I feel my tone has been pragmatic, but not overly conciliatory.

Simon nods and softly says, "Yeah, I agree."

I want to shout, What do you mean, *you* agree! All these years we never agreed on anything, and now you agree? But I say nothing, and even congratulate myself for being able to keep my ill feelings in check, to not show how much I hurt. A second later, I am overwhelmed with sadness. Being able to restrain my emotions isn't a great victory—it's the pitiful proof of lost love.

Every word, every gesture is now loaded with ambiguity, nothing can be taken at face value. We speak to each other from a safe distance, pretending all the years we soaped each other's backs and pissed in front of each other never happened. We don't use any of the baby talk, code words, or shorthand gestures that had been our language of intimacy, the proof that we belonged to each other.

Simon looks at his watch. "I better go. I'm supposed to meet someone by seven."

Is he meeting a woman? This soon? I hear myself say, "Yeah, I have to get ready for a date too." His eyes barely flicker, and I blush, certain that he knows I've told a pathetic lie. As we walk to the door, he glances up.

"I see you finally got rid of that stupid chandelier." He gazes back at the apartment. "The place looks different—nicer, I think, and more quiet."

"Speaking of quiet," I say, and tell him about Paul Dawson, the house terrorist. Simon's the only one I know who can fully appreciate the outcome.

"Dawson?" Simon shakes his head, incredulous. "What a bastard. Why would he do something like that?"

"Loneliness," I say. "Anger. Revenge." And I sense the irony of what I've just said, a poker stabbing the ashes of my heart.

After Simon leaves, the apartment does feel awfully quiet. I lie on the rug in the bedroom and stare at the night sky through a dormer window. I think about our marriage. The weft of our seventeen years together was so easily torn apart. Our love was as ordinary as the identical welcome mats found in the suburbs we grew up in. The fact that our bodies, our thoughts, our hearts had once moved in rhythm with each other had only fooled us into thinking we were special.

And all that talk about the breakup being good for us—who am I trying to fool? I'm cut loose, untethered, not belonging to anything or anybody.

And then I think about Kwan, how misplaced her love for me is. I never go out of my way to do anything for her unless it's motivated by emotional coercion on her part and guilt on mine. I never call her out of the blue to say, "Kwan, how about going to dinner or a movie, just the two of us?" I never take any pleasure in simply being nice to her. Yet there she is, always hinting about our going together to Disneyland or Reno or China. I bat away her suggestions as though they were annoying little flies, saying I hate gambling, or that southern California is definitely not on my list of places to visit in the near future. I ignore the fact that Kwan merely wants to spend more time with me, that I am her greatest joy. Oh God, does she hurt the way I do now? I'm no better than my mother!—careless about love. I can't believe how oblivious I've been to my own cruelty.

I decide to call Kwan and invite her to spend a day, maybe even a weekend, with me. Lake Tahoe, that would be nice. She'll go berserk. I can't wait to hear what she says. She won't believe it.

But when Kwan answers the phone, she doesn't wait for me to explain why I've called. "Libby-ah, this afternoon I talking to my friend Lao Lu. He agree, you *must* go China—you, Simon, me together. This

154

year Dog Year, next year Pig, too late. How you cannot go? This you fate waiting to happen!"

She rambles on, countering my silences with her own irrefutable logic. "You half-Chinese, so must see China someday. What you think? We don't go now, maybe never get another chance! Some mistake you can change, this one cannot. Then what you do? What you think, Libby-ah?"

In hopes that she'll cease and desist, I say, "All right, I'll think about it."

"Oh, I know you change mind!"

"Wait a minute. I didn't say I'd go. I said I'd think about it."

She's off and running. "You and Simon *love* China, guarantee one hundred percent, specially my village. Changmian so beautiful you can't believe. Mountain, water, sky, like heaven and earth come together. I have things I leave there, always want give you. . . ." She goes on for another five minutes, extolling the virtues of her village before announcing, "Oh-oh, doorbell ringing. I call you again later, okay?"

"Actually, I called you."

"Oh?" The doorbell sounds once more. "Georgie!" she cries. "Georgie! Answer door!" Then she shouts, "Virgie! Virgie!" Is George's cousin from Vancouver already living with them? Kwan comes back on the line. "Wait minute. I go answer door." I hear her welcoming someone, and then she's on the line again, slightly breathless. "Okay. Why you call?"

"Well, I wanted to ask you something." I immediately regret what I haven't said yet. What am I getting myself into? I think about Lake Tahoe, being marooned with Kwan in a dinky motel room. "This is sort of last-minute, so I understand if you're too busy—"

"No-no, never too busy. You need something, ask. My answer always yes."

"Well, I was wondering, well"—and then I say, all in a rush—"what are you doing tomorrow for lunch? I have to take care of some business near where you work. But if you're busy, we could do it another day, no big deal."

"Lunch?" Kwan says brightly. "Oh! Lunch!" Her voice sounds heartbreakingly happy. I curse myself for being so stingy with my token gift. And then I listen, flabbergasted, as she turns away from the receiver to announce, "Simon, Simon — Libby-ah call me have lunch tomorrow!" I hear Simon in the background: "Make sure she takes you somewhere expensive."

"Kwan? Kwan, what's Simon doing there?"

"Come over eat dinner. Yesterday I already ask you. You say busy. Not too late, you want come now, I have extra."

I look at my watch. Seven o'clock. So this is his date. I nearly jump for joy. "Thanks," I tell her. "But I'm busy tonight." My same excuse.

"Always too busy," she answers. Her same lament.

Tonight, I make sure my excuse isn't a lie. As penance, I busy myself making a to-do list of unpleasant tasks I've been putting off, one of which is changing my name. That necessitates changing my driver's license, credit cards, voter registration, bank account, passport, magazine subscriptions, not to mention informing our friends and clients. It also means deciding what last name I will use. Laguni? Yee?

Mom suggested I keep the name Bishop. "Why go back to Yee?" she reasoned. "There aren't any other Yees you're related to in this country. So who's going to care?" I didn't remind Mom about her pledge to do honor to the Yee family name.

As I think more about my name, I realize I've never had any sort of identity that suited me, not since I was five at least, when my mother changed our last name to Laguni. She didn't bother with Kwan's. Kwan's name remained Li. When Kwan came to America, Mom said that it was a Chinese tradition for girls to keep their mother's last name. Later, she admitted that our stepfather didn't want to adopt Kwan since she was nearly an adult. Also, he didn't want to be legally liable for any trouble she might cause as a Communist.

Olivia Yee. I say the name aloud several times. It sounds alien, as though I'd become totally Chinese, just like Kwan. That bothers me a little. Being forced to grow up with Kwan was probably one of the reasons I never knew who I was or wanted to become. She was a role model for multiple personalities.

I call Kevin for his opinion on my new name. "I never liked the name Yee," he confesses. "Kids used to yell, 'Hey, Yee! Yeah, you, yee-eye-yee-eye-oh.' "

"The world's changed," I say. "It's hip to be ethnic."

"But wearing a Chinese badge doesn't really get you any bonus points," Kevin says. "Man, they're cutting Asians out, not making more room for them. You're better off with Laguni." He laughs. "Hell, some people think Laguni's Mexican. Mom did."

"Laguni doesn't feel right to me. We don't really belong to the Laguni lineage."

"Nobody does," says Kevin. "It's an orphan's name."

"What are you talking about?"

"When I was in Italy a couple of years ago, I tried to look up some Lagunis. I found out it's just a made-up name that nuns gave to orphans. Laguni—like 'lagoon,' isolated from the rest of the world. Bob's grandfather was an orphan. We're related to a bunch of orphans in Italy."

"Why didn't you ever tell us this before?"

"I told Tommy and Mom. I guess I forgot to tell you because—well, I figured you weren't a Laguni anymore. Anyway, you and Bob didn't get along that much. To me, Bob's the only dad I ever knew. I don't remember anything about our real father. Do you?"

I do have memories of him: flying into his arms, watching him crack open the claws of a crab, riding on his shoulders as he walked through a crowd. Aren't they enough that I should pay tribute to his name? Isn't it time to feel connected to somebody's name?

AT NOON, I go to the drugstore to pick up Kwan. We first spend twenty minutes while she introduces me to everyone in the store—the pharmacist, the other clerk, her customers, all of whom happen to be her "favoritests." I choose a Thai restaurant on Castro, where I can watch the street traffic from a window table while Kwan carries on a one-sided conversation. Today I'm taking it like a good sport; she can talk about China, the divorce, my smoking too much, whatever she wants. Today is my gift to Kwan.

I put on my reading glasses and scan the menu. Kwan scrutinizes the restaurant surroundings, the posters of Bangkok, the purple-and-gold fans on the walls. "Nice. Pretty," she says, as if I had taken her to the finest place in town. She pours us tea. "So!" she proclaims. "Today you not too busy."

"Just taking care of personal stuff."

"What kind personal?"

"You know, renewing my residential parking permit, getting my name changed, that sort of thing."

"Name change? What's name change?" She unfolds her napkin in her lap.

"I have to do all this junk to change my last name to Yee. It's a hassle, going to the DMV, the bank, City Hall. . . . What's the matter?"

Kwan is vigorously shaking her head. Her face is scrunched up. Is she choking?

"Are you all right?"

She flaps her hands, unable to speak, looking frantic.

"Omigod!" I try to recall how to do the Heimlich maneuver.

But now Kwan motions that I should sit down. She swallows her tea, then moans, "Ai-ya, ai-ya. Libby-ah, now I sorry must tell you something. Change name to Yee, don't do this."

I steel myself. No doubt she's going to argue once again that Simon and I shouldn't divorce.

She leans forward like a spy. "Yee," she whispers, "that not really Ba's name."

I sit back, heart pounding. "What are you talking about?"

"Ladies," the waiter says. "Have we decided?"

Kwan points to an item on the menu, asking first how to pronounce it. "Fresh?" she asks. The waiter nods, but not with the enthusiasm that Kwan requires. She points to another item. "Tender?"

The waiter nods.

"Which one better?"

He shrugs. "Everything is good," he says. Kwan looks at him suspiciously, then orders the pad thai noodles.

When the waiter leaves, I ask, "What were you saying?"

"Sometimes menu say fresh—*not* fresh!" she complains. "You don't ask, maybe they serve you yesterday leftovers."

"No, no, not the food. What were you saying about Daddy's name?"

"Oh! Yes-yes." She hunches her shoulders, and drops once again to her spy pose. "Ba's name. Yee not his name, no. This true, Libby-ah! I only telling you so you don't go through life with wrong name. Why make ancestors happy not our own?"

"What are you talking about? How could Yee not be his name?"

Kwan looks from side to side, as if she were about to reveal the identities of drug lords. "Now I going to tell you something, ah. Don't tell anyone, promise, Libby-ah?"

I nod, reluctant but already caught. And then Kwan begins to talk in Chinese, the language of our childhood ghosts.

I'm telling you the truth, Libby-ah. Ba took another person's name. He stole the fate of a lucky man.

During the war, that's when it happened, when Ba was at National Guangxi University, studying physics. This was in Liangfeng, near Guilin. Ba was from a poor family, but his father sent him to a missionary boarding school when he was a young boy. You didn't have to pay anything, just promise to love Jesus. That's why Ba's English was so good.

I don't remember any of this. I'm just telling you what Li Bin-bin, my auntie, said. Back then, my mother, Ba, and I lived in a small room in Liangfeng, near the university. In the mornings, Ba went to his classes. In the afternoons, he worked in a factory, putting together radio parts. The factory paid him by the number of pieces he finished, so he didn't make very much money. My auntie said Ba was more nimble with his mind than with his fingers. At night, Ba and his classmates threw their money together to buy kerosene for a shared lamp. On full-moon nights they didn't need a lamp. They could sit outside and study until dawn. That's what I also did when I was growing up. Did you know that? Can you see how in China the full moon is both beautiful and a bargain?

One night, when Ba was on his way home from his studies, a drunkard stepped out of an alley and blocked his way. He waved a suit coat in his hands. "This coat," he said, "has been in my family for many generations. But now I must sell it. Look at my face, I'm just a common man from the hundred family names. What use do I have for such fancy clothes?"

Ba looked at the suit coat. It was made of excellent cloth, lined and tailored in a modern style. You have to remember, Libby-ah, this was 1948, when the Nationalists and Communists were fighting over China. Who could afford a coat like this? Someone important, a big official, a dangerous man who got all his money taking bribes from scared people. Our Ba didn't have cotton batting for brains. Hnh! He knew the drunkard had stolen the coat and they both could lose their heads trading in such goods. But once Ba put his fingers on that coat, he was like a small fly caught in a big spider's web. He could not let go. A new feeling ran through him. Ah! To feel the seams of a rich man's coat—to think this was the closest he had ever come to a better life. And then this dangerous feeling led to a dangerous desire, and this desire led to a dangerous idea.

He shouted at the drunkard: "I know this coat is stolen, because I know its owner. Quick! Tell me where you got it or I'll call the police!" The guilty thief dropped the coat and ran off.

Back in our little room, Ba showed my mother the coat. She told me later how he slipped his arms into the sleeves, imagining that the power of its former owner now streamed through his own body. In one pocket he found a pair of thick eyeglasses. He put these on and swung out one arm, and in his mind a hundred people leapt to attention and bowed. He clapped his hands lightly, and a dozen servants rushed from his dreams to bring him food. He patted his stomach, full from his make-believe meal. And that's when Ba felt something else.

Eh, what's this? Something stiff was caught in the lining of the suit coat. My mother used her fine scissors to cut away the threads along the seam. Libby-ah, what they found must have caused their minds to whirl like clouds in a storm. From within the lining fell out a stack of papers—official documents for immigrating to America! On the first page there was a name written in Chinese: Yee Jun. Below that, it was in English: Jack Yee.

You have to imagine, Libby-ah, during civil wartime, papers like these were worth many men's lives and fortunes. In our Ba's trembling hands were certified academic records, a quarantine health certificate, a student visa, and a letter of enrollment to Lincoln University in San Francisco, one year's tuition already paid. He looked inside an envelope: it contained a one-way ticket on American President Lines and two hundred U.S. dollars. And there was also this: a study sheet for passing the immigration examination upon landing.

Oh, Libby-ah, this was very bad business. Don't you see what I'm saying? In those days, Chinese money was worthless. It must be that this man Yee had bought the papers for a lot of gold and bad favors. Did he betray secrets to the Nationalists? Did he sell the names of leaders in the People's Liberation Army?

My mother was scared. She told Ba to throw the coat into the Li River. But Ba had a wild-dog look in his eyes. He said, "I can change my fate. I can become a rich man." He told my mother to go live with her sister in Changmian and wait. "Once I'm in America, I will send for you and our daughter, I promise."

My mother stared at the visa photo of the man Ba would soon become, Yee Jun, Jack Yee. He was an unsmiling thin man, only two years older than Ba. He was not handsome, not like Ba. This man Yee had short hair, a mean face, and he wore thick glasses in front of his cold eyes. You can see a person's heart through his eyes, and my mother said this man Yee looked like the sort of person who would say, "Roll out of the way, you worthless maggot!"

That night my mother watched Ba turn himself into this man Yee by putting on his clothes, cutting his hair. She watched him put on the thick eyeglasses. And when he faced her, she saw his tiny eyes, so cold-looking. He had no warm feelings anymore for my mother. She said it was as though he had become this man Yee, the man in the photo, a man who was arrogant and powerful—eager to be rid of his past, in a hurry to start his new fate.

So that's how Ba stole his name. As to Ba's real name, I don't know what it is. I was so young, and then, as you already know, my mother died. You are lucky no such tragedy like this has happened to you. Later, my auntie refused to tell me Ba's real name because he left her sister. That was my auntie's revenge. And my mother wouldn't tell me either, even after she died. But I've often wondered what his name was.

A few times I invited Ba to visit me from the World of Yin. But other yin friends tell me he is stuck somewhere else, a foggy place where people believe their lies are true. Isn't this sad, Libby-ah? If I could learn his real name, I would tell him. Then he could go to the World of Yin, say sorry to my mother, so sorry, and live in peace with our ancestors.

That's why you must go to China, Libby-ah. When I saw that letter yesterday I said to myself, This is your fate waiting to happen! People in Changmian might still remember his name, my auntie for one, I'm sure of it. The man who became Yee, that's what Big Ma, my auntie, always called him. You ask my Big Ma when you go. Ask her what our Ba's real name is.

Ah! What am I saying! You won't know how to ask. She doesn't speak Mandarin. She's so old she never went to school to learn the people's common language. She speaks the Changmian dialect, not Hakka, not Mandarin, something in between, and only people from the village speak that. Also, you have to be very clever how you ask her questions about the past, otherwise she'll chase you away like a mad duck plucking at your feet. I know her ways. What a temper she has!

Don't worry, though, I'm going with you. I already promised. I never forget my promises. You and me, the two of us, we can change our father's name back to its true one. Together we can send him at last to the World of Yin.

And Simon! He must come along too. That way, you can still do the magazine article, get some money to go. Also, we need him to carry the suitcases. I have to bring lots of gifts. I can't go home with empty hands. Virgie can cook for Georgie, her dishes aren't so bad. And Georgie can take care of your dog, no need to pay anyone.

Yes, yes, the three of us together, Simon, you, me. I think this is the most practical, the best way to change your name.

Hey, Libby-ah, what do you think?

## 12

# THE BEST TIME TO
# EAT DUCK EGGS

Kwan doesn't argue to get her own way. She uses more effective methods, a combination of the old Chinese water torture approach and American bait-and-switch.

"Libby-ah," she says. "What month we go China, see my village?"

"I'm not going, remember?"

"Oh, right-right. Okay, what month you think I should go? September, probably still too hot. October, too many tourist. November, not too hot, not too cold, maybe this best time."

"Whatever."

The next day, Kwan says, "Libby-ah, Georgie can't go, not enough vacation time earn up yet. You think Virgie and Ma come with me?"

"Sure, why not? Ask them."

A week later, Kwan says, "Ai-ya! Libby-ah! I already buy three ticket. Now Virgie got new job, Ma got new boyfriend. Both say, Sorry, can't go. And travel agent, she say sorry too, no refund." She gives me a look of agony. "Ai-ya, Libby-ah, what I do?"

I think about it. I could pretend to fall for her routine. But I can't bring myself to do it. "I'll see if I can find someone to go with you," I say instead.

In the evening, Simon calls me. "I was thinking about the China trip. I don't want our breakup to be the reason you miss out on this. Take another writer—Chesnick or Kelly, they're both great on travel pieces. I'll call them for you, if you want."

I'm stunned. He keeps persuading me to go with Kwan, to use her homecoming as a personal angle to the story. I turn over in my head all the permutations of meanings in what he's saying. Maybe there's a chance we can become friends, the kind of buddies we were when we first met. As we continue on the phone, I recall what initially attracted us to each other—the way our ideas grew in logic or hilarity or passion the more we talked. And that's when I feel the grief for what we've lost over the years: the excitement and wonder of being in the world at the same time and in the same place.

"Simon," I say at the end of our two-hour conversation, "I really appreciate this. . . . I think it'd be nice to one day be friends."

"I never stopped being yours," he says.

And at that moment I let go of all restraint. "Well, then, why don't you come to China too?"

ON THE PLANE, I begin to look for omens. That's because Kwan said, when we checked in at the airport: "You, me, Simon—going China! This our fate join together at last."

And I think, Fate as in "the mysterious fate of Amelia Earhart." Fate as in the Latin root of "fatal." It doesn't help matters that the Chinese airline Kwan chose for its discount fare has suffered three crashes in the past six months, two of them while landing in Guilin, where we're headed, after a four-hour stopover in Hong Kong. My confidence in the airline takes another nosedive when we board. The Chinese flight attendants greet us wearing tam-o'-shanters and kilts, an inexplicable fashion choice that makes me question our caretakers' ability to deal with hijackers, loss of engine parts, and unscheduled ocean landings.

As Kwan, Simon, and I struggle down the narrow aisle, I notice there isn't a single white person in coach, unless you count Simon and me. Does this mean something?

Like many of the Chinese people on board, Kwan is gripping a tote bag of gifts in each hand. These are in addition to the suitcase full of presents that has already gone into checked baggage. I imagine tomorrow's television newscast: "An air-pump thermos, plastic food-savers, packets of Wisconsin ginseng—these were among the debris that littered the runway after a tragic crash killed Horatio Tewksbury III of Atherton, who was seated in first class, and four hundred Chinese who dreamed of returning as success stories to their ancestral homeland."

When we see where our assigned seats are, I groan. Center row, smack in the middle, with people on both sides. An old woman sitting at the other end of the aisle stares at us glumly, then coughs. She prays aloud to an unspecified deity that no one will take the three seats next to her, and cites that she has a very bad disease and needs to lie down and sleep. Her coughing becomes more violent. Unfortunately for her, the deity must be out to lunch, because we sit down.

When the drink trolley finally arrives, I ask for relief in the form of a gin and tonic. The flight attendant doesn't understand.

"Gin and tonic," I repeat, and then say in Chinese: "A slice of lemon, if you have it."

She consults her comrade, who likewise shrugs in puzzlement.

*"Ni you* scotch *meiyou?"* I try. "Do you have scotch?"

They laugh at this joke.

Surely you have scotch, I want to shout. Look at the ridiculous costumes you have on!

But "scotch" is not a word I've learned to say in Chinese, and Kwan isn't about to assist me. In fact, she looks rather pleased with my frustration and the flight attendants' confusion. I settle for a Diet Coke.

Meanwhile, Simon sits on my other side, playing Flight Simulator on his laptop. "Whoa-whoa-*whoa!* Shit." This is followed by the sounds of a crash-and-burn. He turns to me. "Captain Bishop here says drinks are on the house."

Throughout the trip, Kwan acts tipsy with happiness. She repeatedly squeezes my arm and grins. For the first time in more than thirty years, she'll be on Chinese soil, in Changmian, the village where she lived until she was eighteen. She'll see her aunt, the woman she calls Big Ma, who brought her up and, according to Kwan, horribly abused her, pinching her cheeks so hard she left her with crescent-shaped scars.

She'll also be reunited with old schoolmates, at least those who survived the Cultural Revolution, which started after she left. She's looking forward to impressing her friends with her English, her driver's license, the snapshots of her pet cat sitting on the floral-patterned sofa she bought recently at a warehouse sale — "fifty percent off for small hole, maybe no one even see it."

She talks of visiting her mother's grave, how she'll make sure it's swept clean. She'll take me to a small valley where she once buried a box filled with treasures. And because I am her darling sister, she wants to show me her childhood hiding place, a limestone cave that contains a magic spring.

The trip presents a number of firsts for me as well. The first time I've gone to China. The first time since I was a child that Kwan will be my constant companion for two weeks. The first time that Simon and I will travel together and sleep in separate rooms.

Now squished into my seat between Simon and Kwan, I realize how crazy it is that I am going — the physical torture of being in planes and airports for almost twenty-four hours, the emotional havoc of going with the very two people who are the source of my greatest heartaches and fears. And yet for the sake of my heart, that's what I have to do. Of course, I have pragmatic reasons for going — the magazine article, finding my father's name. But my main motivation is fear of regret. I worry that if I didn't go, one day I'd look back and wonder, What if I had?

Perhaps Kwan is right. Fate is the reason I'm going. Fate has no logic, you can't argue with it any more than you can argue with a tornado, an earthquake, a terrorist. Fate is another name for Kwan.

WE'RE TEN HOURS from China. My body is already confused as to whether it's day or night. Simon is snoozing, I haven't slept a wink, and Kwan is waking up.

She yawns. In an instant, she's alert and restless. She fidgets with her pillows. "Libby-ah, what you thinking?"

"Oh, you know, business." Before the trip, I made an itinerary and a checklist. I've taken into account jet lag, orientation, location scouting, the possibility that the only lighting available will be fluorescent blue. I've penciled in reminders to get shots of small grocery stores and big supermarkets, fruit stands and vegetable gardens, stoves and cooking utensils, spices and oils. I've also fretted many nights over logistics and budget. The distance to Changmian is a major problem, a three- or four-hour ride from Guilin, according to Kwan. The travel agent wasn't even able to find Changmian on a map. He has us booked into a hotel in Guilin, two rooms at sixty dollars each a night. There might be places that are cheaper and closer, but we'll have to find them after we arrive.

"Libby-ah," Kwan says. "In Changmian, things maybe not too fancy."

"That's fine." Kwan has already told me that the dishes are simple, similar to what she cooks, not like those in an expensive Chinese restaurant. "Actually," I reassure her, "I don't want to take pictures of fancy stuff. Believe me, I'm not expecting champagne and caviar."

"Cavi-ah, what that?"

"You know, fish eggs."

"Oh! Have, *have.*" She looks relieved. "Cavi-egg, crab egg, shrimp egg, chicken egg—all have! Also, thousand-year duck egg. Course, not really thousand year, only one, two, three year most . . . Wah! What I thinking! I know where find you duck egg older than that. Long time ago, I hide some."

"Really?" This sounds promising, a nice detail for the article. "You hid them when you were a girl?"

"Until I twenty."

"Twenty? . . . You were already in the States then."

Kwan smiles secretively. "Not *this* time twenty. *Last* time." She leans her head against the seat. "Duck egg—ahh, so good . . . Miss Banner, she don't like too much. Later, starving time come, eat anything, rat, grasshopper, cicada. She think thousand-year *yadan* taste better than eat those. . . . When we in Changmian, Libby-ah, I show you where hide them. Maybe some still there. You and me go find, ah?"

I nod. She looks so damn happy. For once, her imaginary past does not bother me. In fact, the idea of searching for make-believe eggs in China sounds charming. I check my watch. Another twelve hours and we'll be in Guilin.

"Mmm," Kwan murmurs. *"Yadan . . ."*

I can tell that Kwan is already there, in her illusory world of days gone by.

D uck eggs, I loved them so much I became a thief. Before breakfast, every day except Sunday, that's when I stole them. I wasn't a terrible thief, not like General Cape. I took only what people wouldn't miss, one or two eggs, that sort of thing. Anyway, the Jesus Worshippers didn't want them. They liked the eggs of chickens better. They didn't know duck eggs were a great luxury—very expensive if you bought them in Jintian. If they knew how much duck eggs cost, they'd want to eat them all the time. And then what? Too bad for me!

To make thousand-year duck eggs, you have to start with eggs that are very, very fresh, otherwise, well, let me think . . . otherwise . . . I don't know, since I used only fresh ones. Maybe the old ones have bones and beaks already growing inside. Anyway, I put these very fresh eggs into a jar of lime and salt. The lime powder I saved from washing clothes. The salt was another matter, not cheap like today. Lucky for me, the foreigners had lots. They wanted their food to taste as if it were dipped in the sea. I liked salty things too, but not *everything* salty. When they sat down to eat, they took turns saying "Please pass the salt," and added even more.

I stole the salt from the cook. Her name was Ermei, Second Sister, one daughter too many of a family with no sons. Her family gave her to the missionaries so they wouldn't have to marry her off and pay a dowry. Ermei and I had a little back-door business. The first week, I gave her one egg. She then poured salt into my empty palms. The next week, she wanted two eggs for the same amount of salt! That girl knew how to bargain.

One day, Dr. Too Late saw our exchange. I walked to the alleyway where I did the wash. When I turned around, there he was, pointing to the little white mound lying in the nest of my palms. I had to think fast. "Ah, this," I said. "For stains." I was not lying. I needed to stain the eggshells. Dr. Too Late frowned, not understanding my Chinese. What could I do? I dumped all that precious salt into a bucket of cold water. He was still watching. So I pulled something from the basket of ladies' private things, threw that in the bucket, and began to scrub. "See?" I said, and held up a salty piece of clothing. Wah! I was holding Miss Mouse's panties, stained at the bottom with her monthly blood! Dr. Too Late—ha, you should have seen his face! Redder than those stains. After he left, I wanted to cry for having spoiled my salt. But when I fished out Miss Mouse's panties—ah?—I saw I'd been telling the truth! That bloodstain, it was gone! It was a Jesus miracle! Because from that day on, I could help myself to as much salt as I needed, one handful for stains, one handful for eggs. I didn't have to go to Ermei through the back door. But every now and then, I still gave her an egg.

I put the lime, salt, and eggs into earthen jars. The jars I got from a one-eared peddler named Zeng in the public lane just outside the alleyway. One egg traded for a jar that was too leaky for oil. He always had plenty of cracked jars. This made me think that man was either very clumsy, or crazy about duck eggs. Later, I learned he was crazy for me! It's true! His one ear, my one eye, his leaky jars, my tasty eggs—maybe that's why he thought we were a good match. He didn't say he wanted me to become his wife, not in so many words. But I knew he was thinking this, because one time he gave me a jar that was not even cracked. And when I pointed this out to him, he picked up a stone, knocked a little chip off the mouth of the jar, and gave it back to me. Anyway, that's how I got jars and a little courtship.

After many weeks, the lime and the salt soaked through the eggshells. The whites of the eggs became firm green, the yellow yolks hard black. I knew this because I sometimes ate one to be certain the others were ready to go into their mud coats. Mud, I didn't have to steal that. In the Ghost Merchant's garden I could mix plenty. While the mud-coated eggs were still wet, I wrapped them in paper, pages torn from those pamphlets called "The Good News." I stuck the eggs into a small drying oven I had made out of bricks. I didn't steal the bricks. They had fallen out of the wall and were cracked. Along every crack, I smeared glue squeezed from a sticky poisonous plant. That way the sun could flow through the cracks, the bugs got stuck and couldn't eat my eggs. The next week, when the clay coats were hard, I put my eggs once more in the curing jar. I buried them in the northwest corner of the Ghost Merchant's garden. Before the end of my life, I had ten rows of jars, ten paces long. That's where they still might be. I'm sure we didn't eat them all. I saved so many.

To me, a duck egg was too good to eat. That egg could have become a duckling. That duckling could have become a duck. That duck could have fed twenty people in Thistle Mountain. And in Thistle Mountain, we rarely ate a duck. If I ate an egg—and sometimes I did—I could see twenty hungry people. So how could I feel full? If I hungered to eat one, but saved it instead, this satisfied me, a girl who once had nothing. I was thrifty, not greedy. As I said, every now and then I gave an egg to Ermei, to Lao Lu as well.

Lao Lu saved his eggs too. He buried them under the bed in the gatehouse, where he slept. That way, he said, he could dream about tasting them one day. He was like me, waiting for the best time to eat those eggs. We didn't know the best time would later be the worst.

ON SUNDAYS, the Jesus Worshippers always ate a big morning meal. This was the custom: long prayer, then chicken eggs, thick slices of salty pork, corn cakes, watermelon, cold water from the well, then another long prayer. The foreigners liked to eat cold and hot things together, very unhealthy. The day that I'm now talking about, General Cape ate plenty. Then he stood up from the table, made an ugly face, and announced he had a sour stomach, too bad he couldn't visit God's House that morning. That's what Yiban told us.

So we went to the Jesus meeting, and while I was sitting on the bench, I noticed Miss Banner could not stop tapping her foot. She seemed anxious and happy. As soon as the service was over, she picked up her music box and went to her room.

During the noonday meal of cold leftovers, General Cape didn't come to the dining room. Neither did Miss Banner. The foreigners looked at his empty chair, then hers. They said nothing, but I knew what they were thinking, mm-hmm. Then the foreigners went to their rooms for the midday nap. Lying on my straw mat, I heard the music box playing that song I had grown to hate so much. I heard Miss Banner's door open, then close. I put my hands over my ears. But in my mind I could see her rubbing Cape's sour stomach. Finally, the song stopped.

I awoke hearing the stableman shout as he ran along the passage-way: "The mule, the buffalo, the cart! They're gone." We all came out of our rooms. Then Ermei ran from the kitchen and cried: "A smoked pork leg and a sack of rice." The Jesus Worshippers were confused, shouting for Miss Banner to come and change the Chinese words into English. But her door stayed closed. So Yiban told the foreigners what the stableman and the cook had said. Then all the Jesus Worshippers flew to their rooms. Miss Mouse came out, crying and pulling at her neck; she had lost her locket with the hair of her dead sweetheart. Dr. Too Late couldn't find his medicine bag. For Pastor and Mrs. Amen, it was a silver comb, a golden cross, and all the mission money for the next six months. Who had done such a thing? The foreigners stood like stat-ues, unable to speak or move. Maybe they were wondering why God let this happen on the day they worshipped him.

By this time, Lao Lu was banging on General Cape's door. No an-swer. He opened the door, looked in, then said one word: Gone! He knocked on Miss Banner's door. Same thing, gone.

Everyone began to talk all at once. I think the foreigners were try-ing to decide what to do, where to look for those two thieves. But now they had no mule, no buffalo cow, no cart. Even if they did have them, how would they know where to look? Which way did Cape and Miss Banner go? To the south into Annam? To the east along the river to Can-ton? To Guizhou Province, where wild people lived? The nearest *yamen* for reporting big crimes was in Jintian, many hours' walking distance from Changmian. And what would the *yamen* official do when he heard that the foreigners had been robbed by their own kind? Laugh ha-ha-ha.

That evening, during the hour of insects, I sat in the courtyard, watching the bats as they chased after mosquitoes. I refused to let Miss Banner float into my mind. I was saying to myself, "Nunumu, why should you waste one thought on Miss Banner, a woman who favors a traitor over a loyal friend? Nunumu, you remember from now on, foreigners cannot be trusted." Later I lay in my room, still not thinking about Miss Banner, refusing to give her one piece of my worry or anger or sadness. Yet something leaked out anyway, I don't know how. I felt a twist in my stomach, a burning in my chest, an ache in my bones, feelings that ran up and down my body, trying to escape.

The next morning was the first day of the week, time to wash clothes. While the Jesus Worshippers were having a special meeting in God's House, I went into their rooms to gather their dirty clothes. Of course, I didn't bother with Miss Banner's room. I walked right past it. But then my feet started walking backward and I opened her door. The first thing I saw was the music box. I was surprised. Must be she thought it was too heavy for her to carry. Lazy girl. I saw her dirty clothes lying in the basket. I looked in her wardrobe closet. Her Sunday dress and shoes were gone, also her prettiest hat, two pairs of gloves, the necklace with a woman's face carved on orange stone. Her stockings with the hole in one heel, they were still there.

And then I had a bad thought and a good plan. I wrapped a dirty blouse around the music box and put it in the basket of clothes. I carried this down the passageway, through the kitchen, then along the hall to the open alleyway. I walked through the gate into the Ghost Merchant's garden. Along the northwest wall, where I kept my duck eggs, that's where I dug another hole and buried the box and all memories of Miss Banner.

As I was patting dirt over this musical grave, I heard a low sound, like a frog: "Wa-*ren*! Wa-*ren*!" I walked along the path, and above the crunch-crunch of leaves I heard the sound again, only now I knew it was Miss Banner's voice. I hid behind a bush and looked up at the pavilion. Wah! There was Miss Banner's ghost! Her hair, that's what made me think this, it was wild-looking, flowing to her waist. I was so scared I fell against the bush, and she heard my noise.

"Wa-*ren*? Wa-*ren*?" she called, as she ran down the pathway with a wild, lost look on her face. I was crawling away as fast as I could. But then I saw her Sunday shoes in front of me. I looked up. I knew right away she wasn't a ghost. She had many mosquito bites on her face, her neck, her hands. If there had also been *ghost* mosquitoes out there, they might have done that. But I didn't think of that until just now. Anyway, she was carrying her leather bag for running away. She scratched at her itchy face, asked me in a hopeful voice: "The general—has he come back for me?"

So then I knew what had happened. She had been waiting in the pavilion since the day before, listening for every small sound. I shook my head. And I felt both glad and guilty to see misery crawl over her face. She collapsed to the ground, then laughed and cried. I stared at the back of her neck, the bumpy leftovers where mosquitoes had feasted, the proof that her hope had lasted all night long. I felt sorry for her, but also I was angry.

"Where did he go?" I asked. "Did he tell you?"

"He said Canton. . . . I don't know. Maybe he lied about that as well." Her voice was dull, like a bell that is struck but doesn't ring.

"You know he stole food, money, lots of treasures?"

She nodded.

"And still you wanted to go with him?"

She moaned to herself in English. I didn't know what she was saying, but it sounded as if she was pitying herself, sorry she was not with that terrible man. She looked up at me. "Miss Moo, whatever should I do?"

"You didn't respect my opinion before. Why ask me now?"

"The others, they must think I'm a fool."

I nodded. "Also a thief."

She was quiet for a long time. Then she said, "Perhaps I should hang myself—Miss Moo, what do you think?" She began laughing like a crazy person. Then she picked up a rock and placed this in my lap. "Miss Moo, please do me the favor of smashing my head in. Tell the Jesus Worshippers that the devil Cape killed me. Let me be pitied instead of despised." She threw herself on the dirt, crying, "Kill me, please kill me. They'll wish me dead anyway."

"Miss Banner," I said, "you are asking me to be a murderer?"

And she answered: "If you are my loyal friend, you would do me this favor."

Loyal friend! Like a slap in the face! I said to myself, "Who is she to talk about being a loyal friend?" Kill me, Miss Moo! Hnh! I knew what she really wanted—for me to soothe her, tell her how the Jesus Worshippers would not be angry, how they would understand that she'd been fooled by a bad man.

"Miss Banner," I said, choosing my words very carefully, "don't be an even bigger fool. You don't really want me to smash your head. You're pretending."

She answered: "Yes, yes, kill me! I want to die!" She beat her fist on the ground.

I was supposed to persuade her against this idea at least one or two more times, arguing until she agreed, with much reluctance, to live. But instead I said, "Hm. The others will hate you, this is true. Maybe they will even kick you out. Then where will you go?"

She stared at me. Kick her out? I could see this idea running through her mind.

"Let me think about this," I said. After a few moments, I announced in a firm voice: "Miss Banner, I've decided to be your loyal friend."

Her eyes were two dark holes swimming with confusion.

"Sit with your back against this tree," I told her. She didn't move. So I grabbed her arm and dragged her to the tree and pushed her down. "Come, Miss Banner, I'm only trying to help you." I put the hem of her Sunday dress between my teeth and ripped it off.

"What are you doing!" she cried.

"What does it matter?" I said. "Soon you'll be dead anyway." I tore her hem into three pieces of cloth. I used one strip to tie her hands behind the skinny tree trunk. By now she was trembling a lot.

"Miss Moo, please let me explain—" she started to say, but then I tied another strip around her mouth. "Now, even if you must scream," I said, "no one will hear you." She was mumbling uh-uh-uh. I wrapped the other strip over her eyes. "Now you can't see the terrible thing I must do." She began to kick her feet. I warned her: "Ah, Miss Banner, if you struggle like this, I may miss, and smash only your eye or nose. Then I would have to do it again. . . ."

She was making muffled cries, wagging her head and bouncing on her bottom.

"Are you ready, Miss Banner?"

She was making the uh-uh-uh sounds and shaking her head, her whole body, the tree, shaking so hard the leaves started to fall as if it were autumn. "Farewell," I said, then touched her head lightly with my fist. Just as I thought she would, she fainted right away.

What I had done was mean but not terrible. What I did next was kind but a lie. I walked over to a flowering bush. I broke off a thorn and pricked my thumb. I squeezed and dribbled blood onto the front of her dress, along her brow and nose. And then I ran to get the Jesus Worshippers. Oh, how they praised and comforted her. Brave Miss Banner!—tried to stop the General from stealing the mule. Poor Miss Banner!—beaten, then left to die. Dr. Too Late apologized that he had no medicine to put on the bumps on her face. Miss Mouse said it was so sad that Miss Banner had lost her music box. Mrs. Amen made her invalid soup.

When she and I were alone in her room, Miss Banner said, "Thank you, Miss Moo. I don't deserve such a loyal friend." Those were her words, I remember, because I was very proud. She also said, "From now on, I'll always believe you." Just then Yiban entered the room without knocking. He threw a leather bag on the floor. Miss Banner gasped. It was her bag of clothes for running away. Now her secret had been discovered. All my meanness and kindness were for nothing.

"I found this in the pavilion," he said. "I believe it belongs to you. It contains your hat, also some gloves, a necklace, a lady's hairbrush." Yiban and Miss Banner stared at each other a long time. Finally he said, "Lucky for you, the General forgot to take it with him." That's how he let her know that he too would keep her pitiful secret.

All that week as I did my work, I asked myself, Why did Yiban save Miss Banner from disgrace? She had never been his friend, not like me. I thought about that time I pulled Miss Banner from the river. When you save a person's life, that person becomes a part of you. Why is that? And then I remembered that Yiban and I had the same kind of lonely heart. We both wanted someone to belong to us.

Soon Yiban and Miss Banner were spending many long hours together. Mostly they spoke in English, so I had to ask Miss Banner what they said. Oh, she told me, nothing very important: their life in America, their life in China, what was different, what was better. I felt jealous, knowing she and I had never talked about these not very important things.

"What is better?" I asked.

She frowned and searched her mind. I guessed she was trying to decide which of the many Chinese things she loved should be mentioned first. "Chinese people are more polite," she said, then thought some more. "Not so greedy."

I waited for her to continue. I was sure she would say that China was more beautiful, that our thinking was better, our people more refined. But she did not say these things. "Is there anything better in America?" I asked.

She thought a little bit. "Oh . . . comfort and cleanliness, stores and schools, walkways and roadways, houses and beds, candies and cakes, games and toys, tea parties and birthdays, oh, and big loud parades, lovely picnics on the grass, rowing a boat, putting a flower in your hat, wearing pretty dresses, reading books, and writing letters to friends . . ." On and on she went, until I felt myself growing small and dirty, ugly, dumb, and poor. Often I have not liked my situation. But this was the first time I had this feeling of not liking myself. I was sick with envy—not for the American things she mentioned, but that she could tell Yiban what she missed and he could understand her old desires. He belonged to her in ways that I could not.

"Miss Banner," I asked her, "you feel something for Yiban Johnson, ah?"

"Feel? Yes, perhaps. But just as a friend, though not as good a friend as you. Oh! And not with the feeling between a man and woman—no, no, *no!* After all, he's Chinese, well, not completely, but half, which is almost worse. . . . Well, in our country, an American woman can't possibly . . . What I mean is, such romantic friendships would *never* be allowed."

I smiled, all my worries put to rest.

Then, for no reason, she began to criticize Yiban Johnson. "I must tell you, though, he's awfully serious! No sense of humor! So gloomy about the future. China is in trouble, he says, soon even Changmian will not be safe. And when I try to cheer him up, tease him a little, he won't laugh. . . ." For the rest of the afternoon, she criticized him, mentioning all his tiny faults and the ways she could change them. She had so many complaints about him that I knew she liked him better than she said. *Not* just a friend.

The next week, I watched them sitting in the courtyard. I saw how he learned to laugh. I heard the excited voices of boy-girl teasing. I knew something was growing in Miss Banner's heart, because I had to ask many questions to find out what it was.

I'll tell you something, Libby-ah. What Miss Banner and Yiban had between them was love as great and constant as the sky. She told me this. She said, "I have known many kinds of love before, never this. With my mother and brothers, it was tragic love, the kind that leaves you aching with wonder over what you might have received but did not.

With my father, I had uncertain love. I loved him, but I don't know if he loved me. With my former sweethearts, I had selfish love. They gave me only enough to take back what they wanted from me.

"Now I am content," Miss Banner said. "With Yiban, I love and am loved, fully and freely, nothing expected, more than enough received. I am like a falling star who has finally found her place next to another in a lovely constellation, where we will sparkle in the heavens forever."

I was happy for Miss Banner, sad for myself. Here she was, speaking of her greatest joy, and I did not understand what her words meant. I wondered if this kind of love came from her American sense of importance and had led to conclusions that were different from mine. Or maybe this love was like an illness—many foreigners became sick at the slightest heat or cold. Her skin was now often flushed, her eyes shiny and big. She was forgetful of time passing. "Oh, is it that late already?" she often said. She was also clumsy and needed Yiban to steady her as she walked. Her voice changed too, became high and childlike. And at night she moaned. Many long hours she moaned. I worried that she had caught malaria fever. But in the morning, she was always fine.

Don't laugh, Libby-ah. I had never seen this kind of love in the open before. Pastor and Mrs. Amen were not like this. The boys and girls of my old village never acted like this, not in front of other people, at least. That would have been shameful—showing you care more for your sweetheart than for all your family, living and dead.

I thought that her love was another one of her American luxuries, something Chinese people could not afford. For many hours each day, she and Yiban talked, their heads bent together like two flowers reaching for the same sun. Even though they spoke in English, I could see that she would start a thought and he would finish it. Then he would speak, stare at her, and misplace his mind, and she would find the words that he had lost. At times, their voices became low and soft, then lower and softer, and they would touch hands. They needed the heat of their skin to match the warmth of their hearts. They looked at the world in the courtyard—the holy bush, a leaf on the bush, a moth on the leaf, the moth he put in her palm. They wondered over this moth as though it were a new creature on earth, an immortal sage in disguise. And I could see that this life she carefully held was like the love she would always protect, never let come to harm.

By watching all these things, I learned about romance. And soon, I too had my own little courtship—you remember Zeng, the one-eared peddler? He was a nice man, not bad-looking, even with one ear. Not too old. But I ask you: How much exciting romance can you have talking about cracked jars and duck eggs?

Well, one day Zeng came to me as usual with another jar. I told him, "No more jars. I have no eggs to cure, none to give you."

"Take the jar anyway," he said. "Give me an egg next week."

"Next week I still won't have any to give you. That fake American general stole the Jesus Worshippers' money. We have only enough food to last until the next boat from Canton comes with Western money."

The next week Zeng returned and brought me the same jar. Only this time, it was filled with rice. So heavy with feelings! Was this love? Is love rice in a jar, no need to give back an egg?

I took the jar. I didn't say, Thank you, what a kind man you are, someday I'll pay you back. I was like—how do you say it?—a *diplomat*. "Zeng-ah," I called as he started to leave. "Why are your clothes always so dirty? Look at all those grease spots on your elbows! Tomorrow you bring your clothes here, I'll wash them for you. If you're going to court me, at least you should look clean."

You see? I knew how to do romance too.

WHEN WINTER CAME, Ermei was still cursing General Cape for stealing the pork leg. That's because all the cured meat was gone, and so was the fresh. One by one, she had killed the pigs, the chickens, the ducks. Every week, Dr. Too Late, Pastor Amen, and Yiban walked many hours down to Jintian to see if the boat from Canton had come, bearing them money. And every week, they walked home with the same long faces.

One time, they returned with blood running down their long faces. The ladies went running toward them, screaming and crying: Mrs. Amen to Pastor Amen, Miss Mouse to Dr. Too Late, Miss Banner to Yiban. Lao Lu and I ran to the well. While the ladies fussed and washed off the blood, Pastor Amen explained what happened and Yiban translated for us.

"They called us devils, enemies of China!"

"Who? Who?" the ladies cried.

"The Taiping! I won't call them God Worshippers anymore. They're madmen, those Taiping. When I said, 'We're your friends,' they threw rocks at me, tried to kill me!"

"Why? Why?"

"Their eyes, because of their eyes!" Pastor shouted more things, then fell to his knees and prayed. We looked at Yiban and he shook his head. Pastor began punching the air with his fists, then prayed again. He pointed to the mission and wailed, prayed more. He pointed to Miss Mouse, who started to cry, patting Dr. Too Late's face, even though there was no more blood to wipe away. He pointed to Mrs. Amen, spit more words out. She stood up, then walked away. Lao Lu and I were like deaf-mutes, still innocent of what he had said.

At night, we went to the Ghost Merchant's garden to find Yiban and Miss Banner. I saw their shadows in the pavilion on top of the little hill, her head on his shoulder. Lao Lu would not go up there, because of the ghost. So I hissed until they heard me. They walked down, holding hands, letting go after they saw me. By the light of a melon slice of moon, Yiban told us the news.

He had talked to a fisherman when he went with Pastor and Dr. Too Late to the river to learn about the arrival of boats. The fisherman told him, "No boats, not now, not soon, maybe never. The British boats choked off the rivers. No coming in, no going out. Yesterday the foreigners fought for God, today for the Manchus. Maybe tomorrow China will break into little pieces and the foreigners will pick them up, sell them along with their opium." Yiban said there was fighting from Suzhou to Canton. The Manchus and foreigners were attacking all the cities ruled by the Heavenly King. Ten-ten thousand Taiping killed, babies and children too. In some places, all a man could see were rotting Taiping bodies; in other cities, only white bones. Soon the Manchus would come to Jintian.

Yiban let us think about this news. "When I told Pastor what the fisherman said, he went to his knees and prayed, just as you saw him do this afternoon. The God Worshippers threw stones at us. Dr. Too Late and I began to run, calling Pastor, but he wouldn't come. Stones hit his back, his arm, a leg, then his forehead. When he fell to the ground, blood and patience ran out of his head. That's when he lost his faith. He cried, 'God, why did you betray me? Why? Why did you send us the fake general, let him steal our hopes?' "

Yiban stopped talking. Miss Banner said something to him in English. He shook his head. So Miss Banner continued. "This afternoon, when you saw him fall to his knees, he again let the bad thoughts spill out of his brain. Only now he had lost not just his faith, but also his mind. He was shouting, 'I hate China! I hate Chinese people! I hate their crooked eyes, their crooked hearts. They have no souls to save.' He said, 'Kill the Chinese, kill them all, just don't let me die with them.' He pointed to the other missionaries and cried, 'Take her, take him, take her.' "

After that day, many things changed, just like my eggs. Pastor Amen acted like a little boy, complaining and crying often, acting stubborn, forgetting who he was. But Mrs. Amen was not angry with him. Sometimes she scolded him, most times she tried to comfort him. Lao Lu said that night she let Pastor curl against her. Now they were like husband

and wife. Dr. Too Late let Miss Mouse nurse his wounds long after there was nothing more to heal. And late at night, when everyone was supposed to be asleep but was not, a door would open, then close. I heard footsteps, then Yiban's whispers, then Miss Banner's sighs. I was so embarrassed to hear them that soon after that I dug up her music box and gave it back. I told her, "Look what else General Cape forgot to take."

One by one the servants left. By the time the air was too cold for mosquitoes to come out at night, the only Chinese who remained at the Ghost Merchant's House were Lao Lu and I. I'm not counting Yiban, because I no longer thought he was more Chinese than Johnson. Yiban stayed because of Miss Banner. Lao Lu and I stayed because we still had our duck-egg fortunes buried in the Ghost Merchant's garden. But we also knew that if we left, none of those foreigners would know how to stay alive.

Every day Lao Lu and I searched for food. Since I had once been a poor girl in the mountains, I knew where to look. We poked in the places beneath tree trunks where cicadas slept. We sat in the kitchen at night, waiting for insects and rats to come out for crumbs we couldn't see. We climbed up the mountains and picked wild tea and bamboo. Sometimes we caught a bird that was too old or too stupid to fly away fast enough. In the springtime, we plucked locusts and grasshoppers hatching in the fields. We found frogs and grubs and bats. Bats you have to chase into a small place and keep them flying until they fall from exhaustion. We fried what we caught in oil. The oil I got from Zeng. Now he and I had more to talk about than just cracked jars and eggs—funny things, like the first time I served Miss Banner a new kind of food.

"What's this?" she asked. She put her nose to the bowl, looked and sniffed. So suspicious. "Mouse," I said. She closed her eyes, stood up, and left the room. When the rest of the foreigners demanded to know what I had said, Yiban explained in their language. They all shook their heads, then ate with good appetites. I later asked Yiban what he told them. "Rabbit," he said. "I said Miss Banner once had a rabbit for a pet."

After that, whenever the foreigners asked what Lao Lu and I had cooked, I had Yiban tell them, "Another kind of rabbit." They knew not to ask whether we were telling the truth.

I'm not saying we had plenty to eat. You need many kinds of rabbits to feed eight people two or three times a day. Even Mrs. Amen grew thin. Zeng said the fighting was getting worse. We kept hoping one side would win, one side would lose, so we could return to life being better. Only Pastor Amen was happy, babbling like a baby.

One day Lao Lu and I both decided everything had become worse and worse, until now it was the worst. We agreed that this was the best time to eat duck eggs. We argued a little over how many eggs to give each person. This depended on how long Lao Lu and I thought the worst time would last and how many eggs we had to make things better. Then we had to decide whether to give the eggs to people in the morning or at night. Lao Lu said the morning was best, because we could have dreams of eating eggs and have them come true. This, he said, would make us glad if we woke up and discovered we were still alive. So every morning, we gave each person one egg. Miss Banner, oh, she loved those green-skinned eggs—salty, creamy, better than rabbits, she said.

Help me count, Libby-ah. Eight eggs, every day for almost one month, that's what?—two hundred and forty duck eggs. Wah! I made that many! If I sold those today in San Francisco, ah, what a fortune! Actually, I made even more than that. By the middle of summer, the end of my life, I had at least two jars left. The day we died, Miss Banner and I were laughing and crying, saying we should have eaten more eggs.

But how can a person know when she's going to die? If you knew, what would you change? Can you crack open more eggs and avoid regrets? Maybe you'd die with a stomachache.

Anyway, Libby-ah, now that I think of this, I don't have regrets. I'm glad I didn't eat all those eggs. Now I have something to show you. Soon we can dig them up. You and I, we can taste what's left.

# 13

# YOUNG GIRL'S WISH

**M**y first morning in China, I awake in a dark hotel room in Guilin and see a figure leaning over my bed, staring at me with the concentrated look of a killer. I'm about to scream, when I hear Kwan saying in Chinese, "Sleeping on your side — so *this* is the reason your posture is so bad. From now on, you must sleep on your back. Also do exercises."

She snaps on the light and proceeds to demonstrate, hands on hips, twisting at the waist like a sixties PE teacher. I wonder how long she's stood by my bed, waiting for me to waken so she can present her latest bit of unsolicited advice. Her bed is already made.

I look at my watch and say in a grumpy voice, "Kwan, it's only five in the morning."

"This is China. Everyone else is up. Only you're asleep."

"Not anymore."

We've been in China less than eight hours, and already she's taking control of my life. We're on her terrain, we have to go by her rules, speak her language. She's in Chinese heaven.

Snatching my blankets, she laughs. "Libby-ah, hurry and get up. I want to go see my village and surprise everyone. I want to watch Big

Ma's mouth fall open and hear her words of surprise: 'Hey, I thought I chased you away. Why are you back?' "

Kwan pushes open the window. We're staying at the Guilin Sheraton, which faces the Li River. Outside it's still dark. I can hear the *trnnng! trnnng!* of what sounds like a noisy pachinko parlor. I go to the window and look down. Peddlers on tricycle carts are ringing their bells, greeting one another as they haul their baskets of grain, melons, and turnips to market. The boulevard is bristling with the shadows of bicycles and cars, workers and schoolchildren—the whole world chirping and honking, shouting and laughing, as though it were the middle of the day. On the handlebar of a bicycle dangle the gigantic heads of four pigs, roped through the nostrils, their white snouts curled in death grins.

"Look." Kwan points down the street to a set of stalls lit by low-watt bulbs. "We can buy breakfast there, cheap and good. Better than paying nine dollars each for hotel food—and for what? Doughnut, orange juice, bacon, who wants it?"

I recall the admonition in our guidebooks to steer clear of food sold by street vendors. "Nine dollars, that's not much," I reason.

"Wah! You can't think this way anymore. Now you're in China. Nine dollars is lots of money here, one week's salary."

"Yeah, but cheap food might come with food poisoning."

Kwan gestures to the street. "You look. All those people there, do they have food poisoning? If you want to take pictures of Chinese food, you have to taste real Chinese food. The flavors soak into your tongue, go into your stomach. The stomach is where your true feelings are. And if you take photos, these true feelings from your stomach can come out, so that everyone can taste the food just by looking at your pictures."

Kwan is right. Who am I to begrudge carrying home a few parasites? I slip some warm clothes on and go into the hallway to knock on Simon's door. He answers immediately, fully dressed. "I couldn't sleep," he admits.

In five minutes, the three of us are on the sidewalk. We pass dozens of food stalls, some equipped with portable propane burners, others with makeshift cooking grills. In front of the stalls, customers squat in semi-circles, dining on noodles and dumplings. My body is jittery with exhaustion and excitement. Kwan chooses a vendor who is slapping what look like floury pancakes onto the sides of a blazing-hot oil drum. "Give me three," she says in Chinese. The vendor pries the cooked pancakes off with his blackened bare fingers, and Simon and I yelp as we toss the hot pancakes up and down like circus jugglers.

"How much?" Kwan opens her change purse.

"Six yuan," the pancake vendor tells her.

I calculate the cost is a little more than a dollar, dirt cheap. By Kwan's estimation, this is tantamount to extortion. "Wah!" She points to another customer. "You charged him only fifty fen a pancake."

"Of course! He's a local worker. You three are tourists."

"What are you saying! I'm also local."

"You?" The vendor snorts and gives her a cynical once-over. "From where, then?"

"Changmian."

His eyebrows rise in suspicion. "Really, now! Who do you know in Changmian?"

Kwan rattles off some names.

The vendor slaps his thigh. "Wu Ze-min? You know Wu Ze-min?"

"Of course. As children, we lived across the lane from each other. How is he? I haven't seen him in over thirty years."

"His daughter married my son."

"Nonsense!"

The man laughs. "It's true. Two years ago. My wife and mother opposed the match—just because the girl was from Changmian. But they have old countryside ideas, they still believe Changmian is cursed. Not me, I'm not superstitious, not anymore. And now a baby's been born, last spring, a girl, but I don't mind."

"Hard to believe Wu Ze-min's a grandfather. How is he?"

"Lost his wife, this was maybe twenty years ago, when they were sent to the cowsheds for counterrevolutionary thinking. They smashed his hands, but not his mind. Later he married another woman, Yang Ling-fang."

"That's not possible! She was the little sister of an old schoolmate of mine. I can't believe it! I still see her in my mind as a tender young girl."

"Not so tender anymore. She's got *jiaoban* skin, tough as leather, been through plenty of hardships, let me tell you."

Kwan and the vendor continue to gossip while Simon and I eat our pancakes, which are steaming in the morning chill. They taste like a cross between focaccia and a green-onion omelet. At the end of our meal, Kwan and the vendor act like old friends, she promising to send greetings to family and comrades, he advising her on how to hire a driver at a good price.

"All right, older brother," Kwan says, "how much do I owe you?"

"Six yuan."

"Wah! Still six yuan? Too much, too much. I'll give you two, no more than that."

"Make it three, then."

Kwan grunts, settles up, and we leave. When we're half a block away, I whisper to Simon, "That man said Changmian is cursed."

Kwan overhears me. "Tst! That's just a story, a thousand years old. Only stupid people still think Changmian is a bad-luck place to live."

I translate for Simon, then ask, "What kind of bad luck?"

"You don't want to know."

I am about to insist she tell me, when Simon points to my first photo opportunity—an open-air market overflowing with wicker baskets of thick-skinned pomelos, dried beans, cassia tea, chilies. I pull out my Nikon and am soon busy shooting, while Simon jots down notes.

"Plumes of acrid breakfast smoke mingled with the morning mist," he says aloud. "Hey, Olivia, can you do a shot from this direction? Get the turtles, the turtles would be great."

I inhale deeply and imagine that I'm filling my lungs with the very air that inspired my ancestors, whoever they might have been. Because we arrived late the night before, we haven't yet seen the Guilin landscape, its fabled karst peaks, its magical limestone caves, and all the other sites listed in our guidebook as the reasons this is known in China as "the most beautiful place on earth." I have discounted much of the hype and am prepared to focus my lens on the more prosaic and monochromatic aspects of communist life.

No matter which way we go, the streets are chock-full of brightly dressed locals and bloated Westerners in jogging suits, as many people as one might see in San Francisco after a 49ers Super Bowl victory. And all around us is the hubbub of a free-market economy. There they are, in abundance: the barterers of knickknacks; the hawkers of lucky lottery tickets, stock market coupons, T-shirts, watches, and purses with bootlegged designer logos. And there are the requisite souvenirs for tourists — Mao buttons, the Eighteen Lohan carved on a walnut, plastic Buddhas in both Tibetan-thin and roly-poly models. It's as though China has traded its culture and traditions for the worst attributes of capitalism: rip-offs, disposable goods, and the mass-market frenzy to buy what everyone in the world has and doesn't need.

Simon sidles up to me. "It's fascinating and depressing at the same time." And then he adds, "But I'm really glad to be here." I wonder if he's also referring to being with me.

Looking up toward cloud level, we can still see the amazing peaks, which resemble prehistoric shark's teeth, the clichéd subject of every Chinese calendar and scroll painting. But tucked in the gums of these ancient stone formations is the blight of high-rises, their stucco exteriors grimy with industrial pollution, their signboards splashed with garish red and gilt characters. Between these are lower buildings from an earlier era, all of them painted a proletarian toothpaste-green. And here and there is the rubble of prewar houses and impromptu garbage dumps. The whole scene gives Guilin the look and stench of a pretty face marred by tawdry lipstick, gapped teeth, and an advanced case of periodontal disease.

"Boy, oh boy," whispers Simon. "If Guilin is China's most beautiful city, I can't wait to see what the cursed village of Changmian looks like."

We catch up with Kwan. "Everything is entirely different, no longer the same." Her voice seems tinged with nostalgia. She must be sad to see how horribly Guilin has changed over the past thirty years. But then Kwan says in a proud and marveling voice: "So much progress, everything is so much better."

A couple of blocks farther on, we come upon a part of town that screams with more photo opportunities: the bird market. Hanging from tree limbs are hundreds of decorative cages containing singing finches, and exotic birds with gorgeous plumage, punk crests, and fanlike tails. On the ground are cages of huge birds, perhaps eagles or hawks, magnificent, with menacing talons and beaks. There are also the ordinary fowl, chickens and ducks, destined for the stew pot. A picture of them, set against a background of beautiful and better-fated birds, might make a nice visual for the magazine article.

I've shot only half another roll at the bird market, when I see a man hissing at me. "Ssssss!" He sternly motions me to come over. What is he, the secret police? Is it illegal to take pictures here? If he threatens to take my camera away, how much should I offer as a bribe?

The man solemnly reaches underneath a table and brings out a cage. "You like," he says in English. Facing me is a snowy-white owl with milk-chocolate highlights. It looks like a fat Siamese cat with wings. The owl blinks its golden eyes and I fall in love.

"Hey, Simon, Kwan, come here. Look at this."

"One hundred dollar, U.S.," the man says. "Very cheap."

Simon shakes his head and says in a weird combination of pantomime and broken English: "Take bird on plane, not possible, customs official will say stop, not allowed, must pay big fine—"

"How much?" the man asks brusquely. "You say. I give you morning price, best price."

"There's no use bargaining," Kwan tells the man in Chinese. "We're tourists, we can't bring birds back to the United States, no matter how cheap."

"Aaah, who's talking about bringing it back?" the man replies in rapid Chinese. "Buy it today, then take it to that restaurant across the street, over there. For a small price, they can cook it tonight for your dinner."

"Omigod!" I turn to Simon. "He's selling this owl as food!"

"That's disgusting. Tell him he's a fucking goon."

"You tell him!"

"I can't speak Chinese."

The man must think I am urging my husband to buy me an owl for dinner. He zeroes in on me for a closing sales pitch. "You're very lucky I even have *one*. The cat-eagle is rare, very rare," he brags. "Took me three weeks to catch it."

"I don't believe this," I tell Simon. "I'm going to be sick."

Then I hear Kwan saying, "A cat-eagle is not that rare, just hard to catch. Besides, I hear the flavor is ordinary."

"To be honest," says the man, "it's not as pungent as, say, a pangolin. But you eat a cat-eagle to give you strength and ambition, not to be fussy over taste. Also, it's good for improving your eyesight. One of my customers was nearly blind. After he ate a cat-eagle, he could see his wife for the first time in nearly twenty years. The customer came back and cursed me: 'Shit! She's ugly enough to scare a monkey. Fuck your mother for letting me eat that cat-eagle!'"

Kwan laughs heartily. "Yes, yes, I've heard this about cat-eagles. It's a good story." She pulls out her change purse and holds up a hundred-yuan note.

"Kwan, what are you doing?" I cry. "We are *not* going to eat this owl!"

The man waves away the hundred yuan. "Only American money," he says firmly. "One hundred *American* dollars."

Kwan pulls out an American ten-dollar bill.

"Kwan!" I shout.

The man shakes his head, refusing the ten. Kwan shrugs, then starts to walk away. The man shouts to her to give him fifty, then. She comes back and holds out a ten and a five, and says, "That's my last offer."

"This is insane!" Simon mutters.

The man sighs, then relinquishes the cage with the sad-eyed owl, complaining the whole time: "What a shame, so little money for so much work. Look at my hands, three weeks of climbing and cutting down bushes to catch this bird."

As we walk away, I grab Kwan's free arm and say heatedly: "There's no way I'm going to let you eat this owl. I don't care if we are in China."

"Shh! Shh! You'll scare him!" Kwan pulls the cage out of my reach. She gives me a maddening smile, then walks over to a concrete wall overlooking the river and sets the cage on top. She meows to the owl. "Oh, little friend, you want to go to Changmian? You want to climb with me to the top of the mountain, let my little sister watch you fly away?" The owl twists his head and blinks.

I almost cry with joy and guilt. Why do I think such bad things about Kwan? I sheepishly tell Simon about my mistake and Kwan's generosity. Kwan brushes off my attempt to apologize.

"I'm going back to the bird market," says Simon, "to take some notes on the more exotic ones they're selling for food. Want to come?"

I shake my head, content to admire the owl Kwan has saved.

"I'll be back in ten or fifteen minutes."

Simon strides off, and I notice how American his swagger looks, especially here on foreign soil. He walks in his own rhythm; he doesn't conform to the crowd.

"See that?" I hear Kwan say. "Over there." She's pointing to a cone-shaped peak off in the distance. "Just outside my village stands a sharp-headed mountain, taller than that one even. We call it Young Girl's Wish, after a slave girl who ran away to the top of it, then flew off with a phoenix who was her lover. Later, she turned into a phoenix, and together, she and her lover went to live in an immortal white pine forest."

Kwan looks at me. "It's a story, just superstition."

I'm amused that she thinks she has to explain.

Kwan continues: "Yet all the girls in our village believed in that tale, not because they were stupid but because they wanted to hope for a better life. We thought that if we climbed to the top and made a wish, it might come true. So we raised little hatchlings and put them in cages we had woven ourselves. When the birds were ready to fly, we climbed to the top of Young Girl's Wish and let them go. The birds would then fly to where the phoenixes lived and tell them our wishes."

Kwan sniffs. "Big Ma told me the peak was named Young Girl's Wish because a crazy girl climbed to the top. But when she tried to fly, she fell all the way down and lodged herself so firmly into the earth she became a boulder. Big Ma said that's why you can see so many boulders at the bottom of that peak — they're all the stupid girls who followed her kind of crazy thinking, wishing for hopeless things."

I laugh. Kwan stares at me fiercely, as if I were Big Ma. "You can't stop young girls from wishing. No! Everyone must dream. We dream to give ourselves hope. To stop dreaming — well, that's like saying you can never change your fate. Isn't that true?"

"I suppose."

"So now you guess what I wished for."

"I don't know. What?"

"Come on, you guess."

"A handsome husband."

"No."

"A car."

She shakes her head.

"A jackpot."

Kwan laughs and slaps my arm. "You guessed wrong! Okay, I'll tell you." She looks toward the mountain peaks. "Before I left for America, I raised three birds, not just one, so I could make three wishes at the top of the peak. I told myself, If these three wishes come true, my life is complete, I can die happy. My first wish: to have a sister I could love with all my heart, only that, and I would ask for nothing more from her. My second wish: to return to China with my sister. My third wish"—Kwan's voice now quavers—"for Big Ma to see this and say she was sorry she sent me away."

This is the first time Kwan's ever shown me how deeply she can resent someone who's treated her wrong. "I opened the cage," she continues, "and let my three birds go free." She flings out her hand in demonstration. "But one of them beat its wings uselessly, drifting in half-circles, before it fell like a stone all the way to the bottom. Now you see, two of my wishes have already happened: I have you, and together we are in China. Last night I realized my third wish would never come true. Big Ma will never tell me she is sorry."

She holds up the cage with the owl. "But now I have a beautiful cat-eagle that can carry with him my new wish. When he flies away, all my old sadnesses will go with him. Then both of us will be free."

Simon comes bounding back. "Olivia, you won't believe the things people here consider food."

We head to the hotel, in search of a car that will take one local, two tourists, and a cat-eagle to Changmian village.

# 14
# HELLO
# GOOD-BYE

By nine, we've procured the services of a driver, an amiable young man who knows how to do the capitalist hustle. "Clean, cheap, fast," he declares in Chinese. And then he makes an aside for Simon's benefit.

"What'd he say?" Simon asks.

"He's letting you know he speaks English."

Our driver reminds me of the slick Hong Kong youths who hang out in the trendy pool halls of San Francisco, the same pomaded hair, his inch-long pinkie nail, perfectly manicured, symbolizing that his lucky life is one without back-breaking work. He flashes us a smile, revealing a set of nicotine-stained teeth. "You call me Rocky," he says in heavily accented English. "Like famous movie star." He holds up a tattered magazine picture of Sylvester Stallone that he has pulled out of his Chinese–English dictionary.

We stash a suitcase of gifts and my extra camera gear into the trunk of his car. The rest of the luggage is at our hotel. Rocky will have to take us back there tonight, unless Kwan's aunt insists that we stay at her place—always a possibility with Chinese families. With this in mind, I've tucked an overnight kit into my camera bag. Rocky opens the door with a flourish, and we climb into a black Nissan, a late-model sedan that curiously lacks seat belts and safety headrests. Do the Japanese think Chinese lives aren't worth saving? "China has either better drivers or no liability lawyers," Simon concludes.

Having learned that we're Americans, Rocky happily assumes we like loud music. He slips in a Eurythmics tape, which was a gift from one of his "excellent American customers." And so with Kwan in the front seat, and Simon, the owl, and me in back, we start our journey to Changmian, blasted by the beat of "Sisters Are Doing It for Themselves."

Rocky's excellent American customers have also taught him select phrases for putting tourists at ease. As we traverse the crowded streets of Guilin, he recites them to us like a mantra: "Where you go? I know it. Jump in, let's go." "Go faster? Too fast? No way, José." "How far? Not far. Too far." "Park car? Wait a sec. Back in flash." "Not lost. No problem. Chill out." Rocky explains that he is teaching himself English so he can one day fulfill his dream and go to America.

"My idea," he says in Chinese, "is to become a famous movie actor, specializing in martial arts. For two years I've practiced tai chi chuan. Of course, I don't expect a big success from the start. Maybe when I first arrive I'll have to take a job as a taxi driver. But I'm hardworking. In America, people don't know how to be as hardworking as we Chinese. We also know how to suffer. What's unbearable to Americans would be ordinary conditions for me. Don't you think that's true, older sister?"

Kwan gives an ambiguous "Hm." I wonder whether she is thinking of her brother-in-law, a former chemist, who immigrated to the States and now works as a dishwasher because he's too scared to speak English lest people think he is stupid. Just then Simon's eyes grow round, and I shout, "Holy shit," as the car nearly sideswipes two schoolgirls holding hands. Rocky blithely goes on about his dream:

"I hear you can make five dollars an hour in America. For that kind of money, I'd work ten hours a day, every day of the year. That's fifty dollars a day! I don't make that much in a month, even with tips." He looks at us in the rearview mirror to see if we caught this hint. Our guide-book says tipping in China is considered insulting; I figure the book must be out-of-date.

"When I live in America," Rocky continues, "I'll save most of my money, spend only a little on food, cigarettes, maybe the movies every now and then, and of course a car for my taxi business. My needs are simple. After five years, I'll have almost one hundred thousand American dollars. Here that's a half-million yuan, more if I exchange it on the streets. Even if I don't become a movie star in five years, I can still come back to China and live like a rich man." He's grinning with happiness at the prospect. I translate for Simon what Rocky has said.

"What about expenses?" says Simon. "There's rent, gas, utilities, car insurance."

"Don't forget income taxes," I say.

And Simon adds: "Not to mention parking tickets and getting mugged. Tell him most people would probably starve in America on fifty dollars a day."

I'm about to translate for Rocky, when I remember Kwan's story about Young Girl's Wish. You can't stop people from hoping for a bet-ter life.

"He'll probably never make it to America," I reason to Simon. "Why spoil his dreams with warnings he'll never need?"

Rocky looks at us through the rearview mirror and gives us a thumbs-up. A second later, Simon grips the front seat, and I shout, "Holy Jesus shit!" We are about to hit a young woman on a bicycle with her baby perched on the handlebar. At the last possible moment, the bi-cyclist wobbles to the right and out of our way.

Rocky laughs. "Chill out," he says in English. And then he explains in Chinese why we shouldn't worry. Kwan turns around and translates for Simon: "He said in China if driver run over somebody, driver always at fault, no matter how careless other person."

Simon looks at me. "This is supposed to reassure us? Did something get lost in the translation?"

"It doesn't make any sense," I tell Kwan, as Rocky veers in and out of traffic. "A dead pedestrian is a dead pedestrian, no matter whose fault it is."

"Tst! This American thinking," Kwan replies. The owl swings his head and stares at me, as if to say, Wise up, gringa, this is China, your American ideas don't work here. "In China," Kwan goes on, "you always responsible for someone else, no matter what. You get run over, this my fault, you my little sister. Now you understand?"

"Yeah," Simon says under his breath. "Don't ask questions." The owl pecks at the cage.

We drive by a strip of shops selling rattan furniture and straw hats. And then we're in the outskirts of town, both sides of the road lined with mile after mile of identical one-room restaurants. Some are in the stages of being built, their walls layers of brick, mud plaster, and whitewash. Judging from the garish billboard paintings on the front, I guess that all the shops employ the same artist. They advertise the same specialties: orange soda pop and steamy-hot noodle soup. This is competitive capitalism taken to a depressing extreme. Idle waitresses squat outside, watching our car whiz by. What an existence. Their brains must be atrophied from boredom. Do they ever rail against the sheer randomness of their lot in life? It's like getting the free space on the bingo card and nothing else. Simon is furiously jotting down notes. Has he observed the same despair?

"What are you writing?"

"Billions and billions unserved," he answers.

A few miles farther on, the restaurants give way to simple wooden stalls with thatched roofs, and even farther, peddlers without any shelter from the damp chill. They stand by the side of the road, yelling at the top of their lungs, waving their string bags of pomelos, their bottles of homemade hot sauce. We are moving backward in the evolution of marketing and advertising.

As we drive through one village, we see a dozen or so men and women dressed in identical white cotton jackets. Next to them are stools, buckets of water, wooden tool chests, and hand-painted signboards. Being illiterate in Chinese, I have to ask Kwan what the signs say. " 'Expert haircut,' " she reads. "Also each one can drain boil, clip off corns, remove earwax. Two ears same price as one."

Simon is taking more notes. "Whew! How'd you like to be the tenth person offering to remove earwax, when no one is stopping for the first? That's my definition of futility."

I remember an argument we once had, in which I said you couldn't compare your happiness with someone else's unhappiness and Simon said why not. Perhaps we were both wrong. Now, as I watch these people waving at us to stop, I feel lucky I'm not in earwax removal. Yet I'm also afraid that the core of my being, stripped of its mail-order trappings, is no different from that of the tenth person who stands on the road wishing for someone to stop and single her out. I nudge Simon. "I wonder what they hope for, if anything."

He answers mock-cheery: "Hey, the sky's the limit—as long as it doesn't rain."

I imagine a hundred Chinese Icaruses, molding wings out of earwax. You can't stop people from wishing. They can't help trying. As long as they can see sky, they'll always want to go as high as they can.

The stretches between villages and roadside bargains grow longer. Kwan is falling asleep, her head bobbing lower and lower. She half awakens with a snort every time we hit a pothole. After a while, she emits long rhythmical snores, blissfully unaware that Rocky is driving faster and faster down the two-lane road. He routinely passes slower vehicles, clicking his fingers to the music. Each time he accelerates, the owl opens his wings slightly, then settles down again in the cramped cage. I'm gripping my knees, then sucking air between clenched teeth whenever

Rocky swings into the left lane to pass. Simon's face is tense, but when he catches me looking at him, he smiles.

"Don't you think we should tell him to slow down?" I say.

"We're fine, don't worry." I take Simon's "don't worry" to be patronizing. But I resist the urge to argue with him. We are now tailgating a truck filled with soldiers in green uniforms. They wave to us. Rocky honks his horn, then swerves sharply to pass. As we go by the truck, I can see an oncoming bus bearing down on us, the urgent blare of its horn growing louder and louder. "Oh my God, oh my God," I whimper. I close my eyes and feel Simon grab my hand. The car jerks back into the right lane. I hear a *whoosh*, then the blare of the bus horn receding.

"That's it," I say in a tense whisper. "I'm going to tell him to slow down."

"I don't know, Olivia. He might be offended."

I glare at Simon. "What? You'd rather die than be rude?"

He affects an attitude of nonchalance. "They all drive like that."

"So mass suicide makes it okay? What kind of logic is that?"

"Well, we haven't seen any accidents."

The knot of irritation in my throat bursts. "Why do you always think it's best not to say anything? Tell me, who gets to pick up the pieces after the damage is done?"

Simon stares at me, and I can't tell whether he is angry or apologetic. At that moment, Rocky brakes abruptly. Kwan and the owl awake with a flutter of arms and wings. Perhaps Rocky has picked up the gist of our argument—but no, we are now almost at a standstill in bumper-to-bumper traffic. Rocky rolls down the window and sticks out his head. He curses under his breath, then starts punching the car horn with the heel of his hand.

After a few minutes, we can see the source of our delay: an accident, a bad one, to judge from the spray of glass, metal, and personal belongings that litter the road. The smells of spilled gasoline and scorched rubber hang in the air. I am about to say to Simon, "See?" But now our car is inching by a black minivan, belly up, its doors splayed like the broken wings of a squashed insect. The front passenger section is obliterated. There is no hope for anyone inside. A tire lies in a nearby vegetable field. Seconds later, we go by the other half of the impact: a red-and-white public bus. The large front window is smashed, the hound-nosed hood is twisted and smeared with a hideous swath of blood, and the driver's seat is empty, a bad sign. About fifty gawkers, farm tools still in hand, mill around, staring and pointing at various parts of the crumpled bus as if it were a science exhibit. And then we are passing the other side of the bus and I can see a dozen or so injured people, some clutching themselves and bellowing in pain, others lying quietly in shock. Or perhaps they are already dead.

"Shit, I can't believe this," says Simon. "There's no ambulance, no doctors."

"Stop the car," I order Rocky in Chinese. "We should help them." Why did I say that? What can I possibly do? I can barely look at the victims, let alone touch them.

"Ai-ya." Kwan stares at the field. "So many yin people." Yin people? Kwan is saying there are dead people out there? The owl coos mournfully and my hands turn slippery-cold.

Rocky keeps his eyes on the road ahead, driving forward, leaving the tragedy behind us. "We'd be of no use," he says in Chinese. "We have no medicine, no bandages. Besides, it's not good to interfere, especially since you're foreigners. Don't worry, the police will be along soon."

I'm secretly relieved he isn't heeding my instructions.

"You're Americans," he continues, his voice deep with Chinese authority. "You're not used to seeing tragedies. You pity us, yes, because you can later go home to a comfortable life and forget what you've seen. For us, this type of disaster is commonplace. We have so many people.

This is our life, always a crowded bus, everyone trying to squeeze in for himself, no air to breathe, no room left for pity."

"Would someone please tell me what's going on!" Simon exclaims. "Why aren't we stopping?"

"Don't ask questions," I snap. "Remember?" Now I'm glad Rocky's dreams of American success will never come true. I want to tell him about illegal Chinese immigrants who are duped by gangs, who languish in prison and then are deported back to China. I'll fill his ear with stories about homeless people, about the crime rate, about people with college degrees who are standing in unemployment lines. Who is he to think his chances of succeeding are any better than theirs? Who is he to assume we know nothing about misery? I'll rip up his Chinese–English dictionary and stuff it in his mouth.

And then I feel literally sick with disgust at myself. Rocky is right. I can't help anyone, not even myself. I weakly ask him to pull over so I can throw up. As I lean out of the car, Simon pats my back. "You're okay, you're going to be fine. I feel queasy too."

When we get back on the open road, Kwan gives Rocky some advice. He solemnly nods, then slows down.

"What'd she say?" Simon asks.

"Chinese logic. If we're killed, no payment. And in the next lifetime, he'll owe us big time."

ANOTHER THREE HOURS PASS. I know we have to be getting close to Changmian. Kwan is pointing out landmarks. "There! There!" she cries huskily, bouncing up and down like a little child. "Those two peaks. The village they surround is called Wife Waiting for Husband's Return. But where is the tree? What happened to the tree? Right there, next to that house, there was a very big tree, maybe a thousand years old."

She scans ahead. "That place there! We used to hold a big market there. But now look, it's just an empty field. And there—that mountain up ahead! That's the one we called Young Girl's Wish. I once climbed all the way to the top."

Kwan laughs, but the next second she seems puzzled. "Funny, now that mountain looks so small. Why is that? Did it shrink, washed down by the rain? Or maybe the peak was worn down by too many girls running up there to make a wish. Or maybe it's because I've become too American and now I see things with different eyes, everything looking smaller, poorer, not as good."

All at once, Kwan shouts to Rocky to turn down a small dirt road we just passed. He makes an abrupt U-turn, knocking Simon and me into each other, and causing the owl to shriek with indignity. Now we are rumbling along a rutted lane, past fields with pillows of moist red dirt. "Turn left, turn left!" Kwan orders. She has her hands clasped in her lap. "Too many years, too many years," she says, as if chanting.

We approach a stand of trees, and then, as soon as Kwan announces, "Changmian," I see it: a village nestled between two jagged peaks, their hillsides a velvety moss-green with folds deepening into emerald. More comes into view: crooked rows of buildings whitewashed with lime, their pitched tile roofs laid in the traditional pattern of dragon coils. Surrounding the village are well-tended fields and mirrorlike ponds neatly divided by stone walls and irrigation trenches. We jump out of the car. Miraculously, Changmian has avoided the detritus of modernization. I see no tin roofs or electrical power lines. In contrast to other villages we passed, the outlying lands here haven't become dumping grounds for garbage, the alleys aren't lined with crumpled cigarette packs or pink plastic bags. Clean stone pathways crisscross the village, then thread up a cleft between the two peaks and disappear through a stone archway. In the distance is another pair of tall peaks, dark jade in color, and beyond those, the purple shadows of two more. Simon and I stare at each other, wide-eyed.

"Can you fucking believe this?" he whispers, and squeezes my

204

hand. I remember other times he has said those same words: the day we went to City Hall to be married, the day we moved into our co-op. And then I think to myself: Happy moments that became something else.

I reach into my bag for my camera. As I look through the viewfinder, I feel as though we've stumbled on a fabled misty land, half memory, half illusion. Are we in Chinese Nirvana? Changmian looks like the carefully cropped photos found in travel brochures advertising "a charmed world of the distant past, where visitors can step back in time." It conveys all the sentimental quaintness that tourists crave but never actually see. There must be something wrong, I keep warning myself. Around the corner we'll stumble on reality: the fast-food market, the tire junkyard, the signs indicating this village is really a Chinese fantasyland for tourists: Buy your tickets here! See the China of your dreams! Unspoiled by progress, mired in the past!

"I feel like I've seen this place before," I whisper to Simon, afraid to break the spell.

"Me too. It's so perfect. Maybe it was in a documentary." He laughs. "Or a car commercial."

I gaze at the mountains and realize why Changmian seems so familiar. It's the setting for Kwan's stories, the ones that filter into my dreams. There they are: the archways, the cassia trees, the high walls of the Ghost Merchant's House, the hills leading to Thistle Mountain. And being here, I feel as if the membrane separating the two halves of my life has finally been shed.

From out of nowhere we hear the din of squeals and cheers. Fifty tiny schoolchildren race toward the perimeter of a fenced-in yard, hailing our arrival. As we draw closer, the children shriek, turn on their heels, and run back to the school building laughing. After a few seconds, they come screaming toward us like a flock of birds, followed by their smiling teacher. They stand at attention, and then, through some invisible signal, shout all together in English, "A-B-C! One-two-three! How are you! Hello good-bye!" Did someone tell them American guests were coming? Did the children practice this for us?

The children wave and we wave back. "Hello good-bye! Hello good-bye!" We continue along the path past the school. Two young men on bicycles slow down and stop to stare at us. We keep walking and round a corner. Kwan gasps. Farther up the path, in front of an arched gateway, stand a dozen smiling people. Kwan puts her hand to her mouth, then runs toward them. When she reaches the group, she grabs each person's hand between her two palms, then hails a stout woman and slaps her on the back. Simon and I catch up with Kwan and her friends. They are exchanging friendly insults.

"Fat! You've grown unbelievably fat!"

"Hey, look at you—what happened to your hair? Did you ruin it on purpose?"

"This is the style! What, have you been in the countryside so long you don't recognize good style?"

"Oh, listen to her, she's still bossy, I can tell."

"You were always the bossy one, not—"

Kwan stops in mid-sentence, transfixed by a stone wall. You would think it's the most fascinating sight she's ever seen.

"Big Ma," she murmurs. "What's happened? How can this be?"

A man in the crowd guffaws. "Ha! She was so anxious to see you she got up early this morning, then jumped on a bus to meet you in Guilin. And now look—you're here, she's there. Won't she be mad!"

Everyone laughs, except Kwan. She walks closer to the wall, calling hoarsely, "Big Ma, Big Ma." Several people whisper, and everyone draws back, frightened.

"Uh-oh," I say.

"Why is Kwan crying?" Simon whispers.

"Big Ma, oh, Big Ma." Tears are streaming down Kwan's cheeks. "You must believe me, this is not what I wished. How unlucky that you died on the day that I've come home." A few women gasp and cover their mouths.

I walk over to Kwan. "What are you saying? Why do you think she's dead?"

"Why is everyone so freaked?" Simon glances about.

I hold up my hand. "I'm not sure." I turn back to her. "Kwan?" I say gently. "Kwan?" But she does not seem to hear me. She is looking tenderly at the wall, laughing and crying.

"Yes, I knew this," she is saying. "Of course, I knew. In my heart, I knew all the time."

IN THE AFTERNOON, the villagers hold an uneasy homecoming party for Kwan in the community hall. The news has spread through Changmian that Kwan has seen Big Ma's ghost. Yet she has not announced this to the village, and since there is no proof that Big Ma has died, there is no reason to call off a food-laden celebration that evidently took her friends days to prepare. During the festivities, Kwan does not brag about her car, her sofa, her English. She listens quietly as her former childhood playmates recount major events of their lives: the birth of twin sons, a railway trip to a big city, and the time a group of student intellectuals was sent to Changmian for reeducation during the Cultural Revolution.

"They thought they were smarter than us," recounts one woman whose hands are gnarled by arthritis. "They wanted us to raise a fast-growing rice, three crops a year instead of two. They gave us special seeds. They brought us insect poison. Then the little frogs that swam in the rice fields and ate the insects, they all died. And the ducks that ate the frogs, they all died too. Then the rice died."

A man with bushy hair shouts: "So we said, 'What good is it to plant three crops of rice that fail rather than two that are successful?'"

The woman with arthritic hands continues: "These same intellectuals tried to breed our mules! Ha! Can you believe it? For two years, every week, one of us would ask them, 'Any luck?' And they'd say, 'Not yet, not yet.' And we'd try to keep our faces serious but encouraging. 'Try harder, comrade,' we'd say. 'Don't give up.' "

We are still laughing when a young boy runs into the hall, shouting that an official from Guilin has arrived in a fancy black car. Silence. The official comes into the hall, and everyone stands. He solemnly holds up the identity card of Li Bin-bin and asks if she belonged to the village. Several people glance nervously at Kwan. She walks slowly toward the official, looks at the identity card, and nods. The official makes an announcement, and a ripple of moans and then wails fills the room.

Simon leans toward me. "What's wrong?"

"Big Ma's dead. She was killed in that bus accident we saw this morning."

Simon and I walk over and each put a hand on one of Kwan's shoulders. She feels so small.

"I'm sorry," Simon stammers. "I . . . I'm sorry you didn't get to see her again. I'm sorry we didn't meet her."

Kwan gives him a teary smile. As Li Bin-bin's closest relative, she has volunteered to perform the necessary bureaucratic ritual of bringing the body back to the village the next day. The three of us are returning to Guilin.

As soon as Rocky sees us, he stubs out his cigarette and turns off the car radio. He must have heard the news. "What a tragedy," he says. "I'm sorry, big sister, I should have stopped. I'm to blame—"

Kwan waves off his apologies. "No one's to blame. Anyway, regrets are useless, always too late."

When Rocky opens the car door, we see that the owl is still in his cage on the backseat. Kwan lifts the cage gently and stares at the bird. "No need to climb the mountain anymore," she says. She sets the cage on the ground, then opens its door. The owl sticks out his head, hops to the edge of the doorway and onto the ground. He twists his head and, with a great flap of wings, takes off toward the peaks. Kwan watches him until he disappears. "No more regrets," she says. And then she slips into the car.

As Rocky warms the engine, I ask Kwan, "When we passed the bus accident this morning, did you see someone who looked like Big Ma? Is that how you knew she'd died?"

"What are you saying? I didn't know she was dead until I saw her yin self standing by the wall."

"Then why did you tell her that you knew?"

Kwan frowns, puzzled. "I knew what?"

"You were telling her you knew, in your heart you knew it was true. Weren't you talking about the accident?"

"Ah," she says, understanding at last. "No, not the accident." She sighs. "I told Big Ma that what *she* was saying was true."

"What did she say?"

Kwan turns to the window, and I can see the reflection of her stricken face. "She said she was wrong about the story of Young Girl's Wish. She said all my wishes had already come true. She was always sorry she sent me away. But she could never tell me this. Otherwise I wouldn't have left her for a chance at a better life."

I search for some way to console Kwan. "At least you can still see her," I say.

"Ah?"

"I mean as a yin person. She can visit you."

Kwan stares out the car window. "But it's not the same. We can no longer make new memories together. We can't change the past. Not until the next lifetime." She exhales heavily, releasing all her unsaid words.

As our car rumbles along the road, the children in the playground run toward us and press their faces against the slat fence. "Hello goodbye!" they cry. "Hello good-bye!"

# 15

# THE
# SEVENTH DAY

Kwan is devastated, I can tell. She isn't crying, but when I suggested earlier that we simply order hotel room service rather than troop outside for a bargain, she readily agreed.

Simon offers her a few more awkward condolences. He kisses her on the cheek, then leaves the two of us alone in our room. We're dining on lasagne, twelve dollars a plate, wildly extravagant by Chinese standards. Kwan stares at her dinner, her face blank, a windswept plain before the storm. For me, lasagne is comfort food. I'm hoping it will fortify me enough to comfort Kwan.

What should I say? "Big Ma—she was a great lady. We're all going to miss her"? That would be insincere, since Simon and I never met her. And Kwan's stories of Big Ma's mistreating her always sounded to me like material for an *Auntie Dearest* memoir. Yet here is Kwan, grieving over this vile woman who literally left her with scars. Why do we love the mothers of our lives even if they were lousy caretakers? Are we born with blank hearts, waiting to be imprinted with any imitation of love?

I think about my own mother. Would I be desolate if she died? I feel terrified and guilty even pondering the question. Think about it, though: Would I revisit my childhood to cull happy memories and find they are as rare as ripe blackberries on a well-picked bush? Would I stumble into thorns, stir up the queen wasp surrounded by her adoring drones? Upon my mother's death, would I forgive her, then breathe a sigh of relief? Or would I go to an imaginary dell where my mother is now perfect, attentive and loving, where she embraces me and says, "I'm sorry, Olivia. I was a terrible mother, really shitty. I wouldn't blame you if you never forgave me." That's what I want to hear. I wonder what she would in fact tell me.

"Lasagne," Kwan says out of the blue.

"What?"

"Big Ma ask what we eating. Now she say big regret don't have time try American food."

"Lasagne is Italian."

"Shh! Shh! I know, but you tell her that, then regret don't have time see Italy. Already too many regret."

I lean toward Kwan and say sotto voce, "Big Ma doesn't understand English?"

"Just Changmian dialect and a little heart-talk. After she dead longer, learn more heart-talk, maybe even some English. . . ."

Kwan keeps talking, and I'm glad she's not drowning in grief, because I wouldn't know how to save her.

". . . Yin people, after while, just speak heart-talk. Easier, faster that way. No misconfusion like with words."

"What does heart-talk sound like?"

"I already tell you."

"You did?"

"Many time. Don't just use tongue, lip, teeth for speaking. Use hundred secret sense."

"Oh, right, right." I recall snatches of conversations we've had about this: the senses that are related to primitive instincts, what humans had before their brains developed language and the higher functions—the ability to equivocate, make excuses, and lie. Spine chills and musky scents, goose bumps and blushing cheeks—those are the vocabulary of the secret senses. I think.

"The secret senses," I say to Kwan. "Is it like your hair standing on end means you're afraid?"

"Mean someone you *love* now afraid."

"Someone you love?"

"Yes, secret sense always between two people. How you can have secret just you know, ah? You hair raise up, you know someone secret."

"I thought you meant that they were secret because people have forgotten they have these senses."

"Ah, yes. People often forget until die."

"So it's a language of ghosts."

"Language of love. Not just honey-sweetheart kind love. Any kind love, mother-baby, auntie-niece, friend-friend, sister-sister, stranger-stranger."

"Stranger? How can you love a stranger?"

Kwan grins. "When you first meet Simon, he stranger, right? First time I meet you, you stranger too. And Georgie! When I first see Georgie, I say myself, 'Kwan, where you know this man from?' You know what? Georgie my sweetheart from last lifetime!"

"Really? Yiban?"

"No, Zeng!"

Zeng? I draw a blank.

And she answers in Chinese: "You know—the man who brought me oil jars."

"Yes, I remember now."

"Wait, Big Ma, I'm telling Libby-ah about my husband." Kwan looks past me. "Yes, you know him—no, not in this lifetime, the last, when you were Ermei, and I gave you duck eggs, and you gave me salt."

As I poke my fork into the lasagne, Kwan is happily chatting away, distracted from grief by her memories of a make-believe past.

The last time I saw Zeng before he became Georgie, that was ... ah, yes, the day before I died.

Zeng brought me a small bag of dried barley, and some bad news. When I handed him his clean clothes, he gave me back nothing to wash. I was standing near my steaming pots, boiling the clothes.

"No need to worry about what's clean or dirty anymore," he told me. He was looking at the mountains, not at me. Ah, I thought, he's saying our courtship is over. But then he announced: "The Heavenly King is dead."

Wah! This was like hearing a thunderclap when the sky is blue. "How could this happen? The Heavenly King can't die, he's immortal!"

"No longer," Zeng said.

"Who killed him?"

"Died by his own hand, that's what people are saying."

This news was even more shocking than the first. The Heavenly King didn't allow suicide. Now he had killed himself? Now he was admitting he wasn't baby brother to Jesus? How could a Hakka man disgrace his own people that way? I looked at Zeng, his gloomy face. I guessed he had my same feelings. He was Hakka too.

I thought about this as I drew the heavy, wet clothes out of the water. "At least the battles will now end," I said. "The rivers will flow with boats again."

That's when Zeng gave me the third piece of news, even worse than the other two. "The rivers are already flowing, not with boats but with blood." When someone says "not with boats but with blood," you don't just listen and say, "Oh, I see." I had to nudge him to get every piece of information, like begging for a bowl of rice one grain at a time. He was so stingy with words. Little bit by little bit, this is what I learned.

Ten years before, the Heavenly King had sent a tide of death from the mountains to the coast. Blood flowed, millions died. Now the tide was returning. In the port cities, the Manchus had slaughtered all the God Worshippers. They were moving inland, burning down houses, digging up graves, destroying heaven and earth at the same time.

"All dead," Zeng told me. "No one is spared. Not even babies."

When he said that, I saw so many crying babies. "When will they come to our province?" I whispered. "Next month?"

"Oh no. The messenger reached our village only a few paces ahead of death."

"Ai-ya! Two weeks? One? How long?"

"Tomorrow the soldiers will destroy Jintian," he said. "The day after that—Changmian."

All feeling drained from my body. I leaned against the grinding mill. In my head, I could already see the soldiers marching along the road. As I was imagining swords dripping with blood, Zeng asked me to marry him. Actually, he didn't use this word "marry." He said in a rough voice: "Hey, tonight I'm going to the mountains to hide in the caves. You want to come with me or not?"

To you, this may sound clumsy, not so romantic. But if someone offers to save your life, isn't that as good as going to church in a white dress and saying "I do"? If my situation had been different, that's what I would have said: I do, let's go. But I had no room in my mind to think about marriage. I was wondering what would happen to Miss Banner, Lao Lu, Yiban—yes, even the Jesus Worshippers, those white faces of Pastor and Mrs. Amen, Miss Mouse and Dr. Too Late. How strange, I thought. Why should I care what happens to them? We have nothing in common—no language, no ideas, no same feelings about the earth and sky. Yet I could say this about them: Their intentions are sincere. Maybe some of their intentions are not so good to begin with, they lead to bad results. Still, they try very hard. When you know this about a person, how can you not have something in common?

Zeng broke into my thoughts. "You coming or not?"

"Let me consider this awhile," I answered. "My mind is not as quick as yours."

"What's left to consider?" Zeng said. "You want to live, or you want to die? Don't think too much. That makes you believe you have more choices than you do. Then your mind becomes confused." He went over to the bench next to the passageway wall, put his hands behind his head, and lay down.

I threw the wet clothes on the grinding mill. I rolled the stone to squeeze out the water. Zeng was right; I was confused. In one corner of my mind, I was thinking, Zeng is a good man. For the remainder of my life, I may never get another chance like this, especially if I die soon.

Then I went to another corner of my mind: If I go with him, then I'll have no more questions or answers of my own. I can no longer ask myself, Am I a loyal friend? Should I help Miss Banner? What about the Jesus Worshippers? These questions would no longer exist. Zeng would decide what should concern me, what should not. That's how things are between a man and a woman.

My mind was going back and forth, this way, that way. A new life with Zeng? Old loyalty to friends? If I hide in the mountains, will I suffer from fear, then die no matter what? If I stay, will my death be quick? Which life, which death, which way? It was like chasing a chicken, then becoming the chicken being chased. I had only one minute to decide which feeling was strongest. And that was the one I followed.

I looked at Zeng lying on the bench. His eyes were closed. He was a kind person, not too clever, but always honest. I decided to end our courtship the same way I started it. I would be a diplomat and make him think it was his idea to stop.

"Zeng-ah," I called.

He opened his eyes, sat up.

I started hanging the wet clothes. "Why should we run away?" I said. "We're not Taiping followers."

He put his hands on his knees. "Listen to your friend, ah," he said, very patient with me. "The Manchus need only a hint that you're friends with God Worshippers. Look where you live. That's enough for a death sentence."

I knew this, but instead of agreeing, I argued: "What are you saying? The foreigners don't worship the Heavenly King. Many times, I heard them say, 'Jesus has no Chinese baby brother.'"

Zeng huffed at me, as if he had never realized what a stupid girl I was. "Say that to a Manchu soldier, your head will already be rolling on the ground." He sprang to his feet. "Don't waste time talking anymore. Tonight I'm leaving. Are you coming?"

I continued my foolish talk: "Why not wait a little longer? Let's see what really happens. The situation can't be as bad as you think. The Manchus will kill some people here and there, but only a few, to set an example. As for the foreigners, the Manchus won't bother them. They have a treaty. Now that I think of this, maybe it's safer to stay here. Zeng-ah, you come live with us. We have room."

"Live here?" he shouted. "Wah! Maybe I should cut my own throat right now!" Zeng squatted and I could see his mind was bubbling like my laundry pots. He was saying all kinds of impolite things, loud enough for me to hear: "She's an idiot. Only one eye—no wonder she can't see what's the right thing to do!"

"Hey! Who are you to criticize me?" I said. "Maybe a fly has flown into your one ear and filled your head with locust fever." I held up the tip of my little finger and made zigzags in the air. "You hear *zzz-zzz*, you think clouds of disaster are coming from behind. Scared for no reason."

"No reason!" Zeng shouted. "What's happened to your mind? Have you been living in foreign holy clouds so long you think you're immortal?" He stood up, looked at me with disgust a few moments, then said, "Pah!" He turned around and walked away. Instantly, my heart was hurting. As his voice drifted off, I heard him say, "What a crazy girl! Lost her mind, now she's going to lose her head. . . ."

I kept hanging the laundry, but now my fingers were trembling. How quickly good feelings turn to bad. How easily he was fooled. A tear was burning my eye. I pushed it back. No self-pity. Crying was a weak person's luxury. I started to sing one of the old mountain songs, which one I don't remember now. But my voice was strong and clear, young and sad.

"All right, all right. No more arguing." When I turned around, there Zeng was, a tired look on his face. "We can take the foreigners to the mountains too," he said.

Take them with us! I nodded. As I watched him walk away, he started to sing the boy's answer to my song. This man was smarter than I had thought. What a clever husband he would make. With a good voice too. He stopped and called to me: "Nunumu?"

"Ah!"

"Two hours after the sun goes down, that's when I'll come. Tell everyone to be ready in the main courtyard. Do you understand?"

"Understood!" I shouted.

He walked a few more steps, then stopped again. "Nunumu?"

"Ah!"

"Don't wash any more clothes. The only one left to wear them will be a corpse."

So you see? He was already being bossy, making decisions for me. That's how I knew we were married. That's how he told me *I do*.

AFTER ZENG LEFT, I went into the garden and climbed up to the pavilion where the Ghost Merchant died. I looked over the wall and saw the rooftops of many houses, the little pathway leading to the mountains. If you had just come to Changmian for the first time, you might think, Ah, what a beautiful place. So quiet. So peaceful. Maybe I should do my honeymoon here.

But I knew this stillness meant the season of danger was now ending, and disaster would soon begin. The air was thick and damp, hard to breathe. I saw no birds, I saw no clouds. The sky was stained orange and red, as if the bloodshed had already reached into the heavens. I was nervous. I had a feeling that something was crawling on my skin. And when I looked, creeping on my arm was one of the five evils, a centipede, its legs marching in a wave! Wah! I whipped out my arm to shake it off, then crushed that centipede flat as a leaf. Even though it was dead, my foot kept stomping on it, up and down, until it was a dark smear on the stone floor. And still I couldn't get rid of this feeling that something was crawling on my skin.

After a while, I heard Lao Lu ringing the dinner bell. Only then did I come to my senses. In the dining room, I took a seat next to Miss Banner. We didn't have separate tables for Chinese and foreigners anymore, not since I started sharing my duck eggs. Same as usual, Mrs. Amen said the mealtime prayer. Same as usual, Lao Lu brought out a dish of fried grasshoppers, which he said was chopped-up rabbit. I was going to wait until we had finished eating, but my thoughts burst from my mouth: "How can I eat when tomorrow we might die!"

When Miss Banner finished translating my bad news, everyone was quiet for a moment. Pastor Amen leapt out of his chair, held up his arms, and cried to God in a happy voice. Mrs. Amen led her husband back to the table and made him sit down. Then she spoke, and Miss Banner translated her words: "Pastor can't go. You see how he is, still feverish. Out there he would call attention to himself, bring danger to others. We'll stay here. I'm sure the Manchus won't harm us, since we're foreigners."

Was this bravery or stupidity? Maybe she was right and the Manchus would not kill the foreigners. But who could be sure?

Miss Mouse spoke next. "Where is this cave? Do you know how to find it? We might become lost! Who is this man Zeng? Why should we trust him?" She couldn't stop worrying. "It's so dark! We should stay here. The Manchus can't kill us. It's not allowed. We are subjects of the Queen. . . ."

Dr. Too Late ran to Miss Mouse and took her pulse. Miss Banner whispered to me what he said: "Her heart beats too fast. . . . A journey into the mountains would kill her. . . . Pastor and Miss Mouse are his patients. . . . He will stay with them. . . . Now Miss Mouse is crying and Dr. Too Late is holding her hand. . . ." Miss Banner was translating things I could see for myself. That's how dazed she was.

Then Lao Lu spoke up: "I'm not staying. Look at me. Where's my long nose, my pale eyes? I can't hide behind this old face. At least in the mountains there are a thousand caves, a thousand chances. Here I have none."

Miss Banner stared at Yiban. So much fright in her eyes. I knew what she was thinking: That this man she loved looked more Chinese than Johnson. Now that I think about this, Yiban's face was similar to Simon's, sometimes Chinese, sometimes foreign, sometimes mixed up. But that night, to Miss Banner he looked very Chinese. I know this, because she turned to me and said: "What time will Zeng come for us?"

We didn't have wristwatches back then, so I said something like, "When the moon has risen halfway into the night sky," which meant around ten o'clock. Miss Banner nodded, then went to her room. When she came out, she was wearing all her best things: her Sunday dress with the torn hem, the necklace with a woman's face carved into orange stone, gloves of very thin leather, her favorite hairpins. They were tortoiseshell, just like that soap dish you gave me for my birthday. Now you know why I loved it so much. Those were the things she decided to wear in case she died. Me, I didn't care about my clothes, even though that night was supposed to be like my honeymoon. Also, my other trousers and blouse were still wet, hanging in the garden. And they were no better than what I had on.

THE SUN WENT DOWN. The half-moon rose, then climbed even higher. We grew feverish, waiting in the dark courtyard for Zeng to come. To be honest, we didn't have to wait for him. I knew the way into the mountains as well as he did, maybe even better. But I didn't tell the others that.

Finally, we heard a fist pounding on the gate. *Bom! Bom! Bom!* Zeng was here! Before Lao Lu reached the gate, the sound came again: *Bom! Bom!* So Lao Lu shouted: "You made us wait, now you can do the same while I take a piss!" He opened one side of the gate, and instantly two Manchu soldiers with swords sprang inside, knocking him to the ground. Miss Mouse gave out one long scream — *"Aaaaahhhhh!"* — followed by many fast ones, *"Aahh-aahh-aahh!"* Dr. Too Late put his hand over her noisy mouth. Miss Banner pushed Yiban away, and he crept behind a bush. I did nothing. But in my heart, I was crying, What's happened to Zeng? Where's my new husband?

Just then, someone else walked into the courtyard. Another soldier. This one was of high rank, a foreigner. His hair was short. He had no beard, no cape. But when he spoke — shouting "Nelly!" while tapping his stick — we knew who this traitor thief was. There he stood, General Cape, searching the courtyard for Miss Banner. Did he look sorry for what he had done? Did the Jesus Worshippers run over and beat him with their fists? He held out his arm to Miss Banner. "Nelly," he said once again. She didn't move.

And then everything wrong happened all at once. Yiban came out from behind the bush and walked angrily toward Cape. Miss Banner rushed past Yiban and threw herself into Cape's arms, murmuring, "Waren." Pastor Amen began to laugh. Lao Lu shouted: "The bitch can't wait to fuck the dog!" A sword flashed down — *crack!* — then again — *whuck!* And before any of us could think to cry stop, a head came rolling toward me, its lips still formed in a yell. I stared at Lao Lu's head, waiting to hear his usual curse. Why didn't he speak? Behind me, I heard the foreigners, their whimpers and moans. And then a howl rose out of my chest and I threw myself on the ground, trying to bring these two pieces together as Lao Lu again. Useless! I jumped to my feet, glared at

Cape, ready to kill and be killed. I took only one step and my legs went soft, as if they had no bones inside. The night grew darker, the air even heavier, as the ground rose up and smashed against my face.

When I opened my eye, I saw my hands and brought them to my neck. My head was there, so was a big bump on the side. Had someone struck me down? Or had I fainted? I looked around. Lao Lu was gone, but the dirt nearby was still wet with his blood. In the next moment, I heard shouts coming from around the other end of the house. I scurried over and hid behind a tree. From there, I could see into the open windows and doors of the dining room. It was like watching a strange and terrible dream. Lamps were burning. Where did the foreigners find the oil? At the small table where the Chinese used to eat sat the two Manchu soldiers and Yiban. In the middle of the foreigner table lay a large shank bone, its blackened meat still smoking from the fire. Who brought this food? General Cape held a pistol in each hand. He lifted one and aimed it at Pastor Amen, who was sitting next to him. The pistol made a loud click but no explosion. Everybody laughed. Pastor Amen then began tearing off pieces of meat with his bare hands.

Soon, Cape barked to his soldiers. They picked up their swords, walked briskly across the courtyard, opened the gate, and went outside. Cape then stood up and bowed to the Jesus Worshippers as if to thank them for being his honored guests. He held out his hand to Miss Banner, and just like emperor and empress they strolled down the corridor until they reached her room. Soon enough, I heard the awful sounds of her music box.

My eye flew back to the dining room. The foreigners were no longer laughing. Miss Mouse had her face pressed against the palms of her hands. Dr. Too Late was comforting her. Only Pastor Amen was smiling as he examined the shank bone. Yiban was already gone.

So many bad thoughts whirled through my head. No wonder the foreigners are called white devils! They had no morals. They couldn't be trusted. When they say to turn the other cheek, they really mean they have two faces, one tricky, the other false. How could I be so stupid as to think they were my friends! And now where was Zeng? How could I have risked his life for theirs?

A door swung open and Miss Banner stepped out, holding a lantern in her hand. She called back to Cape in a teasing voice, then closed the door and walked toward the courtyard. *"Nuli!"* she cried sharply in Chinese. *"Nuli,* come! Don't keep me waiting!" Oh, I was mad. Who does she think she's calling slave girl? She was searching for me, turning in circles. My hand scraped along the ground for a stone. But all I found was a pebble, and clutching this tiny weapon, I told myself, This time I'll smash her head in for sure.

I came out from behind the tree. *"Nuwu!"* I answered back.

As soon as I called her witch, she spun around, the lantern glowing on her face. She still couldn't see me. "So, witch," I said, "you know your name." One of the soldiers opened the gate and asked if anything was the matter. Cut off her head, I expected Miss Banner to say. But instead she answered in a calm voice: "I was calling for my servant."

"You want us to look for her?"

"Ah! No need, I've already found her. See, she's over there." She was pointing to a dark spot at the opposite end of the courtyard. *"Nuli!"* she shouted to the empty corner. "Quick now, bring me the key to my music box!"

What was she saying? I wasn't there. The soldier stepped back outside, banging the gate closed. Miss Banner turned around and hurried toward me. In a moment, her face was near mine. By lantern light I could see the anguish in her eyes. "Are you still my loyal friend?" she asked in a soft, sad voice. She held up the music box key. Before I could think what she meant, she whispered, "You and Yiban must leave tonight. Let him despise me, otherwise he won't leave. Make sure he is safe. Promise me this." She squeezed my hand. "Promise," she said again. I nodded. Then she opened my fist and saw the pebble in my palm. She took this and replaced it with the key. "What?" she shouted. "You left the key in the pavilion? Stupid girl! Now take this lantern, go to the garden. Don't you dare come back until you find it."

I was so happy to hear her say these meaningless things. "Miss Banner," I whispered. "You come with us — now."

She shook her head. "Then he'll kill us all. After he's gone, we'll find each other." She let go of my hand and walked in the dark, back to her room.

I FOUND YIBAN in the Ghost Merchant's garden, burying Lao Lu.

"You are a good person, Yiban." I covered the dirt with old leaves so the soldiers would not find his grave.

When I finished, Yiban said, "Lao Lu knew how to keep the gate closed to everything except his own mouth."

I nodded, then remembered my promise. So I said in an angry voice: "It's Miss Banner's fault he's dead. Throwing herself in the traitor's arms!" Yiban was staring at his fists. I nudged his arm. "Hey, Yiban, we should leave, run away. Why die for the sins of these foreigners? None of them are any good."

"You're mistaken," Yiban said. "Miss Banner only pretends to give Cape her heart, to save us all." You see how well he knew her? Then you also know how strongly I had to lie.

"Hnh! Pretend!" I said. "I'm sorry to have to tell you the truth. Many times she's told me she wished he would come back for her. Of course she was fond of you, but only half as much as she is fond of Cape. And you know why? You are only half a foreigner! That's how these Americans are. She loves Cape because he is her same kind. You can't easily change ruts that have been carved in mud."

Yiban's fists were still clenched, and his face grew sad, very sad. Lucky for me, I didn't have to tell too many more lies about Miss Banner. He agreed we should leave. But before we did that, I went to the northwest corner and reached into an open jar that had two duck eggs left. There was no time to dig up more. "We'll go to Hundred Caves Mountain," I said. "I know how to find it." I blew out the lantern Miss Banner had given me and handed it to Yiban. Then the two of us slipped through the alleyway gate.

We did not take the path through the village. We crept along the foot of the mountain, where prickly bushes grew. As we began to climb toward the first ridge and its wall, my heart was pounding hard with worry that the soldiers would see us. Even though I was a girl and Yiban a man, I climbed faster. I had my mountain legs. When I reached the archway, I waited for him to catch up. From there my eye searched for the Ghost Merchant's House. It was too dark. I imagined Miss Banner gazing into the night, wondering if Yiban and I were safe. And then I thought of Zeng. Had he seen Cape and his soldiers? Did he flee to the mountains by himself? Just as I thought this, I heard his voice calling me from behind.

"Nunumu?"

"Ah!" I turned around. I saw his shadow at the end of the archway tunnel. How happy I was. "Zeng, there you are! I've been worried to pieces about you. We waited, and then the soldiers came—"

He cut me off. "Nunumu, hurry. Don't waste time talking. Come this way." He was still bossy, no time to say, "Oh, my little treasure, at last I have found you." As I walked through the arch, I let him know I was glad to see him, by complaining in a teasing way: "Hey, when you didn't come, I thought you had changed your mind, taken another woman, one with two eyes." I stepped out of the archway tunnel. Zeng was walking along the ridge beside the wall. He waved for me to follow.

"Don't travel through the valley," he said. "Stay high along the mountain."

"Wait!" I said. "Another person is coming." He stopped. I turned around to see if Yiban was following. And then I heard my new husband say, "Nunumu, tonight the soldiers killed me. Now I will wait for you forever."

"Ai-ya!" I grumbled. "Don't joke like that. Tonight the soldiers killed Lao Lu. I've never seen a more terrible sight—"

At last, Yiban came out of the archway. "Who are you speaking to?" he asked.

"Zeng," I said. "He's here. See?" I turned around. "Zeng? I can't see you. Wave your hand. . . . Hey, where are you? Wait!"

"I will wait for you forever," I heard him whisper in my ear. Ai-ya! That's when I knew Zeng wasn't joking. He was dead.

Yiban came next to me. "What's wrong? Where is he?"

I bit my lips to keep from crying out. "I was mistaken. I saw a shadow, that's all." My eye was burning and I was grateful for the dark. What did it matter if I died now rather than later? If I had not made a promise to Miss Banner, I would have gone back to the Ghost Merchant's House. But now here was Yiban, waiting for me to decide which way to go.

"High along the mountain," I said.

As Yiban and I pushed past bushes and stumbled over rocks, we said nothing to each other. I think he was like me, hurting over people he had lost. He and Miss Banner might one day be together again. No such hope for Zeng and me. But then I heard Zeng say, "Nunumu, how can you decide the future? What about the next lifetime? Can't we marry then?" Wah! Hearing this, I almost tumbled down the mountain. Marry! He used the word "marry"!

"Nunumu," he continued, "before I leave, I'll take you to a cave where you should hide. Use my eyes in the dark."

Right away, I could see through the patch of my blind eye. And before me was a small path, cast with dusk light. The land everywhere else was hidden by night. I turned to Yiban. "Quick now," I said, and I marched ahead as bravely as any soldier.

After several hours, we were standing in front of a bush. As I pulled back the branches, I saw a hole just big enough for one person to squeeze through. Yiban climbed in first. He called back: "It's too shallow. It ends a few paces in."

I was surprised. Why would Zeng take us to such a poor cave? My doubt insulted him. "It's not too shallow," he said. "On the left side are two boulders. Reach down between them." I climbed in and found a cool opening that slanted down.

"This is the right cave," I said to Yiban. "You just didn't look carefully enough. Light the lantern and climb down after me."

That hole was the beginning of a long, twisty passageway with a small stream running along one side. Sometimes the tunnel split into two directions. "Where one way goes up, the other down," Zeng said, "always go lower. Where one has a stream, and the other is dry," Zeng said, "follow the water. Where one is narrow, the other wide," Zeng said, "squeeze in." The farther we went, the cooler the air became, very refreshing.

We turned one corner after another, until we saw a celestial light. What was this? We were in a place, like a palace room, that could have held a thousand people. It was very bright. In the middle of the floor was a lake—with water that glowed. It was a greenish-golden color, and not like light that comes from a candle, a lamp, or the sun. I thought it was the beams of the moon shining through a hole in the world.

Yiban thought it might be a volcano bubbling underneath. Or ancient sea creatures with shining eyes. Or perhaps a star that broke in two, fell to earth, and splashed into the lake.

I heard Zeng say, "Now you can find the rest of the way yourself. You won't get lost."

Zeng was leaving me. "Don't go!" I shouted.

But only Yiban answered back: "I haven't moved."

And then I could no longer see out of my blind eye. I waited for Zeng to speak again. Nothing. Gone like that. No "Good-bye, my little heart-liver. Soon I will meet you in the next world." That's the trouble with yin people. Unreliable! They come when they want, go when they please. After I died, Zeng and I had a big argument about that.

And then I told him what I am telling you now, Big Ma: That with your death, I know too late what I have truly lost.

# 16
# BIG MA'S
# PORTRAIT

I listened to Kwan talk to Big Ma for half the night. Now I'm bleary-eyed. She's as perky as can be.

Rocky is driving us to Changmian in a trouble-prone van. Big Ma's shrouded body is lying across the bench in the back. At every intersection, the van coughs to a stop, belches, and dies. Rocky then jumps out, flings open the hood, and bangs on various metallic parts, while bellowing in Chinese, "Fuck your ancestors, you lazy worm." Miraculously, this incantation works, much to our relief and that of the honking drivers behind us. Inside, the van feels like an icebox; out of consideration to Big Ma and her sad condition, Rocky has kept the heater turned off. Staring out the windows, I can see fog rising off the banks of irrigation ditches. The peaks have blended into the thick mist. This does not look like the beginning of a good day.

Kwan is sitting in the back, chatting loudly to Big Ma's body as though they were girls on their way to school. I am one bench up, and Simon is sitting on the seat behind Rocky, maintaining proletarian camaraderie and, I suspect, keeping an eye on dangerous driving maneuvers. Earlier this morning, after we checked out of the Sheraton and loaded the luggage into the van, I told Simon, "Thank God this will be the last ride we have to make with Rocky." Kwan gave me a horrified look: "Wah! Don't say 'last.' Bad luck to say such a thing." Bad luck or not, at least we won't have to make the daily commute to and from Changmian. We are going to live in the village for the next two weeks, rent-free, courtesy of Big Ma, who, according to Kwan, "invite us to stay her place, even before she die."

Above the metallic rattles of the van, I can hear Kwan bragging to the dead woman: "This sweater, see, it looks like wool, doesn't it? But it's *crylic-ah*, mm-hmm, *machine wash*." She says "acrylic" and "machine washable" in her version of English, then explains how washing machines and dryers figure into the American judicial system: "In California, you can't hang laundry from your balcony or window, oh no. Your neighbors will call the police for shaming them. America doesn't have as much freedom as you think. So many things are forbidden, you would not believe it. I think some rules are good, though. You can't smoke except in jail. You can't throw an orange peel on the road. You can't let your baby poop on the sidewalk. But some rules are ridiculous. You can't talk in a movie theater. You can't eat too many fatty foods. . . ."

Rocky revs the engine and speeds down the bumpy road. Now I'm concerned not only for Kwan's state of mind but also at the possibility that Big Ma's body will soon go hurtling onto the floor.

"Also, you can't make your children work," Kwan is saying with absolute authority. "I'm telling the truth! Remember how you made me gather twigs and sticks for fuel? Oh yes, I remember. I had to run all over the place in the wintertime, up and down, back and forth, here and there! My poor little fingers, swollen stiff with cold. And then you sold my bundles to other households and kept the money yourself. No, I'm not blaming you, not now. Of course, I know, in those days everyone had to work hard. But in America, they would have put you in jail for treating me this way. Yes, and for slapping my face so many times and pinching my cheeks with your sharp fingernails. You don't remember?

See the scars, here on my cheek, two of them, like a rat bite. And now that I'm remembering this, I'm telling you again, I didn't give those moldy rice cakes to the pigs. Why should I lie now? Just as I told you then, the one who stole them was Third Cousin Wu. I know because I watched her cutting off the green mold, one little rice cake at a time. Ask her yourself. She must be dead by now. Ask her why she lied and said I threw them away!"

Kwan is unusually quiet for the next ten minutes, and I figure that she and Big Ma are giving each other the Chinese silent treatment. But then I hear Kwan shout to me in English: "Libby-ah! Big Ma ask me can you take her picture? She say there no good picture of her when she still alive." Before I can answer, Kwan does more yin-speak translation: "This afternoon, she say best time take picture. After I put on best clothes, best shoes." Kwan smiles broadly at Big Ma, then turns to me. "Big Ma say she proud beyond words have such famous photographer in family."

"I'm not famous."

"Don't argue with Big Ma. To her, you famous. That's what matter."

Simon wobbles toward the back and sits next to me, whispering, "You're not actually going to take a picture of a corpse, are you?"

"What am I supposed to say? — 'I'm sorry, I don't do dead people, but I can refer you to someone who does'?"

"She might not be very photogenic."

"No kidding."

"You realize this is Kwan's wish for a photo, not Big Ma's."

"Why are you saying things that are completely unnecessary?"

"Just checking, now that we're in China. A lot of weird stuff has already happened, and it's only the second day."

WHEN WE ARRIVE in Changmian, four elderly women snatch our luggage and wave off our protests with laughter and assertions that each

230

is stronger than the three of us combined. Unencumbered, we wend our way through a maze of stone-paved lanes and narrow alleyways to reach Big Ma's house. It is identical to every other house in the village: a one-story walled hut made out of mud bricks. Kwan opens the wooden gate and Simon and I step over the threshold. In the middle of an open-air courtyard, I see a tiny old woman draining water from a hand pump into a bucket. She looks up, first with surprise, then with delight, in seeing Kwan. "Haaaa!" she cries, her open mouth releasing clouds of moist breath. One of her eyes is pinched shut, the other turned outward like that of a frog on the alert for flies. Kwan and the woman grab each other by the arms. They poke at each other's waistlines and then break into rapid Changmian dialect. The old woman gestures toward a crumbling wall, throws a deprecating scowl at her untended fire. She seems to be apologizing for the poor condition of the house and her failure to have ready a banquet and forty-piece orchestra to hail our arrival.

"This Du Lili, my old family friend," Kwan tells Simon and me in English. "Yesterday she gone to mountainside, pick mushrooms. Come back, find out I already come and gone."

Du Lili crinkles her face into an expression of agony, as if she understood this translation of her disappointment. We nod in sympathy.

Kwan continues: "Long time ago we live together, this same house. You speak Mandarin to her. She understand." Kwan turns back to her friend and explains on our behalf: "My little sister, Libby-ah, she speaks a strange kind of Mandarin, American style, her thoughts and sentences running backward. You'll see. And this one here, her husband, Simon, he's like a deaf-mute. English, that's all he speaks. Of course, they're only half Chinese."

"Ahhhhh!" Du Lili's tone suggests either shock or disgust. "Only half! What do they speak to each other?"

"American language," Kwan answers.

"Ahhhhh." Another note of apparent revulsion. Du Lili inspects me as if the Chinese part of my face were going to peel off any second.

"You can understand a little?" she asks me slowly in Mandarin. And when I nod, she complains in more rapid speech: "So skinny! Why are you so skinny? Tst! Tst! I thought people in America ate lots. Is your health poor? Kwan! Why don't you feed your little sister?"

"I try," Kwan protests. "But she won't eat! American girls, they all want to be skinny."

Next, Du Lili gives Simon the once-over: "Oh, like a movie star, this one." She stands on tiptoe for a better view.

Simon looks at me with raised eyebrows. "Translation, please."

"She says you'd make a good husband for her daughter." I wink at Kwan and try to keep a straight face.

Simon's eyes widen. This is a game he and I used to play in the early days of living together. I'd give him bogus translations, and both of us would play out the lie until one of us broke down.

Du Lili takes Simon's hand and leads him inside, saying, "Come, I want to show you something."

Kwan and I follow. "She needs to check your teeth first," I tell Simon. "It's a custom before the betrothal." We find ourselves in an area about twenty feet by twenty feet, which Du Lili calls the central room. It is dark, and sparsely furnished with a couple of benches, a wooden table, and a scattering of jars, baskets, and boxes. The ceiling is peaked. From the rafters hang dried meat and peppers, baskets, and no light fixtures. The floor is made of tamped earth. Du Lili points toward a plain wooden altar table pushed against a back wall. She asks Simon to stand next to her.

"She wants to see if the gods approve of you," I say. Kwan rounds her mouth, and I wink at her.

Tacked above the table are pink paper banners with faded inscriptions. In the middle is a picture of Mao with yellowed tape across his torn forehead. On the left is a cracked gilt frame containing a portrait of Jesus, hands raised to a golden ray of light. And on the right is what Du Lili wants Simon to see: an old calendar photo featuring a Bruce Lee look-alike in ancient warrior costume, guzzling a green-colored soda pop. "See this movie star?" Du Lili says. "I think you look like him — thick hair, fierce eyes, strong mouth, the same, oh, very handsome."

I peer at the photo and then at Simon, who is waiting for my translation. "She says you resemble this criminal who's on China's most-wanted list. Forget the marriage. She's going to collect a thousand yuan for turning you in."

He points to the calendar photo, then to himself, mouthing, "Me?" He shakes his head vigorously and protests in pidgin English: "No, no. Wrong person. Me American, nice guy. This man bad, someone else."

I can't hold on to the façade any longer. I burst out laughing.

"I win," Simon gloats. Kwan translates our silliness to Du Lili. For a few seconds, Simon and I smile at each other. It's the first warm moment we've shared in a long time. At what point in our marriage did our teasing drift into sarcasm?

"Actually, what Du Lili said was, you're as handsome as this movie star."

Simon clasps his hands together and bows, thanking Du Lili. She bows back, glad that he finally understands her compliment.

"You know," I tell him, "for some reason, in this light, you do look, well, different."

"Hmm. How so?" His eyebrows dance flirtatiously.

I feel awkward. "Oh, I don't know," I mumble, my face growing warm. "Maybe you look more Chinese or something." I turn away and pretend to be absorbed in the picture of Mao.

"Well, you know what they say about people who are married, how we become more and more alike over the years."

I keep staring at the wall, wondering what Simon is really thinking. "Look at this," I say, "Jesus right next to Mao. Isn't this illegal in China?"

"Maybe Du Lili doesn't know who Jesus is. Maybe she thinks he's a movie star selling light bulbs."

I am about to ask Du Lili about the Jesus picture, when Kwan spins around and calls to some dark figures standing in the bright doorway. "Come in! Come in!" She becomes all bustle and business. "Simon, Libby-ah, quick! Help the aunties with our luggage." Our elderly bell-hops push us aside and with mighty huffs finish dragging in our suit-cases and duffel bags, the bottoms of which are spattered with mud.

"Open your purse," Kwan says, and before I can comply she is ri-fling through my bag. She must be looking for money for a tip. But in-stead she pulls out my Marlboro Lights and gives the women the whole damn pack. One of the women gleefully passes the pack around, then pockets the rest. The old ladies start puffing away. And then, in a cloud of smoke, they leave.

Kwan drags her suitcase into a dark room on the right. "We sleep here." She motions me to follow. I expect a grim communist bedroom, decor that will match the minimalist look of the rest of the house. But when Kwan opens a window to let in the late-morning sun, I spot an or-nately carved marriage bed, enclosed with a shredded canopy of grayed mosquito netting. It is a wonderful antique, almost exactly like one I cov-eted in a shop on Union Street. The bed is made up in the same way Kwan does hers at home: a sheet pulled taut over the mattress, the pil-low and folded quilt stacked neatly at the foot end. "Where did Big Ma get this?" I marvel.

"And this." Simon brushes his hand along a marble-topped dresser, its mirror showing more silver than reflection. "I thought they got rid of all this imperialist furniture during the revolution."

"Oh, those old things." Kwan gives them a dismissive wave, full of pride. "Been in our family long time. During Cultural Revolution time, Big Ma hid them under lots a straw, in shed. That's how everything saved."

"Saved?" I ask. "Then where did our family get them originally?"

"Original, missionary lady give our mother's grandfather, payment for big debt."

"What big debt?"

"Very long story. This happen, oh, one hundred year —"

Simon cuts in. "Could we talk about this later? I'd like to get settled in the other bedroom."

Kwan lets out a derisive snort.

"Oh." Simon's face goes blank. "I take it there's no other bedroom."

"Other bedroom belong Du Lili, only one small bed."

"Well, where are we all going to sleep?" I search the room for an extra mattress, a cushion.

Kwan gestures nonchalantly toward the marriage bed. Simon smiles at me and shrugs in an apologetic manner that is clearly insincere.

"That bed's barely big enough for two people," I say to Kwan. "You and I can sleep there, but we're going to have to find a spare bed for Simon."

"Where you can find spare bed?" She stares at the ceiling, palms up, as if beds might materialize out of thin air.

Panic grows in my throat. "Well, somebody must have an extra mattress pad or *something*."

She translates this to Du Lili, who also turns her palms up. "See?" Kwan says. "Nothing."

"It's okay, I can sleep on the floor," Simon offers.

Kwan translates this to Du Lili as well, and it elicits chuckles. "You want sleep with bugs?" says Kwan. "Biting spiders? Big rats? Oh yes, many rats here, chew off you finger." She makes chomping-teeth sounds. "How you like that, ah? No. Only way, we three sleep same bed. Anyway, only for two weeks."

"That's not a solution," I reply.

Du Lili looks concerned and whispers to Kwan. Kwan whispers back, tilts her head toward me, then Simon. *"Bu-bu-bu-bu-bu!"* Du Lili cries, the nos punctuated by rapid shakes of her head. She grabs my arm, then Simon's, and pushes us together as though we were two squabbling toddlers. "Listen, you two hotheads," she scolds in Mandarin. "We don't have enough luxuries for your American kind of foolishness. Listen to your auntie, ah. Sleep in one bed, and in the morning you'll both be warm and happy as before."

"You don't understand," I say.

"*Bu-bu-bu!*" Du Lili waves off any lame American excuses.

Simon blows out a sigh of exasperation. "I think I'll go take a short walk while you three figure this out. Me, I'm amenable to three's a crowd or rats on the floor. Really, whatever you decide."

Is he angry with me for protesting so much? This isn't my fault, I want to shout. As Simon walks out, Du Lili follows him, scolding him in Chinese: "If you have troubles, you must fix them. You're the husband. She'll listen to your words, but you must be sincere and ask forgiveness. A husband and wife refusing to sleep together! This is not natural."

When we are alone, I glower at Kwan: "You planned this whole thing, didn't you?"

Kwan acts offended. "This not plan. This China."

After a few moments of silence, I grumpily excuse myself. "I have to use the bathroom. Where is it?"

"Down lane, turn left, you see small shed, big pile black ash—"

"You mean there's *no* bathroom in the house?"

"What I tell you?" Kwan answers, now grinning victoriously. "This China."

WE EAT a proletarian lunch of rice and yellow soybeans. Kwan insisted that Du Lili throw together some simple leftovers. After lunch, Kwan returns to the community hall so she can prepare Big Ma for her portrait session. Simon and I take off in different directions to explore the village. The route I choose leads to an elevated narrow stone lane that cuts through soggy fields. In the distance, I see ducks waddling in a line parallel to the horizon. Are Chinese ducks more orderly than American ones? Do their quacks differ? I click off a half-dozen shots with my camera, so I can remind myself later of what I was thinking at the moment.

When I return to the house, Du Lili announces that Big Ma has been waiting for her picture to be taken for more than half an hour. As we walk toward the hall, Du Lili takes my hand and speaks to me in Mandarin: "Your big sister and I once splashed together in those rice paddies. See, over there."

I imagine Du Lili as a younger woman caring for a child-size version of Kwan.

"Sometimes we caught tadpoles," she says, acting girlish, "using our headscarves as nets, like this." She makes scooping motions, then pretends she is wading in mud. "In those days, our village leaders told married women that swallowing a lot of tadpoles was good for birth control. Birth control! We didn't even know what that was. But your sister said, 'Du Lili, we must be good little Communists.' She ordered me to eat the black creatures."

"You didn't!"

"How could I not obey? She was older than I was by two months!"

*Older?* My mouth drops. How can Kwan be older than Du Lili? Du Lili looks ancient, at least a hundred. Her hands are rough and callused. Her face is heavily furrowed and several of her teeth are missing. I guess that's what happens when you don't use Oil of Olay after a long, hard day in the rice paddies.

Du Lili smacks her lips. "I swallowed a dozen, maybe more. I could feel them wiggling down my throat, swimming in my stomach, then sliding up and down my veins. They squirmed all around my body, until one day I fell down with a fever and a doctor from the big city said, 'Hey, Comrade Du Lili, have you been eating tadpoles? You have blood flukes!'"

She laughs, and a second later turns somber. "Sometimes I wonder if that's why no one wanted to marry me. Yes, I think that's the reason. Everybody heard I ate tadpoles and could never bear a son."

I glance at Du Lili's wandering eye, her sun-coarsened skin. How unfair life has been to her. "Don't worry." She pats my hand. "I'm not blaming your sister. Many times I'm glad I never married. Yes, yes — what a lot of trouble, taking care of a man. I heard that half a man's brain lies between his legs — hah!" She grabs her crotch and ambles forward in a drunken manner. Then she grows serious again. "Some days, though, I say to myself, Du Lili, you would have been a good mother, yes, watchful and strict about morals."

"Sometimes children are a lot of trouble too," I say quietly.

She agrees. "A lot of heartaches."

We walk in silence. Unlike Kwan, Du Lili seems sensible, down-to-earth, someone you can confide in. She doesn't commune with the World of Yin, or at least she doesn't talk about it. Or does she?

"Du Lili," I say. "Can you see ghosts?"

"Ah, you mean like Kwan? No, I don't have yin eyes."

"Does anyone else in Changmian see ghosts?"

She shakes her head. "Only your big sister."

"And when Kwan says she sees a ghost, does everyone believe her?" Du Lili looks away, uncomfortable. I urge her to be open with me: "Myself, I don't believe in ghosts. I think people see what they wish in their hearts. The ghosts come from their imaginations and longings. What do you think?"

"Ah! What does it matter what I think?" She won't meet my eye. She bends down and wipes the toe of her muddied shoe. "It's like this. For so many years, others have been telling us what to believe. Believe in gods! Believe in ancestors! Believe in Mao Tse-tung, our party leaders, dead heroes! As for me, I believe whatever is practical, the least trouble. Most people here are the same way."

"So you don't really believe Big Ma's ghost is here in Changmian." I want to pin her down.

Du Lili touches my arm. "Big Ma is my friend. Your sister is also my friend. I would never damage either friendship. Maybe Big Ma's ghost is here, maybe not. What does it matter? Now do you understand? Ah?"

"Hmm." We keep walking. Will Chinese thinking ever take root in my brain? As if she heard me, Du Lili chuckles. I know what she's thinking. I'm like those intellectuals who came to Changmian, so smart, so sure of their own ideas. They tried to breed mules and ended up making asses out of themselves.

WE ARRIVE at the gateway to the community hall just as a heavy rain begins pelting the ground so violently my chest thumps, urgent and panicky. We dash across the open yard, through double doors leading into a large room that is bone-chillingly cold. The air holds an old, musty dampness, which I imagine to be the byproduct of hundreds of years of moldering bones. The balmy autumn weather, for which Guilin is supposedly known, has taken an early exodus, and although I have on as many layers of clothes as I can fit under my Gore-Tex parka, my teeth are chattering, my fingers are numb. How am I going to shoot any pictures this afternoon?

A dozen people are in the hall, painting white funeral banners and decorating the walls and tables with white curtains and candles. Their loud voices rise above the rain, echo in the room. Kwan is standing next to the coffin. As I approach, I find myself loath to see my photo subject. I imagine she'll look fairly battered. I nod to Kwan when she sees me.

When I look in the coffin, I'm relieved to see that Big Ma's face is covered with a white paper sheet. I try to keep my voice respectful. "I guess the accident damaged her face."

Kwan seems puzzled. "Oh, you mean this paper," she says in Chinese. "No, no, it's customary to cover the face."

"Why?"

"Ah?" She cocks her head, as if the answer would descend from heaven and fall into her ear. "If the paper moves," she says, "then the person is still breathing, and it's too soon to bury the body. But Big Ma is dead for sure, she just told me." Before I can prepare myself, Kwan reaches over and removes the sheet.

Big Ma certainly looks lifeless, although not horribly so. Her brow is bunched into a worried expression and her mouth is twisted into an eternal grimace. I've always thought that when people die, their facial muscles relax, giving them a look of grateful tranquility.

"Her mouth," I say in awkward Chinese. "The way it's crooked. It looks like her dying time was very painful."

Kwan and Du Lili lean forward in unison to stare at Big Ma. "That might be," Du Lili says, "but right now she looks very much as she did when she was alive. The turn in her mouth, that's what she always wore."

Kwan agrees. "Even before I left China, her face was this way, worried and dissatisfied at the same time."

"She was very heavy," I note.

"No, no," Kwan says. "You only think so because now she's dressed for her journey to the next world. Seven layers for her top half, five for the bottom."

I point to the ski jacket Kwan selected as the seventh layer. It's iridescent purple with flashy southwestern details, one of the gifts she bought on sale at Macy's, hoping to impress Big Ma. The price tag is still attached, to prove the jacket isn't a hand-me-down. "Very nice," I say, wishing I were wearing it right now.

Kwan looks proud. "Practical too. All waterproof."

"You mean it rains in the next world?"

"Tst! Of course not. The weather is always the same. Not too hot, not too cold."

"Then why did you say the jacket is waterproof?"

She stares at me blankly. "Because it is."

I cup my numb fingers near my mouth and blow on them. "If the weather's so nice in the other world, why so many clothes, seven and five layers?"

Kwan turns to Big Ma and repeats my question in Chinese. She nods as if listening on a telephone. "Ah. Ah. Ah. Ah-ha-ha-ha!" then translates the answer for my mortal ears: "Big Ma says she doesn't know. Ghosts and yin people were forbidden by the government for so long, now even she's forgotten all the customs and their meanings."

"And now the government *allows* ghosts?"

"No, no, they just don't fine people anymore for letting them come back. But this is the correct custom, seven and five, always two more on top than on the bottom. Big Ma thinks seven is related to the seven days of the week, one layer for each day. In the old days, people were supposed to mourn their relatives seven weeks, seven times seven, forty-nine days. But nowadays, we're just as bad as foreigners, a few days is enough."

"But why only five layers on her lower half?"

Du Lili cracks a smile. "It means that two days a week Big Ma must wander about with her bottom naked in the underworld."

She and Kwan laugh so hard that people in the hall turn and stare. "Stop! Stop!" Kwan cries, trying to stifle her giggles. "Big Ma is scolding us. She says she hasn't been dead long enough for us to make such jokes." When she regains her composure, Kwan goes on: "Big Ma isn't sure, but she thinks five is for all the common things that attach mortals to the living world—the five colors, the five flavors, the five senses, the five elements, the five emotions—"

And then Kwan stops. "Big Ma, there are seven emotions, ah, not just five." She counts them on her hand, beginning with her thumb: "Joy, anger, fear, love, hate, desire . . . One more—what is it? Ah, yes, yes! Sorrow! No, no, Big Ma, I didn't forget. How could I forget? Of course

I have sorrow now that you are leaving this world. How can you say such a thing? Last night I cried, and not just to show off. You saw me. My sorrow was genuine, not fake. Why do you always believe the worst about me?"

"Ai-ya!" Du Lili cries to Big Ma's body. "Don't fight anymore now that you're dead." She looks at me and winks.

"No, I won't forget," Kwan is telling Big Ma. "A rooster, a dancing rooster, not a hen or a duck. I already know this."

"What's she saying?" I ask.

"She wants a rooster tied to the lid of her coffin."

"Why?"

"Libby-ah wants to know why." Kwan listens for a minute, then explains. "Big Ma can't remember exactly, but she thinks her ghost body is supposed to enter the rooster and fly away."

"And you believe that?"

Kwan smirks. "Of course not! Even Big Ma doesn't believe it. This is just superstition."

"Well, if she doesn't believe it, why do it?"

"Tst! For tradition! Also, to give something scary for children to believe. Americans do the same thing."

"No we don't."

Kwan gives me a superior big-sister look. "You don't remember? When I first arrived in the United States, you told me rabbits laid eggs once a year and dead people came out of caves to look for them."

"I did not."

"Yes, and you also said if I did not listen to you, Santa Claus would come down the chimney and put me in a bag, then take me to a very cold place, colder than a freezer."

"I never said that." And even as I protest, I vaguely recall a Christmas joke I once played on Kwan. "Maybe you just misunderstood what I meant."

Kwan sticks out her lower lip. "Hey, I'm your big sister. You think

242

I don't understand your meaning? Hnh! Ah, never mind. Big Ma says no more chitter-chatter. Time to take the picture."

I try to clear my head by doing a routine reading with the light meter. Definitely, time for the tripod. Aside from the illumination of a few white candles near a spirit table, the available light is northern, glary, and coming through dirty windows. There are no ceiling fixtures, no lamps, no wall outlets for strobes. If I use a flash unit, I won't be able to control the amount of light I want, and Big Ma might come out looking even more ghoulish. A chiaroscuro effect is what I prefer anyway, a combination of airiness and murkiness. A full second at f/8 will produce nice detail on one half of Big Ma's face, the shadow of death on the other.

I take out the tripod, set up my Hasselblad, and attach a color Polaroid back to do a test. "Okay, Big Ma," I say, "don't move." Am I losing my mind? I'm talking to Big Ma as if I too believe she can hear me. And why am I making such a big deal over a photo of a dead woman? I'm not going to be able to use it in the article. Then again, everything matters, or should. Every frame should be the best I can shoot. Or is this another one of those myths in life, passed along by high achievers so that everyone else will feel like a perpetual failure?

Before I can ponder this further, a dozen people gather around me, clamoring to see what's come out of the camera. No doubt many of them have seen tourist photo stands, the ones offering instant pictures at extortionist prices.

"Hold on, hold on," I say, as they crowd closer. I place the print against my chest to speed up the developing. The villagers fall silent; they must think noise will disturb the process. I peel off the top and look at the test. The contrast is too sharp for my taste, but I show them the photo anyway.

"Very realistic!" one person exclaims.

"Fine quality!" another says. "See how Big Ma looks—like she's about to wake up and feed her pigs."

Someone jokes: " 'Wah!' she'll say. 'Why are so many people around my bed?' "

Du Lili steps up. "Libby-ah, now take my picture." She is flattening a bristly cowlick with her palm, tugging on her jacket sleeve to smooth out the wrinkles. I look through the viewfinder. She has assumed the stiff posture of a soldier on guard, her face turned toward me, her wandering eye pointed upward. The camera whirs. As soon as I pull the Polaroid test off, she snatches it from my hands and hugs it to her chest, tapping her foot and grinning madly.

"The last time I saw a photograph of myself was many years ago," she says with excitement. "I was very young." When I give her the okay signal, she yanks off the top layer and whips the picture up to her eager face. She squints with her turned-out eye and blinks several times. "So this is what I look like." Her expression speaks of reverence for the miracle of photography. I'm touched, proud in an "aw, shucks" way.

Du Lili carefully hands Kwan the photo as if it were a newly hatched chick. "A good likeness," Kwan says. "What did I tell you? My little sister is very skillful." She passes the Polaroid around for the others to see.

"Very true to life," a man says enthusiastically. The others chime in:

"Exceptionally clear."

"Extraordinarily realistic."

The Polaroid comes around to Du Lili again. She cradles it in her palms. "Then I don't look so good," she says in a wan voice. "I'm so old. I never thought I was so old, so ugly. Am I really that ugly, that stupid-looking?"

A few people laugh, thinking Du Lili is making a joke. But Kwan and I can see that she is genuinely shocked. She wears the face of someone betrayed, and I am the one who has wounded her. Certainly she must have seen herself recently in a mirror? But then the way we see our reflections from changing angles allows us to edit out what we don't like. The camera is a different sort of eye, one that sees a million present particles of silver on black, not the old memories of a person's heart.

Du Lili wanders off, and I want to say something to comfort her, to tell her that I am a bad photographer, that she has wonderful qualities a camera can never see. I start to follow her, but Kwan takes my arm and shakes her head. "Later I will talk to her," she says, and before she can say anything else, I am surrounded by a dozen people, all of them pleading that I take their photos as well. "Me first!" "Take one of me with my grandson!"

"Wah!" Kwan scolds. "My sister is not in the business of giving away free portraits." The people keep insisting: "Just one!" "Give me a photo too!" Kwan holds up her hands and yells sternly: "Quiet! Big Ma just told me everyone must leave right away." The shouts dwindle. "Big Ma says she needs to rest before her journey to the next world. Otherwise she might go crazy with grief and stay here in Changmian." Her comrades quietly absorb this proclamation, then file out, grousing good-naturedly.

When we are alone, I grin my thanks to Kwan. "Did Big Ma really say that?" Kwan gives me a sidelong glance and bursts into laughter. I join her, grateful for her quick thinking.

Then she adds: "The truth is, Big Ma said to take more photos of her, but this time from another angle. She said the last one you took makes her look almost as old as Du Lili."

I'm taken aback. "That's a mean thing to say."

Kwan acts clueless. "What?"

"Saying Du Lili looks older than Big Ma."

"But she is older, at least five or six years."

"How can you say that! She's younger than you are."

Kwan tilts her head, attentive. "Why do you think this?"

"Du Lili told me."

Kwan is now reasoning with Big Ma's lifeless face: "I know, I know. But because Du Lili has mentioned this, we must tell her the truth." Kwan walks up to me. "Libby-ah, now I must tell you a secret."

A stone drops in my stomach.

"Almost fifty years ago, Du Lili adopted a little girl she found on the road during civil war time. Later, that daughter died and Du Lili was so crazy with sorrow she believed she became her daughter. I remember this, because the little girl was my friend, and yes, if she had lived, she would have been two months younger than I am now and not the seventy-eight-year-old woman that Du Lili is today. And now that I am telling you this—" Kwan breaks off and begins to argue with Big Ma again. "No, no, I can't tell her that, it's too much."

I stare at Kwan. I stare at Big Ma. I think about what Du Lili has said. Who and what am I supposed to believe? All the possibilities whirl through my brain, and I feel I am in one of those dreams where the threads of logic between sentences keep disintegrating. Maybe Du Lili is younger than Kwan. Maybe she's seventy-eight. Maybe Big Ma's ghost is here. Maybe she isn't. All these things are true and false, yin and yang. What does it matter?

Be practical, I tell myself. If the frogs eat the insects and the ducks eat the frogs and the rice thrives twice a year, why question the world in which they live?

# 17
# THE YEAR
## OF NO FLOOD

Why question the world, indeed? Because I'm not Chinese like Kwan. To me, yin isn't yang, and yang isn't yin. I can't accept two contradictory stories as the whole truth. When Kwan and I walk back to Big Ma's house, I quietly ask, "How did Du Lili's daughter die?"

"Oh, it's a very sad story," Kwan answers in Chinese. "Maybe you don't want to know."

We continue in silence. I know she is waiting for me to ask again, so finally I say, "Go ahead."

Kwan stops and looks at me. "You won't be scared?"

I shake my head while thinking, How the hell would I know if I'm not going to be scared? As Kwan begins to speak, I shiver, and it is not due to the cold.

Her name was Buncake and we were five years old when she drowned. She was as tall as I was, eye to eye, her quiet mouth to my noisy one. That's what my auntie complained, that I talked too much. "If you let go with one more word," Big Ma would warn, "I'll send you away. I never promised your mother I'd keep you."

Back then, I was skinny, nicknamed Pancake, *bao-bing*—"a flimsy piece of fritter," Big Ma called me—always with four scabby bites on my knees and elbows. And Buncake, she was plump, her arms and legs creased like a steamed stuffed *bao-zi*. Du Yun was the one who found her on the road—that was Du Lili's name back then, Du Yun. Big Ma was the one who named Buncake Lili, because when she first came to our village, *lili-lili-lili* was the only sound she could make, the warbling of an oriole. *Lili-lili-lili,* that's what came out of the pucker of her small red mouth, as if she had just bitten into a raw persimmon, expecting sweet, tasting bitter. She watched the world like a baby bird, her eyes round and black, looking for danger. Why she was like this nobody knew except me, because she never talked, not with words at least. But in the evening, when lamplight danced on the ceiling and walls, her little white hands spoke. They would glide and swoop with the shadows, soar and float, those pale birds through clouds. Big Ma would watch and shake her head: Ai-ya, how strange, how strange. And Du Yun would laugh like an idiot watching a play. Only I understood Buncake's shadow talk. I knew her hands were not of this world. You see, I also was a child, still close to the time before this life. And so I too remembered I had once been a spirit who left this earth in the body of a bird.

To Du Yun's face, everyone in the village would smile and tease, "That little Buncake of yours, she's peculiar, ah?" But outside our courtyard, they would whisper rotten words, and these sounds would drift over our wall and into my ears.

"That girl is so spoiled she's turned crazy," I heard neighbor Wu say. "Her family must have been bourgeois-thinking. Du Yun should beat her often, at least three times a day."

"She's possessed," another said. "A dead Japanese pilot fell from the sky and lodged in her body. That's why she can't speak Chinese, only grunt and twirl her hands like a suicide plane."

"She's stupid," yet another neighbor said. "Her head is as hollow as a gourd."

But to Du Yun's way of thinking, Buncake didn't speak because Du Yun could speak for her. A mother always knows what's best for her daughter, she'd say, isn't that true?—what she should eat, what she should think and feel. As to Buncake's shadow-dancing hands, this was proof, Du Yun once said—genuine proof!—that her ancestors had been ladies of the court. And Big Ma replied, "Wah! Then she has counter-revolutionary hands, hands that will be chopped off one day. Better that she learn how to press one finger to her nostril and blow snot into her palm."

Only one thing about Buncake made Du Yun sad. Frogs. Buncake didn't like springtime frogs, green-skinned frogs as small as her fist. At dusk, that's when you could hear them, groaning like ghost gates: *Ahh-wah, ahh-wah, ahh-wah.* Big Ma and Du Yun would grab buckets and nets, then wade into the watery fields. And all those frogs held their breath, trying to disappear with their silence. But soon they could not hold in their wishes any longer: *Ahh-wah, ahh-wah, ahh-wah,* even louder than before, wailing for love to find them.

"Who could love such a creature?" Du Yun used to joke. And Big Ma always answered, "I can—once it is cooked." How easily they caught those lovesick creatures. They put them in buckets, shiny as oil in the rising moonlight. By morning, Big Ma and Du Yun were standing by the road, calling, "Frogs! Juicy frogs! Ten for one yuan!" And there we were, Buncake and I, seated on upturned buckets, chins resting on palms, nothing to do but feel the sun rise, warming one cheek, one arm, one leg.

No matter how good the business, Big Ma and Du Yun always saved at least a dozen frogs for our noon meal. By mid-morning, we trudged home, seven buckets empty, one half-full. In the courtyard kitchen, Big Ma would make a big hot fire. Du Yun would reach into the bucket and grab a frog, and Buncake would hurry behind me, hiding. I could feel her chest heave up and down, fast and hard, just like that frog squirming in Du Yun's hand, puffing its throat in and out.

"Watch closely, ah," Du Yun would say to Buncake and me. "This is the best way to cook a frog." She would turn the frog on its back and—quick!—stick the sharp end of a pair of scissors up its anus—*szzzzzzz!*—slicing all the way to its throat. Her thumb would dip under the slit, and with one fast tug, out slid a belly full of mosquitoes and silver-blue flies. With another tug, at the frog's throat, off slipped the skin, snout to tail, and it hung from Du Yun's fingers like the shriveled costume of an ancient warrior. Then chop, chop, chop, and the frog lay in pieces, body and legs, the head thrown away.

While Du Yun peeled those frogs, one after another, Buncake kept her fist wedged hard between her teeth, like a sandbag stopping a leak in a riverbank. So no scream came out. And when Du Yun saw the anguish on Buncake's face, she would croon in a mother's sweet voice: "Baby-ah, wait a little longer. Ma will feed you soon."

Only I knew what words were stuck in Buncake's screamless mouth. In her eyes I could see what she had once seen, as clearly as if her memories were now mine. That this tearing of skin from flesh was how her mother and father had died. That she had watched this happen from a leafy limb, hidden high in a tree where her father had put her. That in the tree an oriole called, warning Buncake away from her nest. But Buncake would not make a sound, not a cry or even a whimper, because she had promised her mother to be quiet. That's why Buncake never talked. She had promised her mother.

In twelve minutes, twelve frogs and skins flew into the pan and crackled in oil, so fresh some of the legs would leap from the pan—wah!—and Du Yun would catch them with one hand, her other hand still stirring. That's how good Du Yun was at cooking frogs.

But Buncake didn't have the stomach to appreciate this. By the dim lamplight, she watched as we greedy ones ate those delicious creatures, our teeth busy searching for shreds of meat on bones as tiny as embroidery needles. The skins were the best, soft and full of flavor. Second best I liked the crunchy small bones, the springy ones just above the feet.

Often Du Yun would look up and urge her new daughter, "Don't play now, eat, my treasure, eat." But Buncake's hands would be flapping and flying, soaring with her shadows. Then Du Yun would become sad that her daughter wouldn't eat the dish she cooked best. You should have seen Du Yun's face — so much love for a leftover girl she had found on the road. And I know Buncake tried to love Du Yun with the leftover scraps of her heart. She followed Du Yun's footsteps around the village, she raised one arm so her new mother could hold her hand. But on those nights when the frogs sang, when Du Yun picked up her swinging buckets, Buncake would run to a corner, press in tight, and begin to sing: *Lili-lili-lili.*

That's how I remember Buncake. She and I were good little friends. We lived in the same house. We slept in the same bed. We were like sisters. Without talking, we each knew what the other was feeling. At such a young age, we knew about sadness, and not just our own. We both knew about the sadness of the world. I lost my family. She lost hers.

The year Du Yun found Buncake on the road, that was a strange year, the year of no flood. In the past, our village always had too much rain, at least one flood in the springtime. Sudden rivers that swept through our homes, washing the floors of insects and rats, slippers and stools, then retching all this into the fields. But the year Buncake came — no flood, just rain, enough for crops and frogs, enough for people in our village to say, "No flood, why are we so lucky? Maybe it was the girl Du Yun found on the road. Yes, she must be the reason."

The following year, there was no rain. In all the villages surrounding ours, rain fell as usual, big rain, small rain, long rain, short rain. Yet in our village, none. No rain for the spring tilling. No rain for the summer harvest. No rain for the fall planting. No rain, no crops. No water to cook the rice that no longer grew, no chaff to feed the pigs. The rice fields cooked hard as porridge crust, and the frogs lay on top, dry as twigs. The insects climbed out of the cracked ground, waving their feelers toward the sky. The ducks withered and we ate them, skin on bones. When we stared too long at the mountain peaks, our hungry eyes saw roasted sweet potatoes with their skins broken open. Such a terrible year, so terrible that people in our village said Buncake, that crazy girl, she must be the reason.

One hot day, Buncake and I were sitting in the hull of a dusty ditch that ran alongside our house. We were waiting for our imaginary boat to take us to the land of fairy queens. Suddenly we heard a groan from the sky, then another groan, then a big crack—*kwahhh!*—and hard rain fell like pellets of rice. I was so happy and scared! More lightning came, more thunder. At last our boat is going, I shouted. And Buncake laughed. For the first time, I heard her laugh. I saw her reach her hands toward the flashes in the sky.

The rain kept gurgling—*gugu-gugu-gugu*—rolling down the mountains, filling their wrinkles and veins. And the hollows couldn't gulp fast enough, there was that much water. Soon, so quick, this friendly ditch-boat became a brown river, pushing against our legs. White water-tails grabbed our little wrists and ankles. Faster and faster we tumbled, arms first, then feet first, until the water spat us out into a field.

Through whispered talk, I later learned what happened. When Big Ma and Du Yun took us out of the water, we both were pale and still, wrapped in weeds, two soggy cocoons with no breath bursting through. They dug the mud out of our nostrils and mouths, they pulled the weeds out of our hair. My thin body was broken to pieces, her sturdy one was not. They dressed us in farewell clothes. Then they went to the courtyard, washed two pig troughs that were no longer needed, broke off the seats of two benches for lids. They put us in these poor little coffins, then sat down and cried.

For two days, we lay in those coffins. Big Ma and Du Yun were waiting for the rain to stop so they could bury us in the rocky soil where nothing ever grew. On the third morning, a big wind came and blew the clouds away. The sun rose, and Du Yun and Big Ma opened the coffins to see our faces one last time.

I felt fingers brushing my cheek. I opened my eyes and saw Du Yun's face, her mouth stretched big with joy. "Alive!" she cried. "She's alive!" She grabbed my hands and rubbed them against her face. And then Big Ma's face was looking down at me too, searching. I was confused, my head as thick as morning fog.

"I want to get up." That's what I first said. Big Ma jumped back. Du Yun dropped my hands. I heard them howl: "How can this be! It can't be!"

I sat up. "Big Ma," I said, "what's the matter?" They began to scream, loud screams, so terrible I thought my head would burst from fright. I saw Big Ma running to the other coffin. She flung open the lid. I saw myself. My poor broken body! And then my head whirled, my body fell, and I saw nothing more until evening came.

When I awoke, I was lying on the cot I once shared with Buncake. Big Ma and Du Yun were standing across the room, in the doorway. "Big Ma," I said, yawning. "I had a nightmare."

Big Ma said, "Ai-ya, look, she speaks." I sat up and slid off the cot, and Big Ma cried, "Ai-ya, look, she moves." I stood up, complained I was hungry and wanted to pee. She and Du Yun backed off from the doorway. "Go away or I'll beat you with peach twigs!" Big Ma cried.

And I said, "Big Ma, we have no peach trees." She clapped her hand to her mouth. At the time, I didn't know that ghosts were supposed to be scared of peach twigs. Later, of course, I learned that this was just superstition. I've since asked many ghosts, and they all laugh and say, "Scared of peach twigs? No such thing!"

Anyway, as I was saying, my bladder was about to burst. I was anxious to pieces, hopping and holding myself in. "Big Ma," I said, more politely this time, "I want to visit the pigs." Next to the pen we had a small pit, a plank of wood on each side for balancing yourself while doing your business, both kinds. That was before our village went through reeducation on collective waste. And after that, it was no longer enough to give your mind, body, and blood to the common good—you had to donate your shit too, just like American taxes!

But Big Ma did not say I could visit the pigs. She walked up to me and spit in my face. This was another superstition about ghosts: Spit on them and they'll disappear. But I did not disappear. I wet my pants, a warm stream dribbling down my legs, a puddle darkening the floor. I was sure that Big Ma would beat me, but instead she said, "Look, she's pissing."

And Du Yun said, "How can that be? A ghost can't piss."

"Well, use your own eyes, you fool. She's pissing."

"Is she a ghost or isn't she?"

They went on and on, arguing about the color, the stink, the size of my puddle. Finally they decided to offer me a little something to eat. This was their thinking: If I was a ghost, I would take this bribe and leave. If I was a little girl, I would stop complaining and go back to sleep, which is what I did after eating a little piece of stale rice ball. I slept and dreamed that all that had happened was part of the same long dream.

When I awoke the next morning, I again told Big Ma that I had suffered a nightmare. "You're still sleeping," she said. "Now get up. We're taking you to someone who will wake you out of this dream."

We walked to a village called Duck's Return, six *li* south of Changmian. In this village lived a blind woman named Third Auntie. She was not really my auntie. She was auntie to no one. It was just a name, Third Auntie, what you call a woman when you should not say the word "ghost-talker." In her youth, she had become famous all around the countryside as a ghost-talker. When she was middle-aged, a Christian missionary redeemed her and she gave up talking to ghosts, all except the Holy Ghost. When she was old, the People's Liberation Army re-formed her, and she gave up the Holy Ghost. And when she grew very old, she no longer remembered whether she was redeemed or reformed. She was finally old enough to forget all she had been told to be.

When we entered her room, Third Auntie was sitting on a stool in the middle of the floor. Big Ma pushed me forward. "What's wrong with her?" Du Yun asked in a pitiful voice. Third Auntie took my hands in her rough ones. She had eyes the color of sky and clouds. The room was quiet except for my breathing. At last, Third Auntie announced: "There's a ghost inside this girl." Big Ma and Du Yun gasped. And I jumped and kicked, trying to rid myself of the demon.

"What can we do?" Du Yun cried.

And Third Auntie said, "Nothing. The girl who lived in this body before doesn't want to come back. And the girl who lives in it now can't leave until she finds her." That's when I saw her, Buncake, staring at me from a window across the room. I pointed to her and shouted, "Look! There she is!" And when I saw her pointing back at me, her puckered mouth saying my words, I realized I was looking at my own reflection.

On the way home, Big Ma and Du Yun argued, saying things a lit-tle girl should never hear.

"We should bury her, put her in the ground where she belongs." This was Big Ma talking.

"No, no," Du Yun moaned. "She'll come back, still a ghost, and angry enough to take you and me with her."

Then Big Ma said, "Don't say she's a ghost! We can't bring home a ghost. Even if she is—wah, what trouble!—we'll have to be reformed."

"But when people see this girl, when they hear the other girl's voice . . ."

By the time we reached Changmian, Big Ma and Du Yun had de-cided they would pretend nothing was the matter with me. This was the attitude people had to take with many things in life. What was wrong was now right. What was right was now left. So if someone said, "Wah, this girl must be a ghost," Big Ma would answer, "Comrade, you are mistaken. Only reactionaries believe in ghosts."

At Buncake's funeral, I stared at my body in the coffin. I cried for my friend, I cried for myself. The other mourners were still confused over who was dead. They wept and called my name. And when Big Ma corrected them, they again wept and called Buncake's name. Then Du Yun would begin to wail.

For many weeks, I scared everyone who heard my voice come out of that puckered mouth. No one talked to me. No one touched me. No one played with me. They watched me eat. They watched me walk down the lane. They watched me cry. One night, I woke up in the dark to find Du Yun sitting by my bed, pleading in a lilting voice. "Buncake, treasure, come back home to your ma." She lifted my hands, moved them near the candlelight. When I yanked them back, she churned the air with her arms—oh, so clumsy, so desperate, so sad, a bird with broken wings. I think that's when she started believing she was her daughter. That's how it is when you have a stone in your heart and you can't cry out and you can't let it go. Many people in our village had swallowed stones like this, and they understood. They pretended I was not a ghost. They pretended I had always been the plump girl, Buncake the skinny one. They pretended nothing was the matter with a woman who now called herself Du Lili.

In time, the rains came again, then the floods, then the new leaders who said we must work harder to wash away the Four Olds, build the Four News. The crops grew, the frogs creaked, the seasons went by, one ordinary day after another, until everything changed and was the same again.

One day, a woman from another village asked Big Ma: "Hey, why do you call that fat girl Pancake?" And Big Ma looked at me, trying to remember. "Once she was skinny," she said, "because she wouldn't eat frogs. Now she can't stop."

You see, everyone decided not to remember. And later, they really did forget. They forgot there was a year of no flood. They forgot that Du Lili was once called Du Yun. They forgot which little girl drowned. Big Ma still beat me, only now I had a body with more fat, so her fists did not hurt me as much as before.

Look at these fingers and hands. Sometimes even I believe they have always been mine. The body I thought I once had, maybe that was a dream I confused with waking life. But then I remember another dream.

In this dream, I went to the World of Yin. I saw so many things. Flocks of birds, some arriving, some leaving. Buncake soaring with her mother and father. All the singing frogs I had ever eaten, now with their skin coats back on. I knew I was dead, and I was anxious to see my mother. But before I could find her, I saw someone running to me, anger and worry all over her face.

"You must go back," she cried. "In seven years, I'll be born. It's all arranged. You promised to wait. Did you forget?" And she shook me, shook me until I remembered.

I flew back to the mortal world. I tried to return to my body. I pushed and shoved. But it was broken, my poor thin corpse. And then the rain stopped. The sun was coming out. Du Yun and Big Ma were opening the coffin lids. Hurry, hurry, what should I do?

So tell me, Libby-ah, did I do wrong? I had no choice. How else could I keep my promise to you?

# 18

# SIX-ROLL
# SPRING CHICKEN

"Now you remember?" Kwan asks.

I am transfixed by her plump cheeks, the crease of her small mouth. Looking at her is like viewing a hologram: locked beneath the shiny surface is the three-dimensional image of a girl who drowned.

"No," I say.

Is Kwan—that is, this woman who claims to be my sister—actually a demented person who *believed* she was Kwan? Did the flesh-and-blood Kwan drown as a little girl? That would account for the disparity between the photo of the skinny baby our father showed us and the chubby girl we met at the airport. It would also explain why Kwan doesn't resemble my father or my brothers and me in any way.

Maybe my wish from childhood came true: The real Kwan died, and the village sent us this other girl, thinking we wouldn't know the difference between a ghost and someone who thought she was a ghost. Then again, how can Kwan not be my sister? Did a terrible trauma in childhood cause her to believe she had switched bodies with someone else? Even if we aren't genetically related, isn't she still my sister?

Yes, of course. Yet I want to know what parts of her story might be true.

Kwan smiles at me, squeezing my hand. She points to birds flying overhead. If only she said they were elephants. Then, at least, her madness would be consistent. Who can tell me the truth? Du Lili? She isn't any more reliable than Kwan. Big Ma is dead. And no one else in the village who would be old enough to remember speaks anything other than Changmian. Even if they did speak Mandarin, how can I ask? "Hey, tell me, is my sister really my sister? Is she a ghost or just insane?" But I have no time to decide what to do. Kwan and I are now walking through the gate to Big Ma's house.

In the central room, we find Simon and Du Lili carrying on a spirited conversation in the universal language of charades. Simon rolls down an imaginary car window and shouts, "So I stuck my head out and said, 'Come on, move your ass!'" He leans on an invisible horn, and then — *"Bbbbrr-ta-ta! Bbbbbrrr-ta-ta!"* — imitates an Uzi-wielding thug blowing up his tires.

Du Lili says in Changmian what sounds like the equivalent of "Hnh! That's nothing." She acts out a pedestrian lugging bags of groceries — heavy bags, we are asked to observe, that stretch her arms like noodle dough. Suddenly she glances up, leaps back nearly onto Simon's toes, and launches her heavy bags just as a car zigzagging like a snake flies past the tip of her nose and plows into a crowd of people. Or maybe she means a stand of trees. In any case, some sort of limbs are flying this way and that through the air. To end her little drama, she walks over to the driver and spits in his face, which in this reenactment is the bucket next to Simon's shoe.

Kwan bursts into hoots and cheers, I clap. Simon pouts like the second runner-up in *Queen for a Day*. He accuses Du Lili of exaggerating — maybe the car was *not* going fast like a snake, no indeed, but slow as a lame cow. *"Bu-bu-bu!"* she cries, giggling and stamping her foot. Yes, and maybe she was walking with her head in the clouds and *she* caused the accident. *"Bu-bu-bu!"* As she pummels his back, Simon cowers: "All right, you win! Your drivers are worse!"

Except for their age difference, they look like new lovers who flirt with each other, bantering, provoking, finding excuses to touch. I feel a twitch in my heart, although it can't be jealousy, because who could ever think that those two— Well, whether or not Kwan's story about Du Lili and her dead daughter is true, one thing is certain: Du Lili is way past old.

The charades now over, she and Kwan drift toward the courtyard, discussing what they are going to make for dinner. When they are out of earshot, I pull Simon aside.

"How did you and Du Lili get on the topic of bad drivers, of all things?"

"I started off trying to tell her about yesterday's trip here with Rocky, about the accident."

Makes sense. I then recount to him what Kwan told me. "So what do you think?"

"Well, number one, Du Lili doesn't seem crazy to me, nor does Kwan. And number two, they're the same old stories you've heard all your life."

"But this one's different. Don't you see? Maybe Kwan really isn't my sister."

He frowns. "How can she *not* be your sister? Even if she isn't blood-related, she's still your sister."

"Yeah, but that means there was another girl who was *also* my sister."

"Even so, what would you do? Disown Kwan?"

"Of course not! It's just that—well, I need to know for sure what really happened."

He shrugs. "Why? What difference would it make? All I know is what I see. To me, Du Lili seems like a nice lady. Kwan is Kwan. The village is great. And I'm glad to be here."

"So what about Du Lili? Do you believe her when she says she's fifty? Or do you believe Kwan, who says Du Lili is—"

Simon breaks in: "Maybe you didn't understand what Du Lili was saying. You said it yourself, your Chinese isn't all that great."

I'm annoyed. "I just said I couldn't *speak* it as well as Kwan."

"Maybe Du Lili used an expression like—well, 'young as a spring chicken.'" His voice has the assured tone of masculine reason. "Maybe you took her literally to mean she thought she was a chicken."

"She didn't say she was a chicken." My temples are pounding.

"See, now you're taking even me too literally. I was only giving an example of—"

I lose it. "Why do you always have to prove you're so goddamn right?"

"Hey, what is this? I thought we were just talking here. I'm not trying to—"

And then we hear Kwan shout from the courtyard: "Libby-ah! Simon! Hurry come! We cook now. You want take picture, yes?"

Still irritated, I run into Big Ma's room to retrieve my photo gear. There it is again: the marriage bed. Don't even think about it, I tell myself. I look out the window, then at my watch: almost dusk, the golden half-hour. If ever there were a time and a place to allow gut passion into my work, this is it, in China, where I have no control, where everything is unpredictable, totally insane. I pick up the Leica, then stuff ten rolls of high-speed film into my jacket pocket.

In the courtyard, I take out a numbered roll and load it. After the heavy rain, the sky has drained itself to a soft gouache blue, splotches of powder-puff clouds swimming behind the peaks. I inhale deeply and smell the woody kitchen smoke of Changmian's fifty-three households. And beneath that bouquet wafts the ripe odor of manure.

I scope out the elements of the scene. The mud-brick walls of the courtyard will serve well as overall backdrop. I like the orange tinge, the rough texture. The tree in the middle has anemic-looking leaves — avoid that. The pigpen has definite foreground potential — nicely positioned on the right side of the courtyard under an eave of thatched twigs. It's rustically simple, like a manger in a kids' Christmas play. But instead of Jesus, Mary, and Joseph, there are three pigs rooting in muck. And a half-dozen chickens, one lacking a foot, another with part of its beak missing. I dance in an expanding then shrinking arc around my subject. Out of the corner of my eye, I see a slop bucket full of grayish rice gruel and flies. And a pit with a terrible stench, a dark watery hole. I lean over and glimpse a gray-furred creature, along with clumps of puffy rice that writhe — maggots, that's what they are.

Life in Changmian now seems futile. I should be "previsualizing" the moment I want, willing spontaneity to coincide with what's given. But all I see in my head are well-heeled readers flipping through a chic travel magazine that specializes in bucolic images of third world countries. I know what people want to see. That's why my work usually feels unsatisfying, pre-edited into safe dullness. It isn't that I want to take photos that are deliberately unflattering. What's the point in that? There's no market for them, and even if there were, hard realism would give people the wrong impression, that *all* of China is this way, backward, unsanitary, miserably poor. I hate myself for being American enough to make these judgments. Why do I always edit the real world? For whose sake?

Screw the magazine. To hell with right and wrong impressions. I check the light, the f-stop. I'll just do my best to capture a moment, the sense of it as it happens. And that's when I spot Du Lili crouched next to the hand pump, draining water into a pan. I circle her, focus, and begin to shoot. But upon seeing my camera, she jumps up to pose and tugs at the bottom of her old green jacket. So much for spontaneity.

"You don't have to stand still," I call to her. "Move around. Ignore me. Do what you want."

She nods, then walks around the courtyard. And in her diligence to forget the camera's presence, she admires a stool, gestures toward baskets hanging from a tree, marvels over an ax covered with mud, as if she were displaying priceless national treasures. "One, two, three," I count stiffly in Chinese, then take a few posed shots to satisfy her. "Good, very good," I say. "Thank you."

She looks puzzled. "I did it wrong?" she asks in a plaintive child's voice. Ah—she's been waiting for a flash, the click of the shutter, neither of which the Leica will produce. I decide to tell a small lie.

"I'm not really taking pictures," I explain. "I'm only looking—just practice."

She gives me a relieved smile and walks back to the pigpen. As she opens the gate, the pigs snort and run toward her, snouts raised, sniffing for handouts. A few hens warily circle her for the same reason. "A nice fat one," Du Lili says, considering her choices. I skulk around the courtyard like a thief, trying to remain unobtrusive, while I search for the best combination of subject, light, background, and framing. The sun sinks another degree and sends filtered rays through the twig roof, throwing warm light on Du Lili's gentle face. With this bit of serendipity, my instincts take over. I can feel the shift, the power that comes from abandoning control. I'm shooting now between breaths. Unlike other cameras, which leave me blind while the shutter's open, the Leica lets me see the moment I'm capturing: the blur of Du Lili's hand grabbing a chicken, the flurry of the other chickens, the pigs turning in unison like a marching band. And Simon—I shoot a few pictures of him taking notes for possible captions. This is like the old days, the way we used to work in rhythm with each other. Only now he isn't in his business-as-usual mode. His eyes are wonderfully intense. He glances at me and smiles.

I turn my camera back to Du Lili. She is walking toward the hand pump, the squawking chicken in her grip. She holds it over a white enamel bowl that sits on a bench. Her left hand firmly clutches the chicken's neck. In her other hand is a small knife. How the hell is she going to lop off the chicken's head with that? Through the viewfinder, I see her pressing the blade against the bird's neck. She slowly saws. A thin ribbon of blood springs up. I'm as stunned as the chicken. She dangles the bird so that its neck is extended downward, and blood starts to trickle into the white bowl.

In the background, I can hear the pigs screaming. They are actually *screaming*, like people in terror. Someone once told me that pigs can go into a deadly fever when they're being led to the slaughterhouse, that they are smart enough to know what awaits them. And now I wonder if they also could have sympathy for the pain of a dying chicken. Is that evidence of intelligence or a soul? In spite of all the open-heart surgeries and kidney transplants I've photographed, I feel queasy. Yet I keep shooting. I notice Simon is no longer writing captions.

When the bowl is half filled with blood, Du Lili lets the chicken fall to the ground. For several agonizing minutes, we watch as it stumbles and gurgles. At last, with dazed eyes, it slumps over. Well, if Du Lili believes she is Buncake, she certainly must have lost her compassion for birds.

Simon comes over to me. "That was fucking barbaric. I don't know how you could keep shooting."

His remark irritates me. "Stop being so ethnocentric. You think killing chickens in the States is more humane? Anyway, she probably did it that way so the meat will be free of toxins. It's like a tradition, a kosher process or something."

"Kosher my ass! Kosher is killing the animal quickly so it *doesn't* suffer. And the blood's drained after the animal's dead, then thrown away."

"Well, I still think she did it that way for health reasons." I turn to Du Lili and ask her in Chinese.

"*Bu-bu,*" she replies, shaking her head with a laugh. "After I have enough blood, I usually cut off the head right away. But this time I let the chicken dance a bit."

"Why?"

"For you!" she says happily. "For your photos! More exciting that way, don't you agree?" Her eyebrows flick up as she waits for my thanks. I fake a smile.

"Well?" says Simon.

"It's . . . Well, you're right, it's not kosher." And then I can't help it, seeing that smug look on his face. "Not kosher in a Jewish sense," I add. "It's more of an ancient Chinese ritual, a spiritual cleansing . . . for the chicken." I return my attention to the viewfinder.

Du Lili dumps the chicken into a pot of boiling water. And then, with her bare hands, she begins dipping the bird as though she were washing a sweater. She has so many calluses they cover her palms like asbestos gloves. At first she seems to be petting the dead chicken, consoling it. But with each stroke, a handful of feathers comes away, until the bird emerges from its bath pimply-skinned pink.

Simon and I follow Du Lili as she carries the carcass across the courtyard to the kitchen. The roof is so low we have to crouch to avoid brushing our heads against the thatching. From a dark corner in the back, Kwan pulls out a bundle of twigs, then feeds them into the mouth of a blazing mud-brick hearth. Over the fire sits a wok big enough to cook a boar. She grins at me. "Good picture?"

How could I have had any doubts she is my sister? They're all stories, I tell myself. She just has a crazy imagination.

Kwan guts the chicken in one motion, then chops it up, head, feet, and tail, and dumps the pieces into a bubbling broth. Into this mixture, she tosses several handfuls of greens, what looks like chard. "Fresh," she notes in English to Simon. "Everything always fresh."

"You went to the market today?"

"What market? No market. Only backyard, pick youself." Simon writes this down.

Du Lili is now bringing in the bowl of chicken blood. It has congealed to the color and consistency of strawberry gelatin. She cuts the blood into cubes, then stirs them into the stew. As I watch the red swirls,

I think of the witches of *Macbeth*, their faces lit by fire, with steam rising from the caldron. How did the line go? "For a charm of powerful trouble," I recite, "like a hell-broth boil and bubble."

Simon looks up. "Hey, that's what I was just thinking." He leans over to smell the stew. "This is great material."

"Don't forget, we have to eat this great material."

When the fire dies down, so does my available light. I slip the Leica into a jacket pocket. God! I'm hungry! If I don't eat the chicken and its bloody broth, what are my other choices? There's no ham and cheese in the fridge—there's no fridge. And if I wanted ham, I'd have to slaughter the screaming pigs first. But there isn't time to consider alternatives. Kwan is now at a half-crouch, grabbing the handles of the giant wok. She does a dead lift. "Eat," she announces.

In the center of the courtyard, Du Lili has made a small twig fire within an iron ring. Kwan sets the wok on top and Du Lili passes out bowls, chopsticks, and cups for tea. Following her lead, we squat around our improvised dinner table. "Eat, eat," Du Lili says, motioning to Simon and me with her chopsticks. I eye the pot, looking for something that resembles my supermarket version of packaged meat. But before I can find it, Du Lili plucks a chicken's foot from the stew and plops it in my bowl.

"No, no. You take that," I protest in Chinese. "I can help myself."

"Don't be polite," she argues. "Eat before it gets cold."

Simon smirks. I transfer the foot to his bowl. "Eat, eat," I say with a gracious smile, then help myself to a thigh. Simon stares morosely at the once dancing foot. He takes a tentative bite and chews with a thoughtful expression. After a while, he nods politely to Du Lili and says, "Hmm-mmm. Good, very good." The way she beams, you'd think she's just won a cook-off.

"That was nice of you to say that."

"It *is* good," he says. "I wasn't just being polite."

I ease my teeth on the edge of the thigh and take a puppy nip. I chew, let it roll onto my tongue. No taste of blood. The meat is amazingly flavorful, velvety! I eat more, down to the bone. I sip the broth, so clean-tasting yet buttery rich. I reach into the pot and fish out a wing. I chew, and conclude that Chinese courtyard chickens taste better than American free-range. Does the tastiness come from what they eat? Or is it the blood in the broth?

"How many rolls did you shoot?" Simon asks.

"Six," I say.

"Then we'll call this six-roll spring chicken."

"But it's autumn."

"I'm naming it in honor of Du Lili, who ain't no spring chicken, as you pointed out." Simon quivers and pleads, Quasimodo style: "Please, Mistress, don't beat me."

I make the sign of the cross over his head. "All right. You're forgiven, you jerk."

Du Lili holds up a bottle of colorless liquor. "When the Cultural Revolution ended, I bought this wine," she proclaims. "But for the last twenty years, I've had no reason to celebrate. Tonight, I have three." She tips the bottle toward my cup, sighs a protracted "ahhhh," as if she were relieving her bladder, not pouring us wine. When all of our cups are filled, she lifts hers — *"Gan-bei!"* — and sips noisily, her head tilting back slowly until she has emptied the contents.

"You see?" Kwan says in English. "Must keep cup going back, back, back, until all finish." She demonstrates by chugging hers. "Ahhhh!" Du Lili pours herself and Kwan another round.

Well, if Kwan, the queen of the teetotalers, can drink this, it must not be very strong. Simon and I clink glasses, then toss the liquor down our throats, only to gasp immediately like city slickers in a cowboy saloon. Kwan and Du Lili slap their knees and chortle. They point to our cups, still half full.

"What is this?" Simon gasps. "I think it just removed my tonsils."

"Good, ah?" Kwan tops his cup before he can refuse.

"It tastes like sweat socks," he says.

"Sweet suck?" Kwan takes another sip, smacks her lips, and nods in agreement.

Three rounds and twenty minutes later, my head feels clear, but my feet have gone to sleep. I stand up and shake my legs, wincing as they tingle. Simon does the same.

"That tasted like shit." He stretches his arms. "But you know, I feel *great.*"

Kwan translates for Du Lili: "He says, Not bad."

"So what do you call this drink, anyway?" Simon asks. "Maybe we should take some with us when we go back to the States."

"This drink," says Kwan, and she pauses to look at her cup with great respect, "this drink we call pickle-mouse wine, something like that. Very famous in Guilin. Taste good, also good for health. Take long time make. Ten, maybe twenty year." She motions to Du Lili and asks her to show the bottle. Du Lili holds up the bottle and taps the red-and-white label. She passes it to Simon and me. It's nearly empty.

"What's this at the bottom?" Simon asks.

"Mouse," says Kwan. "That's why call pickle-mouse wine."

"What is it really?"

"You look." Kwan points to the bottom of the bottle. "Mouse."

We look. We see something gray. With a tail. Somewhere in my brain I know I should retch. But instead, Simon and I look at each other and we both start laughing. And then we can't stop. We laugh until we choke, clutching our aching stomachs.

"Why are we laughing?" Simon is panting.

"We must be drunk."

"You know, I don't feel drunk. I feel, well, happy to be alive."

"Me too. Hey, look at those stars. Don't they seem bigger? Not just brighter, but bigger? I feel like I'm shrinking and everything else is getting bigger."

"You see like tiny mouse," Kwan says.

Simon points to the shadows of mountains jutting above the court-yard wall. "And those," he says. "The peaks. They're huge."

We stare in silence at the mountains, and then Kwan nudges me. "Now maybe you see dragon," she says. "Two side-by-side dragon. Yes?"

I squint hard. Kwan grabs my shoulders and repositions me. "Squeeze-close eyes," she orders. "Sweep from mind American ideas. Think Chinese. Make you mind like dreaming. Two dragon, one male, one female."

I open my eyes. It's as though I'm viewing the past as the fore-ground, the present as a faraway dream. "The peaks going up and down," I say, tracing in the air, "those are their two spines, right? And the way the two front peaks taper into those mounds, those are their two heads, with the valley tucked between their two snouts."

Kwan pats my arm, as if I were a student who has recited her geography lessons well. "Some people think, 'Oh, village sit right next to dragon mouth — what bad *feng shui*, no harmony.' But to my way thinking, all depend what type dragon. These two dragon very loyal, good *chi* — how you say in English, good *chi*?"

"Good vibes," I say.

"Yes-yes, good vibe." She translates for Du Lili what we are talk-ing about.

Du Lili breaks into a huge grin. She chatters something in Chang-mian and starts humming: "Daaa, dee-da-da."

Kwan sings back: "Dee, da-da-da." Then to us she says, "Okay-okay. Simon, Libby-ah, sit back down. Du Lili say I should tell you dragon love-story." We're like kindergartners around a campfire. Even Du Lili is leaning forward.

"This the story," Kwan begins, and Du Lili smiles, as if she under-stood English. "Long time ago two black dragon, husband and wife, live below ground near Changmian. Every springtime, wake up, rise from earth like mountain. Outside, these two dragon look like human person, only black skin, also very strong. In one day, two together can dig ditch all around village. Water run down mountain, caught in ditch. That way, no rain come, doesn't matter, plenty for grow plants. Libby-ah, what you call this kind watering, flow by itself?"

"Irrigation."

"Yes-yes. What Libby-ah say, irritation—"

"Irrigation."

"Yes-yes, irrigationing, they make this for whole village. So everybody love these two black dragon people. Every year throw big feast, celebrate them. But one day, Water God, real low-level type, he get mad—'Hey, somebody took water from my river, not asking permission.'"

"Darn." Simon snaps his fingers. "Water rights. It's always water rights."

"Yes-yes. So big fight, back and forth. Later Water God hire some wild people from other tribe, not our village, somewhere else, far away. Maybe Hawaii." She elbows Simon. "Hey. Joke, I just joke! Not Hawaii. I don't know where from. Okay, so people use arrow, kill dragon man and woman, pierce their body all over every place. Before die, crawl back inside earth, turn into dragon. See! Those two backs now look-alike six peaks. And where arrows gone in, make ten thousand cave, all twist together, lead one heart. Now when rain come, water flow through mountain, pour through holes, just like tears, can't stop running down. Reach bottom—flood! Every year do this."

Simon frowns. "I don't get it. If there's a flood every year, what's the good *chi*?"

"Tst! Flood not big flood. Only little flood. Just enough wash floor clean. In my lifetime, only one bad flood, one long drought. So pretty good luck."

I could remind her that she lived in Changmian for only eighteen years before moving to America. But why ruin her story and our good time? "What about the Water God?" I ask.

"Oh, that river—no longer. Flood wash him away!"

Simon claps and whistles, startling Du Lili out of her doze. "The happy ending. All right!" Du Lili stands up and stretches, then begins clearing away the remnants of our chicken feast. When I try to help, she pushes me down.

"So who told you that story?" I ask Kwan.

She's placing more twigs on top of the fire. "All Changmian people know. For five thousand year, every mother singing this story to little children, song call 'Two Dragon.'"

"Five thousand years? How do you know that? It couldn't be written down anywhere."

"I know, because—well, I tell you something, secret. Between two dragon, in small valley after this one, locate small cave. And this little cave lead to other cave, so big you can't believe almost. And inside that big cave—lake, big enough for boat ride! Water so beautiful you never seen, turquoise and gold. Deep, glowing too! You forget bring lamp, you still see entire ancient village by lakeside—"

"Village?" Simon comes over. "You mean a real village?"

I want to tell him it's another one of Kwan's stories, but I can't catch his eye.

Kwan is pleased by his excitement. "Yes-yes, ancient village. How old, don't know exact. But stone house still standing. No roof, but wall, little doorway to crawl inside. And inside—"

"Wait a second," Simon interrupts. "You've been in this cave, you've seen this village?"

Kwan goes on rather cockily: "Course. And inside stone house, many thing, stone chair, stone table, stone bucket with handle, two dragon carve on top. You see—two dragon! That story same age stone village. Maybe older, maybe five thousand year not right. Maybe more like ten thousand. Who know how old for sure."

A prickle of goose bumps rises along my back. Maybe she's talking about a different cave. "How many people have been to this village?" I ask.

"How many? Oh, don't know exact amount. House very small. Not too many people can live there one time."

"No, what I mean is, do people go there now?"

"Now? No, don't think so. Too scared."

"Because—"

"Oh, you don't want know."

"Come on, Kwan."

"Okay-okay! But you get scared, not my fault."

Simon leans against the water pump. "Go ahead."

Kwan takes a deep breath. "Some people say, you go inside, not just this cave, any cave this valley, never come back." She hesitates, then adds: "Except as ghost." She checks us for a reaction. I smile. Simon is transfixed.

"Oh, I get it." I try again to catch Simon's attention. "This is the Changmian curse that man mentioned yesterday."

Simon is pacing. "God! If this is true . . ."

Kwan smiles. "You think true, I'm ghost?"

"Ghost?" Simon laughs. "No, no! I meant the part about the cave itself—if *that's* true."

"Course, true. I already telling you, I see so myself."

"I'm only asking because I read somewhere, what was it? . . . I remember now. It was in the guidebook, something about a cave with Stone Age dwellings inside. Olivia, did you read about that?"

I shake my head. And now I'm wondering if I've taken Kwan's story about Nunumu and Yiban too skeptically. "You think this is the cave?"

"No, that's some big tourist attraction closer to Guilin. But the book said that this mountain area is so riddled with caves there are probably thousands no one's ever seen before."

"And the cave Kwan's talking about might be another—"

"Wouldn't that be incredible?" Simon turns to Kwan. "So you think no one else has been there before?"

Kwan frowns. "No-no. I not saying this. Lots people been."

Simon's face falls. He rolls his eyes. Oh well.

"But now all dead," Kwan adds.

"Whoa." Simon holds up his hand, stop sign–like. "Let's see if we can get this straight." He starts pacing again. "What you're telling us is, no one *living* knows about the cave. Except you, of course." He waits for Kwan to confirm what he's said so far.

"No-no. Changmian people know. Just don't know where locate."

"Ah!" He slowly walks around us. "No one knows where the cave is located. But they know *about* the cave."

"Course. Many Changmian stories concerning this. Many."

"For example." He motions for Kwan to take the floor.

She furrows her brow and crinkles her nose, as if searching through her extensive repository of ghost stories, all of them secrets we would be sworn never to reveal. "Most famous ones," she says after this pause, "always concerning foreigner. When they die cause so much trouble!"

Simon nods sympathetically.

"Okay, one story go like this. This happen maybe one hundred year ago. So I didn't see, only hear Changmian people talk. Concerning four missionaries, come from England, riding in little wagons, big umbrella on top, just two mule in front pulling those fat people. Hot day too. Jump out two Bible ladies, one young and nervous, one old and bossy, also two men, one has beard, other one, oh, so fat no one from our village can believe. And these foreigners, they wearing Chinese clothes—yes!— but still look strange. Fat man, he speak Chinese, little bit, but very hard understanding him. He say something like, 'Can we do picnic here?' Everybody say, 'Welcome-welcome.' So they eat, eat, eat, eat, eat, so much food."

I interrupt Kwan. "You're talking about Pastor Amen?"

"No-no. Entirely different people. I already told you, didn't see, only hear. Anyway, after they done eating, fat man ask, 'Hey, we hear you have famous cave, ancient city inside. You show us?' Everybody make excuse: 'Oh, too far. Too busy. Nothing see.' So old Bible lady, she hold up pencil—'Whoever want it, take me see cave, you can have!' Those days, long time ago, our people never yet seen pencil—writing brush, course, but pencil, no. Course, probably Chinese people invent pencil, we invent so many things—gunpowder but not for killing, noodle too. Italian people always say they invent noodle—not true, only copy Chinese from Marco Polo time. Also, Chinese people invent zero for number. Before zero, people don't know have nothing. Now everybody have zero." Kwan laughs at her own joke. " . . . What I saying before?"

"You were talking about the Bible lady with the pencil."

"Ah, yes. In our poor village, no one seen pencil. Bible lady, she show them can make mark just like that, no need mixing ink. One young man, family name Hong—he always dreaming he better than you—he took that pencil. Today, his family still have, on altar table, same pencil cost his life." Kwan crosses her arms, as if to suggest pencil greediness deserved death.

Simon picks up a twig. "Wait a minute. We're missing something here. What happened to the missionaries?"

"Never come back."

"Maybe they went home," I reason. "Nobody saw them leave."

"That young man also don't come back."

"Maybe he became a Christian and joined the missionaries."

Kwan gives me a doubtful look. "Why someone do that? Also, why those missionaries don't take their wagons, their mules? Why Bible church later send all kinds foreign soldiers searching for them? Causing so much trouble, knock on this door, that door—'What happen? You don't tell us what, burn you down.' Pretty soon, everybody got same idea, they say, 'Oh, so sad, bandits, that's what.' And now, today, everyone still know this story. If someone acting like better than you, you say, 'Huh! You don't watch, maybe you later turn into pencil man.' "

"Hear that?" I poke Simon.

Kwan sits up straight and cocks her ear toward the mountains. "Ah, you hear?"

"What?" Simon and I say at the same time.

"Singing. Yin people singing."

We fall quiet. After a few moments, I hear a slight whishing sound. "Sounds like wind to me."

"Yes! To most people, just wind—*wu! wu!*—blow through cave. But you have big regret, then hear yin people calling you, 'Come here, come here.' You grow more sad, they sing more louder: 'Hurry! Hurry!' You go see inside, oh, they so happy. Now you take someone place, they can leave. Then they fly to Yin World, peace at last."

"Sort of a tag-you're-it kind of place," Simon adds.

I pretend to laugh, but I'm bothered. Why does Kwan have so many stories about switching places with dead people?

Kwan turns to me. "So now you know why village name become Changmian. *Chang* mean 'sing,' *mian* mean 'silk,' something soft but go on forever like thread. Soft song, never ending. But some people pronounce 'Changmian' other way, rising tone change to falling, like this: *Chang.* This way *chang* mean 'long,' *mian* mean 'sleep.' Long Sleep. Now you understand?"

"You mean songs that put you to sleep," says Simon.

"No-no-no-no-no. Long Sleep—this another name for *death.* That's why everybody say, 'Changmian cave, don't go there. Doorway to World of Yin.' "

My head tingles. "And you believe that?"

"What believe? I already there. I know. Lots yin people stuck there, waiting, waiting."

"So why is it you were able to come back?" I catch myself before she can answer. "I know, you don't have to tell me." I don't want Kwan to go into the whole story of Buncake or Zeng now. It's late. I need sleep, and I don't want to feel I'm lying next to someone who's possessed a dead girl's body.

Simon crouches next to me. "I think we should go see this cave."

"You're kidding."

"Why not?"

"Why not! Are you nuts? People die in there!"

"You believe that stuff about ghosts?"

"Of course not! But there must be something bad in there. Gas fumes, cave-ins, who knows what else."

"Drowning," adds Kwan. "Lots sad people drown themself, fall to bottom, down, down, down."

"Hear that, Simon? Drowning, down, down, down!"

"Olivia, don't you realize? This could be an incredible find. A prehistoric cave. Stone Age houses. Pottery—"

"And bone," Kwan offers, looking helpful.

"And bones!" reiterates Simon. "What bones?"

"Mostly foreigner bone. They lose way, then lose mind. But don't want die. So lie by lakeside long time, until body become stone."

Simon stands up, facing the peaks.

I say to him: "People lose their minds in there. They turn to stone."

But Simon isn't listening anymore. I know he's mentally wending his way into the cave and into the world of fame and fortune. "Can you imagine what the magazine editors will say when they see our story? Shit! From chicken soup to major archaeological find! Or maybe we should call *National Geographic* or something. I mean, it's not like we owe *Lands Unknown* the rights to this story. And we should also take some of the pottery back with us as proof, definitely."

"I'm not going in there," I say firmly.

"Fine. I'll go by myself."

I want to shout, I forbid you. But how can I? I don't have an exclusive claim anymore on his body, mind, or soul. Kwan is looking at me, and I want to shout at her as well: This is your fault! You and your damn stories! She gives me that annoying sisterly look, pats my arm, trying to calm me down. I yank my arm away.

She turns to Simon. "No, Simon. Can't go youself."

He spins around. "What do you mean?"

"You don't know where cave locate."

"Yeah, but you'll show me." He states this like a fact.

"No-no, Libby-ah right, too dangerous."

Simon scratches his neck. I figure he is gathering his arguments to beat us both down, but instead he shrugs. "Well, maybe. But why don't we all sleep on it?"

I LIE in the middle of the crowded marriage bed, as stiff as Big Ma in her coffin. My limbs ache in my effort not to touch Simon. We are in the same bed for the first time in nearly ten months. He's wearing silk thermal underwear. Every now and then I feel the sharp ridge of his shins or the cleft of his butt against my thigh, and I carefully ease away, only to be rebuffed by Kwan's knees, her jabbing toes. I have the sneaking suspicion she's pushing me toward Simon.

Strange groaning sounds erupt. "What was that?" I whisper.

"I didn't hear anything," Simon answers. So he's still awake too.

Kwan yawns. "Singing from cave. I already tell you this."

"It sounds different now, like someone complaining."

She rolls over to her side. In a few minutes, she's snoring, and after a while, Simon's breathing deeply. So there I am, crammed between two people, yet alone, wide awake, staring at the dark, seeing the moments of the past twenty-four hours: The refrigerated van ride and Big Ma's ski parka. Buncake and Kwan in their coffins. The poor chicken and its death dance. The dead mouse in the wine, the dead missionaries in the cave. And Simon's face, his excitement when we looked at the dragon peaks together. That was nice, special. Was it the old feeling we once had? Maybe we could become friends. Or maybe it meant nothing. Maybe it was only the pickle-mouse wine.

I flip onto my side and Simon follows suit. I make myself as straight as a chopstick to avoid touching him. The body, however, isn't meant to be stiff and still, except in death. I long to bend my body into his, to allow myself this comfort. But if I do, maybe he'll assume too much, think that I'm forgiving him. Or admitting that I need him. He smacks his lips and snuffles—the sounds he always makes as he enters into deep sleep. And soon I can feel his breath rolling in waves on my neck.

I've always envied the way he can sleep solidly through the night, undisturbed by car alarms, earthquakes, and now, those persistent scratching sounds beneath the bed. Or is it more like sawing? Yes, that's the teeth of a saw, the sawteeth of a rat, chewing on a bedpost, sharpening its fangs before climbing up here. "Simon," I whisper, "do you hear that? Simon!" And then, as in the old days, he loops one arm over my hip and nuzzles his face against my shoulder. I instantly stiffen. Is he asleep? Did he do this by instinct? I wiggle my hip slightly to see if he'll rouse and remove his hand. He groans. Maybe he's testing me.

I lift his hand from my hip. He stirs and says in a groggy voice, "Mmm, sorry," then extricates himself, snorts, and turns over. So his embrace was an accident of sleep. He meant nothing by it. My throat tightens, my chest hurts.

I remember how he always wanted to cuddle and make love after an argument, as if connecting our bodies that way mended whatever rift was between us. I resented the easy supposition of all's well that ends well. And yet I'd resist only slightly when he'd raise my chin. I'd hold in my anger and my breath as he nibbled my lips, my nose, my brow. The more upset I was, the more places he'd woo: my neck, my nipples, my knees. And I'd let him—not because I weakened and wanted sex, but because it would have been spiteful, beyond redemption, not to allow us this hope.

I planned to talk about the problems later. How he saw avoidance as normal and I saw it as a warning. How we didn't know how to talk to each other anymore, how in protecting our own territory we were losing common ground. Before it was too late, I wanted to say that whatever love had brought us together had dwindled and now needed to be restocked. At times I feared that our love had never overflowed into plenty, that it had been enough for a few years but was never meant to last a lifetime. We mistook a snack for a recurring harvest. We were two people starved for abundant love but too tired to say so, leg-ironed together until time passed us by and we left this world, two vague hopes without dreams, just another random combination of sperm and egg, male and female, once here now gone.

I used to think these things while he undressed me, resenting the fact that he saw nakedness as intimacy. I'd let him stroke me where he knew me best, which was my body and not my heart. He'd be seeking my rhythm, saying, "Relax, relax, relax, relax." And I'd slip, let go of all that was wrong. I'd yield to my rhythm, his rhythm, our rhythm, love by practice, habit, and reflex.

In the past, after we made love, I would feel better, no longer quite as upset. I'd try to remember the worries once again—about harvests and abundance, fruitless love and hopeless death—and they were no longer feelings but notions, silly, even laughable.

Now that our marriage is over, I know what love is. It's a trick on the brain, the adrenal glands releasing endorphins. It floods the cells that transmit worry and better sense, drowns them with biochemical bliss. You can know all these things about love, yet it remains irresistible, as beguiling as the floating arms of long sleep.

I'm jolted out of sleep by screams—young girls being raped or killed or both! Then Du Lili's voice cries out, "Wait, wait, you greedy things." And the pigs shriek even louder as she coos: "Eat, eat. Eat and grow fat."

Before I can relax, I sense another unpleasant eye-opener. During the night, my body must have gravitated toward the nearest heat source, that being Simon. More precisely, my butt is now snuggled against the springy nest of his groin, which, I notice, is sprouting a morning erection, what we once fondly referred to as "the alarm cock." Kwan's third of the bed is empty, her indentation already cool to the touch. When did she leave? Oh yes, I know what she's up to, the sneak. And Simon, he really asleep? Is he secretly laughing?

The awful truth is, I'm aroused. In spite of everything I thought the night before, my lower body has a pulsing, heat-seeking, rub-craving itch. And the rest of me longs for comfort. I curse myself: You have a fucking brainless burrow! The IQ of a pop-bead! I slide away from danger and hop out of Kwan's side of the bed. Simon stirs. Shivering in my nightshirt, I hurry to the foot of the bed, where I dumped my luggage yesterday. The air temperature must be forty-five degrees. My hands go trawling for warm clothes.

Simon yawns, sits up and stretches, then peels back the mosquito netting. "I slept well," he says ambiguously. "How 'bout you?"

I pull out my parka and drape it over my shoulders. It's so stiff with cold it crackles. My teeth are chattering as I speak: "So how does one take a shower or bath around here?" Simon has an amused look on his face. Does he suspect anything?

"There's a public bathhouse next to the toilet shack," he says. "I checked it out yesterday while you were shooting. It has an Esalen-spa charm to it. Gender neutral. One trough, no waiting. But I don't think anyone's used it for ages. The water's kind of scummy. And if you want a warm bath, bring a pail of hot water."

I was prepared for bad, but not incredibly bad. "They use the same bathwater—all day?"

"All week, it looks like. God, I know, we're so *wasteful* in the States."

"What are you grinning at?" I ask.

"You. I know how obsessed you are about cleanliness."

"No I'm not."

"Oh? Then why is it that when you stay in a hotel, you pull down the bedspread first thing?"

"Because they don't get changed that often."

"So?"

"So I'm not fond of lying on top of someone else's skin flakes and dried-up bodily fluids."

"Aha! I rest my case. Now go to the bathhouse. I dare you."

For a moment, I weigh which is worse, bathing in the common broth or going funky for the next two weeks.

"Of course, you could fill a basin and take a sponge bath right here. I could be your water boy."

I pretend not to hear him. My cheek muscles are nearly spastic from trying not to smile. I pull out two pairs of leggings. I reject the thin cotton, choose the Polarfleece, regretting I didn't bring more. Simon's suggestion is a good one, the part about the sponge bath, that is. Water boy, yeah, fat chance. I can just picture it, Simon as Egyptian slave, wearing one of those twisted-cloth jockstraps, a look of excruciating desire on his face as he silently ladles warm water over my breasts, my stomach, my legs. And heartless me, I'd treat him like a faucet: More hot! More cold! Hurry up!

"By the way," he says, interrupting my thoughts, "you were talking in your sleep again."

I avoid meeting his eye. Some people snore. I sleep-talk, not in mumbles but in complete, well-articulated sentences. Nightly. Loudly. Sometimes I even wake myself up. Simon's heard me tell knock-knock jokes, order a three-course meal of desserts, shout for Kwan to keep her ghosts from me.

Simon lifts one eyebrow. "Last night, what you said was certainly revealing."

Shit. What the hell did I dream? I always remember my dreams. Why can't I now? Was Simon in the dream? Did we have sex? "Dreams don't mean anything," I say. I take out a thermal undershirt and bottle-green velour top. "They're just flotsam and jetsam."

"Don't you want to know what you said?"

"Not really."

"It relates to something you *love* to do."

I throw down the clothes and snap, "I don't love it as much as you think!"

Simon blinks twice, then starts laughing. "Oh yes you do! Because you said, 'Simon, wait. I haven't paid for this yet!' " He allows five seconds for this to sink in. "You were shopping. What did you think I was referring to?"

"Shut up." My face is burning. I thrust my hand into the suitcase and angrily grab some woolen socks. "Turn around. I want to get dressed."

"I've already seen you naked a thousand times."

"Well, it's not going to be a thousand and one. Turn around."

With my back to him, I whip off the parka and my nightshirt, still berating myself for being taken in by him. He baited me! And what an idiot I was, going for it. I should have known he'd trick me. And then I sense something else. I spin around.

"You don't have to suck your tummy in." He's holding up the gauzy curtain. "You look great. You always have. I never get tired of looking at you."

"You shithead!"

"What! We're still married!"

I wad up a sock and throw it at him. He ducks, letting go of the mosquito netting, which must be a hundred years old, because when the sock hits, the mesh blows apart—poof!—and wispy tufts are lofted high into the air.

We both stare at the damage. I feel like a kid who's broken a neighbor's window with a baseball, wickedly thrilled.

"Uh-oh." I cover my mouth and snicker.

Simon shakes his head. "Bad girl."

"It's your fault."

"What do you mean! You threw the sock."

"You were looking!"

"I still am."

And there I am, standing stark naked, freezing my ass off.

I throw the other sock at him, then my leggings, the velour top, my nightshirt. Clutching a slipper, I fly toward Simon and strike him on the back. He grabs my hand and we both fall onto the bed, where we tussle and roll, slap and shove, so grateful finally to have this excuse to touch each other. And when we exhaust ourselves with this playful joust, we look at each other, silently, eye to eye, no smiles, nothing more to be said. All at once, we both leap, like wolf mates reunited, searching for that which identifies us as belonging to each other: the scent of our skin, the taste of our tongues, the smoothness of our hair, the saltiness of our necks, the ridges of our spines, the slopes and creases we know so well yet feel so new. He is tender and I am wild, nuzzling and nipping, both of us tumbling until we lose all memory of who we were before this moment, because at this moment we are the same.

WHEN I WALK out to the courtyard, Kwan gives me one of her innocent but knowing grins. "Libby-ah, why you smiling?"

I look at Simon. "No rain," I answer. No matter who Kwan really is, sister or not, I'm glad that she suggested we come to China.

In front of her, on the ground, is an open suitcase, stuffed with various gizmos and gadgets. According to Kwan, Big Ma bequeathed these gifts to Du Lili, everything except a wooden music box that plays a tinkly version of "Home on the Range." I pull out my camera and begin shooting.

Kwan picks up the first item. Simon and I lean forward to see. It's a Roach Motel. "In America," she explains to Du Lili with a serious face, "they call this a guesthouse for roaches." She points to the label.

"Wah!" cries Du Lili. "Americans are so rich they make toy houses for insects! Tst! Tst!" She shakes her head, her mouth turned down in proletarian disgust. I tell Simon what she said.

"Yes, and Americans feed them delicious food." Kwan peers into the motel's door. "And the food is so good, the bugs never want to leave. They stay forever."

Du Lili slaps Kwan's arm and pretends to be angry. "You're so bad! You think I don't know what this is?" She then says to me in an excited voice, "Chinese people have the same thing. We use pieces of bamboo, cut open like this and filled with sweet sap. Your big sister and

I used to make them together. Our village held contests to see who could catch the most pests — the most flies, the most rats, the most roaches. Your big sister was often praised for catching the most roaches. Now she's trying to catch me with a prank."

Kwan unveils more treasures, and it's obvious that many of them have come from a sporting goods store. First, there's a day pack. "Strong enough to carry bricks, with many pockets, on the sides, underneath, here, there, see. Unzip them like this — Wah, what's in here?" She pulls out a portable water purifier, a tiny backpacking stove, a small medical kit, an inflatable cushion, resealable baggies, heavy-duty trash liners, a space blanket, and — "Wah! Unbelievable!" — even more things: a waterproof match holder, a flashlight, and a Swiss Army knife with a built-in toothpick, "very practical." Like an Avon Lady, Kwan explains the particular use of each item.

Simon examines the stash. "Amazing. How'd you think of all this?"

"Newspaper," Kwan answers. "They have article on earthquake, if big one come, this what you need for survive. In Changmian, you see, no need wait for earthquake. Already no electricity, no running water, no heat."

Next Kwan lifts from the suitcase a plastic sweater box, the kind used for storing junk under the bed, and out come gardening gloves, gel-filled insoles, leggings, towels, T-shirts. Du Lili exclaims and sighs and laments that Big Ma did not live long enough to enjoy such luxuries. I take a picture of Du Lili surrounded by her inheritance. She is wearing wraparound sunglasses and a 49ers Super Bowl cap, the word "Champs" studded in rhinestones.

After a simple breakfast of rice porridge and pickled vegetables, Kwan brings out stacks of photos that document her thirty-two years of American life. She and Du Lili sit on a bench, poring over them. "Look here," Kwan says. "This is Libby-ah, only six years old. Isn't she cute? See the sweater she's wearing? I knit it myself before I left China."

"These little foreigner girls" — Du Lili points — "who are they?"

"Her schoolmates."

"Why are they being punished?"

"Punished? They're not being punished."

"Then why are they wearing the tall dunce hats?"

"Ah-ha-ha-ha! Yes, yes, tall hats for punishing counterrevolutionaries, that's what they look like! In America, foreigners wear tall hats to celebrate birthdays, also New Year's. This is a party for Libby-ah's birthday. It's a common American custom. The schoolmates offer gifts, nothing useful, just pretty things. And the mother makes a sweet cake and puts flaming candles on top. The child plants a wish in her head, and if she can blow out the candles all at once, the wish will grow true. Then the children feast on sweet cake, guzzle sweet drinks, eat sweet candy, so much sweetness their tongues roll back and they can't swallow any more."

Du Lili rounds her mouth in disbelief. "Tst! Tst! A party for every birthday. A simple charm for a birthday wish. Why do Americans still wish so much, when they already have too much? For me, I don't even need a party. A wish once every twenty years would be enough. . . ."

Simon pulls me aside. "Let's go for a walk."

"Where to?"

He leads me out of the courtyard, then points to the archway between the mountains, the entrance to the next valley.

I wag my finger at him like a nursery school teacher. "Simon, you aren't still thinking about that cave, are you?"

He returns a phony look of offense. "*Moi?* Of course not. I just thought it would be nice to go for a walk. We have things to talk about."

"Oh? Like what?" I say coyly.

"You know." He takes my hand, and I call out over the wall: "Kwan! Simon and I are going for a walk."

"Where?" she shouts back.

"Around."

"When you return?"

"You know, whenever."

"How I know what time worry?"

"Don't worry." And then I have second thoughts about where we might be headed. So I add, "If we're not back in two hours, call the police."

I hear her happily grumbling to Du Lili in Chinese: "She says if they're lost, telephone the police. What telephone? We have no telephone. . . ."

We walk quietly, holding hands. I'm thinking of what I should say. I'm sure Simon is doing the same. I'm not going to settle for patching things up automatically. I want a commitment to become closer, to be intimate with our minds and not just our bodies. And so with our own yet-to-be-spoken thoughts, we head in the general direction of the stone wall that separates Changmian from the next valley.

Our meandering takes us through private alleyways that interlace related compounds, and we apologize to those families who stare at us with curiosity, then apologize again when they run to their doorways, showing us coins for sale, green tarnished disks they claim are at least five hundred years old. I shoot a couple of frames and imagine a caption that would suit them: "Changmian residents staring at intruders." We peek into the open gates of courtyards and see old men coughing, smoking the stubs of cigarettes, young women holding babies, their fat cheeks bright pink from the pinching cold. We pass an old woman with a huge bundle of kindling balanced on her shoulders. We smile at children, several of whom have cleft palates or clubfeet, and I wonder if this is the result of inbreeding. We see this together, two aliens in the same world. Yet what we see is also different, because I wince at such hardship, the life that Kwan once had, that I could have had. And Simon remarks, "You know, they're sort of lucky."

"What do you mean?"

"You know, the small community, family histories linked for generations, focused on the basics. You need a house, you get your friends to help you slap a few bricks together, no bullshit about qualifying for a loan. Birth and death, love and kids, food and sleep, a home with a view—I mean, what more do you need?"

"Central heating."

"I'm serious, Olivia. This is . . . well, this is *life*."

"You're being sentimental. This is the pits, this is basic survival."

"I still think they're lucky."

"Even if they don't think so?"

He pauses, then raises his lower lip like a bulldog. "Yeah." His smart-ass tone is begging for an argument. And then I think, What's the matter with me? Why do I have to escalate everything into a moral battle of right and wrong? The people here don't care what we think. Let it go, I tell myself.

"I guess I can see your point," I say. And when Simon smiles, the embers of my irritation are fanned once again.

The path leads up the hill. As we round the top, we spot two little girls and a boy, all around five or six years old, playing in the dirt. About ten yards beyond them is the high stone wall and its archway, blocking our view of what lies beyond. The children look up, cautious and alert, their faces and clothes covered with mud.

*"Ni hau?"* Simon says in a flat American accent—"How are you?" being one of the few Chinese phrases he knows. Before the children notice, I bring out the Leica and fire off five shots. The children giggle, then return to their play. The boy is patting out the finishing touches on a mud fortress, his thumbprints still visible on the walls and gate. One girl is using her fingers to tweeze small blades of grass. The other girl delicately transfers the green slivers to the thatched roof of a miniature hut. And crawling near the hut are several brown grasshoppers, the captive residents of this elaborate compound. "Aren't those kids smart?" I say. "They made toys out of nothing."

"Smart and messy," Simon answers. "I'm kidding. They're cute." He points to the smaller girl. "That one sort of looks like you at age six, you know, the birthday party snapshot."

As we walk toward the archway, the children jump up. "Where are you going?" the boy says gruffly in his childish Mandarin.

"To see what's over there." I point to the tunnel. "Do you want to come?" They run ahead of us. But when they arrive at the entrance, they turn around and look at us. "Go ahead," I tell them. "You go first." They don't budge, only shake their heads solemnly. "We'll go together." I extend my hand to the smaller girl. She backs away and stands behind the boy, who says, "We can't." The bigger girl adds, "We're scared." The three of them huddle together even more closely, their huge eyes fixed on the archway.

After I translate this for Simon, he says, "Well, I'm going through now. If they don't want to come, fine." The moment he steps into the archway, the children scream, turn on their heels, and flee at top speed. "What was that about?" Simon's voice echoes in the rounded entrance.

"I don't know." My eyes follow the children until they drop behind the hill. "Maybe they've been warned not to talk to strangers."

"Come on," he calls. "What are you waiting for?"

I'm looking at the walls along the ridge. Unlike the mud-brick ones in the village, these are made out of huge blocks of cut stone. I imagine the laborers from long ago hauling them into place. How many died of exhaustion? Were their bodies used as mortar, the way workers' bodies were when the Great Wall was built? In fact, this looks like a miniature version of the Great Wall. But why is it here? Was it also built as a barrier during the days of warlords and Mongolian invaders? As I step through the archway, the pulse in my neck pounds. My head begins to float. I stop in the middle of the tunnel and put my hand on the wall. The tunnel is about five feet long and five feet high, tomblike. I imagine ghostly warring troops waiting for us on the other side.

What I see instead is a small, flat valley, a rain-soaked pasture on one side, a sectioned field on the other, with the pathway we are on continuing straight down the middle like a flat brown ribbon. Flanking both sides of the valley are dozens of loaf-shaped mountains much smaller than the two peaks ahead of us. It would be the perfect setting for a pastoral romance, if not for the fact that I can't get the faces of those scared children out of my mind. Simon is already walking down the hill.

"Do you think we're trespassing?" I say. "I mean, maybe this is private property."

He looks back at me. "In China? Are you kidding? They don't call it communist for nothing, you know. It's all public land."

"I don't think that's true anymore. People can own houses and even their own businesses now."

"Hey, don't worry. If we're trespassing, they're not going to shoot us. They'll just tell us to get out and we'll get out. Come on. I want to see what's in the valley after this one."

I keep expecting an angry farmer to come charging at us with an upraised hoe. But the lush pasture is empty, the fields are quiet. Isn't this a workday? Why isn't anyone out here? And those high stone walls, why are they there, if not to keep someone out? Why is it so deathly quiet? No sign of life, not even a peeping bird. "Simon," I start to say, "doesn't it seem, well—"

"I know, isn't it amazing, more like the fields of an English country manor, a scene out of *Howards End.*"

In an hour, we've traveled the length of the valley. We begin walking up another hill, this one steeper and rockier than the last. The path narrows to a rough trail of switchbacks. I can see the wall and the second archway above, the limestone peaks looking like sharp coral thrust up from an ancient ocean floor. Dark clouds whirl in front of the sun, and the air turns chilly. "Maybe we should head back," I suggest. "It looks like rain."

"Let's see what's at the top first." Without waiting for me to agree, Simon climbs the path. As we wind our way up, I think about Kwan's story of the missionaries, how the villagers said they were killed by bandits. Maybe there's truth in the lie. Just before we left the hotel in Guilin — when was that? only yesterday? — I picked up *The China Daily*, the English-language newspaper. On the front page was a report that violent crime, once unheard of in China, is now on the increase, especially in tourist locales such as Guilin. In one village of only two hundred seventy-three people, five men were executed by firing squad a couple of days ago, one for rape, two for robbery, two for murder, crimes committed all in the last year. Five violent crimes, five executions — and from one tiny village! That's swift justice for you: accused, found guilty, kaboom. The newspaper further reported that the crime wave stemmed from "Western pollution and degenerative thinking." Before being executed, one of the hooligans confessed that his mind had rotted after he watched a bootlegged American movie called *Naked Gun 33⅓*. He swore, however, that he was innocent of murder, that hillside bandits had killed the Japanese tourist and his crime lay only in buying the dead woman's stolen Seiko watch. Remembering this account, I do an appraisal of our robbery potential. My watch is a cheap plastic Casio. Although who knows, maybe hillside bandits crave digital watches with built-in calculators the size of thumbnails. I left my passport at Big Ma's house, thank God. I heard passports are worth about five thousand U.S. dollars each on the black market. Thieves would kill for those.

"Where's your passport?" I ask Simon.

"Right here." He pats his fanny pack. "What, you think we'll run into the border patrol or something?"

"Shit, Simon! You shouldn't carry your passport with you!"

"Why not?"

Before I can answer, we hear rustling in the bushes, followed by a clop-clop sound. I picture bandits on horseback. Simon keeps walking ahead. "Simon! Come back here."

"In a sec." He rounds the bend, out of sight.

And then I hear him yelp: "Hey, there. Whoa! Wait . . . hey, wait!"

He comes scrambling down the path, yelling, "Olivia, get out—" then flies into me so hard he knocks the wind out of me. As I lie in the dirt, my mind detaches itself from my body. Strange, I'm so lucid and calm. My senses seem sharper. I examine the knot on my lower shin, the popped-out vein on my kneecap. No pain. No pain! I *know* without any doubt or fear that this is a sign that death is around the bend. I've read this in how-to books on dying, that somehow you *know*, although you can't explain why. The moments slow. This is the one-second flashback that dying people have, and I'm surprised how long the second is lasting. I seem to have an infinite amount of time to sum up what's been important in my life—laughter, unanticipated joy, Simon . . . even Simon. And yes, love, forgiveness, a healing inner peace, knowing I'm not leaving behind any big rifts or major regrets. I laugh: Thank God I have on clean underwear, although who in China would care? Thank God Simon is with me, that I'm not alone in this terrible yet wonderful moment. Thank God he'll be by my side later—that is, if there is a heaven or World of Yin, whatever. And if there is indeed a whatever, what if . . . what if Elza is there? Into whose angelic arms will Simon fly? My thoughts aren't quite as lucid or healing anymore, the seconds tick at their usual workaday pace, and I jump to my feet, saying to myself, Fuck this shit.

That's when they appear, our would-be assassins, a cow and her calf, so startled by my scream they skid to a mud-flying stop. "What's the matter?" Simon asks. The cow gives me a big-gummed moo. If self-humiliation were fatal, that's what I would have died of. My big spiritual epiphany is a joke on me. And I can't even laugh about it. How stupid I feel. I can no longer trust my perceptions, my judgments. I know how schizophrenics must feel, trying to find order in chaos, inventing bootstrap logic that would hold together what might otherwise further unravel.

The cow and her calf lope off. But just as we step back onto the path, a young man strides down, stick in hand. He wears a gray sweater over a white shirt, new blue jeans, and clean-white sneakers. "He must be the cow herder," says Simon.

I'm wary of making any assumptions now. "He could be a bandit, for all we know."

We stand off to the side to let him pass. But when the young man is in front of us, he stops. I keep expecting him to ask us a question, yet he says nothing. His expression is bland, his eyes intense, observant, almost critical.

*"Ni hau!"* Simon waves, even though the guy is standing right in front of us.

The young man remains silent. His eyes flick up and down. I begin to babble in Chinese. "Are those your cows? They scared me to death. Maybe you heard me scream. . . . My husband and I, we're Americans, from San Francisco. Do you know the place? Yes? No? . . . Well, now we're visiting my sister's aunt in Changmian. Li Bin-bin."

Still no answer.

"Do you know her? Actually, she's dead. Yesterday, that's when she died, before we could meet her, a real pity. So now we want to make a, a . . ." I'm so flustered I can't think of the Chinese word for "funeral," so I say, "Make a party for her, a sad party." I laugh nervously, ashamed of my Chinese, my American accent.

He stares me straight in the eye. And I say to him in my mind, Okay, buster, if you want to play this game, I'll stare too. But after ten seconds I look down.

"What's with this guy?" Simon asks. I shrug. The cow herder does not look like other men we have seen in Changmian, the ones with cold-coarsened hands and home-chopped hair. He's groomed, his fingernails are clean. And he looks arrogantly smart. In San Francisco, he could pass for a doctoral student, a university lecturer, a depressed poet-activist. Here he's a cow herder, a cow herder who disapproves of us for reasons I can't fathom. And because of that, I want to win him over, make him smile, assure myself I'm not as ridiculous as I feel.

"We're taking a walk," I continue in Mandarin. "Having a look around. It's very pretty here. We want to see what lies between those mountains." I point toward the archway, just in case he doesn't understand.

He looks up, then turns back to us with a scowl. Simon smiles at him, then leans toward me. "He obviously doesn't know what you're talking about. Come on, let's go."

I persist. "Is that all right?" I say to the cow herder. "Do we need to receive permission from someone? Is it safe? Can you advise us?" I wonder how it would feel to be smart but to have your prospects go no further than a pasture in Changmian. Maybe he envies us.

As if he heard my thoughts, he smirks. "Assholes," he says in perfectly enunciated English, then turns and walks down the path. For a few seconds, we're too stunned to say anything.

Simon starts walking. "That was weird. What did you say to him?"

"I didn't say anything!"

"I'm not accusing you of saying anything wrong. But what did you say?"

"I said we were going for a walk. Okay? I asked if we needed permission to be here."

We trudge up the hill again, no longer holding hands. The two strange encounters, first with the kids and now with the cow herder, have put a pall on any sort of romantic talk. I try to dismiss them, but unable to make any sense of them, I worry. This is a warning. It's as clear as smelling a bad odor, knowing it leads to something rotten, dead, decayed.

Simon puts his hand on the small of my back. "What is it?"

"Nothing." Yet I long to confide in him, to have our fears if not our hopes be in synch. I stop walking. "This is going to sound silly, but actually I was wondering—maybe these things are like omens."

"What things?"

"The kids telling us not to go in here—"

"They said *they* couldn't go in. There's a difference."

"And that guy. His evil chuckle, like he knows we shouldn't go into the next valley, but he's not going to say."

"His laugh wasn't evil. It was a laugh. You're acting like Kwan, linking two coincidences and coming up with a superstition."

I explode: "You asked me what I was thinking, and I told you! You don't have to contradict everything I say and make fun of me."

"Hey, hey, easy. I'm sorry. . . . I was only trying to put your mind at ease. Do you want to go back now? Are you really that nervous?"

"God, I hate it when you say that!"

"What! Now what'd I do?"

" '*That* nervous,' " I say testily. "You only say it about women and yappy little dogs. It's condescending."

"I don't mean it that way."

"You never describe men as nervous."

"All right, all right! Guilty as charged. You're not nervous, you're . . . you're hysterical! How's that?" He grins. "Come on, Olivia, lighten up. What's the matter?"

"I'm just . . . well, I'm concerned. I'm concerned we might be trespassing, and I don't want to come across as ugly Americans, you know, presuming we can do anything we want."

He puts his arm around me. "Tell you what. We're almost at the top. We'll have a quick look, then head back. If we see anyone, we'll apologize and leave. Of course, if you really are nervous, I mean, *concerned*—"

"Would you stop!" I give him a shove. "Go on. I'll catch up."

He shrugs, then climbs the path with big strides. I stand there for a moment, mentally lashing myself for not saying what I feel. But I'm irked that Simon can't sense what I really want. I shouldn't have to spell it out like a demand, making me the bitch of the day and him the all-suffering nice guy.

When I reach the top, he is in the second archway, which is nearly identical to the first, except that it seems older, or perhaps battered.

Part of the wall has caved in, and it looks as though it happened not through gradual decay but rather with the sudden force of a cannon or a ramrod.

"Olivia!" Simon shouts from the other side. "Come here. You won't believe this!"

I hurry over, and when I emerge from the archway and look down, I see a landscape that both chills and mesmerizes me, a fairy-tale place I've seen in nightmares. It is completely unlike the smooth, sunlit valley we just crossed. This is a deep and narrow ravine shaped by violent upheavals, as lumpy as an unmade bed, a scratchy blanket of moss with patches of light and pockets of shadows, the faded hues of a perpetual dusk.

Simon's eyes are glazed with excitement. "Isn't this great?"

Sprouting here and there are mounds of rocks, stacked high as men. They look like monuments, cairns, an army of petrified soldiers. Or perhaps they are the Chinese version of Lot's salty wife, pillars of human weakness, the fossilized remains of those who entered this forbidden place and dared to look back.

Simon points. "Look at those caves! There must be hundreds."

Along the walls, from the bottom of the ravine to the tops of the peaks, are cracks and fissures, pockmarks and caves. They look like the shelves and storage bins of a huge prehistoric mortuary.

"It's incredible!" Simon exclaims. I know he's thinking about Kwan's cave. He goes down a trail of sorts, more gully than path, with rocky footholds that give under his weight.

"Simon, I'm tired. My feet are starting to hurt."

He turns around. "Just wait there. I'll look around for about five minutes. Then we'll go back together. Okay?"

"No more than five minutes!" I yell. "And don't go in any caves."

He is clambering down the trail. What is it that makes him so oblivious to danger? Probably one of those biological differences between men and women. Women's brains use higher and more evolved functions, which account for their sensitivity, their humaneness, their worry, whereas men rely on more primitive functions. See rock, chase. Danger, sniff, go find. Smoke cigar later. I resent Simon's carelessness. And yet, I have to admit, I find it seductive, his boyish disregard of peril, his pursuit of fun without consequences. I think about the type of men I consider sexy: they are always the ones who climb the Himalayas, who paddle through alligator-infested jungle rivers. It isn't that I consider them brave. They are reckless, unpredictable, maddeningly unreliable. But like rogue waves and shooting stars, they also lend thrills to a life that otherwise would be as regular as the tide, as routine as day passing into night.

I look at my watch. Five minutes have dragged by. Then it becomes ten, fifteen, twenty. Where the hell is Simon? The last time I saw him he was making his way toward a cluster of those cairns, or whatever they are. He walked behind a bush, and then I couldn't follow where he went. A raindrop hits my cheek. Another splatters on my jacket. In an instant, it's pouring. "Simon!" I yell. "Simon!" I expect my voice to echo loudly, but it is muffled, absorbed by the rushing rain. I duck under the archway. The rain is falling so fast and hard it makes a hazy curtain. The air smells metallic, minerals flushed from rocks. The peaks and hillsides are turning dark, glistening. Rain streams along their sides, and small rivulets send loose rocks down. Flash flood, what if there's a flash flood? I curse Simon for making me worry about him. But within another minute, my worry spills into panic. I have to leave the shelter and search for him. I pull the parka hood over my head, step into the downpour, and march toward the slope.

I'm counting on altruistic courage to seize hold of me and guide me down. Yet when I lean toward the dark ravine, fear slips into my veins, paralyzes my limbs. My throat tightens and I plead out loud: "Please, dear God, or Buddha, whoever's listening. Make him return right now. I can't stand it anymore. Make him return, and I promise—"

Simon's face pops into view. His hair, his down jacket, his jeans are soaking wet, and there he is, panting like a dog who wants to play more fetch. My one second of gratitude dissolves into anger.

We run for the archway. Simon slips off his jacket and twists the sleeves, releasing a small flood onto the ground. "Now what are we going to do?" I grouse.

"Keep each other warm." His teeth are chattering. He leans against the tunnel wall, then pulls me toward him, my back against his chest, his arms wrapped around me. His hands are icy. "Come on, relax." He rocks me slightly. "There, that's better."

I try to recall the morning's lovemaking, the unexpected joy, the welling up of emotion we both had. But throughout my body, bundles of muscles tighten and cramp—my jaw, my chest, my forehead. I feel restrained, stifled. I ask myself, How can I relax? How can I let go of everything that's happened? You need complete trust to do that.

And then a bad thought lands on my brain: Has Simon slept with other women since our separation? Of course he has! The guy can't go without sex for more than a couple of days. One time—this was a few years ago—we came across a magazine questionnaire, "Your Lover's Inner Sex Life," something stupid like that. I read the first question out loud to Simon: "How often does your lover masturbate?" And I was mentally checking "never or seldom" when Simon said, "Three or four times a week. It depends."

"It depends?" I blurted. "On what? Sunny weather?"

"Boredom, as much as anything," he answered. And I thought, Twice a week with me is *boring*?

And now I'm wondering, How many women has he been *bored* by since we broke up?

Simon massages my neck. "God, you're so tight in here. Can you feel that?"

"Simon, this morning, you know?"

"Hmm, that was nice."

"But don't you think we should have used a condom?" I'm hoping he'll say, "What for? I'm shooting blanks. You know that." But instead he catches his breath. His fingers stop kneading. And then he rubs one of my arms briskly.

"Hmm. Yeah. I guess I forgot."

My eyes lock. I try to breathe calmly. I'm going to ask him. But whatever he says next, I can take it. Besides, I'm not so holy myself. I slept with that creepy marketing director, Rick—or rather, we groped, never needed the condom lying on the nightstand, because "the big bruiser," as my date called his flaccid penis, went on strike, something it had never done, he assured me, ever. And of course, I felt sexually humiliated, especially after pretending with well-timed sighs and shivers that I was aroused.

Simon's mouth is near my ear. His breathing reminds me of the rushing sea sounds you can hear in a nautilus, a memory now endlessly trapped in a spiral.

"Simon, about the condom—are you saying you slept with someone else?"

His breathing stops. He lifts his head away from my ear. "Well . . . well, if I did, I don't remember anymore." He squeezes me. "Anyway, they don't matter. Only you." He strokes my hair.

"They? How many is *they*?"

"Uh . . . Hell, I don't know."

"Ten? Twelve?"

He laughs. "Gimme a break."

"Three? Four?"

He's quiet. I'm quiet. He exhales, shifts his posture slightly. "Hmm. Maybe something like that."

"Which is it? Three or four?"

"Olivia, let's not talk about this. It'll only get you upset."

I pull away from him. "I'm already upset. You slept with four other women and you didn't even bother to use a goddamn condom this morning!" I walk to the opposite side of the archway and glare at him with my shit-detector eyes.

"It was three." He's looking at his feet. "And I was careful. I didn't catch anything. I used a condom every time."

"*Every* time! Boxes and boxes of condoms! How thoughtful of you to be thinking of me."

"Come on, Olivia. Stop it."

"Who were they? Someone I know? Tell me." And then I think of a woman I despise, Verona, a free-lance art director we hired last year for one project. Everything about her was fake, her name, her eyelashes, her fingernails, her breasts. I once told Simon her breasts were too symmetrical to be real. He laughed and said, "Well they sure squished like the real thing." And when I asked how he knew that, he said that whenever they looked at the layouts together, she leaned over his shoulder and pressed her tits into his back. "Why didn't you say something?" I asked. He said that that would only have called more attention to the fact she was flirting, that it was better to just ignore it, since he wasn't going to do anything about it anyway.

"Was one of them Verona?" I hold my arms tightly across my chest in an effort to stop trembling. He opens his mouth slightly, then closes it, resigned. "You did, didn't you? You fucked that bitch."

"I'm not saying that, you are."

I'm crazed. "So tell me, were they real? Did she have squishy tits?"

"Come on, Olivia. Quit. Why on earth is this so important to you? It shouldn't mean a damn thing."

"It means you never intended to get back together with me! It means I can't trust you. I've never been able to trust you." I'm raging, drowning, needing to take Simon down with me. "I've never been important to you! I only tricked myself into thinking I was. And Kwan tricked you with her stupid ghost tricks, that séance. Yeah, remember that? What

Elza said? You were supposed to forget her, move on with your life. And you know what? Kwan made that up. She lied! I told her to."

Simon gives a small laugh. "Olivia, you're acting crazy. Do you actually think I *believed* that séance shit? I thought we were both just humoring Kwan."

I'm sobbing: "Right, barrels of laughs . . . Only it wasn't a joke, Simon, she was there! I swear, she was, I saw her. And you know what she was saying? Forget her? Fuck no! She was begging you to forget *me*. She said to wait—"

Simon claps his hand to his forehead. "You just never give up, do you?"

"*Me* give up? You've never given *her* up!"

Simon's eyes narrow. "You want to know what the real problem is? You use Elza as a scapegoat for all your insecurities. You've made her a bigger deal in your life than she ever was in mine. You never even knew her, but you project every doubt about yourself onto her. . . ."

I put my hands over my ears. And as he continues to heap his pseudo-analytic garbage on me, I rack my brain for another weapon, a final, fatal bullet to the heart. And that's when I recall secretly reading some letters Elza had written Simon, their pet names, their youthful promises. I turn to him. "You think I'm crazy? Well, maybe I am, because I can see her right now! Yeah, Elza! She's standing right in front of you. She just said, 'Angel Buns, what do you mean I was no big deal?'" Simon's face freezes. "You were supposed to wait, we were supposed to plant those trees together, one for every year."

Simon tries to cover my mouth with his hand. I jump back.

"Don't you see?" I wail. "She's here! She's in your head. She's in your heart! She's always here, right now, in this stupid fucking place, with her stupid fucking omens, telling us we're doomed, Simon, we're doomed!"

At last, Simon has a stricken look on his face I've never seen before.

It scares me. He's shaking. Drops are running down his cheeks—are they rain or tears?

"Why are you doing this?" he howls.

I turn and race out of the archway, into the rain. I run across the valley, gasping, pushing my heart to burst. By the time I reach Big Ma's house, the rain has stopped. I walk through the courtyard, and Kwan gives me one of her knowing looks.

"Libby-ah, oh, Libby-ah," she moans. "Why you crying?"

# 20

# THE VALLEY
# OF STATUES

Simon still isn't back. I look at my watch. An hour has gone by. I figure he's fuming by himself. Fine, let him freeze his ass out there. It's not quite noon. I pull out a paperback and climb into the bed. The trip to China is now a debacle. Simon will have to leave. That makes the most sense. After all, he doesn't speak any Chinese. And this is Kwan's village, and she's *my* sister. As for the magazine piece, I'll just have to take notes from here on out and find someone back home to polish it into an article.

Kwan calls out that it's time for lunch. I muster my composure, ready to face the Chinese inquisition. "Where Simon?" she'll ask. "Ai-ya, why you fight too much?" Kwan is in the central room, putting a steaming bowl on the table. "See? Tofu, tree ear, pickled green. You want take picture?" I have no desire to eat, or shoot photos. Du Lili bustles into the room with a pot of rice and three bowls. We begin to eat, or rather, they do, eagerly, critically.

"First not salty enough," Kwan complains. "Now too salty." Is this some sort of veiled message about Simon and me? A few minutes later she says to me, "Early this morning big sun, now look, rain come back."

Is she making a sneaky analogy to my fight with Simon? But through-out the rest of the meal, she and Du Lili don't even mention his name. Instead, they gossip animatedly about people in the village, thirty years' worth of marriages and diseases, unexpected tragedies and hilarious out-comes, all of which I have no interest in. My ear is attuned to the gate, waiting for the creak and slam of Simon's return. I hear only the mean-ingless spatter of rain.

After lunch, Kwan says she and Du Lili are going to the commu-nity hall to visit Big Ma. Do I want to come? I imagine Simon return-ing to the house, searching for me, growing uneasy, worried, maybe even frantic. Shit, he wouldn't worry, that's what *I* do. "I think I'll stay here," I tell Kwan. "I need to reorganize my camera gear and enter some notes on what I've taken so far."

"Okay. You get done later, come visit Big Ma. Last chance. To-morrow we do funeral."

When I'm finally alone, I sort through my baggies of film, checking for moisture. Damn this weather! It's so damp and chilly that even with four layers of clothing, my skin feels clammy, my toes practically numb. Why did I let pride take precedence over warm clothes?

Before we left for China, Simon and I discussed what we should bring. I packed a large suitcase, a duffel, and my camera bag. Simon said he had two carry-ons, and then he goaded me: "By the way, don't count on me to lug your extra junk." I shot back: "Who asked you to?" And he retaliated with another taunt: "You never *ask*, you *expect*." After that remark, I decided I wouldn't let Simon help me—even if he *insisted*. Like a pioneer faced with a dead team of oxen and a desert to cross, I took a long, hard look at my travel inventory. I was determined to reduce my luggage to complete self-sufficiency: one wheeled carry-on and my cam-era bag. I pitched everything that was not absolutely essential. Out went the portable CD player and CDs, the exfoliant, skin toner, and re-juvenating cream, the hair dryer and conditioner, two pairs of leggings and matching tunic tops, half my stash of underwear and socks, a couple of novels I'd been meaning to read for the last ten years, a bag of prunes, two out of three rolls of toilet paper, a pair of fleece-lined boots, and the saddest omission, a purple down vest. In deciding what should go in my allotted space, I bet on tropical weather, hoped for the occasional night of Chinese opera, and didn't even question whether there would be electricity.

And so, among the things I packed and now resent seeing in my tiny suitcase are two silk tanktops, a pair of canvas shorts, a clothes steamer, a pair of sandals, a swimsuit, and a neon-pink silk blazer. The only opera I'll wear that to is the soap going on in my own little courtyard. At least I have the waterproof shell. Small consolation, big regret. I long for the down vest the way a person adrift in the sea deliriously dreams of water. Warmth—what I would give for it! Damn this weather! Damn Simon for being nice and toasty in his own down jacket. . . .

His down jacket—it's drenched, sopping and useless. Just before I left him, he was shaking, with anger, I thought at the time. Now I wonder. Oh God! What are the signs of hypothermia? A vague memory about cold and anger strays across my mind. When was that, five or six years ago?

I was shooting photos in an emergency room, the usual dramatic stock for a hospital's annual report. A team of paramedics wheeled in a shabbily dressed woman who reeked of urine. Her speech was slurred, she complained she was burning up and had to take off a mink coat she didn't have. I assumed she was drunk or high on drugs. And then she started convulsing. "Defibrillator!" someone shouted. I later asked one of the nurses what I should put in the caption—heart attack? alcoholism? "Put down that she died of January," the nurse said angrily. And because I didn't understand, he said, "It's January. It's cold. She died of hypothermia, just like six other homeless people this month."

That won't happen to Simon. He's healthy. He's always too warm. He rolls down the car window when other people are freezing, and he doesn't even ask. He's inconsiderate that way. He keeps people waiting. He doesn't even think they might be worried. He'll be here any minute. He'll arrive with that irritating grin of his, and I'll be pissed for worrying without reason.

After five minutes of trying to convince myself of these things, I run to the community hall to find Kwan.

IN THE TUNNEL of the second archway, Kwan and I find Simon's jacket crumpled on the ground like a broken corpse. Stop whimpering, I tell myself. Crying means you expect the worst.

I stand at the top of the ledge that leads into the ravine and look down, searching for movement. Various scenarios play in my head. Simon, now delirious, wandering half clothed in the ravine. Rocks tumbling down from the peaks. The young man, who is not a cow herder at all but a modern-day bandit, stealing Simon's passport. I blurt out to Kwan: "We ran into some kids, they screamed at us. And later this guy with some cows, he called us assholes. . . . I was tense. I went a little crazy, and Simon . . . he was trying to be nice, but then he got mad. And what I said, well, I didn't mean it." In the coved tunnel, my words sound confessional and hollow at the same time.

Kwan listens quietly, sadly. She doesn't say anything to take away my guilt. She doesn't respond with false optimism that all will be well. She unzips the day pack that Du Lili insisted we bring along. She spreads the space blanket on the ground, inflates the cushion, lays out the little camping stove and an extra canister of fuel.

"If Simon returns to Big Ma's house," she reasons in Chinese, "Du Lili will send someone to let us know. If he comes to this place, you will be here to help him get warm." She opens her umbrella.

"Where are you going?"

"A short look around, that's all."

"What if you get lost too?"

*Meiyou wenti.*" Don't worry, she's telling me. "This is my childhood home. Every rock, every twist and turn in the hills, I know them all like old friends." She steps outside, into the drizzle.

I call to her: "How long will you be gone?"

"Not long. Maybe one hour, no more."

I look at my watch. It's almost four-thirty. At five-thirty, the golden half-hour will come, but now dusk scares me. By six, it will be too dark to walk.

After she leaves, I pace between the archway's two openings. I look out on one side, see nothing, then repeat the process on the opposite side. You're not going to die, Simon. That's fatalistic bullshit. I think of people who beat the odds. The lost skier at Squaw Valley who dug a snow cave and was saved three days later. And that explorer who was trapped on an ice floe—was it John Muir?—who did jumping jacks all night long to stay alive. And of course, there was that Jack London tale about a man caught in a blizzard who manages to build a fire out of wet twigs. But then I remember the ending: A clump of snow slides off the branch above and extinguishes his hope below. And then other endings come to mind: The snowboarder who fell into a tree well and was found dead the next morning. The hunter who sat down to rest one day on the Italian–Austrian border and wasn't discovered until spring thaw thousands of years later.

I try meditating to block out these negative thoughts: palms open, mind open. But all I can think about is how cold my fingers are. Is that how cold Simon is?

I imagine myself as Simon, standing in the same archway, overheated from our argument, muscles tight, wanting to bolt in any dangerous direction. I've seen that happen before. When he learned that our friend Eric had been killed in Vietnam, he went meandering alone and wound up lost in the eucalyptus groves of the Presidio. The same thing happened when we visited some friends of friends in the country, and one man started telling racist jokes. Simon stood up and announced that the guy had his head screwed on wrong. At the time, I was angry that he had created a scene and left me to deal with the aftermath. But now, recalling this moment, I feel a mournful admiration for him.

The rain has stopped. That's what he too must be seeing. "Hey," I imagine him saying, "let's check out those rocks again." I walk outside to the ledge, look down. He wouldn't see stomach-churning steepness the way I do. He wouldn't see a hundred ways to crack your skull open. He'd just walk down the trail. So I do. Did Simon go this way? About halfway down, I look back, then around. There isn't any other way into this place, unless he threw himself over the ledge and dropped seventy feet to the bottom. Simon isn't suicidal, I tell myself. Besides, suicidal people talk about killing themselves before they do it. And then I remember reading a story in the *Chronicle* about a man who parked his new Range Rover on the Golden Gate Bridge during rush hour, then threw himself over the railing. His friends expressed the usual shock and disbelief. "I saw him at the health club just last week," one was reported as saying. "He told me he held two thousand shares of Intel stock at twelve that were now trading at seventy-eight. Man, he was talking about the *future.*"

Toward the bottom of the ravine, I check the sky for the amount of daylight still left. I see dark birds fluttering like moths; they fall suddenly, then flap upward again. They're making shrill, high-pitched noises, the sounds of frightened creatures. Bats—that's what they are! They must have escaped from a cave, now out for a flight at dusk, the hour of insects. I saw bats in Mexico once—*mariposas,* the waiters called them, butterflies, so as not to scare the tourists. I wasn't afraid of them then, nor am I now. They are harbingers of hope, as welcome as the dove that brought a leafy twig to Noah. Salvation is nearby. Simon is nearby too. Perhaps the bats soared out because he entered their lair and disturbed their upside-down slumber.

I follow the twisty, uneven path, trying to see where the bats are coming from, where they return. My foot slides, and I wrench my ankle. I hobble over to a rock and sit down. "Simon!" I expect my yelling to carry as if in an amphitheater. But my cries are sucked into the hollows of the ravine.

At least I'm not cold anymore. There's hardly any wind down here. The air is still, heavy, almost oppressive. That's strange. Isn't the wind supposed to blow *faster*? What was in that brochure Simon and I did on Measure J, the one against Manhattanization—the Bernoulli effect, how forests of skyscrapers create wind tunnels, because the smaller volume through which air passes decreases pressure and increases velocity—or does it increase pressure?

I look at the clouds. They're streaming along. The wind is definitely blowing up there. And the more I watch, the more unsteady the ground feels, like the bottom of a salad spinner. And now the peaks, the trees, the boulders grow enormous, ten times larger than they were a minute ago. I stand and walk again, this time careful of my footing. Although the ground appears level, it's as if I were climbing a steep incline. A force seems to push me back. Is this one of those places on earth where the normal properties of gravity and density, volume and velocity have gone haywire? I grab on to the cracks of a rocky mound and strain so hard to pull myself up I'm sure a blood vessel in my brain will burst.

And then I gasp. I'm standing on a crest. Below is an abrupt drop of twenty feet or so, as if the earth collapsed like a soufflé, creating a giant sinkhole. Stretching out to the mountains at the other end of the ravine is a bumpy wasteland pincushioned with those things I saw earlier—cairns, monuments, whatever they are. It alternately resembles a petrified forest of burnt trees and a subterranean garden of stalagmites from a former cave. Did a meteor fall here? The Valley of the Shadow of Death, that's what this is.

I go up to one of the formations and circle it like a dog, then circle it again, attempting to make sense of it. Whatever this is, it sure does not grow that way naturally. Someone deliberately stacked these rocks—and at angles that don't look balanced. Why don't the rocks fall? Large boulders perch on the points of small spires. Other rocks tilt on dime-size spots, as if they were iron filings latched on to a magnet. They could pass for modern art, sculptures of lamps and hat racks, precisely planned to give them a haphazard look. On one pile the topmost rock looks like a misshapen bowling ball, its holes suggesting vacant eyes and a screaming mouth, like the person in that Edvard Munch painting. I see other formations with the same features. When were these made? By whom and why? No wonder Simon wanted to come down here. He came back to investigate further. As I continue walking, this strange gathering of rocks resembles more and more the blackened victims of Pompeii, Hiroshima, the Apocalypse. I'm surrounded by an army of these limestone statues, bodies risen from the calcified remains of ancient sea creatures.

A dank, fusty odor hits my nose and panic rises in my throat. I look around for signs of decay. I've smelled this same stench before. But where? When? It feels overwhelmingly familiar, an olfactory version of déjà vu—déjà senti. Or perhaps it's instinctive, like the way animals know that smoke comes from fire and fire leads to danger. The odor is trapped in my brain as visceral memory, emotional residue of stomach-cramping fear and sadness, but without the reason that caused it.

I hurry past another stack of rocks. But my shoulder catches a jutting edge, and I scream as the entire load collapses. I stare at the rubble. Whose magic did I just destroy? I have the uneasy feeling I have broken a spell and these metamorphisms will soon begin to sway and march. Where is the archway? Now there seem to be more rock mounds — have they multiplied? — and I must weave through this maze, my legs going one direction, my mind arguing that I should go another. What would Simon do? Whenever I've become uncertain about accomplishing a physical feat, he's been the reasoning voice, assuring me I can run another half-mile, or hike to the next hill, or swim to the dock. And there were times in the past when I believed him, and was grateful that he believed in me.

I imagine Simon urging me on now. "Come on, Girl Scout, move your ass." I look for the stone wall and archway to orient myself. But nothing is distinct. I see only gradations of flat-light shadows. Then I remember those times I became angry with Simon because I listened to him and failed. When I yelled at him after I tried rollerblading and fell on my butt. When I cried because my backpack was too heavy.

I sit on the ground in exasperation, whimpering. Fuck this, I'm calling a taxi. Look how dopey I've become. Do I really believe I can stick my hand up, hail a taxi, and get out of this mess? Is that all that I've managed to store in the emergency section of my inner resources—my willingness to pay cab fare? Why not a limo? I must be losing my mind!

"Simon! Kwan!" Hearing the panic in my voice, I grow even more panicked. I try to move more quickly but my body feels heavy, pulled to the earth's core. I bump into one of the statues. A rock topples, grazes my shoulder. And just like that, all the terror I've been holding in bubbles out of my mouth and I begin to cry like an infant. I can't walk. I can't think. I sink to the ground and clutch myself. I'm lost! They're lost! All three of us are trapped in this terrible land. We'll die here, rot and slough, then petrify and become other faceless statues! Shrill voices accompany my screams. The caves are singing, songs of sorrow, songs of regret.

I cover my ears, close my eyes, to shut out the craziness of the world, my mind, both. You can make it stop, I tell myself. I'm straining hard to believe this; I can feel a cord in my brain stretching taut, and then it rips and I'm soaring, free of my body and its mortal fears, growing light and giddy. So this is how people become psychotic, they simply let go. I can see myself in a boring Swedish movie, slow to react to painfully obvious ironies. I howl like a madwoman at how ridiculous I look, how stupid it is to die in a place like this. And Simon will never know how *nervous* I became. He's right. I'm hysterical!

A pair of hands grabs my shoulders, and I yell.

It's Kwan, her face full of worry. "What happen? Who you talk-ing to?"

"Oh God!" I jump up. "I'm lost. I thought you were too." I'm snif-fling and babbling between staccato breaths. "I mean, are we? Are we lost?"

"No-no-no," she says. I notice then that she has a wooden box tucked under one arm and balanced on her hip. It looks like an old chest for silverware.

"What's that?"

"Box." With her free hand, Kwan helps me onto my rubbery legs.

"I *know* it's a box."

"This way." She guides me by the elbow. She says nothing about Simon. She is strangely solemn, unusually taciturn. And fearing that she might have bad news to tell me, I feel my chest tighten.

"Did you see —" She cuts me off by shaking her head. I'm relieved, then disappointed. I no longer know how I should feel from moment to moment. We're edging our way past the strange statues. "Where'd you get that box?"

"Found it."

I am beyond being frustrated. "Really!" I snap. "I thought you bought it at Macy's."

"This my box I hide long time ago. Already tell you this. This box always want show you."

"Sorry. I'm just frazzled. What's inside?"

"We go up there, open and see."

We walk quietly. As my fear ebbs, the landscape begins to look more benign. The wind pushes against my face. I was perspiring earlier, and now I'm growing chilled. The path is still uneven and tricky, but I no longer sense any strange gravitational pull. I berate myself: Girl, the only thing haywire in this place is your mind. I went through nothing more dangerous than a panic attack. Rocks, I was scared of rocks.

"Kwan, what are these things?"

She stops and turns around. "What thing?"

I gesture to one of the piles.

"Rocks." She starts walking again.

"I *know* they're rocks. I mean, how did they get here, what are they supposed to be? Do they mean something?"

She stops once more, casts her eye over the gully. "This secret."

The hair rises on the back of my neck. I put some casual bluff in my voice. "Come on, Kwan. Are they like gravestones? Are we walking across a cemetery or something? You can tell me."

She opens her mouth, about to answer. But then a stubborn look crosses her face. "I tell you later. Not now."

"Kwan!"

"After we back." She points to the sky. "Dark soon. See? Don't waste time talk." And then she adds softly: "Maybe Simon already come back."

My chest swoops with hope. She knows something I don't, I'm sure of it. I concentrate on this belief as we thread our way up and around several boulders, down a gully, then past a high-walled crevasse. Soon we are at the small trail leading to the top. I can see the wall and the archway.

I scramble ahead of Kwan, heart pounding. I'm convinced Simon is there. I believe that the forces of chaos and uncertainty will allow me another chance to make amends. At the top, my lungs are nearly bursting. I'm dizzy with joy, crying with relief, because I feel the clarity of peace, the simplicity of trust, the purity of love.

And there!—the day pack, the stove, the damp jacket, everything as we left it, nothing more or less. Fear nicks my heart, but I cling to the absolute strength of faith and love. I walk to the other end of the tunnel, knowing that Simon will be there, he *has* to be.

The ledge is empty, nothing out there but the wind, its slap. I lean against the tunnel wall and slump to the ground, hugging my knees. I look up. Kwan's there. "I'm not leaving," I tell her. "Not until I find him."

"I know this." She sits on top of the wooden chest, opens the day pack, and takes out a glass jar of cold tea and two tins. One contains roasted peanuts, the other fried fava beans. She cracks open a peanut and offers it to me.

I shake my head. "You don't need to stay. I know you have to get ready for Big Ma's funeral tomorrow. I'll be okay. He'll probably show up soon."

"I stay with you. Big Ma already tell me, delay funeral two three day, still okay. Anyway, more time cook food."

An idea hits me. "Kwan! Let's ask Big Ma where Simon is." As soon as I say this, I realize how desperate I've become. This is how parents of dying children react, turning to psychics and New Age healers, anything as long as there is a thread of possibility somewhere in this universe or the next.

Kwan gives me a look so tender I know I have hoped for too much. "Big Ma doesn't know," she says quietly in Chinese. She pulls off the cup that covers the camping stove, and lights the burner. Blue flames shoot through tiny slots with a steady hiss. "Yin people," she now says in English, "not know everything, not like you thinking. Sometimes they lost themself, don't know where should go. That's why some yin people come back so often. Always looking, asking, 'Where I lose myself? Where I go?' "

I'm glad Kwan can't see how dejected I feel. The camp stove throws only enough light to outline us as shadows. "You want," she says softly, "I ask Big Ma help us go look. We make like FBI search party. Okay, Libby-ah?"

I'm touched by her eagerness to help me. That's all that makes sense out here.

"Anyway, no funeral tomorrow. Big Ma have nothing else can do."

Kwan pours cold tea into the metal stove cup and sets this on the burner. "Of course, I can't ask her tonight," she says in Chinese. "It's already dark—ghosts, they scare her to death, even though she's a ghost herself. . . ."

I absently watch blue and orange flame tips licking at the bottom of the metal cup.

Kwan holds her palms toward the stove. "Once a person has the bad habit of being scared of ghosts, it's hard to break. Me, I'm lucky, I never started this habit. When I see them, we just talk like friends. . . ."

At that moment, a dreadful possibility grips me. "Kwan, if you saw Simon, I mean, as a yin person, you would tell me, wouldn't you? You wouldn't pretend—"

"I don't see him," she answers right away. She strokes my arm. "Really, I'm telling the truth."

I allow myself to believe her, to believe that she wouldn't lie and he isn't dead. I bury my head in the nest of my arms. What should we do next, what rational, efficient plan should we use in the morning? And later, say by noon, if we still haven't found him, then what? Should one of us call the police? But then I remember there are no phones, no car. Maybe I could hitchhike and go directly to the American consulate. Is there a branch in Guilin? How about an American Express office? If there is, I'll lie and tell them I'm a Platinum Card member, charge me for whatever is needed, search and rescue, emergency airlift.

I hear scraping sounds and raise my head. Kwan is poking the Swiss Army knife into the keyhole on the front of the chest. "What are you doing?"

"Lost key." She holds up the knife, searching among its tools for a better implement. She chooses the plastic toothpick. "Long time ago, I put many thing inside here." She inserts the toothpick into the hole. "Libby-ah, flashlight in bag, you get for me, okay?"

With the light, I can see that the box is made of a dark reddish wood and trimmed in tarnished brass. On the lid is a bas-relief carving of thick trees, a Bavarian-looking hunter, a small dead deer slung over his shoulders, and a dog leaping in front of him.

"What's in there?"

There's a click and Kwan sits up. She smiles, gestures toward the box. "You open, see youself."

I grasp a small brass latch and slowly pull up the lid. Tinkling sounds burst out. Startled, I let the lid drop. Silence. It's a music box.

Kwan titters. "Hnh, what you thinking—ghost in there?"

I lift the lid again, and the plucked sounds of a silvery tune fill our small tunnel, sounding jarringly cheerful, a jaunty military march for prancing horses and people in bright costumes. Kwan hums along, obviously familiar with the melody. I aim the light toward the interior of the box. In one corner, under a panel of glass, is the apparatus that makes the music, a metal comb brushing against the pins of a rolling cylinder. "It doesn't sound very Chinese," I tell Kwan.

"Not Chinese. German-made. You like music?"

"Very pleasant." So this is the source of her music box story. I'm relieved to know there's at least some basis for her delusions. I too hum along with the tune.

"Ah, you know song?"

I shake my head.

"I once give you music box, wedding present. Remember?"

Abruptly, the music stops; the tune hangs in the air a few seconds before it fades away. There is only the awful hissing of the stove, a reminder of rain and cold, of Simon's being in danger. Kwan slides open a wooden panel in the box. She takes out a key, inserts it into a slot, and begins cranking. The music resumes, and I'm grateful for its artificial comfort. I glance at the section of the box that is now exposed. It's a knickknack drawer, a catchall for loose buttons, a frayed ribbon, an empty vial—things once treasured but eventually forgotten, things meant to be repaired, then put aside for too long.

When the music stops again, I wind the box myself. Kwan is examining a kidskin glove, its fingers permanently squeezed into a brittle bunch. She puts it to her nose and sniffs.

I pick up a small book with deckled edges. *A Visit to India, China, and Japan* by Bayard Taylor. Inserted between two pages is a bookmark of sorts, the torn flap of an envelope. A phrase on one of the pages is underlined: "Their crooked eyes are typical of their crooked moral vision." What bigot owned this book? I turn over the envelope flap. Written in brown ink is a return address: Russell and Company, Acropolis Road, Route 2, Cold Spring, New York. "Did this box belong to someone named Russell?" I ask.

"Ah!" Kwan's eyes grow big. "Russo. You remember!"

"No." I point the flashlight at the envelope flap. "It says here 'Russell and Company.' See?"

Kwan seems disappointed. "At that time, I didn't know English," she says in Chinese. "I couldn't read it."

"So this box belonged to Mr. Russell?"

*"Bu-bu."* She takes the envelope flap and stares at it. "Ah! Russell. I thought it was 'Russo' or 'Russia.' The father worked for a company named Russell. His name was . . ." Kwan looks me in the eye. "Banner," she says.

I laugh. "Oh, right. Like Miss Banner. Of course. Her father was a merchant seaman or something."

"Opium boat."

"Yeah, I remember now. . . ." And then the oddity of this strikes me, that we're no longer talking about a bedtime story of ghosts. Here is the music box, here are the things that supposedly belonged to them. I can barely speak. "This was Miss Banner's music box?"

Kwan nods. "Her first name—ai-ya!—now it's run out of my head." She reaches into the knickknack drawer and removes a small tin. "Tst! Her name," she keeps saying to herself, "how can I forget her name?" From the tin, she removes a small black brick. I think it is an inkstone, until she pinches off a piece and adds it to the tea, now boiling on the stove.

"What's that?"

"Herb." She switches to English. "From special tree, new leaf only, very sticky. I make for Miss Banner myself. Good for drinking, also just for smelling. Loosen you mind. Make you feel peace. Maybe give me memory back."

"Is this from the holy tree?"

"Ah! You remember!"

"No. I remember the story you told." My hands are shaking. I have a terrible craving for a cigarette. What the hell is going on? Maybe I have become as crazy as Kwan. Maybe the water in Changmian is contaminated with a hallucinogen. Or maybe I've been bitten by a Chinese mosquito that infects the brain with insanity. Maybe Simon isn't missing. And I don't have things in my lap that belong to a woman from a childhood dream.

The mist and sharp scent of the tea waft upward. I hover over the cup, the steam dampening my face, close my eyes, and inhale the fragrance. It has a calming effect. Maybe I am actually asleep. This is a dream. And if it is, I can pull myself out. . . .

"Libby-ah, look."

Kwan gives me a hand-stitched book. The cover is made of soft, floppy suede, sepia-colored. OUR SUSTENANCE, it says in embossed gothic lettering. Traces of gold flake rim the bottoms of the letters. As I turn the cover, bits of endpaper crumble off and I see from the exposed leather underneath that the now faded covers were once a somber purple, a color that reminds me of a Bible picture from childhood: a wild-looking Moses, standing on a boulder against a purple sky, breaking the tablets in front of a crowd of turban-headed heathens.

I open the book. On the left side of one page is a message typeset in cramped, uneven lines: "Trust in the Lord delivers us from temptations of the Devil. If you are overflowing with the Spirit, you cannot be fuller." On the opposite page are the typeset words "The Amen Corner." And beneath that, in a scrawl full of ink smears and sputters, is a quirky list: "Rancid beans, putrid radishes, opium leaf, pigweed, shepherd's purse, artemisia, foul cabbage, dried seeds, stringy pods, and woody bamboo. Much served cold or adrift in a grim sea of castor oil. God have mercy." The pages that follow contain similar juxtapositions, Christian inspiration related to thirst and salvation, hunger and fulfillment, answered by an Amen Corner listing foods that the owner of this journal obviously found offensive yet useful for heretic humor. Simon would love seeing this. He can use it in our article.

"Listen." I read aloud to Kwan: " 'Canine cutlets, bird fricassee, stewed holothuria, worms, and snakes. A feast for honourable guests. In the future, I shall strive to be less than honourable!' " I put the journal down. "I wonder what holothuria is."

"Nelly."

I look up. "Holothuria means Nelly?"

She laughs, spanks my hand lightly. "No-no-no! Miss Banner, her first name Nelly. But I always call her Miss Banner. That's why almost don't remember whole name. Ha. What bad memory! Nelly Banner." She chuckles to herself.

I grip the journal. My ears are ringing. "When did you know Miss Banner?"

Kwan shakes her head. "Exact date, let me see —"

"*Yi ba liu si.*" I recall the Chinese words from one of Kwan's bedtime stories. "Lose hope, slide into death. One eight six four."

"Yes-yes. You good memory. Same time Heavenly King lose Great Peace Revolution."

The Heavenly King. I remember that part as well. Was there actually someone called the Heavenly King? I wish I knew more about Chinese history. I rub my palm on the soft cover of the journal. Why can't they make books like this today? — books that feel warm and friendly in your hands. I turn to another page and read the entry: " 'Biting off the heads of lucifer matches (agonizing). Swallowing gold leaf (extrava-gant). Swallowing chloride of magnesium (foul). Eating opium (pain-less). Drinking unboiled water (my suggestion). Further to the topic of suicide, Miss Moo informed me that it is strictly forbidden among Tai-ping followers, unless they are sacrificing themselves in the battle for God.' "

*Taiping. Tai* means "great." *Ping* means "peace." *Taiping*, Great Peace. That took place — when? — sometime in the mid–nineteenth century. My mind is being pulled and I'm resisting, but barely hanging on. In the past, I've always maintained enough skepticism to use as an antidote to Kwan's stories when necessary. But now I'm staring at sepia ink on yel-lowed paper, a tarnished locket, the bunched glove, the cramped letters: OUR SUSTENANCE. I'm listening to the music, its lively, old-fashioned melody. I examine the box to see if there is any indication of a date. And then I remember the journal. On the back of the title page, there it is: Glad Tidings Publishers, MDCCCLIX. In Latin, damn it! I corral the letters into numbers: 1859. I flip open the Bayard Taylor book: G. P. Putnam, 1855. So what do these dates prove? That doesn't mean Kwan knew someone named Miss Banner during the Taiping Rebellion. It's just coincidence, the story, the box, the dates on the book.

But in spite of all my logic and doubt, I can't dismiss something larger I know about Kwan: that it isn't in her nature to lie. Whatever she says, she believes is true. Like what she said about Simon, that she hadn't seen him as a ghost, which means he's alive. I believe her. I have to. Then again, if I believe what she says, does that mean I now believe she has yin eyes? Do I believe that she talks to Big Ma, that there ac-tually is a cave with a Stone Age village inside? That Miss Banner, General Cape, and One-half Johnson were real people? That she was Nunumu? And if that's all true, the stories she told throughout these years . . . well, she must have told me for a reason.

I know the reason. I've known since I was a child, really I have. Long ago I buried that reason in a safe place, just as she had done with her music box. Out of guilt, I listened to her stories, all the while holding on to my doubts, my sanity. Time after time, I refused to give her what she wanted most. She'd say, "Libby-ah, you remember?" And I'd always shake my head, knowing she hoped I would say, "Yes, Kwan, of course I remember. I was Miss Banner. . . ."

"Libby-ah," I hear Kwan say now, "what you thinking?"

My lips are numb. "Oh. You know. Simon. I keep thinking, and everything I think about gets worse and worse."

She scoots over so that we are sitting side by side. She massages my cold fingers, and instant warmth flows through my veins.

"How 'bout we talk? Nothing to talk about, that's what we talk. Okay? Talk movie we seen. Talk book you reading. Or talk weather— no-no, not this, then you worry again. Okay, talk political things, what I vote, what you vote, maybe argue. Then you don't think too much."

I'm confused. I return a half-smile.

"Ah! Okay. Don't talk. I talk. Yes, you just listen. Let see, what I talk about? . . . Ah! I know. I tell you story of Miss Banner, how she decide give me music box."

I catch my breath. "Okay. Sure."

Kwan switches to Chinese: "I have to tell you this story in Mandarin. It's easier for me to remember that way. Because when this happened, I couldn't speak any English. Of course, I didn't speak Mandarin then, only Hakka, and a little bit of Cantonese. But Mandarin lets me think like a Chinese person. Of course, if you don't understand a word here and there, you ask me, I'll try to think of the English word. Let me see, where should I start? . . .

"Ah, well, you already know this about Miss Banner, how she was not like other foreigners I knew. She could open her mind to different opinions. But I think sometimes this made her confused. Maybe you know how that is. You believe one thing. The next day, you believe the opposite. You argue with other people, then you argue with yourself. Libby-ah, do you ever do that?"

Kwan stops and searches my eyes for an answer. I shrug and this satisfies her. "Maybe too many opinions is an American custom. I think Chinese people don't like to have different opinions at the same time. We believe one thing, we stick to it for one hundred years, five hundred years. Less confusion that way. Of course, I'm not saying Chinese people never change their minds, not so. We can change if there's a good reason. I'm just saying we don't change back and forth, right and left, whenever we like, just to be interesting. Actually, maybe today, Chinese people are changing too much, whichever way the money is blowing, that's the direction they'll chase."

She nudges me. "Libby-ah, don't you think that's true? In China today people grow more capitalist ideas than pigs. They don't remember when capitalism was the number-one enemy. Short memory, big profits."

I respond with a polite laugh.

"Americans have short memories too, I think. No respect for history, only what's popular. But Miss Banner, she had a good memory, very unusual. That's why she learned to speak our language so quickly. She could hear something just once, then repeat it the next day. Libby-ah, you have a memory like this—don't you?—only it's with your eyes not your ears. What do you call this kind of memory in English? . . . Libby-ah, are you asleep? Did you hear what I asked?"

"Photographic memory," I answer. She's pressing all the buttons now. She's not going to let me hide this time.

"Photographic, yes. Miss Banner didn't have a camera, so she was not photographic, but she did have the memory part. She always could remember what people said, just like a tape recorder. Sometimes this was good, sometimes bad. She could remember what people said at dinnertime, how they said something completely different the next week.

She remembered things that bothered her, could not let them out of her mind. She remembered what people prayed for, what they got instead. Also, she was very good at remembering promises. If you made her a promise, oh, she would never let you forget. This was like her memory specialty. And she also remembered promises she made to other people. To some people, making a promise is not the same thing as doing the promise. Not Miss Banner. To her a promise was forever, not just one lifetime. Like the vow she made to me, after she gave me the music box, when death marched toward us. . . . Libby-ah, where you going?"

"Fresh air." I walk to the archway, trying to push out of my mind what Kwan is telling me. My hands are trembling, and I know it isn't because of the cold. This is the promise Kwan always talked about, the one I never wanted to hear, because I was afraid. Of all times, why does she have to tell me this now? . . .

And then I think: What am I afraid of? That I might believe the story is true—that I made a promise and kept it, that life repeats itself, that our hopes endure, that we get another chance? What's so terrible about that?

I survey the night sky, now clear of rain clouds. I remember another night long ago with Simon, when I said something stupid about the night sky, how the stars were the same that the first lovers on earth had seen. I had been hoping with all my soul that someday he would love me above all others, above all else. But it was for just a brief moment, because my hope felt too vast, like the heavens, and it was easier to be afraid and keep myself from flying out there. Now I'm looking at the heavens again. This is the same sky that Simon is now seeing, that we have seen all our lives, together and apart. The same sky that Kwan sees, that all her ghosts saw, Miss Banner. Only now I no longer feel it is a vacuum for hopes or a backdrop for fears. I see what is so simple, so obvious. It holds up the stars, the planets, the moons, all of life, for eternity. I can always find it, it will always find me. It is continuous, light within dark,

dark within light. It promises nothing but to be constant and mysterious, frightening and miraculous. And if only I can remember to look at the sky and wonder about this, I can use this as my compass. I can find my way through chaos no matter what happens. I can hope with all my soul, and the sky will always be there, to pull me up. . . .

"Libby-ah, you thinking too much again? Should I talk more?"

"I was just wondering."

"Wondering what?"

I keep my back to her, still searching the sky, finding my way from star to star. Their shimmer and glow have traveled a million light-years. And what I now see is a distant memory, yet as vibrant as life can ever be.

"You and Miss Banner. Did you ever look at the sky together on a night like this?"

"Oh yes, many times." Kwan stands up and walks over to me. "Back then, we had no TV of course, so at night the only thing to do was watch the stars."

"What I mean is, did you and Miss Banner ever have a night like this, when you were both scared and you didn't have any idea what would happen?"

"Ah . . . yes, this is true. She was scared to die, scared also because she had lost someone, a man she loved."

"Yiban."

Kwan nods. "I was scared too. . . ." She pauses before saying in a hoarse whisper: "I was the reason he wasn't there."

"What do you mean? What happened?"

"What happened was—ah, maybe you don't want to know."

"Is it . . . is it sad?"

"Sad, yes, happy too. Depends on how you remember."

"Then I want to remember."

Kwan's eyes are wet. "Oh, Libby-ah, I knew someday you would remember with me. I always wanted to show you I really was your loyal friend." She turns away, gathers herself, then squeezes my hand and smiles. "Okay, okay. Now this is a secret. Don't tell anyone. Promise, Libby-ah. . . . Ah yes, I remember the sky was dark, hiding us. Between those two mountains over there, it was growing brighter and brighter. A big orange fire was burning. . . ."

And I listen, no longer afraid of Kwan's secrets. She's offered me her hand. I'm taking it freely. Together we're flying to the World of Yin.

# WHEN HEAVEN
# BURNED

Earlier I was with Yiban, in the cave — the one with the glowing lake, a stone village by its shore. And when I was there, Libby-ah, I did a terrible thing, that led to another. I made my last day on earth a day of lies.

First, I broke my promise to Miss Banner. I did so to be kind. I told Yiban the truth: "Miss Banner was pretending with Cape. She wanted to protect you, make sure you were safe. And see, now here you are."

You should have seen his face! Relief, joy, rage, then alarm — like the turning of leaves, all the seasons happening at once. "What good is it to have me alive when she's not with me?" he cried. "I'll kill that bastard Cape." He jumped up.

"Wah! Where are you going?"

"To find her, bring her here."

"No, no, you must not." And then I told my first lie of the day: "She knows how to come here. She and I have been here many times." Inside, I was worried about Miss Banner, because of course this was not true. So then I told my second lie. I excused myself, saying I needed a girl's privacy, meaning I had to find a dark place to pee. I picked up the lantern, because I knew that if I took this, Yiban would not be able to find his way out of the cave. And then I hurried through the twists and turns of the tunnel, vowing I would bring Miss Banner back.

As I climbed out of the mountain's womb, I felt I was being born into the world again. It was day, but the sky was white not blue, drained of color. Around the sun was a ring of many pale colors. Had the world already changed? What lay beyond these mountains—life or death?

When I reached the archway just above Changmian, I saw the village was there, the crowded marketplace, everything looking the same as before. Alive! Everyone was alive! This gave me hope about Miss Banner, and I cried. As I hurried down the path, I bumped into a man leading his buffalo ox. I stopped him, told him the news, and asked him to warn his family and others: "Remove all signs of 'The Good News,' God, and Jesus. Speak quietly and do not cause alarm. Otherwise the soldiers will see what we are doing. Then disaster will visit today instead of tomorrow."

I ran toward other people and said the same thing. I banged on the gate to the roundhouses where Hakkas lived, ten families under one roof. I went quickly from household to household. Hah! I thought I was so clever, warning the village in such a calm and orderly way. But then I heard a man shouting, "Death is coming for you, you shit-eating worm!" And his neighbor cried back, "Accuse me, will you? I'll tell the Manchus you're bastard brother to the Heavenly King."

At that instant—*ki-kak!*—we all heard it, like the cracking of dry wood. Everyone fell quiet. Then came another crack, this one like the splitting of a tall tree at its thick trunk. Nearby, a man howled, "Guns! The soldiers are already here!" And in an instant people began spilling out of their houses, grabbing on to the sleeves of those fleeing down the street.

"Who's coming?"

"What! A death warrant for all Hakkas?"

"Go! Go! Find your brothers. We're running away!"

The warnings turned into shouts, the shouts into screams, and above that, I could hear the high-pitched wails of mothers calling for their children. I stood in the middle of the lane, bumped by people running this way and that. Look what I had done! Now the entire village would be killed with a single volley of gunfire. People were climbing into the mountains, spreading across like stars in the sky.

I raced down the lane, toward the Ghost Merchant's House. Then came another gunshot, and I knew it had come from within those walls. When I reached the back alleyway gate, there was another explosion, this one echoing through the lanes. I darted inside the back courtyard, then stood still. I was breathing and listening, then listening to my breathing. I scampered to the kitchen, pressed my ear against the door that led into the dining room. No sounds. I pushed the door open, ran to the window facing the courtyard. From there I could see the soldiers by the gate. What luck!—they were sleeping. But then I looked again. One soldier's arm was twisted, the other's leg was bent. Ai! They were dead! Who did this? Had they angered Cape? Was he now killing everybody? And where was Miss Banner?

When I turned down the corridor toward her room, I saw a man's naked body, smashed facedown on the ground. Flies were feasting in the fresh gourd of his brains. Ai-ya! Who was this unlucky person? Dr. Too Late? Pastor Amen? I crept past the body, as if he might awake. A few steps later, I saw last night's dinner, the shank bone now brown with hair and blood. General Cape must have done this. Who else had he killed? Before I could wonder too much longer, I heard sounds coming from God's House. The music box was playing, and Pastor was singing, as if this Seventh Day were like any other. As I hurried across the courtyard toward God's House, Pastor's singing turned to sobs, then the bellow of an animal. And above this, I heard Miss Banner— still alive!—scolding as if she were talking to a naughty child. But a moment later, she began to wail, "No, no, no, no!" before a big explosion cut her off. I raced into the room, and what I saw made my body turn to stone, then sand. By the altar, lying bent and crooked—Miss

Banner in her yellow dress, the Jesus Worshippers in shiny Sunday black—like a butterfly and four beetles squashed dead on the stone floor. Wah! Gone so fast—I could still hear their cries echoing in the room. I listened more carefully. These were not echoes but— "Miss Banner?" I called. She lifted her head. Her hair was unbound, her mouth a silent dark hole. Blood was spattered on her bosom. Ai, maybe she really was dead.

"Miss Banner, are you a ghost?"

She moaned like one, then shook her head. She held out her arm. "Come help me, Miss Moo. My leg is broken."

As I walked toward the altar, I thought the other foreigners would rise too. But they remained still, holding hands, forever sleeping in pools of bright blood. I squatted beside her. "Miss Banner," I whispered, searching the corners of the room. "Where is Cape?"

"Dead," she answered.

"Dead! Then who killed—"

"I can't bear to talk about that now." Her voice was shaky, nervous, which of course made me wonder if she— But no, I couldn't imagine Miss Banner killing anyone. And then I heard her ask with a scared face: "Tell me, quick. Yiban—where is Yiban?"

When I said he was safe in a cave, her face sagged with relief. She sobbed, unable to stop. I tried to soothe her. "Soon you'll be reunited with him. The cave is not so far away."

"I can't walk even one step. My leg." She lifted her skirt, and I saw her right leg was swollen, a piece of bone sticking out. Now I told my third lie: "This is not so bad. Where I grew up, a person with a leg like this could still walk all over the mountain, no problem. Of course, being a foreigner, you are not as strong. But as soon as I find a way to bind your leg, we'll escape from here."

She smiled, and I was grateful to know that a person in love will believe anything as long as it gives hope. "Wait here," I said. I ran to her room and searched through the drawer containing her private ladies' things. I found the stiff garment she used for pinching in her waist and pushing up her bosom, also her stockings with the holes at the heels. I ran back and used these clothes to splint her leg. And when I was done, I helped her stand and limp to the bench at the back of God's House. Only then, away from those who were alive just a short while before, was she able to say how and why each person was killed.

She began by telling me what happened after Lao Lu lost his head and I fell senseless to the ground. The Jesus Worshippers, she said, joined hands and sang the music box song: "When Death turns the corner, our Lord we shall meet."

"Stop singing!" Cape then ordered. And Miss Mouse—you know how she was always so nervous—she shouted at Cape, "I don't fear you or death, only God. Because when I die, I'm going to heaven like this poor man you killed. And you, bastard of the devil, you'll roast in hell." Yes! Can you imagine Miss Mouse saying that? If I had been there, I would have cheered.

But her words did not frighten Cape. "Roast?" he said. "I'll show you what the devil likes to roast." He called his soldiers: "Cut off this dead man's leg and cook it over a fire." The soldiers laughed, thinking this was a joke. Cape barked out the order again, and the soldiers leapt forward to obey. The foreigners cried and tried to leave. How could they watch such an evil sight? Cape growled that if they didn't watch and laugh, each of their right hands would be next to go over the fire. So the foreigners stayed and watched. They laughed and vomited at the same time. Everyone was scared to death of Cape, everyone except Lao Lu, since he was already dead. And when he saw his leg turning on a spit— well, how much can a ghost stand before he turns to revenge?

Early in the morning, before the sun came up, Miss Banner heard a knock on her door. She rose and left Cape sleeping soundly in her bed. From outside, she heard an angry voice. It sounded familiar yet not. It was a man, shouting in the Cantonese of rough workingmen. "General Fake! General Fake! Get up, you lazy dog! Come and see! Brother

Jesus has arrived. He's come to drag your carcass to hell." Wah! Who could this be? Certainly not one of the soldiers. But who else sounded like a coarse-talking *kuli?*

Cape then cursed: "Damn you, man, I'll kill you for ruining my sleep."

The Chinese voice yelled back: "Too late, you son of a bastard dog. I'm already dead."

Cape jumped out of bed, grabbed his pistol. But when he threw open the door, he began to laugh. There was Pastor Amen, the crazy man. He was cursing like a fifth-generation *kuli,* the shank bone from last night's dinner balanced on his shoulder. Miss Banner thought to herself, How strange that Pastor can now speak the native tongue so well. Then she rushed to the door to warn the madman to go away. When Cape turned to push her back, Pastor swung the shank bone and cracked open the fake general's skull. He struck him again and again, his swings so wild that one of them caught Miss Banner on the shin. Finally Pastor threw the bone down and shouted at his enemy, long past dead: "I'll kick you with my good leg when we meet in the other world."

That's when Miss Banner suspected Lao Lu's ghost had jumped into Pastor's empty mind. She watched this man who was both living and dead. He picked up Cape's pistol and ran across the courtyard, and called to the soldiers guarding the gate. From where Miss Banner lay, she heard one explosion. Soon another came. And then she heard Pastor cry in his foreigner's tongue: "Dear God! What have I done?" All that noise had wakened him from his cloudy dreams.

Miss Banner said that when she saw Pastor next, he had the face of a living ghost. He staggered toward his room, but came across Cape's body first, then Miss Banner with her broken leg. She cowered as if he would strike her again.

For many hours, Pastor and the other Jesus Worshippers discussed what had happened, what they must do. Miss Banner listened to their talk of doom. If the Manchus saw what Pastor had done, Miss Mouse pointed out, he and the rest of them would be tortured alive. Which of them had the strength to lift the bodies and bury them? None. Should they run away? To where? There was no place they knew of where they could hide. Then Dr. Too Late suggested they end their suffering by killing themselves. But Mrs. Amen argued, "Taking our own lives would be a great sin, the same as murdering someone else."

"I'll put us all to rest," said Pastor. "I'm already condemned to hell for killing those three. At least let me be the one to deliver you to peace."

Only Miss Banner tried to persuade them against this idea. "There's always hope," she said. And they told her that any hope now lay beyond the grave. So she watched as they prayed in God's House, as they ate Mrs. Amen's stale Communion bread, as they drank water, pretending it was wine. And then they swallowed Dr. Too Late's pills to forget all their pains.

What happened after that you already know.

Miss Banner and I had no strength to bury the Jesus Worshippers. Yet we could not leave them as an easy meal for hungry flies. I went to the garden. I pulled down the white clothes I had washed the day before. I thought about all the terrible things that had happened during the time the laundry had changed from wet to dry. As I wrapped our friends in those hurry-up funeral shrouds, Miss Banner went to their rooms and tried to find a remembrance of each to put in her music box. Since Cape had already stolen their treasures, all that was left were pitiful scraps. For Dr. Too Late, it was a little bottle that once contained his opium pills. For Miss Mouse, a leather glove she always clutched when in fear. For Mrs. Amen, the buttons she popped off her blouses when she sang out loud. For Pastor Amen, a travel book. And for Lao Lu, the tin with leaves from the holy tree. She placed these things in the box, along with the album where she wrote her thoughts. Then we lighted the altar candles that had melted to stubs. I took from my pocket the key Miss Banner had given me the night before. I wound the box, we played the song. And Miss Banner sang the words the foreigners loved so much.

When the song was over, we prayed to their God. This time I was sincere. I bowed my head. I closed my eyes. I said out loud, "I lived with them for six years. They were like my family, although I didn't know them very well. But I can honestly say they were loyal friends of your son, also to us. Please welcome them to your home. Pastor too."

HOW MUCH TIME did we have before the Manchus would come? I did not know then, but I can tell you now. It was not enough.

Before we escaped, I tore off the skirt of Miss Banner's everyday dress and made a sling for the music box. I threw this over my left shoulder, Miss Banner leaned on my right, and we two hobbled out as one. But when we reached the door to leave God's House, a sudden wind blew past us. I turned around and saw the clothes of the Jesus Worshippers billowing as if their bodies were renewed with breath. Stacks of "The Good News" scattered, and those papers that flew on top of the burning candles burst into flame. Soon I could smell the Ghost Merchant, chili and garlic, very strong, as if a welcome-home banquet were being prepared. And maybe this was imagination that springs from too much fear. But I saw him—Miss Banner did not—his long robes, and beneath that, his two new feet in thick-soled shoes. He was walking and nodding, finally back in his unlucky house.

Hop by hop, Miss Banner and I climbed into those mountains. Sometimes she would stumble and land on her bad leg, then cry, "Leave me here. I can't go on."

"Stop this nonsense," I would scold each time. "Yiban is waiting, and you've already made us late." That was always enough to make Miss Banner try again.

At the top of the first archway, I looked back at the empty village.

Half of the Ghost Merchant's House was on fire. A great black cloud was growing above it, like a message to the Manchus to hurry to Chang-mian.

By the time we reached the second archway, we heard the explosions. There was no way to hurry ourselves except in that place where our stomachs churned. It was growing dark, the wind had stopped. Our clothes were sweat-drenched from our struggle to come this far. Now we had to climb along the rocky side of the mountain, where one misstep could send us tumbling into the ravine. "Come, Miss Banner," I urged. "We're almost there." She was looking at her bad leg, now swollen to the size of two.

I had an idea. "Wait here," I told her. "I'll hurry to the cave where Yiban is. Then the two of us can carry you in." She grasped my hands, and I could see in her eyes that she was frightened of being left alone.

"Take the music box," she said. "Put it in a safe place."

"I'm coming back," I answered. "You know this, don't you?"

"Yes, yes, of course. I only meant you should take it now so that there is less to carry later on." I took her box of memories and staggered forward.

At each cave or crevice I passed, a voice would cry out, "This one's already taken! No room!" That's where people in the village had gone. The caves were plugged up with fear, a hundred mouths holding their breath. I climbed up, then down, searching for the cave hidden by a rock. More explosions! I began to curse like Lao Lu, regretting every wasted moment going by. And then—at last!—I found the rock, then the opening, and lowered myself in. The lamp was still there, a good sign that other people had not come in and that Yiban had not gone out. I put down the music box and lighted the lamp, and groped slowly through the twisty bowels of the cave, hoping with each step that my exhausted mind would not take me the wrong way. And then I saw the glow ahead, like dawn light in a trouble-free world. I burst into the room with the shining lake, crying, "Yiban! Yiban! I'm back. Hurry, come and help Miss Banner! She's standing outside, between safety and death."

No answer. So I called again, this time louder. I walked around the lake. A dozen fears pinched my heart. Had Yiban tried to make his way out and gotten lost? Had he fallen in the lake and drowned? I searched near the stone village. What was this? A wall had been knocked over. And along another part of the ledge, blocks of stone had been piled high. My eye traveled upward, and I could see where a person could grab here, step up there, all the way to a crack in the roof, an opening wide enough for a man to squeeze through. And I could see that through that hole all our hopes had flown out.

When I returned, Miss Banner was sticking her head out of the archway, calling, "Yiban, are you there?" When she saw I was alone, she cried, "Ai-ya! Has he been killed?"

I shook my head, then told her how I had broken my promise. "He's gone to find you," I said in a sorry voice. "This is my fault." She did not say what I was thinking: that if Yiban had still been in that cave, all three of us could have been saved. Instead, she turned, limped to the other side of the archway, and searched for him in the night. I stood behind her, my heart in shreds. The sky was orange, the wind tasted of ash. And now we could see small dots of light moving through the valley below, the lanterns of soldiers, bobbing like fireflies. Death was coming, we knew this, and it was terrible to wait. But Miss Banner did not cry. She said, "Miss Moo, where will you go? Which place after death? Your heaven or mine?"

What a peculiar question. As if I could decide. Didn't the gods choose for us? But I did not want to argue, on this, our last day. So I simply said, "Wherever Zeng and Lao Lu have gone, that's where I'll go too."

"That would be your heaven, then." We were quiet for a few moments. "Where you are going, Miss Moo, do you have to be Chinese? Would they allow me in?"

This question was even stranger than the last! "I don't know. I have never talked to anyone who has been there and back. But I think if you speak Chinese, maybe this is enough. Yes, I'm sure of it."

"And Yiban, since he is half-and-half, where would he go? If we choose the opposite—"

Ah, now I understood all her questions. I wanted to comfort her. So I told her the last lie: "Come, Miss Banner. Come with me. Yiban already told me. If he dies, he will meet you again, in the World of Yin."

She believed me, because I was her loyal friend. "Please take my hand, Miss Moo," she said. "Don't let go until we arrive."

And together we waited, both happy and sad, scared to death until we died.

## 22

# WHEN LIGHT
# BALANCES
# WITH DARK

By the time Kwan finishes talking, the pinpricks of stars have dulled against the lightening sky. I stand at the ridge, searching among the bushy shadows for movement of any kind.

"You remember how we die?" Kwan asks from behind.

I shake my head, but then recall what I always thought was a dream: spears flashing by firelight, the grains of the stone wall. Once again, I can see it, feel it, the chest-tightening dread. I can hear the snorting of horses, their hooves stamping impatiently as a rough rope falls upon my shoulder blades, then scratches around my neck. I'm gulping air, the vein in my neck is pumping hard. Someone is squeezing my hand—Kwan, but I am surprised to see she is younger and has a patch over one eye. I'm about to say don't let go, when the words are jerked from my mouth, and I soar into the sky. I feel a snap, and my fears fall back to earth as I continue to rush through the air. No pain! How wonderful to be released! And yet I'm not, not entirely. For there is Kwan, still holding tight on to my hand.

She squeezes it again. "You remember, ah?"

"I think we were hanged." My lips are sluggish in the morning chill.

Kwan frowns. "Hang? Hmm. Don't think so. Back then, Manchu soldier don't hang people. Take too much trouble. Also, no tree."

I'm strangely disappointed to be told I'm wrong. "Okay, so how'd it happen?"

She shrugs. "Don't know. That's why ask you."

"What! *You* don't remember how we died?"

"Happen so fast! One minute stand here, next minute wake up there. Long time already gone by. By time I realize, I already dead. Same like when I gone hospital, got electric shock. I wake up, Hey, where am I? Who knows, last lifetime maybe lightning come down, send you me fast to other world. Ghost Merchant think he die same way. *Pao!* Gone! Only two feet leave behind."

I laugh. "Shit! I can't believe you told me this whole story, and you don't know the ending?"

Kwan blinks. "Ending? You die, that's not end story. That only mean story not finish. . . . Hey, look! Sun almost come up." She stretches her legs and arms. "We go find Simon now. Bring flashlight, blanket too." She plows ahead, sure of the way back. I know where we are headed: the cave, where Yiban promised he would remain, where I hope Simon might have gone.

We hike along the crumbly ridge, gingerly testing each foothold before bearing down with our full weight. My cheeks sting as warmth floods them. At last I'll see this damn cave that is both curse and hope. And what will we find? Simon, shivering but alive? Or Yiban, forever waiting for Miss Banner? While thinking this, I trip on a shifting pile of scree and land on my rear.

"Careful!" Kwan cries.

"Why do people say careful after it's too late?" I pick myself up.

"Not too late. Next time, maybe you don't fall. Here, take hand."

"I'm fine." I flex my leg. "See. No broken bone." We continue climbing, Kwan looking back at me every few seconds. Soon I come upon a cave. I peer in, search for signs of former life, prehistoric or more recently departed. "Say, Kwan, what became of Yiban and the people from Changmian?"

"I was already dead," she answers in Chinese, "so I don't know for sure. What I know comes from gossip I heard during this lifetime. So who knows what's true? People from other villages always added a bit of their own exaggeration and let the rumors trickle down the mountain like a roof leak. At the bottom, everybody's hearsay turned into one ghost story, and from there it spread throughout the province that Changmian was cursed."

"And—what's the story?"

"Ah, wait a little, let me catch my breath!" She sits on top of a flat boulder, huffing. "The story is this. People say that when the Manchu soldiers came, they heard people crying in the caves. 'Come out!' they ordered. No one did—would you? So the soldiers gathered dried twigs and dead bushes, then placed them near the mouths of those caves. When the fires started, the voices in the caves began to scream. All at once, the caves breathed a huge groan, then vomited a black river of bats. The sky was thick with the flying creatures, so many it was as though the ravine had been darkened by an umbrella. They fanned the fire, and then the whole valley burst into flame. The archway, the ridge—everywhere was surrounded by a burning wall. Two or three soldiers on horses got away, but the rest could not. One week later, when another troop came to Changmian, they found no one, either dead or alive. The village was empty, so was the Ghost Merchant's House, no bodies. And in the ravine, where the soldiers had gone, there was nothing but ash and the stone pilings of hundreds of graves." Kwan stands up. "Let's keep walking." And she's off.

I hurry after her. "The villagers died?"

"Maybe, maybe not. One month later, when a traveler from Jintian passed through Changmian, he found the village full of life on a busy market day. Dogs were lying in the gutter, people were arguing, children were toddling behind their mothers, as if life there had passed from one day to the next without any interruption. 'Hey,' the traveler said to the village elder, 'what happened when the soldiers marched into Changmian?' And the elder wrinkled his face and said, 'Soldiers? I have no memory of soldiers coming here.' So the traveler said, 'What about that mansion there? It's been blackened by fire.' And the villagers said, 'Oh, that. Last month, the Ghost Merchant came back and threw a banquet for us. One of the ghost chickens roasting on the stove flew up to the roof and set the eaves on fire.' By the time the traveler returned to Jintian, there was a pathway of people, from the top of the mountain to the bottom, all saying that Changmian was a village of ghosts. . . . What? Why are you laughing?"

"I think Changmian became a village of liars. They *let* people think they were ghosts. Less trouble than going to the caves during future wars."

Kwan slaps her hands together. "What a smart girl. You're right. Big Ma told me a story once about an outsider who asked a young man from our village, 'Hey, are you a ghost?' The man frowned and swept out his arm toward an ungroomed field of rocks: 'Tell me, could a ghost have grown such a fine crop of rice?' The outsider should have realized the man was fooling him. A real ghost wouldn't brag about rice. He'd lie and say peaches instead! Ah?"

Kwan waits for me to acknowledge the logic of this. "Makes sense to me," I lie in the best Changmian tradition.

She goes on: "After a while, I think the village grew tired of everyone thinking they were ghosts. No one wanted to do business in Changmian. No one wanted their sons or daughters to marry into Changmian families. So later they told people, 'No, we're not ghosts, of course not. But there's a hermit who lives in a cave two mountain ridges over. He might be a ghost, or perhaps an immortal. He has long hair and a beard like one. I've never seen him myself. But I heard he appears only at dawn and dusk, when light balances with dark. He walks among the graves, looking for a woman who died. And not knowing which grave is hers, he tends them all."

"Were they talking about . . . Yiban?" I hold my breath.

Kwan nods. "Maybe this story started when Yiban was still alive, waiting for Miss Banner. But when I was six years old—this was shortly after I drowned—I saw him with my yin eyes, among the graves. By then, he really was a ghost. I was in this same ravine, gathering dried twigs for fuel. At the half-hour when the sun goes down, I heard two men arguing. I wandered among the graves and found them stacking rocks. 'Old uncles,' I said to be polite, 'what are you doing?'

"The bald one was very bad-tempered. 'Shit!' he said. 'Use your eyes, now that you have two. What do you think we're doing?' The long-haired man was more polite. 'See here, little girl,' he said. He held up a stone shaped like the head of an ax. 'Between life and death, there is a place where one can balance the impossible. We're searching for that point.' He placed the stone carefully on top of another one. But they both fell and struck the bald man on the foot.

" 'Fuck!' cursed the bald man. 'You nearly chopped off my leg. Take your time. The right place isn't in your hands, you fool. Use your whole body and mind to find it.' "

"That was Lao Lu?"

She grins. "Dead over a hundred years and still cursing! I found out that Lao Lu and Yiban were stuck, unable to go to the next world, because they had too many future regrets."

"How can you have a *future* regret? That doesn't make any sense."

"No? You think to yourself, If I do this, then this will happen, then I will feel this way, so I shouldn't do it. You're stuck. Like Lao Lu. He was sorry he made Pastor believe he had killed Cape and the soldiers. To teach himself a lesson, he decided he would become Pastor's wife in the next lifetime. But whenever he thought about his future—that he would have to listen to Amen this and Amen that, every Sunday—he would start cursing again. How can he become a pastor's wife when his foul temper is still foul? That's why he's stuck."

"And Yiban?"

"When he couldn't find Miss Banner, he thought she had died. He grew sad. Then he wondered if she had gone back to Cape. He grew even sadder. When Yiban died, he flew to heaven to find Miss Banner, and because she was not there, he believed she was with Cape in hell."

"He never considered that she'd gone to the World of Yin?"

"See! That's what happens when you become stuck. Do good things enter your mind? Mm-mm. Bad things? Plenty."

"So he's still stuck?"

"Oh no-no-no-no-no! I told him about you."

"Told him what?"

"Where you were. When you would be born. And now he's waiting for you again. Somewhere here."

"Simon?"

Kwan flashes a huge smile and gestures toward a large rock. Behind it, barely visible, is a narrow opening.

"This is the cave with the lake?"

"The same."

I poke my head in and yell: "Simon! Simon! Are you in there? Are you all right?"

Kwan grabs my shoulders and gently pulls me back. "I go in, get him," she says in English. "Where flashlight?"

I fish it out of the day pack and click it on. "Shit, it must have been left on all night. The battery's dead."

"Let me see." She takes the flashlight and it immediately brightens. "See? Not dead. Okay!" She presses herself into the cave and I follow.

"No-no, Libby-ah! You stay outside."

"Why?"

"In case . . ."

"In case what?"

"Just in case! Don't argue." She clutches my hand so hard it hurts. "Promise, ah?"

"All right. Promise."

She smiles. The next moment, her face bunches up into an expression of pain, and tears spill down her round cheeks.

"Kwan? What is it?"

She squeezes my hand again and blubbers in English, "Oh, Libby-ah, I so happy can finally pay you back. Now you know all my secret. Give me peace." She throws her arms around me.

I'm flustered. I've always felt awkward with Kwan's emotional outpourings. "Pay me back—for what? Come on, Kwan, you don't owe me anything."

"Yes-yes! You my loyal friend." She's sniffling. "For me, you go Yin World, because I tell you, Sure-sure, Yiban follow you there. But no, he go heaven, you not there. . . . So you see, because me, you lost each other. That's why I so happy first time I meet Simon. Then I know, ah, at last! —"

I back away. My head is buzzing. "Kwan, that night you met Simon, do you remember talking to his friend Elza?"

She wipes her eyes with her sleeve. "Elza? . . . Ah! Yes-yes! Elsie. I remember. Nice girl. Polish-Jewish. Drown after lunch."

"What she said, that Simon should forget about her—did you make that up? Didn't she say something else?"

Kwan frowns. "Forget her? She say that?"

"You said she did."

"Ah! I remember now. Not 'forget.' *Forgive.* She want him forgive her. She done something make him feel guilty. He think his fault she die. She say no, her fault, no problem, don't worry. Something like that."

"But didn't she tell him to wait for her? That she was coming back?"

"Why you think this?"

"Because I saw her! I saw her with those secret senses you always talk about. She was begging Simon to see her, to know what she was feeling. I saw—"

"Tst! Tst!" Kwan puts her hand on my shoulder. "Libby-ah, Libby-ah! This not secret sense. This you own sense doubt. Sense worry. This nonsense! You see you own ghost self begging Simon, Please hear me, see me, love me. . . . Elsie not saying that. Two lifetime ago, you her daughter. Why she want you have misery life? No! She *help* you. . . ."

I listen, stunned. Elza was my mother? Whether that was true or not, I feel lighthearted, giddy, a needless load of resentment removed, and with it a garbage pile of fears and doubts.

"All this time you think she chasing you? Mm-mm. You chase yourself! Simon know this too." She kisses my cheek. "I go find him now, let him tell you hisself." I watch her squeeze into the cave.

"Kwan?"

She turns around. "Ah!"

"Promise you won't get lost. You'll come back."

"Yes, promise-promise! Course." She is lowering herself into the next chamber. "Don't worry." Her voice returns, deep and resonant. "I find Simon, be back soon. You wait for us. . . ." She trails off.

I wrap the space blanket around my shoulders and sit, leaning against the boulder that hid the entrance to the cave. Hope, nothing wrong with that. I scan the sky. Still gray. Is it going to rain again? And with that single unhappy possibility, bleakness and common sense take over. Did I become hypnotized while listening to Kwan's story? Am I as delusional as she is? How could I let my sister go into the cave by herself? I scramble to my feet and stick my head into the entrance. "Kwan! Come back!" I crawl into the mouth of the dark chamber. "Kwan! Kwan! Goddamnit, Kwan, answer me!" I venture forward, bump my head against the low ceiling, curse, then holler again. A few steps later, the light tapers, and at the next turn disappears. It's as if a thick blanket had been thrown over my eyes. I don't panic. I've worked in darkrooms half my life. But in here, I don't know the boundaries of the dark. The blackness is like a magnet drawing me in. I backtrack toward the cave opening, but I'm disoriented, with no sense of direction, not in or out, nor up or down. I shout for Kwan. My voice is growing hoarse, and I'm gasping for breath. Has all the air been sucked out of the cave?

"Olivia?"

I choke a yelp.

"Are you okay?"

"Oh God! Simon! Is that really you? . . ." I start to sob. "Are you alive?"

"Would I be talking to you if I weren't?"

I laugh and cry at the same time. "You never know."

"Here, reach out your hand."

I swat at the air until I touch flesh, his familiar hands. He pulls me toward him and I wrap my arms around his neck, leaning against his chest, rubbing his spine, assuring myself he is real. "God, Simon, what happened yesterday—I was insane. And later, when you didn't come back—did Kwan tell you what I've been through?"

"No, I haven't been back to the house yet."

I stiffen. "Oh God!"

"What's wrong?"

"Where's Kwan? Isn't she behind you?"

"I don't know where she is."

"But . . . she went in to find you. She went into the cave! And I've been calling for her! Oh God! This can't be happening. She promised she wouldn't get lost. She promised to come back. . . ." I keep babbling as Simon leads me out.

We stumble into the open, where the light is so hard I can't see. I blindly pat Simon's face, half expecting that when I can see the world again, he'll be Yiban and I'll be wearing a yellow dress stained with blood.

IV

# 23

# THE FUNERAL

Kwan disappeared two months ago. I don't say "died," because I haven't yet allowed myself to think that's what happened.

I sit in my kitchen, eating granola, staring at the pictures of missing kids on the back of the milk carton. "Reward for any information," it reads. I know what the mothers of those children feel. Until proven otherwise, you have to believe they're somewhere. You have to see them once more before it's time to say good-bye. You can't let those you love leave you behind in this world without making them promise they'll wait. And I have to believe it's not too late to tell Kwan, I was Miss Banner and you were Nunumu, and forever you'll be loyal and so will I.

Two months ago, the last time I saw her, I waited by the cave, certain that if I believed her story, she'd come back. I sat on the music box, with Simon beside me. He tried to appear optimistic, yet never cracked a joke, which was how I knew he was worried. "She'll turn up," he assured me. "I just wish you didn't have to go through this agony, first with me, now with Kwan."

As it turned out, he had been safe all along. After our fight, he too had left the archway. He was trudging back to Big Ma's house when he ran into the cow herder who had called us assholes. Only the guy was not a cow herder but a graduate student from Boston named Andy, the American nephew of a woman living in a village farther down the mountain. The two of them went to his aunt's house, where they chugged shots of *maotai* until their tongues and brains went numb. Even if he hadn't passed out, Simon would have been all right, and it pained him to admit this had been so. In his fanny pack, he had a wool cap, which he put on after I ran away. And then he had raged, pitching rocks into the ravine until he worked up a sweat.

"You worried for nothing," he said, devastated.

And I said, "Better than finding out I worried for *something*." I reasoned that if I was grateful that Simon had never been in any real danger, similar luck would be granted me any minute with regard to Kwan. "Sorry-sorry, Libby-ah," I imagined she'd say. "I took wrong turn in cave, lost. Took me whole morning come back! You worry for nothing." And later, I made adjustments in my hopes to account for the passing of time. "Libby-ah, where my head go? I see lake, can't stop dreaming. I think only one hour pass by. Ha!—don't know was ten!"

Simon and I stayed by the cave all night. Du Lili brought us food, blankets, and a tarp. We pushed away the boulder blocking the entrance of the cave, then climbed in and huddled in the shallow cove. I stared at the sky, a sieve punctured with stars, and considered telling him Kwan's story of Miss Banner, Nunumu, and Yiban. But then I became afraid. I saw the story as a talisman of hope. And if Simon or anyone else discounted even part of it, then some possibility out in the universe, the one I needed, might be removed.

On the second morning of Kwan's disappearance, Du Lili and Andy organized a search party. The older folks were too scared to go into the cave. So those who showed up were mostly young. They brought oil lamps and bundles of ropes. I tried to recall the directions to the cavern with the lake. What had Zeng said? Follow the water, stay low, choose the shallow route over the wide. Or was it narrow instead of deep? I didn't have to ask Simon not to go into the cave. He stayed close to me, and together we watched grimly as one man tied the rope around his waist and burrowed into the cave, while another man stood outside, holding the other end of the rope taut.

By the third day, the searchers had navigated a labyrinth that led them to dozens of other caves. But no trace yet was seen of Kwan. Du Lili went to Guilin to notify the authorities. She also sent a telegram that I had carefully written to George. In the afternoon, four vans arrived bearing green-uniformed soldiers and black-suited officials. The following morning, a familiar sedan rolled up the road, and out stepped Rocky and a somber old scholar. Rocky confided to me that Professor Po was the right-hand man to the paleontologist who discovered the Peking Man. The professor entered the intricate maze of caves, now explored more easily with the addition of guide ropes and lamps. When he emerged many hours later, he announced that many dynasties ago, the inhabitants of this area had excavated through dozens of caves, creating intentional dead ends, as well as elaborate interconnecting tunnels. It was likely, he theorized, the people of Changmian invented this maze to escape from Mongolians and other warring tribes. Those invaders who entered the labyrinth became lost, and scurried about like rats in a death trap.

A team of geologists was brought in. In the excitement that ensued, nearly everyone forgot about Kwan. Instead, the geologists found jars for grain and jugs for water. They barged into bat lairs and sent thousands of the frightened creatures shrieking into the blinding sun. They made an important scientific discovery of human shit that was at least three thousand years old!

On the fifth day, George and Virgie arrived from San Francisco. They had received my various telegrams with their progressively dire messages. George was confident that Kwan wasn't actually missing; it was only my poor Mandarin that had caused us to become temporarily separated. By evening, however, George was a wretched mess. He picked up a sweater that belonged to Kwan, buried his face in it, not caring who watched him cry.

On the seventh day, the search teams located the shining lake and the ancient village beside its shore. Still no Kwan. But now the village was crawling with officials of every rank, as well as a dozen more scientific teams, all of them trying to determine what caused the cave water to glow.

On each of those seven days, I had to give a report to yet another bureaucrat, detailing what had happened to Kwan. What was her birthdate? When did she become an overseas Chinese? Why did she come back here? Was she sick? You had a fight? Not with her but with your husband? Was your husband angry with her too? Is that why she ran away? Do you have a photo of her? You took this picture? What kind of camera do you use? You are a professional photographer? Really? How much money can a person make taking a picture like this? Is that so? That much? Can you take a picture of me?

At night, Simon and I hugged each other tightly in the marriage bed. We made love, but not out of lust. When we were together this way, we could hope, we could believe that love wouldn't allow us to be separated again. With each passing day, I didn't lose hope. I fought to have more. I recalled Kwan's stories. I remembered those times when she bandaged my wounds, taught me to ride a bike, placed her hands on my feverish six-year-old forehead and whispered, "Sleep, Libby-ah, sleep." And I did.

Meanwhile, Changmian had become a circus. The entrepreneurial guy who had tried to sell Simon and me so-called ancient coins was charging curiosity-seekers ten yuan for admission through the first archway. His brother charged twenty to go through the second. Many of the tourists trampled the ravine, and Changmian residents hawked rocks from the graves as souvenirs. An argument broke out between the village leaders and officials over who owned the caves and who could take what they contained. At that point, two weeks had gone by, and Simon and I couldn't stomach any more. We decided to take the plane home on the scheduled day.

BEFORE WE LEFT, Big Ma finally had her funeral. There were only eleven people in attendance that drizzly morning—two hired hands to transport the casket to the grave, a few of the older villagers, and George, Virgie, Du Lili, Simon, and I. I wondered if Big Ma was miffed at being upstaged by Kwan. The hired hands loaded the casket onto the back of a mule cart. Du Lili tied the requisite screaming rooster to the coffin lid. When we reached the bridge over the first irrigation pond, we found a television news crew blocking our way.

"Move your butts!" Du Lili shouted. "Can't you see? We have a funeral procession going through!" The crew came over and asked her to respect the rights of citizens to hear about the wonderful discovery in Changmian.

"Wonderful bullshit!" said Du Lili. "You're ruining our village. Now get out of our way." A stylish woman in snazzy jeans took Du Lili aside. I saw her offer money, which Du Lili angrily refused. My heart soared with admiration. The woman flashed more money. Du Lili pointed to the crew, then the coffin, complaining loudly again. A bigger wad of bills came out. And Du Lili shrugged. "All right," I heard her say as she pocketed the money. "At least the deceased can use this to buy a better life in the next world." My spirits went into a tailspin. Simon looked grim. We took a long detour, squeezing through alleyways until we reached the communal graveyard, a slope leading up the mountains facing west.

At the grave site, Du Lili cried while caressing Big Ma's parched face. I thought the body was amazingly well preserved after a two-week hiatus between departure and sendoff. "Ai, Li Bin-bin," Du Lili crooned, "you're too young to die. I should have gone before you." I translated this to Simon.

He glanced at Du Lili. "Is she saying she's older than Big Ma?"

"I don't know. I don't want to know what anything means anymore."

As the hired hands closed the coffin lid, I felt that the answers to so many questions were being sealed up forever: where Kwan was, what my father's real name had been, whether Kwan and a girl named Buncake had indeed drowned.

"Wait!" I heard Du Lili cry to the workers. "I almost forgot." She reached into her pocket and pulled out the wad of banknotes. As she wrapped Big Ma's stiff hand around the television crew's bribery money, I cried, my faith restored. And then Du Lili reached into the front of her padded jacket and extracted something else. It was a preserved duck egg. She put this in Big Ma's other hand. "Your favorite," she said. "In case you get hungry on your way there."

*Duck eggs!* "I made so many," I could hear Kwan saying. "Maybe some still left."

I turned to Simon. "I have to go." I clutched my stomach and grimaced, feigning illness.

"You want me to help you?"

I shook my head and went over to Du Lili. "Bad stomach," I said. She gave me an understanding look. As soon as I was sure I was out of their view, I started running. I didn't give a damn about keeping my expectations in check. I was surrendering myself completely to hope. I was elated. I knew that what I believed was what I'd find.

I stopped at Big Ma's house and snatched a rusted hoe. And then I sped over to the community hall. When I reached the gate, I walked through slowly, searching for familiar signs. There! — the bottom bricks of the foundation — they were pockmarked black, and I was sure these were the burnt ruins of the Ghost Merchant's House. I raced through the empty building, glad that everyone was at the ravine gawking at three-thousand-year-old shit. In the back, I saw no garden, no rolling paths or pavilion. Everything had been leveled for the exercise yard. But just as I expected, the stones of the boundary walls were also blackened and blistered. I went to the northwest corner and calculated: Ten jars across, ten paces long. I began to hack at the mud with the hoe. I laughed out loud. If anyone saw me, they'd think I was as crazy as Kwan.

I unearthed a trench of mud five feet long and two feet deep, nearly big enough for a corpse. And then I felt the hoe hit something that was neither rock nor soil. I fell to my knees and frantically scooped out the dark moist dirt with my bare hands. And then I saw it, the lighter clay, firm and smooth as a shoulder. In my impatience, I used the handle of the hoe to break open the jar.

I pulled out a blackened egg, then another and another. I hugged them against my chest, where they crumbled, all these relics of our past disintegrating into gray chalk. But I was beyond worry. I knew I had already tasted what was left.

# 24

# ENDLESS SONGS

George and Virgie have just come back from their honeymoon in Changmian. They claim I wouldn't recognize the place. "Tourist trap everywhere!" George says. "The whole village is now rich, selling plastic sea creatures, the glow-in-the-dark kind. That's why the lake was so bright. Ancient fish and plants living deep in the water. But now no more. Too many people made a wish, threw lucky coins in the lake. And all those sea creatures? Poisoned, went belly-up dead. So the village leaders installed underwater lights, green and yellow, very pretty, I saw them myself. Good show."

I think George and Virgie chose to go to Changmian as an apology to Kwan. To get married, George had to have Kwan declared legally dead. I still have mixed feelings about that. The marriage, I figure, is what Kwan had intended all along. At some level, she must have known she wasn't coming home. She never would have let George go through life without having enough to eat. I think she also would have laughed and said, "Too bad Virgie not better cook."

I've had almost two years to think about Kwan, why she came into my life, why she left. What she said about fate waiting to happen, what she might have meant. Two years is enough time, I know, to layer memories of what was with what might have been. And that's fine, because I now believe truth lies not in logic but in hope, both past and future. I believe hope can surprise you. It can survive the odds against it, all sorts of contradictions, and certainly any skeptic's rationale of relying on proof through fact.

How else can I explain why I have a fourteen-month-old baby girl? Like everyone else, I was astounded when I went to the doctor and he said I was three months along. I gave birth nine months after Simon and I made love in the marriage bed, nine months after Kwan disappeared. I'm sure there were those who suspected the father was some fly-by-night date, that I was careless, pregnant by accident. But Simon and I both know: That baby is ours. Sure, there was a reasonable explanation. We went back to the fertility specialist and he did more tests. Well, what do you know? The earlier tests were wrong. The lab must have made a mistake, switched the charts, because sterility, the doctor said, is not a reversible condition. Simon, he announced, had in fact not been sterile. I asked the doctor, "So how do you explain why I never became pregnant before?"

"You were probably trying too hard," he said. "Look how many women become pregnant after they adopt."

All I know is what I want to believe. I have a gift from Kwan, a baby girl with dimples in her fat cheeks. And no, I didn't name her Kwan or Nelly. I'm not that morbidly sentimental. I call her Samantha, sometimes Sammy. Samantha Li. She and I took Kwan's last name. Why not? What's a family name if not a claim to being connected in the future to someone from the past?

Sammy calls me "Mama." Her favorite toy is "ba," the music box Kwan gave me for my wedding. Sammy's other word is "Da," which is what she calls Simon, "Da" for "Daddy," even though he doesn't live with us all the time. We're still working things out, deciding what's important, what matters, how to be together for more than eight hours at a stretch without disagreeing about which radio station we should put on. On Fridays, he comes over and stays the weekend. We snuggle in bed, Simon and I, Sammy and Bubba. We are practicing being a family, and we're grateful for every moment together. The petty arguments, snipes and gripes, they still crop up. But it's easier to remember how unimportant they are, how they shrink the heart and make life small.

I think Kwan intended to show me the world is not a place but the vastness of the soul. And the soul is nothing more than love, limitless, endless, all that moves us toward knowing what is true. I once thought love was supposed to be nothing but bliss. I now know it is also worry and grief, hope and trust. And believing in ghosts — that's believing that love never dies. If people we love die, then they are lost only to our ordinary senses. If we remember, we can find them anytime with our hundred secret senses. "This a secret," I can still hear Kwan whispering. "Don't tell anyone. Promise, Libby-ah."

I hear my baby calling me. She gurgles and thrusts her hand toward the fireplace, at what I don't know. She insists. "What is it, Sammy? What do you see?" My heart races as I sense it might be Kwan.

"Ba," Sammy coos, her hand still reaching up. Now I see what she wants. I go to the mantel and take down the music box. I wind the key. I lift my baby into my arms. And we dance, joy spilling from sorrow.

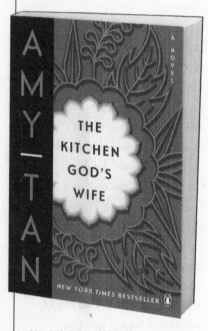